To Mes

Hap~

BLUE
GOLD

DAB

17.xi.17

David Barker
BLUE
GOLD

urbanepublications.com

First published in Great Britain in 2017
by Urbane Publications Ltd
Suite 3, Brown Europe House, 33/34 Gleaming Wood Drive,
Chatham, Kent ME5 8RZ
Copyright © David Barker, 2017

A CIP catalogue record for this book is available
from the British Library.

ISBN 978-1-911331-65-0
MOBI 978-1-911331-67-4
EPUB 978-1-911331-66-7

Design and Typeset by Michelle Morgan

Cover by Author Design Studio

Printed and bound by CPI Group (UK) Ltd, Croydon, CR0 4YY

urbanepublications.com

To Mum and Dad

CONTENTS

PART ONE

We never know the true worth of water until the well is dry

Thomas Fuller, Gnomologia 1732

CHAPTER 1

Snow was ripping away his senses, one by one. The horizon had disappeared and all Sim Atkins could do was focus on the back of the person in front of him. His fingers and toes had gone numb. Thin air and thick snowflakes fought for priority in his nose and throat. Stumbling through knee-high snow drifts, urged on by the muffled cries of a guide, Sim was gasping for oxygen. Big gulps merely delivered a mouthful of snowflakes that melted on his tongue. A welcome sip of water trickled down his throat. *Ahh, a drink of water.* The source of all his troubles, the source of everybody's troubles these days. He tried to control his breathing, deep inhalations through his nose, like a yoga exercise. But the situation was not helping his inner peace, not one jot.

Sim was clipped onto a rope, part of a chain of people trying to get down the mountain as quickly as possible. Gopal, the Ghurka who was leading the line, kept turning around to urge them onwards. The sound of distant explosions echoed off the sides of the mountains, sometimes accompanied by a flurry of movement as dislodged snow cascaded down.

The clouds were starting to part when there was a cry from the back of the human chain. The bald Rabten, who had provided Sim with warm clothes only a few minutes ago, pointed skywards with his pick-axe. "Chopper."

Gopal looked around and spotted a small overhang of rock off to their left up a short, steep incline. "Head for the cover," he shouted.

The helicopter flew closer and a pair of auto cannons opened fire. Bullets bit into the snow around Sim, hissing like hot iron on flesh. Sim's partner, Freda, was lagging behind until Gopal threw her over his shoulder and carried her up the slope. All five of the team made it under the rocky out-crop by the time the helicopter had banked and started coming around for a second attack. The man who hadn't spoken since Sim and Freda had been rescued unslung his sniper rifle and knelt down, using his left knee to steady his aim. He waited while the helicopter flew closer and then squeezed the trigger. The glass on the side of the cabin shattered and the aircraft began to spin out of control. It lost altitude and as it approached the ground swirls of snow gathered around the helicopter until its tail clipped one of the rocks. The aircraft folded in on itself as if it had been made of paper all along. A spark ignited the fuel tank and an orange fireball lit up the snowy scene.

Sim turned to the marksman to offer his congratulations when he heard a rumble like thunder just above the rocks they were cowering under. He stood up to see what was happening but Rabten grabbed hold of his clothes and hauled him down to the ground. Tonnes of snow swept around and over the outcrop for several seconds and then stopped just as quickly as it had started. For a moment the mountainside was quiet and still.

Gopal rose to his feet first. "Come on, there could be more *Black Whirlwinds* around. We need to make the treeline by dusk."

Still clipped together, the group made its way further down the pass. They settled into a steady pace. The delays between distant explosions became longer and longer.

Don't suppose there's much left to destroy now, thought Sim.

They paused as the route down traversed a valley. Some of the snow drifts went up to Sim's waist and the surface ahead was no longer smooth but jagged.

The leader turned to the others. "Probably a glacial tongue under this snow. There may be crevasses, so stick close together."

Walking slowly forward, the group started to edge across the valley. Sim kept his eyes fixed on Freda in front of him, watching carefully where she trod, ready to grab the line in case she started to fall. After twenty minutes, his arms were getting tired from the continuous tension and he was beginning to think that Gopal had mis-diagnosed the lie of the land. His mind began to wander back to that prison cell. With a jolt on the rope, Freda flew out of sight. Not down into a yawning chasm but upwards. How was that possible? Then he realised why - he was the one falling, bumping down a face of rough ice. He thrashed his pick-axe in front of him, trying to grab a purchase on anything. At last it bit into the ice and his shoulder was nearly pulled from its socket as the arm took his full weight. Looking down he could see nothing but a dark gap that went further than he cared to imagine. Looking up he saw a thin slither of light and Freda wedged sideways a few metres above him, still clipped to the line, trying to right herself. He had to hold on so that Freda wasn't dragged down with him.

A voice from the surface shouted. "Don't try to move. Just hang on, we'll get you out."

Sim managed to grab the handle of the pick axe with his other hand and hung there staring at the rough, pale blue ice inches from his face. A reflection looked back at him in those moments of terror. A distorted visage: the result of imperfections in the ice; or all that happened to him these past few weeks? Clinging on for his life, in a glacial crevasse on the far side of the world, he was an international OFWAT agent on a mission to save the world. That sounded crazy. Two months ago, the nearest he would have come to a scenario like this would have been one of his favourite virtual reality games.

Was it really only April when I received that phone call?

♦

"Take that, you green lump of shite! Not so tough now are you?" The noise of blood gurgling from the orc's throat was interrupted by a ring tone. Sim took off his game helm, blinked as his eyes adjusted to the real world and picked up the buzzing phone. "Hello?"

"Finally you pick up, Sim. It's Charlie. I've been trying to get hold of you for the last ten minutes, what've you been up to?"

"Just bustin' orc heads."

"On a Friday night? Listen, loser, you need to come look at these readings."

"Can't it wait until Monday?"

"Do you think I would be phoning at this hour if it wasn't urgent?"

"Well if it's urgent, why don't you send the data to my eye patch, man?"

"Ha ha, very funny. Last time I checked there were only 18 people in the UK with a mobile that worked, and neither of us is on that list. Get yourself down to the base. Another satellite's just disappeared."

Sim Atkins put down the phone and walked from his living room to his bedroom in two strides. The pair of round windows either side of the front door – eyes that stared, unblinking, at the Sutherland mountains beyond – cast pools of moonlight onto the hall carpet.

He put on his biking leathers and went into the garage where he kept his blue Triumph Sprint. The ride from his house took him down the A9 across the Dornoch Firth. His headlight picked out an old stone post at the side of road, still claiming north was towards John O'Groats. He smiled; they'd never get round to correcting that one. Past the Glen Morangie distillery, through the back of Tain and out towards the OFWAT satellite tracking office next to the lighthouse at Wilkhaven.

The office was a squat building, with several large radar dishes on the flat roof. Only a couple of hundred metres away, the red and white stripes of Tarbat Ness lighthouse towered above the office as it flashed its warning. As he approached, Sim saw who was on guard duty: Rusty Jimmy. Grey-red hair and a spikey nose always reminded Sim of the old barbed wire running atop the perimeter fence. He doubted either provided much security to the OFWAT base.

"Evening to you Sim, it'll be a late night for you calling in at this hour," said Jimmy in his thick Glaswegian accent as the bike pulled up at the gate and Sim took off his helmet.

"Aye. Charlie's got his knickers in a twist again. Probably having trouble getting the toaster to work."

Jimmy managed a weak grin and lifted the barrier. Sim parked the bike and looked up in the sky on the off-chance he could see any signs of the lost satellite burning up on re-entry. He remembered the first satellite shower he saw seven years ago. A powerful solar flare had disrupted a dozen satellites at once and Sim had caught the news on an astronomy Twitter feed. He had raced outside with his dad to crane his neck at the Scottish night sky just in time to see a series of improbably bright streaks of fire arcing overhead. By the time Sim had finished school there were not many satellites left to fall.

"So Charles, what's so important that you drag me in at this time on a Friday night?" Sim asked as he entered the main room. His colleague was seated at a long desk adorned with a bank of screens and control pads. There were cups of half-drunk coffee strewn about, piles of boxes containing several weeks' worth of cold pizzas and a practice putting hole at the far end of the room.

"It's one of the *Drop Of Water* low-level cameras. We lost contact with it about 25 minutes ago, somewhere over Iceland," said Charlie.

"The 'A' series has always been a bit flaky. Two to five year lifespan at best. What's unusual about that?"

"This one was only launched last year. And there have been no reports of heat expansion in the upper atmosphere or any recent solar activity to account for the loss."

"OK, better take a look at the last communication we had with it."

Charlie pointed at the screen furthest from Sim, who walked past and sat down to browse the rows of code that represented DOW 149A's last set of transmissions.

"This says the temperature went from normal to fatal in less than a second. I always thought re-entry burn-up took thirty seconds minimum. Weird."

"That's what I've been trying to tell you," replied Charlie.

"A fry job then? Tracking data should still be able to see it but this trace just stops. You sure the dish is working?"

"Yep, I ran a full diagnostic just before you arrived."

"But satellites can't just vanish... unless... bloody hell." Sim dragged his fingers through his hair. "An act of war? At the least, extremely sophisticated terrorism. This is not cool, not cool at all."

He reached for the nearest pizza box, opened the lid and examined its contents. Something glistened at him and he re-closed the box. Sim wrote up his findings and zipped them to Birmingham HQ.

"So, any details of your love life you'd like to share?" asked Charlie as they waited to see if HQ responded to Sim's report.

"Some country, or some group of nut-jobs, might've just declared war on us. How can you think about women at a time like this?"

Charlie shrugged his shoulders. "Why not? It's not as if we can do anything about it stuck in this poxy out-post."

"I guess. Hey, I got pretty frisky with this hot elven sorceress the other night. Sadly she turned out to be from Germany – and only 16 – so I don't think there's a future in that relationship."

"I meant a real woman, not some pixellated fantasy."

"Oh, one of those. The barmaid at the Castle Hotel smiled at me last Friday…though that could've been because I gave her a £10 tip by accident."

Charlie grinned. "Hopeless… hang on, that's Rosie, isn't it? You've been soft on her for months. Accidental tip, my arse. When are you going to ask her out?"

Sim raised his hand to object and then looked away, remembering. Rosie had let him walk her home that night. The smell of the pub on her clothes mixed with vanilla perfume. And then a goodnight kiss – just a peck on the cheek – but he could still recall the warm gossamer touch of her lips. He reached for the putter and started practising as he cogitated some more. He was just about to go home for some sleep when the reply came through: report to Overseas Division, Centre City Tower immediately.

Oh crap, somebody actually believed my theory.

He rode home, quickly loaded the bike's top box with some spare clothes, downed a can of Bluebird to fight off his tiredness, and set off on the journey 500 miles north.

CHAPTER 2

Six years earlier. Ethiopian Army Observation Post Guba,
5 kilometres from the Sudan border.

'Praise God for this beautiful morning,' thought Jember Abdi as he watched the sun rise over the low mountain range to his right. The blackened, battered coffee pot on the stove was running low after Abdi's four hours of duty. He shook it disconsolately. Turning back towards the border he had been observing for three years, he raised the binoculars to his eyes once more and noticed a dust cloud had appeared while he'd been watching the dawn break in the opposite direction. That was odd for this time of year. He didn't recall any storm warnings. He turned on the radio.

'And scientists are now saying that the rapid spread of the South Atlantic Anomaly is behind the recent spate of satellite losses. The weakening of the geomagnetic field, which some are calling the Great Flux, is leaving our upper atmosphere vulnerable to solar flares. If you've just sent your friend a text, I'm afraid it might not arrive for the next few years. Over to Makeda for the weather.'

'Thank you Dawit. Well I don't know about delayed text messages, but the rains are certainly late to arrive this year. The forecast is clear blue skies for the rest of the week.'

He clicked off the radio and moved over to the tripod-mounted scope. The dust cloud was much closer now. Forty M1A3 main battle tanks trundled across the border. These were far superior to anything his own army, or the Sudanese, possessed.

Egyptian. How could these abominations be invading from Sudan?

He reached for the phone to alert HQ to the attack. The line was dead. He gulped; he couldn't remember what he was supposed to do if the phone wasn't working.

Abdi looked back through the scope – the invaders were now only two kilometres away. The sweep of tanks formed a crescent as they scythed through the countryside. The third vehicle from the left started to rotate its turret and raise its cannon. Abdi saw a blast of flame and smoke erupt from the end of its barrel.

"Oh my Lord." He turned and sprinted for the door. He was halfway out when two dozen tungsten balls slammed into the building and ripped through the flimsy breeze blocks as if they weren't there. The roof collapsed instantly. The door blew outwards and smashed into the back of Abdi's head, knocking him unconscious as the over-sized shotgun pellets whistled past.

When he woke up everything looked fuzzy and his mouth was full of dust. He wracked his lungs and looked around for his canteen of water. The movement made him wince and he put his hand up to the back of his head. It was sticky, and when he brought his fingers back in front of him they were red. His vision started to focus but the severe headache would not go away. Abdi retrieved his binoculars from the wreckage of the observation post and watched as more vehicles, carrying Egyptian troops, crossed the border. They were following the path gouged through the countryside by the tanks, like a colony of ants following the trail to some distant source of food.

He balled his hands into tight fists. He started to run towards the invaders; he would arm himself with any stick or stone he could find on the way.

If they think they can get away with this…

And then he stopped. He was being stupid. He was unarmed, on foot and the gash at the back of his head needed medical treatment. Getting himself killed was not going to help anybody, especially his… family. They needed to be warned.

It was two or three hours to the nearest town, away from the invasion. He reached it just after sunset. He had emptied his canteen some time ago, his vision was starting to blur again and his stomach refused to let him forget that his last food had been 24 hours ago. He passed many residents who were leaving the town in a hurry. People carrying their elderly relations, a man trying to carry a goat on his back, a girl with a headless, dirty doll in her hands. He smiled at her but she just stared back, a frozen mask. Eventually Abdi found the main hospital where one of the nurses bandaged his head and, fearing concussion, ordered him to stay overnight for observation.

The next morning, he woke up expecting to see the hospital full of casualties and refugees from the war. But as he paced the building doctors and nurses busied themselves as though it were just an ordinary day. There were no patients lying in the corridor, no crowds outside the front door hoping to get in. He caught a news bulletin on one of the hospital's mega-boards.

At least we are still in control of the TV stations, he thought.

The news revealed that the Egyptians had advanced no further than the Grand Ethiopian Renaissance Dam. Abdi's stomach dropped. Hadn't his cousin gone to work on the dam last year?

Attempts to repulse the invasion had failed. Some military experts had been asked onto the news programme and were discussing the likely next development in this invasion. They concluded that the Egyptians simply wanted to prevent phase three of the dam's project, when the Blue Nile would be diverted to the reservoir.

How could they sit there, all dressed up in suits and ties, discussing technical things like 'phase three'? Our homeland has been violated. People are dying. This isn't a game of chess. Why have you let this happen, Lord?

The days ticked by. He couldn't get through to his family or his regiment. Was his cousin alright? Abdi feigned ongoing concussion and stayed in hospital watching the news, hoping for an international response to his country's plight. A big fancy building on the other side of the world flashed up on the screen – the UN headquarters. Politicians discussed the fate of his country like they were haggling over a piece of furniture. The reporter said that the Egyptians had drawn on all their political allies to state their case as powerfully as possible: the 1959 Nile Agreement, the army's use of minimal force, Egypt's desperate need for an uninterrupted flow of the river. The United Nations were divided – the Chinese refused to condemn the Egyptians' transgression – and so the international response was ineffective and half-hearted.

Three days later, as Abdi travelled back towards his home town, the ground shook beneath his feet and then reverberated. At that same moment, the shock wave travelling through the air arrived, squeezed all hope from his chest and silenced his hearing. He knew instantly what it meant: the Egyptians had destroyed the dam. His country's biggest ever construction project – a source of pride throughout the land, their hope for cheap, plentiful electricity for the next one hundred years – had been pulverised.

This was no act of terrorism, this was war.

CHAPTER 3

If the battle for economic and military control of black gold – oil – was a dominant feature of the second half of the twentieth century, the control of blue gold – water – will be the key to the first half of the 21st century. OFWAT Overseas Division was established in 2022 to work alongside MI6 in monitoring and countering water-related terrorism and acts of war.
Serve, Protect, Quench, Ration.
OFWAT Overseas Division Training Manual Introduction

April 27th, 2028. A38(M) Aston Expressway.

After a short stop for fuel and some strong coffee on the M6 near Carlisle, Sim Atkins entered the outskirts of the Birmingham conurbation at dawn. The streets were still quiet – the buzz of a lively spring Saturday was at least three hours away. Sim was glad to be making this trip so early in the morning. Cities intimidated him and the thought of trying to navigate through the maze of roads around Birmingham during rush hour positively scared him.

Security at Centre City Tower was nothing like Wilkhaven. Card and finger print ID checks were overseen by two armed guards. Sim could not even remember having his prints taken during induction week a few years ago, but they were on the system sure enough. The metal roller gate retracted up into the ceiling. Leaving his bike in the basement car park, he took the elevator up to the sixth floor – Overseas Division. He was tired but excited at the prospect of finally getting to see the area where he had wanted to work when he first applied for a career at OFWAT.

There was a young female receptionist waiting for him. His biking leathers squeaked slightly as he approached.

"Hi, I'm the agent they sent for, from Wilkhaven. Urgent business."

She started to say something and then her nostrils flared and her eyebrows lifted. She consulted her terminal. "Follow me please."

Sim followed in silence and was shown into a small conference room where he was offered coffee and biscuits. There was a copy of the Overseas Division training manual on a unit in the corner of the room, which he started to flick through. He managed to complete the introduction before a tall, thin man entered. Sim guessed he was in his early 50s; his hair was peppery grey, matching his crisp suit. The knot on his green silk tie was loose and low and he wore small rimless spectacles which failed to hide the large bags under his eyes.

"Morning Atkins, thank you for coming so promptly. My name is Wardle, head of O.D." The man's nostrils twitched. "Long drive? You'll have a chance to freshen up soon."

"Pleasure to be here, Sir," said Sim as he rose, recollecting similar encounters with officers from the Para regiment. He wished he had had time to at least put on a clean shirt.

"We read your report on the lost DOW satellite. Seemed like a sound piece of analysis, so we dug some more into it. It turns out that several European agencies have reported similar strange losses of satellites in recent weeks. I am assigning one of my Agents to lead the investigation into this. I seem to remember you applied for O.D. work when you joined OFWAT. How do you fancy tagging along and trying to help?"

"Too right! Well, if you think I can help, Sir."

"Brightwell will be along in a moment, she's one of our best."

They sat and waited. Sim tried to make polite conversation but they had little in common, except extreme tiredness. After a few minutes, he heard a strange tip-tap noise coming from the corridor outside and then the door opened. Whatever preconceptions Sim had about O.D. Agents, the person who limped into the room was quite different.

Freda Brightwell appeared to be in her late thirties, smartly dressed and with strawberry blonde hair. Usually her striking colour would have caught Sim's attention but all he really noticed was the walking stick she clutched in her right hand. It was black, telescopic and had a carved silver handle. Freda's eyes followed Sim's gaze to her stick. As she started to say something, Wardle interrupted.

"So what security clearance have you got, Atkins?"

Sim pulled his focus back to his new boss. "Level 3, Sir, standard for my line of work in Sat Dep."

"And what about that background check I asked for last night, Brightwell?"

Freda sat down next to her boss and opened a slim file. "Born March 2003 to Florence and William Atkins. Raised in Edinburgh. Standard schooling followed by university at St Andrews, graduated with a First in Satellite Communications. Internet activity shows he has an unhealthy obsession with online gaming as well as a monthly subscription to Hustler. Other than that seems pretty clean, no sign of political activity or affiliations. Three years part-time military service in the T.A. Commanding officers reviewed him as bright but cocky. Excellent fitness, strength good for his size."

Sim blushed. He thought about protesting that the Hustler subscription was an administrative error. But before he could say anything, Wardle had continued:

"OK, let's raise that security clearance to level two and issue him a sidearm. First port of call for you two is Biggin Hill. MI6 have picked up intelligence: a possible terrorist attack on an airship landing there soon. It's all a bit vague but lucky we got anything at all to go on. We have checked the manifests. Day after tomorrow there is one landing with a cargo of military-grade satellite components. I doubt it's a coincidence."

Freda's eyebrows pinched together. "Sir, are you sure this is a good idea?"

Wardle stood up. "When you become head of the division, you can choose which missions to send your agents on. Until then I expect you to follow orders."

"I meant sending Atkins with me."

"You know most of our agents are busy with the Svalbard incident. Besides, Atkins has experience in the army and expertise in satellites."

Freda lowered her voice, almost whispering. "You know why I'm asking, Sir."

"We don't have any choice," Wardle said.

Sim blinked as his brown eyes started to feel too dry. He was ten years old again, left standing on the side of a football pitch as neither captain wanted him on their team. As they rose to leave, Sim offered his hand to help Freda up.

She ignored him and heaved herself out of the chair. "Come on, you'll need a wash and some rest before we start your induction."

CHAPTER 4

Tourniquets can be used to curtail catastrophic bleeding. They should be tightened until the distal pulse is no longer felt. The patient will likely require painkillers to accept this level of tightness. Periodic loosening should be considered to help prevent permanent nerve damage.

O.D. Training Manual Section 7e

5½ years earlier, Dorset, England.

Sim was tramping along a deeply rutted path, bone-hard ground offering traces of long-evaporated puddles. The purple flowers and dark green leaves of heather spread out on both sides of him as far as the gently undulating horizon. It reminded him of Scotland, except for the temperature. How long it had been since Southern England had experienced significant rainfall? The newspapers reckoned it was the worst drought in twenty years.

"How much further, Sim?"

Sim turned to look at the source of the question. "I've told you Rhys, call me Sarge when we're on exercise."

"Sorry Sarge," replied his friend.

"Squad, hold up." Sim stopped and consulted his map. "This exercise is too easy. How do they expect us to get lost with a map and compass in this terrain?"

"It's about speed, isn't it? Finding the quickest route between way markers. They said there would be obstacles to overcome."

"Yawn. Surely the T.A. could've sent us on an exercise somewhere a bit closer to University? Not the opposite end of the British Isles."

Sim looked up towards the dazzling sun in a cloudless sky and wiped the back of his neck.

"We might stand a chance of winning, if Max was a bit more min," said Rhys.

"Ahh, a maths joke, everybody. Come on, laugh at Rhys' joke. Anyone? Don't give up the degree just yet, taffy," said Sim.

"Did you hear that? He called me taffy. That's nice, isn't boys? Our Sarge is a racist!"

Sim smiled. The Territorial Army weekends wouldn't be the same without his best friend.

After three more miles of slogging across the rock-hard moorland, Sim called a halt for a quick lunch break. The squad unwrapped their rations cautiously; the T.A. was not known for its kindness to taste buds. Sim ruled out a camp fire to brew some tea – it would take too long and would risk setting fire to the heather.

Sim and Rhys sprawled next to each other, trying to make a chaise longue out of the clumps of heather. Rhys pulled out his drinking bottle and gulped noisily. His hand slipped as he went to put the stopper back in and some liquid spilt on the pale ground, disappearing almost instantly.

"This water shortage is only going to get worse, they reckon. Especially on the continent," said Rhys. "Did you read that the government is going to set up some agency to keep an eye on things. WAT OFF or something like that."

"OFWAT," replied Sim. "It's called OFWAT. I'm thinking of applying for a post there, after uni."

"Really? Some glorified inspector? Sounds a bit boring, though. I reckon it's the special forces for me. Hard-core Marines. Tidy."

"We can't solve all the world's problems with guns, Taffy. We need to use our brains too. OFWAT have this overseas division that sounds awesome. It'll be like MI6."

"Dream on, boyo. They'll never take a loser like you."

Sim sat up. "Thanks for— Hey you two, what the hell do you think you're doing?"

Two of the squad were lining up crossbows on a group of rabbits that were huddled together on a patch of pale yellow grass in the distance. One of the men squeezed the trigger: a zing followed by a thud and a rabbit pinned to the ground twitching. The other rabbits scattered.

"Where did you get those relics of torture from?"

The one who had shot the rabbit stood up. "Lighten up, Sarge. We're just doing some target practice. Sheesh, you're always giving us a hard time."

"Taking pot shots at rabbits. Fuckwits! As if they don't have trouble enough, scratching out a life in this drought," replied Sim.

"Screw you, you think you're so high and mighty. Just because you're the lieutenant's pet doesn't make you my boss." The man raised his crossbow once more and scanned the heather for another target.

Sim made a grab for the bow. The weapon danced between them, then there was another zing. Sim let go and looked in the direction the bow had been pointing. Rhys was writhing on the floor, clutching his leg. Sim ran over to his friend whose right thigh was pumping blood out of a gash in his combat trousers.

"Hold still, Rhys, I need to take a proper look at this. Someone get me a med pack, quick." Sim sliced open the trousers and peeled back the cloth. The wound was deep enough to have nicked an artery. The pool of blood beneath Rhys' leg was already the size of a plate and spreading fast. "Christ, this needs proper medical attention." Sim unwrapped a gauze pad and got somebody to squeeze it hard against the wound. Rhys whimpered and the colour drained from his face.

"Hey Rhys, you're gonna be fine. I've got his," said Sim. He took off his belt and formed a tourniquet around the top of Rhys' thigh. The bleeding slowed but didn't stop completely. Sim stood up and put some distance between himself and Rhys, calling over another member of the squad. "We need to call for an evac, he's going to lose a lot of blood. Probably go into shock."

The other soldier, Max, shook his head. "Can't Sarge. Rhys was standing next to the radio, looks like it got smashed by the bolt."

Sim looked across at where Rhys was lying, and sure enough, just behind him was a communicator with a wrecked speaking piece and a bolt embedded into the metal casing. "We'll phone it in then." Sim reached for his mobile phone and checked for signal strength. No bars.

"It's no good," said Max. "I tried looking up the football scores earlier. The Great Flux is screwing up all the networks."

Sim put his hands on his hips, then scratched his forehead, scanning the horizon. "Well, we'll have to carry him to the nearest way point and hope we're not too late. Come on, help me put a stretcher together."

The squad took it turns to carry the stretcher. Sim was leading from the front, trying to push on at a pace that the stretcher-bearers could maintain without risking a stumble.

"Sarge, are you sure this is the best way?" The man whose bow had caused the injury was looking doubtful.

"Don't you think you've caused enough trouble already, Jon? I know how to read a map."

"It's just that there's a lot of smoke over the horizon, and we seem to be heading straight for it."

Jon was right, but Sim was sure it was just a smoke screen that the organisers had laid on – 'obstacles' they had said. He could lead the squad through a smoke screen, no problems. But when they got to the brow of the hill it was a problem, a big one. The heathland stretching out below them was on fire. A line of orange stretched across their field of vision, and beyond that blackened stumps of shrubs were smouldering away.

Sim cursed and looked at the map. A gust of wind pulled it out of his fingers and he had to leap forward to grasp it again. It was upside down, but Sim took a moment before realising why the map made no sense. He could feel the eyes of the squad boring into him. Left or right of the fire? Right looked quicker but took them through a territory marked 'danger' on the map.

Sim went over to the stretcher and felt Rhys' pulse. They didn't have any choice. Time was running out. "This way, men, come on."

Fortunately, the fire had not spread too far in the direction Sim had chosen. The detour would only cost them ten or fifteen minutes. They cut their way through a barbed wire fence and then walked parallel to it for half a mile. The pace was slowing and the squad had to rotate carrying duties more frequently. The sun was still high in the sky, with no signs of clouds to offer any relief. The smoke from the fire at least wasn't blowing towards them. Max stopped for another drink, but his bottle was empty.

"Have the rest of mine," said Sim. "I'm not thirsty."

"Thanks Sarge." Max took a big gulp of water and then kept hold of the bottle. Sim licked his lips and turned away.

A whistling sound streaked overhead and something thudded into the ground a hundred metres ahead and to the right of them.

"What the fuck was that?" said Jon.

Another whistle and a thud. The squad turned to see bright red smoke billowing out from the first impact crater and then the same from the second impact.

"Shit! Get down everybody," said Sim.

A third whistle. Except that this time the impact was not a gentle thud but a blast of earth being thrown upwards and raining down on the surrounding vicinity. Sim coughed as a light shower of soil fell on his face and some went in his mouth.

Jon lifted his head off the ground briefly to look around. "You've taken us through a firing range, you cretin!" Then he ducked back down as another shell flew over, landing a little closer to them than the first. The ground shook again. More soil and bits of heather rained down on the squad. "We're sitting ducks."

Sim tried to think straight amid the shouts and the bombing. Back the way they had come would leave Rhys even further from medical treatment. Crossing over the fence here was impossible – the fire was still blazing strongly just the other side of the wire. If they kept going and crossed the fence further down, that would be the quickest route to medical help, but would take them even closer to the artillery bombardment. A third shell landed and he pressed his face into the earth again.

Think, dammit, think!

Radar. If the artillery boys aren't directly observing this barrage, they must be monitoring it with radar. If we can get the radio to send out a burst of noise, they might pick it up.

Sim ran over to where the others were cowering and grabbed the broken radio set off them, unscrewing the back to get at its innards. He reached for the mobile phone in his pocket and unwound the headphone cord from around it. A fourth shell landed, and the earth shook again, tipping the radio onto its front. Sim blew soil out of the wired compartment. He sliced open the wires of his mobile's headphones and spliced them into the radio. He switched the phone on and tried to select some music.

His fingers were covered in dirt and the screen didn't register his strokes at first.

Work, you stupid screen!

Some spit and a wipe on his trousers solved that problem. He cranked up the volume on his phone to maximum and selected a rock song. He played a short burst then paused the music, another burst then paused again and a final burst then stopped. Another shell burst, this time closer than the others, sent Sim sprawling to the ground. *Why aren't they listening?*

He played three more bursts of music, leaving the song playing a little longer on these occasions. And then three more short bursts. He lay there waiting for the next shell to land. But it didn't come. The others started to get up from the hollows they had pressed themselves into during the barrage, looking around.

"How's Rhys?" shouted Sim to Max.

"Not good. I think the shelling has loosened the tourniquet – he's bleeding again."

Sim went over to do what he could for Rhys. A faint sound in the distance caused him to stop and look up. Definitely getting nearer. Yes! A helicopter. Smoke from the fire was drifting towards them. Sim wasn't sure the helicopter had seen them. He fired a green flare into the air. The aircraft flew straight towards them and set down in a bare patch a hundred metres away from them. It was a small two-seater scout helicopter.

"Come on, let's get Rhys out of here." Sim picked up one end of the stretcher and helped Max carry his friend over to the chopper.

"What the ruddy hell are you lot doing on my firing range?" shouted the Major over the still-whirring blades.

"No time to explain, Sir, this man needs urgent medical attention. I think he needs your seat." Sim lifted his friend off the stretcher and tried to man-handle him into the helicopter, barging the Major out of the way. Sim leant into the cockpit. "Puncture wound to the femoral artery. Lost a lot of blood. Go!"

The Major stepped away from the helicopter with Sim. His face was puce, but as the aircraft lifted off, his breathing slowed and he turned to Sim. "Was that your awful taste in music we could hear back at the battery?" Sim nodded. "Smart thinking, young man. Smart thinking."

CHAPTER 5

Salt Camels are airships that carry large cargoes of hydrogen chloride from the Middle East to the Arctic Ocean. Water scarcity has forced Middle Eastern governments to build increasing numbers of solar-powered desalination plants. A few years ago one of our brightest engineers suggested that Saudi Arabia might like to sell its salt to the United Kingdom to help maintain the correct salinity of the Atlantic conveyor belt (see section 2c on the melting polar icecap). And so these great airships began their regular roundtrips between Riyadh and the Arctic Ocean.
OD Training Manual Section 2c

April 29th, 2028. Biggin Hill Dirigible Airport, outskirts of London.

Sim stamped his feet and rubbed his hands to ward off the chill of a southerly breeze and a drizzly dawn. The slate grey sky did little to enhance the view over Kent. He had been standing with Freda on the outskirts of Biggin Hill airfield, near the north perimeter fence, for over an hour already. Sim had insisted on following Freda's car on his beloved bike but had taken off his biking gloves because they were too bulky for field work.

"Why do you still ride that ancient machine?"

"Petrol and proud. I like something I can repair myself if it breaks down. One of those sit-on hair driers goes phut and you've had it," said Sim. He started blowing on his hands and looking around. "This is cool."

Freda tutted and threw him a pair of black military gloves - warm, waterproof and thin enough not to interfere with any manual tasks.

"Thanks Ma."

"You want me to sew your name in them? What sort of a name is Sim anyway?"

"What's wrong with Sim?" he asked in a voice that was a little too high to do his credibility any good, then paused. Freda stood looking at him. He sighed. "The kids at school used to call me Simple Simon. The more they bricked on me, the harder I found it to concentrate. The more I struggled, the more they teased. When it came to senior school, I made damn sure I was enrolled as Sim."

"You could've just said it's short for Simon."

Damn, she is seriously uptight.

During his crash training over the past 48 hours Freda had barely broken into a smile. He had tried to impress her with the newly issued 9mm automatic Glock pistol on the shooting range, but kept missing the target high and left. She had grabbed the gun off him as he started to complain about the sights being off, laced the target with three rapid shots and handed it back to him. 'It's more powerful than the Browning you used in the TA – learn to handle it.' She had noted down the result on a clipboard and moved on to the next part of his condensed induction.

Sim put on the gloves and looked around. Biggin Hill was on a plateau about 600 metres above sea level on top of the New South Downs. The basic layout was similar to its glory days during the Battle of Britain: a runway and taxiway at right angles to each other, laid out like a giant flexed arm. There was now a very large circle of tarmac in the crook of the elbow so that the airships could always take off into the wind. There were three huge hangars and two sets of mobile docking towers used to tether the airships that landed there. The airfield this morning was buzzing with activity; ground handlers preparing for the three airships due to land here that morning, fuel trucks and cargo tractors on standby to empty and fill the incoming airships. Sim even noticed that the airport's emergency services were on full alert, already kitted out and waiting in their vehicles in case something went wrong.

Several MI6 armed operatives were stationed towards the southern end of the site. This was the direction from which the vast airship carrying the satellite equipment would approach the landing field. Sim was getting so excited at the prospect of some action at last that he needed to take a pee. He hopped from foot to foot trying not to think about his bladder.

"Why are we all the way back here, when the action's going to be at the other end of the airport?" asked Sim.

"Because we get a better view of everything that's going on here, and because we don't even know if *that* airship will be the target. So eyes peeled, focus. And next time you get ready for outdoor duty, wear some proper bloody clothing. I don't want my life endangered because your fingers are too cold to pull a trigger. Got it?"

"Yes boss." Sim felt his cheeks flush and a stiffening of his muscles. He had assumed that it would be another warm spring day, but assumptions are dangerous. He still thought they were in the wrong part of the airfield but it wasn't worth arguing the point. He was even more convinced that she hated having him tag along and was determined to prove his worth somehow before the day was out.

Sim scratched at his new autographer. All agents wore one in the field – a mask that fitted over eyes, ears and chin with a communication device built in, optical enhancement goggles and a camera that recorded everything the agent saw. Sim's had been moulded to his face but the inside had not yet been worn smooth from weeks of use. SPQR was stamped across his skull-cap: Serve, Protect, Quench, Ration. A picture from a school book flashed through his mind. Sim wondered if the legionaries bearing those same initials had felt this uncomfortable waiting to go into battle.

There was a blurt of activity over the short-wave communicators.

"Suspect sighted, perimeter fence, sector B."

"Team 2 circle round to his left."

"Team 1 moving in, suspect is looking up at approaching airship with something in his hand. Permission to use deadly force?"

There was a muffled crack over the communicator.

"Target down, target down. Move in and immobilise."

Sim was itching to go over to the area where the MI6 gunmen were, but Freda held him back. Then:

"Wrong target, I repeat, wrong target. Just a damn balloon spotter. Get an ambulance here fast."

Through the low-level cloud a ship appeared in the distance; it had an unsightly bulge on the top of its bow and aft outer-skin, like a huge grey marrow. The low hum of large propeller turbines turning over at maneouvering speed could just be detected over the hubbub of airfield activity. Freda put her goggles on to 20x magnification.

"That's not her. It's the SC...one...zero...seven. Arriving a bit early, no? What does the manifest say?"

"SC107, inbound from Riyadh, it's not due in until 07:55. Stopping off for a re-fuel and then onwards to the New South Sea near Iceland. It's a Salt Camel." Sim had been reading up about these in the manual the night before.

The airship drew nearer, venting off some gas to become 50 kilograms 'heavy'. The SC107 glided gently towards the runway with its bow lines hanging out ready to be caught and fed into the mechanical winch. Other handlers had the harder job of grabbing the aft line - once the nose was tethered it was difficult for the pilot to hold the airship steady. A slight breeze and change in temperature started the back end twitching. The ground handlers grouped together like a host of ants trying to bring down a massive beetle. When the tail of the ship had been successfully tethered to the second winch, the dirigible was mechanically hauled into the mobile masts which then proceeded slowly along a tramway towards Hangar Bravo.

Sim was fascinated by the whole process – he had never visited a dirigible airport before – but Freda kept scanning the airfield and the skies for anything unusual. She pointed at something for Sim to watch: the ground crew seemed to be having a problem either with the nose of the Salt Camel or with the bow mooring mast; the agents could not tell which.

Another airship appeared through the clouds. The military dirigible carrying the satellite equipment – the MD34 – was far more beautiful than the Salt Camel. Its body was sleek with an outer skin that seemed to shimmer blue-orange like an oil slick. Carbon-fibre engine frames, like something from an Olympic racing bike, complemented two missile launchers and an M232 Chain Gun.

While Freda watched the second ground crew prepare for the imminent landing, Sim switched his attention back to the Salt Camel, which was still having difficulties. One of the ground crew had started to scale the bow mooring mast's internal ladder to see what the problem was. As the military balloon slowly drifted closer to the runway, Sim listened in to the MI6 communicators again:

"No more screw-ups men, call it in by the book."

"Team One, nothing here, sector A clear."

"Team Two, sector B, negative."

"Team Three, main entrance, all quiet."

Sim watched as the ground crewman reached the top of the Salt Camel's bow mooring mast. He started yelling something to his colleagues.

BOOM!

An explosion ripped through the metal structure as a fireball lit up the grey morning. A rag-doll body was flung from the mast as the tower crumpled like matchsticks. The nose of the dirigible was sliced off and despite losing some gas, it also lost a significant part of its outer skeleton, mooring line and fixing points, instantly becoming 100 kilos 'light'. With its tail still moored and the manoeuvring propellers off-line, the front end of the Salt Camel started floating straight up until the whole balloon resembled a fat rocket on a launch pad. There were screams from the vessel's crew who were still inside the dirigible.

One of the windows of the gondola smashed and a flail of limbs fell through. Even as he staggered backwards with the shock wave, Sim tracked the body downwards, unable to take his eyes off those last few seconds of life. The inevitable abrupt ending sent a jolt through Sim's neck, dazing him. He vaguely realised that somebody was on the floor next to him.

Freda was struggling to her feet. "Shit, it's the wrong bloody balloon."

CHAPTER 6

Small, cheap, remote-control drones have become a nightmare for airport authorities. After a spate of terrorist-related attacks on planes and airport infrastructure in the early 20s, defense mechanisms were installed. These included jamming devices to cut off the control signals as well as surface-to-air weaponry for high-value locations.

OD Training Manual Section 6

4 years earlier. Keystone, South Dakota.

Jember Abdi had travelled a long way. Physically as well as mentally since his country had been attacked. As he limped into the dusty bar, he licked his lips. It was so close now, he could taste the victory. But first, help. He couldn't do this alone. As his eyes adjusted from the glaring sun outside to the dimly lit interior, his glance fell briefly on every person in the room. He walked over to the bar and ordered an iced tea and slurped at it straight away. He turned to face the rest of the clientele. One man gave the faintest of nods and Abdi made his way over.

"Hello black man."

"Runs with the sun on his back?"

"Yes, yes, please sit down. Call me Sonny."

Abdi sat and slurped at his drink again. "It's thirsty work, Sonny, walking twenty miles in this heat."

"Why didn't you catch the bus. Or hire a car?"

"Buses have CCTV." Abdi reached into his pocket and pulled out a few coins and two crumpled notes. "And I couldn't afford the car."

"Ahh, our little flying friends. Not cheap, I suppose."

Abdi shook his head. "Shall we talk business? Somewhere a little more private?"

The other man nodded his head, rattling the beads of his wooden necklace. "Come, follow me."

They entered a basement apartment a few hundred yards from the bar. It was sparsely furnished with a couch, a bed, and a small table in front of a kitchenette. The walls were draped with native American craftwork as well as a few faded photographs in cheap plastic frames.

Abdi approached one and peered at the caption below. 'Crazy Horse, 1868.' He pointed. "Is that an original photograph?"

"Of course. The only thing in this junk pile that's worth anything."

"I didn't realise photography had been invented that long ago."

"We didn't come here to discuss the history of the camera, did we?"

Abdi held out his hands, palms outwards. "No, sorry, of course. But. I need to know. You are committed to this?"

The other man clenched his left fist and jabbed his finger towards the picture. "The sons of bitches stole the Black Hills from Crazy Horse. And desecrated the site with those... those abominations."

"I fear we may not make it back. I'm willing to meet my maker for the cause. Are you?"

The native American shrugged. "I've got nothing better to do."

Abdi closed his eyes and muttered a prayer. Then he drew a small, battered map out of his pocket and spread it on the table, carefully flattening out the corners. "Come, let us rain down hell on our enemies."

The entrance to the National Park was busy on Independence Day. The queue of SUVs stretched back some distance. Sonny's vehicle was now sixth in line, older and dirtier than the other ones. Abdi was watching the steward on the entrance, processing each vehicle with a quick glance at the occupants and the issuance of a ticket. The Ethiopian glanced round at their empty back seat and wiped his neck.

"The air-con gave up a few years ago. Sorry, friend."

"I don't mind the heat," said Abdi. "It's our lack of children that worries me. Every other vehicle is a family coming for a day out in the park. What's the ranger going to think when he sees the pair of us? We can't afford to get searched."

Sonny bit his stubby nails while the queue shuffled forward another two cars and then he reached across for Abdi's hand.

Abdi stared at Sonny. "What you doing?"

"Gay men don't have kids to take to the park. Hold my hand when we get to the gate."

Abdi made the sign of the cross on his chest and then nodded. It was their turn. The steward came up to the driver's window and leant forward as Sonny opened it.

"Hi there gentlemen. Fine day for celebrating, ain't it?"

"It most assuredly is, officer," said Sonny in a soft tone. "I can't wait to dive into my friend's picnic box." He screwed up his eyes and stretched his smile as high as it would go.

The officer paused for a moment, looked across at Abdi, and then coughed. "Yes, right, well that'll be fifty dollars for a day ticket. Please stick to the marked roads and only park in designated areas. The gates will be closing at 7pm this evening."

They drove through the gates and went up the road towards the main car park. Many families were disgorging from their SUVs, grabbing armfuls of picnic hampers and accoutrements and then wandering off into the parkland. Nobody paid any attention to one more truck, even if this one did drive straight through the car park and followed a dirt road, past a sign that said 'authorised vehicles only.'

They carried on down the track for a while, around several turns, until they were well out of sight of the day trippers and the track was hemmed in by thick forest.

"Stop the car," Abdi said. He got out and walked a few paces into the trees, gathering an armful of twigs that were scattered on the dry floor. He arranged them in a pile next to a fallen decaying tree, and took out a small plastic bottle and cloth from his pocket. He doused the cloth in a clear fluid from the bottle, stuffed it at the base of the pile of wood and swapped the bottle for a box of matches in his pocket. He struck a match and watched it flare and take hold, mesmerized by the flame for a moment. Then he held the match against the cloth and retreated once the fuel had caught fire. He watched the flames lick higher and then ran back towards Sonny.

"What's that for?" the driver asked.

"Distraction," said Abdi. "Give them other things to worry about."

They drove on for another ten minutes or so and then pulled off the dirt track into a little clearing, tucking the SUV behind a tall pile of tree logs. They took the covering off the flatbed part of the vehicle, revealing dozens of drones that sat there, glistening in the sun like a swarm of flying ants whose nest had just been unearthed.

Sonny whistled. "So how do we control this many drones? I don't see hundreds of remote control handsets."

"No, no. I have pre-programmed them. See the ones with green dots; they take off from point A, the blue ones from point B, red equals C. Come on, we need to get them in place before anybody notices we are here."

It took over an hour to carry and position all the drones. Once this was done, Abdi and Sonny split up, Abdi to the place where the green drones were lying on the floor and Sonny to the red group of flying machines. One by one, the pair started turning on the drones and watched them shudder into life and then fly off, over the top of the trees, towards Mount Rushmore. The sky began to swarm with the micro flying machines, as if it were hatching time for the insects out on the grasslands of Abdi's home country.

The pair re-united at the spot where the blue drones had been left and turned them on as well to follow behind their fellow drones, all streaming towards the highest point in the park.

As the men stared into the bright sky, Sonny pointed off to their right at a column of thick smoke. "Looks like your fire took hold."

"Come on, let's get out of here."

They drove back up the dirt track past the fire. A warden who was parked next to the blazing trees was too busy shouting into his radio to notice the other vehicle drive past. When the pair made it back to the main car park, they left the SUV in a normal parking bay and started walking up towards the monument. A few of the other visitors had seen the column of smoke and were starting to point. A fire engine steamed through the car park heading for the fire. Abdi and Sonny ignored this and carried on up to the main viewing platform. The swarm of drones were starting to close in on the Presidents' faces.

"This is too easy," said Sonny with a grin on his face.

"Not necessarily. The drones aren't there yet," said Abdi leaning in close to Sonny's ear so that only he could hear him. "The defences will kick-in about now."

In the distance, a red beam, bright enough to be visible even in the middle of the afternoon, shot out from some unseen source between the viewing platform and the Mountain. The beam picked out one of the drones and scythed it in two. Both halves tumbled out of the sky into the trees below. Sonny gasped. Another beam flashed out and a second drone fell.

"Now you see why I needed so many," whispered Abdi.

The drones kept flying straight for their destination with no attempt to dodge the red death ray. There were too many for the laser to bring down. The casualty rate may have been as high as 50 per cent, but that still left over fifty drones that got through and settled onto George Washington's face. The President's statue seemed to age and weather as the drones and their shadows discoloured his skin.

"Come on, let's blow this thing and get out of there," said Sonny, grabbing Abdi's arm.

"Careful what you squeeze." Abdi's right hand was holding a large remote control handset inside his jacket, with the long antenna sticking out under his chin. Abdi waited for the last few drones to run the gauntlet of the laser and then pulled the handset out, extended the antenna even further, and flicked a switch. "Let's see how the Americans like it when one of their national monuments is reduced to rubble." He looked up to watch for the reaction and bit his lip.

George Washington's face disappeared in a puff of greyish purple smoke. A second later the noise of a huge bang reached the viewing platform. People gasped and screamed. Some ran instantly. Others reached for their cameras and starting clicking away as the smoke slowly dissipated.

Sonny reached for Abdi's hand again and then dropped it almost at once. "What the hell?"

The President's face had no visible damage on it whatsoever. Abdi jabbed the switch on his remote control unit a couple more times. Nothing. His mouth opened and he started to say something, but no words came out. He just waved his hand towards the mountain.

All of the tourists around him continued to point and stare at the Presidents' faces. All except one. A young man, not quite as dark skinned as Abdi, was looking at the Ethiopian and the equipment in his hands. The young man stared, then looked up at the mountain, and back at Abdi. Sonny was trying to pull Abdi back towards the car park.

"Terrorists!" The young man pointed an accusing finger and started running towards Abdi. That single word was like a gunshot for a herd of nervous sheep. Tourists began screaming and shouting, running for the stairs. Some tripped over, others jumped off the viewing platform, dropping ten feet down to the ground below. More screams from those that landed badly.

The young man was making slow progress towards Abdi, as the tourists were pouring past him in the opposite direction. Abdi and Sonny started running off, heading towards a set of stairs furthest from their accuser. As they reached the bottom of the stairs the young man vaulted over the side of the platform and landed in a roll, springing to his feet almost instantly.

Abdi was barging people out of the way as he ran down the footpath. Sonny was starting to lag behind; it had been too long since he'd taken proper exercise. The young man caught him and threw his arms around Sonny's legs. They both landed in a heap and Sonny tried to kick off his attacker's hold. His boot connected with the young man's cheek, giving him a moment to roll onto his knees. But immediately he was flat on the ground again. The young man had him pinned down, a knee in Sonny's back with an arm in a painful grip that he couldn't break.

The young man looked down at his catch and then along the path at the crowds of people running towards the car parks. Already he had lost sight of the one with the remote control unit. He breathed hard and sat on top of the one he had caught and waited for somebody to arrive.

A few people who had been running for the car park stopped to help the young man pin Sonny to the ground. It was another twenty minutes before somebody of authority came past the citizen's arrest. A man in a dark suit and matching tie, accompanied by a policeman, stopped and crouched down next to Sonny.

"What's the story here, boy?"

The young man replied: "Just trying to make a difference, Sir. I saw this man and another acting suspiciously just as the explosion happened. One of them had a remote control unit: I figured they set the charges off. I'm sorry. I wasn't quick enough to catch both of them."

The man smiled. "Sounds like you did plenty. What's your name?"

"Bo Brunswick."

"Well Bo, anytime you fancy a full-time job catching scum like this, you give me a call, OK?" The man in the suit handed Bo a business card. Bo was just about to reply when there was a loud crack from up on the mountain. Birds broke cover from the trees and screeched as if in echo. All eyes turned towards George Washington's face just as his nose fell off.

CHAPTER 7

Hoverflies are an essential piece of surveillance equipment. These un-manned aerial vehicles can vary in size, depending on the kit on board, from a small plane to a large dragonfly. Range has become somewhat limited since the Great Flux (see section 2a) due to the lack of sufficient satellite bandwidth.

OD Training Manual Section 8d

Sim rolled with the blast wave of the explosion and, as he rose, drew the automatic pistol from its holster panning the gun across the airfield. He spotted two men outside the perimeter fence.

"There they are," he said to Freda. Sim aimed but realised that he was too far away to use his pistol. The men were wearing tracksuits, one blue and one grey, and both had baseball caps. One of them was stuffing something into a rucksack and then they started running towards a motorbike leaning against the trunk of a young oak tree nearby.

"HQ, this is Agent Brightwell, we need eyes in the sky over Biggin Hill, suspects fleeing the scene on motorbike, two Caucasian males, in tracksuits and baseball caps." While she was relaying this information, Sim sprinted towards his own bike. He fired up the Triumph, and came to collect Freda, thrusting his only helmet in her hand as she got on the back to ride pillion. As they approached the exit gates, Sim assessed the quickest way through without pausing to wait for a barrier to rise.

"Lean left," he shouted as he banked the bike into a sharp right turn. They just squeezed through and under a small gap at the end of the barrier, but not without clipping Freda's helmet on the end of the boom. "My bad," Sim said as they raced away from the airfield and turned right onto the A233 heading towards central London.

"How do you know they went south?" shouted Freda above the roar.

"That's where I would go to escape on a bike."

She clicked on her communicator again. "HQ, we're proceeding south along the A233. Where is hovercam?"

"Scrambling now, ETA five minutes."

Sim opened up the throttle some more - they needed to catch up before the terrorists got to the Croydon Road junction where the escape route options multiplied. If they could not see which option the terrorists took at that point, they would have to rely on sheer guesswork. He pulled out from behind a small, slow car into the path of an oncoming lorry. The lorry flashed its lights and slammed on its brakes just as Sim pulled back into the left side of the road. After a couple of miles with a few more near misses on the wrong side of the road, he caught sight of the other motorbike which was also weaving in and out of the slower traffic. Sim watched them approach the A232 and cross straight over.

"Looks like they're heading into London," he said to Freda. "Get the drone pilot to focus on the A21, they'll be on it in a minute." Looking up, Freda could just make out the unmanned craft starting to draw near. As Sim predicted, they soon reached the A21 and the bike in front turned left, heading towards central London. The traffic got worse as they approached Bromley. The bikes kept weaving in and out of slow-moving vehicles but the slaloming was costing each of them time. Sim could see the terrorists pass through some traffic lights just as they were turning amber. He moved into the middle of the road, passing cars that were slowing down. He sped up even as the lights turned red.

"This is going to be tight," he yelled.

The traffic from both of the side roads started to move across the junction as their lights turned green. Sim swerved left then right, just avoiding the front bumper of a white BMW. The car's on-board computer detected an imminent collision and slammed on the brakes. The driver started to swear loudly in the direction of Sim and Freda but then got shunted from behind by a car that still relied on human reactions. A mother driving her kids to school: her latte slipped from her left hand, bounced off the airbag that had instantly inflated, and emptied its contents all over her new Armani dress.

"Phew, that was *really* close," said Sim, looking back to see the chaos he had just caused at the traffic lights. As he turned back to watch the road ahead, a pushchair was wheeled out into the road right in front of him. Sim slammed on the brakes. The tyres skidded but he managed to keep the bike upright. The rear wheel started sliding out to the left. The front of the bike just passed by the pushchair but the rear part of the bike, now sticking out an angle of 30 degrees, smacked straight into it. The buggy flew up into the air and spun over a couple of times before landing with a bounce and rolled over once more as something flopped out onto the road in a sickening, lifeless manner.

"Holy crap," cried Sim.

Freda looked round to see a girl in a light blue school uniform rush out and pick up a large doll lying next to her toy pushchair. "Don't worry, it was just a doll."

The distractions of the traffic lights and pushchair had cost them valuable time. As Sim re-accelerated, he realised that he had lost sight of the other motorbike. "I hope the drone has visual contact," he said. Freda radioed to HQ and was told to keep heading along the A21 towards central London. The suspects were only about half a mile ahead of them.

Sim pushed the bike hard while Freda stayed in contact with the eyes in the sky. They had made up a lot of ground by the time the terrorists crossed the Thames at Westminster Bridge. The traffic got more and more dense, making rapid progress tricky, even on a motorbike.

"This is HQ, we have local police blocking the road ahead. The net should be closing in. Keep tight."

As they crossed Trafalgar Square, Sim could see the row of police cars with flashing lights blocking the road west. A strip of caltrops awaited the wheels of the terrorists' bike. Sim started to ease back on the throttle as the chase came to an inevitable end, but then the bike in front went straight over the spikes without any effect and veered round the police cars by mounting the kerb.

"Damn, they must be on run-flats." Sim detoured around the strip of caltrops, shooing the policemen out of the way. They got to the bottom of Haymarket and saw the others still on the kerb, proceeding up the hill towards Piccadilly Circus. Pedestrians screamed and scattered as the bike ploughed on through them. Sim followed along the now-clear pavement. The terrorists abandoned their bike near one of the entrances to the underground station and bolted down the stairs.

"Crap, the hovercam won't be any use now," shouted Sim. He pulled up to the same underground entrance and jumped off the bike, running for the stairs. Freda followed more slowly, using the handrail to help her slide down the initial set of steps. Sam found himself in the ticket hall to Piccadilly Circus station: a large circular space, with numerous points of access from all directions. Beyond the ticket barriers there were two main sets of escalators, one towards the Piccadilly line and the other towards the Bakerloo and Northern Line. The morning rush hour was in full flow, mostly with people coming up from the underground lines and heading out to their places of work. Going against this flow was not easy. Sim paused to look around and just caught sight of the men they were pursuing: they had vaulted the barriers and were running towards the right-hand set of escalators leading towards the Bakerloo and Northern line.

Freda just caught up. "Bloomin' ada, it's like Piccadilly Circus in 'ere."

Sim ran for the ticket barriers as a couple of surprised station attendants started shouting after the terrorists. The distraction allowed Sim also to vault the barriers and run for the same escalators.

The men ahead had already reached the bottom and turned towards another set leading to the Bakerloo line. As they did so, one of them grabbed a newspaper out of the hands of a startled commuter. The terrorist reached into his pocket and pulled out a flare, banging the bottom of it hard on the side of the escalator. The flare burst into life, burning incandescent red. The man used it to set light to the newspaper and then threw both of them into a bin at the bottom of the moving steps. Flames started to lick out of the top of the bin.

A few metres away, on the up escalators, a man in a pinstripe suit peered up from his copy of the FT and nearly dropped his umbrella. He pointed and shouted "fire". The woman in front of him screamed and nearly lost her footing. Somebody near the top of the down escalators realised that they were being carried towards the flames and pushed the emergency stop button. The sudden lack of motion sent an elderly gentleman toppling down these escalators until he landed on his back at the bottom, next to the fire. A nasty cut on his forehead was already starting to ooze bright red.

There was a stampede from commuters trying to get up and away from the fire as the alarm bells started ringing throughout the station, and Sim found it almost impossible to make progress. He lost sight of the terrorists but managed to get down to where the unconscious old man was lying near the flames. Quickly assessing that the risk of being burnt alive outweighed the risk of spinal injury, Sim picked the man up and put him in a fireman's lift over his shoulder. He carried him onto the Bakerloo line platform and gently laid the man down onto a bench. There was no sign of the terrorists along the rapidly emptying platform.

He trudged back towards the fire and found Freda with her walking stick and a now-empty fire extinguisher, poking through the smouldering newspapers. She picked up the discharged flare in gloved hands and gently blew off a fine layer of soot. Some initials and a long number emerged on the casing. "Let's see what the tech team make of this."

CHAPTER 8

Facial recognition systems use algorithms to extract landmarks from the image of a subject's face, such as the relative position, size and shape of their eyes, nose and jaw. Skin texture analysis, looking for unique lines and blemishes helps improve the accuracy of the matching process.

OD Training Manual Section 8d

"What went wrong?" said Wardle, banging his hand on the table. "You were sent to Biggin Hill to investigate a potential terrorist plot. You failed to prevent the attack and you failed to apprehend the perpetrators afterwards. What exactly was the point of you being there?"

Sim recoiled at the shock of being blamed. They had tried their best.

"Maybe I over-estimated you, Atkins." Wardle jabbed his finger at Sim. "Maybe satellite analysis is all you're good for."

Freda stood up. "It wasn't Sim's fault, sir. If anything, he was the only one who showed any initiative this morning. Without Sim we wouldn't have been able to give chase and we may not have recovered the forensic evidence at the underground station."

"Hmm…still, I'm surprised at you, Brightwell. Normally my best asset in the field." Wardle sat down and wiped his glasses on a cloth.

"We were sent to keep an eye on MD34, not the Salt Camel. The MI6 meat-heads shot an innocent bystander and weren't even at the right end of the airfield when the explosion happened. We do still have a trail to follow, thanks to Sim." She nodded at him and he gave a cautious smile back.

Wardle drummed his fingers on the table, breathing deeply. "Very well, Brightwell, pursue all lines of enquiries. Take Atkins along if you must. But no more screw-ups."

Security camera feeds of the underground station revealed only blurred images of the terrorists' faces, mostly hidden by baseball caps. But the video from Sim's autographer had captured an image of one face at a distance. Even after the tech guys had enhanced and cleaned up the picture it was still too blurry to run through a face-recognition algorithm.

"Let's come at this from another angle," said Freda, sitting across from Sim in the London offices. They had been given a cramped room as a make-shift base for their investigations. "The Salt Camel arrived early, right? Maybe the MD34 was the actual target and the terrorists screwed up."

She tapped her pen on the desk. "And could the terrorists have planted that bomb on site? Or did they have inside help? The police have been interviewing all the witnesses. We should have a trawl through the transcripts."

Sim looked at this watch, it was nearly 8pm already, 15 hours after they had set off that morning.

"Somewhere to go, have we?" Freda called up the transcripts of all the interviews on her desk glass and transferred half the pile to Sim's screen with a swipe of her hand. "I'll get some food and drink sent up. This could take a while."

"Yes, boss," replied Sim.

Sim's eyes were beginning to droop. The adrenalin from earlier in the day had faded, while the boost of energy from a sandwich and coffee at eight was running out. Staring at a computer screen late into the night was hardly new for him, but the subject matter was normally a bit more entertaining. He flicked over the page of a file he was reading and then flicked back again, noticing something about the interviews with the surviving crew of the Salt Camel.

"Where are the details of the Salt Camel manifest? How many crew did she have?"

Freda tabbed through some other files. "Twenty-two able bodies. Why?"

"They lost two crew members. So how come there are only nineteen interviews here? Somebody did a bunk before the police started asking questions."

They double-checked and sure enough, Paul Thomas was neither dead at the scene nor interviewed afterwards. A cook who had been serving on the Salt Camel for two years.

Freda went to the door and called for somebody called David to join them. "Sim, this is David Feinberg, our resident IT expert since Haman kicked him out. David, this is Sim, a satellites expert who's been assigned to me for the Biggin Hill attack."

The two men shook hands. Sim had dozens of questions running through his mind, but Freda spoke again.

"David, we need to track a missing cook, named Paul Thomas. He left Biggin Hill this morning. Must have been around 7:30am. Not much other information at this stage; but we need to trace him urgently."

David nodded and indicated Freda's desk. "May I?" Without waiting for an answer, he sat down and logged into the OD system, swiping and selecting his way through a few screens. "OK, so Paul Thomas, working on the SC107. Yep, I have his bank account details here from the salary transfers. Let's see if he used that to catch public transport this morning."

Freda glanced across at Sim, smiled and raised her eyebrows.

David tapped away at Freda's screen and keypad. "Yep, as I thought. Caught a train into central London at 07:36. London Transport should be able to link his entry point transaction with an exit. Hang on, just need an extra security clearance. Yep, here he is coming out at Leicester Square. No other signs of travel today. I can run an algo on his face but it might take a few minutes to code up and crunch."

"Right, come on Sim, we're not letting this one get away. David, run the local CCTV tapes around Leicester Square. Once you've worked out where he went next, radio me."

Sim got up and spread his hands, palm up, towards his partner. "What about back-up? Rendezvous point? Evac route, if it all goes pear shaped?" Sim had just been reading the manual on operational protocol. Proper spies never just barged in there.

"No time," said Freda. "A true agent knows when to go by the book and when to wing it. Time to fly, Agent Atkins."

Twenty minutes later, Sim and Freda were walking up Greek Street, looking for the entrance to the *Mixin It* Club. Paul Thomas had arrived there a few hours ago, but apparently hadn't re-emerged. The street thronged with young men and women, busy enjoying themselves. The news of another bomb attack in London that morning left little impression on these revellers, it seemed. The doorway to the club, halfway up the street on the left-hand side, clearly stated 'Members Only'.

"Damn it, now what do we do? I want to get in there undercover, not with a warrant and police escort," said Freda.

"Can't David sort something?"

Freda radioed in to HQ. Five minutes later the message came through. "All sorted, we're VIP members now."

After they had negotiated the entrance, and been issued with temporary membership cards (they claimed that they'd left theirs at home), they descended some stairs to a dance floor thick with strong perfume and stale sweat. There was a lot of heavy make-up on display and a thumping beat that seemed to compel the listeners to gyrate their bodies. Freda and Sim scanned the room as best they could in the strobing lights. No sign of the missing crew member. Then Freda noticed a bouncer standing next to a door marked VIP.

"Come on," she shouted, "let's try through there."

Sim's tiredness quickly evaporated as he saw the amount of flesh on display in the next room. Semi-naked gorgeous women were cavorting around poles on stage while a mostly male audience looked on. Around the edge of the room at individual tables, other men were being treated to a more personal dance. There were plenty of casino tokens being flashed about.

"Enjoying the view, sweetheart," said a husky voice to Sim's left. He turned to see a woman in a clinging dress and high heels wrapping her finger around the tresses of her long blonde hair. Something about her face or figure was both intoxicating and alarming at the same time. He was about to reply when Freda pulled him away.

"Trust me, she's not your type. Now stay focused." They scanned this room, but still no sign of Paul Thomas. Then Freda slapped her forehead. "We've been going about this all wrong."

"What do you mean?"

"We're not looking for Paul Thomas any more. We should be looking for Paulette Tom – he's transgender, one of the dancers here." She pointed to a poster on the wall.

Sim looked at the picture, then up on stage, feeling his face redden. The breasts looked so real. *OK, maybe a bit too perfect.* Then he noticed the slight bulge in the dancers' knickers. And the woman who spoke to him earlier – there *had* been an Adam's apple, and the hands *were* too big. "Right, yes, just what I was thinking," he said.

Freda spotted a she-male that could have been Paul/Paulette leading another man by the hand towards a private booth on the far side of the room. The person, wearing a gold diamante bikini, looked back to see if anybody was watching – Sim had to avert his eyes quickly – and then curtains were pulled across.

"What do we do now?" said Sim.

"Order a drink and wait for her to finish. Then we pay for our own private viewing."

As soon as the two agents and Paulette were ensconced behind the curtains, Freda told the dancer to sit down and then jammed her walking stick under the dancer's chin, pinning her by the throat. Paulette's mouth opened wide and she tried to scream but nothing came out. Freda sat on top of Paulette's legs.

"Tell us what you know about the bomb."

"What bomb?"

"Don't play silly buggers. The bomb that blew up your salt camel. We were there. We saw your crewman die." Freda screwed her hand into a fist.

"Don't know what you're talking about. I didn't have nuffin to do with the bomb. I'm pacifisical, me." Paulette looked at Freda and then at Sim, her eyes wide.

"Then why did you leave the airport in such a hurry?" There was no reply. "You don't want us to mess up your pretty face, do you?" Freda pressed her knuckles and rings into the fleshy part of Paulette's cheek, causing her mouth to squish open again.

"Don't. Please. Don't hit me." The dancer began to sob. "I don't know anythink about bombs or terrorists. I was just lucky to have been first off the airship. Nearly shit meself when I heard that explosion. I just carry the ice for some bloke."

Sim leaned forward to listen better. "The ice?"

"The diamonds. Some geezer gives me the stuff in Riyadh disguised as a set of diamante bra and knickers, I hide them in me dancing gear, then come straight here once we land. The first bloke who pays for a private dance with me takes the underwear and that's it. Money appears in me account, next day. End of."

Freda looked at the tears on Paulette's face and then across to Sim. He shrugged his shoulders. While Freda was looking at Sim, Paulette managed to shift her weight on the seat and jammed her knee into a button concealed under the table. Freda slapped her with the back of her hand and got up.

The curtains were pulled apart by a large man in a black suit and tie. "What the fuck you doing to Paulette?"

He lunged for Freda with a thick, slow hand. She dodged the blow, hooked the handle of her stick around his ankle and grabbed his wrist, pulling him forward, off balance. He crashed to the ground, knocking the table over. Paulette screamed and clambered on top of the padding behind the seats. Freda landed knee first onto the small of the back of the toppled bouncer and put one of his arms into a lock. Several other men in black suits started advancing on Sim and Freda.

Sim pulled out his gun. "Stand back now. This is a criminal investigation. This dancer is helping us with our enquiries."

The men hesitated while Freda got up, having put a cable tie around her vanquished foe's wrists.

"Don't make this worse than it already is, guys," said Freda. "Everybody just chill and let us do our job." She flashed her

OFWAT badge. "Sim, put your piece away for chrissake." She turned around, holding out her hand to the dancer. "You need to come with us, Paulette."

Once outside the bar in the street again, they radioed for a car to pick them up. Freda had a tight hold of Paulette's wrist, dangling from an ill-fitting coat. A few minutes later she was in the back of a police van, being taken away for processing.

"Make sure you swab for explosives, guys," Freda called as the policemen headed off.

"Do you think she's telling the truth?" said Sim.

"Almost certainly. Which means we've just wasted the last few hours."

"Wardle's not going to be happy, is he?"

CHAPTER 9

The Golan Heights have always been an important vantage point for the Israeli-Syrian conflicts. Their strategic value comes from the elevated view across the Sea of Galilee and the control of the Jordan River valley, vital to Israel's supply of fresh water. It is said that whoever controls the Golan Heights, controls Israel.

OD Training Manual Section 5b

4 years earlier, Israeli Intelligence Corps HQ

"Hello David, let's play Global Thermonuclear War," said the synthetic voice.

David Feinberg chuckled. "No thanks, Ivan, I'll stick with the usual simulation thanks very much. Golan Heights, with me as defender. Opponent human, local area network." He knew his colleague Saul was in the room next door preparing to play out the same simulation but as the attacker.

David was deep underground in a bomb-proof bunker, a series of chambers that formed part of the Israeli Defense Force's Intelligence Corps, also known as Haman. He was assigned to the high-level strategic planning team and spent most of his time running numerous what-if scenarios covering the defense of Israel and its potential offensive campaigns.

The Israeli spy network had been getting hints recently, snippets of information, that suggested a Syrian attack on the Golan Heights was being planned. So three times a week for the past two months, David and Saul had been playing the same scenario over and over again. They changed the tactics, the mix of forces, changed the weather and changed sides, each time searching for vital lessons about how to defend the heights.

On this particular week of war gaming, the pair had just exhausted a specific avenue of research regarding Syrian offensive tactics and units, and so Saul had been given a blank canvas and was told to come up with a radical new attack plan without letting David know his intentions beforehand. David sat excited as a kid who had just unwrapped a new computer game and was waiting for it to boot up. These were his favourite opportunities to play this game, when he genuinely didn't know what was coming next. The endless iterations on the same plan were a vital part of the research but mind-numbing.

The status read-out on his computer showed low cloud cover, light drizzle; his units were at alertness level 2 out of 5 with no intelligence suggesting imminent Syrian offensive activity. The current mix of IDF units had a large proportion of infantry interspersed with heavy weapons teams and backed up with a small number of tank and artillery units. Very active air cover would be provided by Wing 1 of the Air Force based at Ramat David Airbase.

A day or two passed in the simulation; David sent some recon vehicles out to scout the eastern edge of the Golan Heights plateau, but the units came back with little to report. The weather deteriorated, such that low visibility was interfering with his air cover.

Now this presumably is when the strike will come, making the most of the bad weather. I wonder which flank he'll target and what units he's going to throw at me?

The computer started showing up multiple contacts around Mount Heron, the left flank of his defensive line. He slowed the game's time speed down to just double real-life so he could carefully consider his response.

OK, so waiting for the worst weather was a good idea – that will severely restrict my use of Panther helicopters from 193 Squadron – but I still have plenty of all-weather ground attack aircraft I can use. He must know that. And concentrating on Mount Heron first is a standard tactic, we've each tried that numerous times and it rarely succeeds beyond the first day or so. If this is the best Saul can come up with, he must be having a bad day.

He clicked onto the online chat box which allowed him to swap text messages with his opponent.

> Saul, really, is that the best you can do? The Heron Storm scenario? Yawn, been there, done that like a billion times…

> Saul?

> !

Hmm, no response, no witty comeback, he is having a bad day. Well better get on with the game.

David issued a series of orders to his units on Mount Heron, called up artillery strikes, sent a small detachment of tanks to shore up his left flank and ordered one of his recon units to attempt to scout round the back of the Syrian attack force to check for reinforcements.

But then something curious happened. The recon unit was annihilated when it blundered straight into the main force of the attackers while the artillery strikes missed their targets by several kilometres. Even worse, some of the defending infantry stationed on Mount Heron started withdrawing from their positions and reinforcing units that were neither under attack nor even close to the front line. The computer flashed up a warning:

Intelligence malfunction.

Wow, that's a new one, I don't know how Saul has done that. I didn't even think that was possible. Clever trick, I could be in genuine trouble here.

He needed time to think. He hit the pause button and typed in the chat box:

> Coffee time, I'll pop round to see if you want one.

He got up, left the room and walked the short distance down the corridor to the office where he knew Saul would be sitting at his terminal. As he entered, Saul turned around in surprise. "What are you doing here? We're in the middle of a battle."

"I just paused the game and sent you a chat to see if you wanted a coffee. Didn't you see it?" David could see on Saul's terminal that a battle was raging between Saul's attacking force and some IDF units. But how could that be if the game was paused on his PC? And the battle was taking place miles away from Mount Heron where Saul's units had showed up on his battle map. He stared for a moment.

"Your scenario isn't the same one I'm playing. That's impossible. *Oy Gevalt*. If we aren't playing against each other, who the hell's our opponent?" David's stomach knotted tightly; something somewhere was very, very wrong. Saul looked equally perplexed. His computer had just sprung up the same message:

Intelligence malfunction.

David sprinted back to his computer and as he got there, tiny images of the Syrian flag – the red, white and black stripes along with two green stars – started popping up all over his screen. Slowly at first, one every few seconds, then more frequently as if they were bacteria multiplying in a petri dish. Quickly his whole screen became filled with overlapping flags of the enemy. Still more kept appearing, layer upon layer of the same thing, over and over again. Ivan's voice sprang to life:

"Malfunction, malfunction."

And then a different voice, a human voice, came over the speaker. "Hello David, have you enjoyed our little game this morning? I certainly did. The look on your face when none of your units did what they were told. What a picture. Why, it's almost as if somebody else was controlling them, feeding them false information. Imagine the chaos that would create if it happened for *real*. You might actually lose the war for once. Still not to worry, that would *never* happen. I mean somebody would have to infiltrate the entire Haman network for that to work... Oh wait, I already have. Well must dash, I think there's a battle about to begin on the Golan Heights."

David stood frozen with fear. Everything was *Fakakta*.

This can't be happening. It mustn't be happening.

He wrenched himself away from the computer and raced down the corridor to one of the control rooms of Haman HQ, one that he knew received and distributed real-time information from the frontline. He burst into the room. Several fellow officers turned to face him, their skin ashen and their features deadly serious. David could see dozens of screens filled with tiny Syrian flags.

One of the ancient phones sitting on a desk nobody used any more started ringing. It was hard-wired all the way to a battalion HQ on the Golan Heights. David raced over and picked it up.

"Hello, Haman HQ? Hello? This is 13th Gideon battalion. We are under attack. All systems are down. We have no CCC, we're fighting blind. Please respond. I repeat, we are under attack."

PART TWO

Fear not the boastfully strong,
but those who pretend to be weak.

Matthew Brightwell, 2003

CHAPTER 10

The first Sea States were established in 2020. Each of them was set in international waters, far enough from the coast to avoid the reach of any government. The global recession had caused government deficits to widen rapidly again, and with income inequality still rising, the only viable source of extra revenue was the richest households. It had been tried before, but this time the wealthy came up with a plan to move beyond the reach of any government's tax net.

O.D. Training Manual Section 3b

By the time Sim and Freda had returned from Soho, forensics had come back with their tests on the terrorists' spent flare – no useable fingerprints. The serial code on the flare had been checked and was traced to an old oil tanker. Maritime records showed that it had been bought by a consortium in 2019 and converted for use as a floating habitat to form part of the sea state of Marinus.

Wardle had listened to the Agents' account of the wild goose chase in the nightclub. "That was bad luck. A valid lead that needed to be followed up. Thorough. So, back to square one. Let's focus on the two who fled the scene of the explosion."

Sim was exhausted, but relieved that Wardle had taken the news so well. The Head of Division picked up the phone and punched in a number.

"Sam, it's Wardle, O.D.O. here. I need a favour – I want to borrow one of your Recog's... Yes, I know it's 1am... I would rather be asleep too. This is urgent."

"What do these fellas do?" Sim whispered to Freda.

"A special consultant with the Met – a super recogniser. It's a kind of magic."

The consultant arrived an hour later, bulging out of a dirty tracksuit, a haggard face topped with disheveled hair and no special equipment whatsoever. He mumbled something as he sat down in the room with Wardle, Freda and Sim then fell silent. A minute later a steaming mug of coffee appeared, along with a chocolate bar. The others watched him devour these and then he turned to them.

"Right, what's so bloody urgent that needs my talents at this hour, you pommy bastards?"

"The bombing at Biggin Hill. We've got an image but the computers can't handle it," said Wardle.

"Well I didn't think I was here to discuss the cricket. Come on, show me the blarrie." The Recog was given the print-out of the blurry face. He held it out in front of him and squinted. Then he drew it so close that his nose was almost rubbing on the paper. He tilted it from side to side then closed his eyes. He sat there in complete silence. Sim fidgeted with a button on his shirt and was about to say something when Freda put her finger to her lips. The Australian's eyebrows creased and then a smile spread across his face.

"Got him, you beaut. This guy was lifted for possession of narcotics at a nightclub raid a few years ago. Benjamin Wyploz. Crikey, that was a toughie."

"Man, you did all that just from a blurry picture and memory?" asked Sim.

"It's a knack a few of us have. Getting the face right's tricky to start with. A bit of human imagination helps fill in the missing details from the photo that a computer struggles to do. Then a quick mental wander around me old photo palace, or in this case a long walkabout, before bumping into this guy and his charge sheet."

David was at hand to help follow up with the identified felon. A cross check of the passenger flight details from London airports to the Canary Islands (the nearest place with direct flights to Marinus) shortly after the motorbike chase showed a match to Wyploz in Heathrow. The airport records brought up a clearer picture of him boarding the plane with his travelling companion: Marty Fields. So they had names and faces.

"Let's hope they're still in Marinus," said Wardle.

"Can't we just get in touch with the authorities there and ask them to detain these lads?" said Sim.

"Too risky. We don't know whom they are working for. If the authorities are involved, or at least if the terrorists have someone working on the inside in Marinus, chances are our phone call will give them all the warning they need. They'll be spirited away and likely as not we'll never see them again."

It was agreed that Freda and Sim should fly to the Sea State under the pretext of being a couple on holiday. It was an expensive destination, but not uncommon for British tourists.

Wardle continued. "Remember Freda, this is high priority. The government needs to show that terrorists cannot take pot shots at Britain."

Refreshed after a few hours of sleep, the agents headed for the airport. Once onboard the plane, they settled into their seats and prepared for the four-hour flight. Sim turned to Freda.

"Thanks for sticking up for me in front of Wardle, boss."

"You did OK. For a rookie."

"What's that supposed to mean?"

Freda sighed and started to speak, but then stopped and stared at Sim's mouth. "Are you going to wear that ridiculous bloody moustache for the whole trip?"

There was a pause before Sim almost mumbled his reply. "They wanted me to look older."

"Ahh. Nobody blinks twice at a husband marrying a woman ten years younger than him, but reverse the roles and suddenly everybody has an opinion." She looked at her reflection in her chair's TV screen, pulling the skin taut across her face. There was an awkward silence. Sim started to fiddle with the controls of his seat and to read about the in-flight entertainment.

"Look they have some old classics to watch – *The Hobbit in 3D*."

"You and I have a different definition of 'old classic'. I prefer the really old stuff like Kurosawa's *Seven Samurai*. Amazing cinematography, terrific fight scenes, especially the final showdown in the pouring rain."

"Can't say that I've ever heard of Kurothingy."

Freda ignored him and carried on. "Did you know that the village elder was the inspiration for Yoda in the *Star Wars* films?"

"Who's Yoda?"

"WHAT! Impossible. One of the best sci-fi films of the twentieth century and you haven't even seen *Star Wars*? It's only fifty years old, what's the matter with you?"

"I don't really bother with the old two-dimensional films all that much. They seem so, well, flat. How come you know so much about ancient films? You can't be old enough to remember them. And swords and sci-fi, not a typical female choice."

"It was my dad. When I was growing up he used to read to me a lot at bedtime - old books of course - and he would play me his favourite films on DVD. I guess he just indoctrinated me. In a nice way." Freda looked out of the window and smiled. "One of his best books was a collection of monologues by Marriott Edgar, from the 1930s. Now he could write a funny poem."

"Marriott Edgar, didn't he win the Grand National last year?"

Freda rolled her eyes. "A stick with an 'orse's head handle, the finest that Woolworth's could sell." Her accent had morphed into something Northern English that Sim was unfamiliar with. She was playing her fingers across the silver horse's head that formed the handle of her walking stick, like a blind person caressing the face of a loved one. Sim thought about his dad's taste in music, clothes and the TV programmes that he watched. He shuddered. He was glad none of that rubbed off on him.

"Nice rock by the way. Did the firm lend you that ring for the disguise?"

"No, it's mine."

"Oh, I didn't realise you were engaged. Congratulations. Who's the lucky fella?"

"Shush, I'm meant to be engaged to you, remember."

There was something in Freda's eyes that told Sim there was another reason she did not want to talk about it, but he decided to drop it and the conversation came to an abrupt end.

Once they had landed at Lanzarote, they transferred to the much smaller seaplane that would take them and 18 other passengers the last 500 miles to Marinus. The yellow seaplane was an old Bombardier 415.

One of the fellow passengers was boring his wife with his knowledge of planes. "Of course, strictly speaking this isn't a seaplane, it's a flying boat - the main fuselage of the plane sits in the water, acting as the source of buoyancy. The floats at the tip of each wing are present merely for stability." The wife smiled weakly at her partner.

They were close to the equator now and the sun was very bright. There were few clouds in the sky and the sea below them glistened brightly with small waves scattering the reflected beams of light. The journey was 90 minutes of cramped, noisy conditions. Sim and Freda started their act of pretending to be a couple just in case others were watching. It felt weird for Sim to be holding the hand of his new boss.

"This Marinus must be tiny. Why do people choose to live in such a wee confined space?" asked Sim.

"Wealthy people will go a long way to make sure they keep hold of their money. If that means leaving a country to live in neutral international waters with no taxes, then so be it."

"I'm sure I wouldn't mind paying more taxes if I were that rich."

"That's what everybody says *before* they get rich."

Around four o' clock in the afternoon, after a short descent, the plane banked left and started circling the Sea State. Sim and Freda could see that an oilrig acted as the centre of the habitat, with a large cruise ship docked on one side, and two huge VLCC oil tankers forming a harbour on the other side. The top of one of the VLCCs was turfed and most of it had been made into a decent-sized park, with a path for jogging and cycling around the outside. There was a section devoted to growing fruit and high-yielding compact vegetables. The deck of the other VLCC was mostly given over to photovoltaic solar panels. To the side of the oil rig there was a reddish brown algae farm, encased in a long loop of miniature booms. A pair of large floating tanks to store the fuel produced by the farm was situated at the far side of the loop.

Sim looked down at this odd concoction of sea vessels; they were intertwined like some slow-motion traffic accident, with the algae as the spilt contents of one of the crashed vehicles. The

Bombardier circled and gradually descended to 30 metres before straightening up at right angles to the two oil tankers and then dropping to sea level. The plane skimmed waves a couple of times before the fuselage finally bit into the water and sank down. It taxied to the small harbour amongst a host of luxury yachts. The plane nosed its way gently towards the longest jetty where it was tied up. As the passengers disembarked, the sun was disappearing behind the high sides of the oil tanker next to their quay. It was surprisingly gloomy despite being barely five o' clock.

There was a smell of seaweed mixed with diesel wafting over from the algae farm. For a moment Sim was 14 years old again, being dragged round a whisky distillery on Islay by his dad for the third year in a row. A team of porters hurried over to take care of the luggage, and Sim wondered what his dad would make of a vacation like this.

The holiday-makers were greeted by one of the tourist reps. First they were led to the immigration office just next to the marina for processing: palm print, iris scan and a finger prick of blood. They filled in the guests' arrival form with the aliases the agents had been given: Mr Goodall and Ms White. After bio passport details had been confirmed – thanks to some prior work by David Feinberg – they were shown to their cabin on board the *Ocarinus* cruise ship. A few of the smaller cabins were set aside for tourists on the lower levels. They were taken towards the front of the cruiser and given the keys to suite 267. There was a large bedroom and small bathroom but no sitting area.

"Err, boss?"

"Don't call me that, even in private. You have to get used to using my first name."

"Freda? There's only one bed, and no sofa."

She laughed. "Don't worry, I don't bite."

After a brief visit to one of the bars on the cruise ship to assess the layout and atmosphere of the place they returned to the cabin and got ready for bed in silence. Stripping down to his underwear in front of his boss, Sim felt like being back at school without the correct gym kit. Freda came out of the bathroom in a tight white t-shirt and knickers. For the first time, Sim looked at her without noticing the walking stick and felt a stirring in his pants. *Uh-oh, quick, think of Wardle, think of satellites, anything boring!*

They settled into the bed and Sim lay there trying as hard as possible to stay away from the middle of the mattress. After a tiring day of travel, sleep came quickly for both of them.

Waking up Sim felt warm and comfortable. A little light was streaming in through the tiny portal window of their bedroom. He could smell the peach shampoo Freda had used the night before. As his dream-like state gave way to full alertness he realised that he was spooning with his boss. His morning glory was in full spate and pressing into Freda's lower back. He fell out of bed in his rush to roll away before she noticed. Hurrying to the bathroom, he stubbed his toe and hobbled into the other room cursing the cabin and his libido.

CHAPTER 11

Reverse Osmosis Desalinator plants are used to convert seawater into drinking water. The technique uses a semi-permeable membrane and pressure is applied to overcome the osmotic pressure, reversing the natural tendency of solvents to equalise concentration levels. Very large plants, such as those commonly used by Cruise Liners or Sea States (see section 6) can produce up to 500 tonnes of potable water a day.

O.D. Training Manual Section 2c

After breakfast in one of the luxury restaurants on the *Ocarinus*, Freda and Sim started to explore the cruise ship. In two hours of searching they failed to bump into anybody remotely resembling the men they had chased on motorbikes 48 hours ago. And the only illicit activity they discovered was a pair of male cabin stewards trying to have a dalliance in a storeroom. Watching the various people move around this warren of passages, Sim was reminded of the ants' nest he had at school. Even without uniforms Sim could tell which people on board the ship were the worker ants as they scurried about on duty.

The top two floors of the cruise ship housed all the activity and entertainment suites. There was a static wave machine for those keen on surfing. Rows and rows of 3D golf simulators were full of grey-haired people desperately trying to improve their handicaps. There was a zero-grav simulator where you could pretend to be Superman, flying through the air assisted by a powerful wind generator in the floor, a body suit and 3D wrap-around glasses. *Very good for vestibular exercise* said the hologram playing on a continual loop in the corridor.

The agents also found a synthetic wine generator where, according to the info screen outside, one could recreate at the molecular level any of the great Bordeaux wines and vintages for that special occasion. A pair of women tumbled out of one of the beauty parlours in a fit of giggles. One of them was showing off her new dynamic skin polymer tattoo. The butterfly on her upper arm flapped its wings as she tensed her muscles and rubbed her skin.

"You should see what my tattoo does when I get it warm," said the other woman to her friend. Cue for more guffaws.

"We're definitely not in Kansas anymore, Toto," said Freda in an American accent.

"Sorry?"

"Never mind, just another old film my dad loved." She stopped and put her hands on her hips. "All this sneaking around is taking too long."

"We could sign up for a guided tour. That way we'll get to see the whole place, ask some questions without arousing suspicions. Maybe even figure out where they keep info on all their citizens," said Sim.

Climbing up the spiral stairs inside one of the oilrig's huge legs, the agents found themselves in a large reception room contained within the ground floor of the main accommodation block on the rig. There was an information desk and a wall-mounted plan of the Sea State. There was also a pair of armed security guards – the first that Sim and Freda had noticed – making it clear that access to this part of the habitat would be restricted. The guide – a red-haired woman from New York – appeared and called together the six people who had signed up for the tour.

"Good afternoon ladies and gentlemen and welcome to Marinus, the Sea State where the sun always shines. Often imitated, never bettered. My name is Charnel and today we're going to take a look at the heart of Marinus. Please make sure you stay in the group without wandering off - this is after all a working environment with potentially dangerous machinery. I'm sure you're all going to have a grrreat day." Sim thought he noticed the tour guide looking specifically at them when she talked about not walking off, but it was hard to tell through her saucer-sized sunglasses.

They were first shown the medical facilities on the second floor which included a fully automated operating cell. It looked like an electronic iron maiden, thought Sim, remembering a childhood visit to the London Dungeon many years ago. There was also a 3D printer in the adjacent room, separated from the tourists by airtight doors.

"Vhy do you need a printer? Surely you don't make your surgical instruments here?" asked a German gentleman on the tour.

"Oh, that. No, honey. That is a fourth-generation bio printer. We can grow most body parts here, up to and including major organs. Billionaires do not do transplant waiting lists."

On the level below was the control centre of the power grid. As well as solar panels, the tankers and oil rig had micro wind turbines and diesel generators as alternative sources of power for night and particularly cloudy days. The bio-ethanol produced by the algae farm was stored in large floating tanks well away from the residential areas, and powered the generators. The plant which supplied the entire population with potable water – affectionately known as Rodney according to the guide – was an intensive user of energy.

"Solar panels are at their most efficient here on the equator; one of the reasons this location was chosen," said the guide.

"German, I noticed. Ve make the best in the wurld," said the tourist who had asked about the printer.

Freda moved forward. "Do you ever have problems with pirates trying to steal your gas? Or even worse, robbing your residents? There must be an awful lot of wealth on board this floating island."

"Of course we take the safety of all our residents very seriously. We have our own highly trained defence force, well equipped to deal with any potential threats from pirates. They also acts as the police for us, but really honey, the level of crime here at Marinus is barely noticeable. We all know each other, and besides, where would you hide if you committed a crime?"

The tour moved on to include a visit to the police station with its tiny holding cell, and then upwards to the roof of the main block where there was a chicken farm housing a few hundred hens. Next to the coop was a battery of surface-to-air missiles, and one of the heli-pads was occupied by a fully armed attack helicopter.

"These have to be the best protected chickens in the world," said Freda.

"And the worst cared for. Look how tightly bunched they are in that run," replied Sim.

Across a wide gantry they were shown to a smaller block of offices which housed the government of Marinus. The current leader - Elsa Greenwood - had been in situ almost from day one of the sea state's existence.

The final part of the tour was a descent down the spiral stairs inside a different leg of the oilrig that eventually led out to a platform at sea level. "You sure keep fit on all these stairs," said the guide as her shoes clip-clopped down the metal steps. "Mind your step, young lady," she called back to Freda who was hobbling down, firmly grasping the handrail with her walking stick in the other hand.

"Did you know that medieval spiral stairs vould always go down reverse clockwise? Zat way the defenders could swing their swords freely in their right hand. Ve have many fine castles in my country." The German again.

Each of the rig's legs were connected at this point by a wide gantry, and from each gantry were suspended thick fishing nets that helped to house a large aquatic farm - a staple diet of the residents. A worker was hauling up a line of rope-grown mussels. There was a small platform and hut next to one of the rig's legs at sea level where a scuba diver was getting kitted up.

"At the bottom of the fish farm we have an artificial sea floor that has been stocked with corals and exotic fish" explained the guide. "And occasionally we get a visit from Great Whites - quite a sight as long as you are on the right side of the netting."

The Encyclopedia Germanicus piped up again: "*Carcharodon carcharias*. Very intelligent animals. They are attracted to the constant vibrations of the machinery here, ja?"

"I bet he is just a bundle of hoots at the dinner table," whispered Sim.

"It's not a sin to enjoy knowledge. But that footwear is sinful," replied Freda, looking down at the German's sock and sandal combination.

At the end of the circuit, Sim and Freda thanked Charnel for her guided tour, tipped her a hundred dollars and returned to the cruise ship.

Freda was pacing up and down their small cabin. "Who knows what this private security force gets up to, or where they recruit from? Could be some real pieces of work in that motley crew. There's definitely a dark underbelly to this place. And it's our best chance of finding these bloody terrorists. People like that must do something in the evening. Let's see if we can find out what."

Despite their best intentions they ended up in a fairly respectable bar where they had fresh seafood and kelp wine. Sim sipped his drink suspiciously but was pleasantly surprised. They chatted to the bar-man and gave him a generous tip while hinting at their desire to have some excitement, a gamble perhaps, that night. They discovered that there was a casino on the cruise ship, but if they fancied something a bit racier they should go to the Compass Bar on board the industrial VLCC and speak to Tomas. They thanked him for the advice and set off straight away. As usual this near the equator the transition from dusk to darkness had been rapid. Sim breathed in the cool night air after the heat of the bar and could smell whiskey again. The place hummed gently with diesel generators powering numerous lights that glowed over the gangways. They negotiated one of these out of the cruise ship, across the oilrig at sea level and then into 'Ivey', the industrial tanker.

"This sure looks like a locals' haunt," shouted Sim as they slalomed their way towards the bar and ordered a couple of large, exorbitantly expensive beers over the thumping background music. There was a marked difference in atmosphere down here compared with the daytime serenity of the cruise ship. There was desperation in the air as too many people tried to let off too much steam in too little time and space. A mix of beer, sweat and perfume invaded their nostrils. Sim and Freda looked around. Still no sign of the missing terrorists. A man standing next to them leaned over when he saw what they had ordered.

"You're obviously not from around here, are you? All the local hands know what a rip-off the European beer is. Most of them are drinking vodka – some bright engineer rigged up a still on level five a few years ago. It's rough but it gets the job done at half the price." The man winked ostentatiously, raised his tumbler and gulped down another mouthful of homemade liquor.

Freda flashed the man her brightest smile. "Thanks, I'll remember that next time. Do you know where we can find Tomas?"

Tomas was a blond Dane, who looked like he'd have to duck every time he passed through a bulkhead.

Freda didn't waste any time, sashaying up close to him and tilting her neck back to look into his eyes. "What's a girl got to do to find some excitement on this boat?"

"That depends for what you're looking, pretty lady," he replied, leering down at her.

"Well, I get up to all sorts at this time of night," she purred, walking her fingers up his barrel chest.

Tomas grabbed her buttocks and squeezed her close so that she had to strain her neck even more to look into his face.

"I can tell you know how to treat a lady right, but just now I fancy a wager on something exciting," said Freda, trying to smile despite the uncomfortable hold he had her in.

Tomas let go of her and then creased his face in distaste. "How do I know you're not some journalist trying to dig up dirt on this place? We had one last year – nasty little shit. The boss was not happy."

"Do I look like I'm hiding anything in this dress?" asked Freda.

Tomas looked her up and down, glanced at Sim and quickly swept the bar near them with his eyes. "Level six, forward storeroom on the port side. Entry fee is $200. Each." After Freda had counted out the notes, Tomas told her the password, told her to come back after he was off duty, and then returned to his work at the bar.

"You men are so easy to manipulate."

"Oi, we're not all Vikings, you know," said Sim.

"Come on, let's see what this is all about," said Freda as they made their way towards the storeroom, not knowing quite what to expect. "Keep your wits about you Sim, and don't do anything stupid, OK?"

They found the right door, knocked and gave the password. Another giant of a man, only slightly smaller than Tomas, let them in. Behind him the room opened up to a rectangular space about 10 metres by 20 with around two dozen people present. The room was uncomfortably warm and the smell was not what they were expecting – almost as if somebody had been making a giant omelette here. There was some activity going on at floor level that all the other occupants of the room were engrossed in. A man at the far end was shouting out odds, a few were hollering their wagers to him and still others were screaming for whatever they had just bet on.

Sim and Freda squeezed their way into the ring of spectators and tried not to flinch at the sight that greeted them. The middle section of the floor was marked out by a border of planks. In between the planks the floor was covered in a thick layer of sand, like a miniature beach, except for the end nearest the door where there was a shallow tray of water and a strip-light above it. At the other end of the sand was a small cage from which one of the organisers had just released several baby Green Turtles, each with a number painted on the top of their shells. This was clearly a race from the cage to the water. But to add spice and danger to the 'sporting' event, some bored ship-hand had come up with the idea of tethering a Black Vulture to each side of the pit about halfway along the race track. Their feet were chained but they had just enough freedom of movement to flap down from their perch, scoop up a turtle in their beak and flap back to enjoy an easy meal.

Turtle 1 was in the lead while turtles 3 and 5 had just been grabbed. Sim's eyes were focused on one of the vultures that was struggling to swallow its prey. Two pathetic flippers were caught on the edge of its beak, flailing against a life too short. A memory that Sim thought he had buried long ago burst forth. He was about to jump into the middle of the ring when Freda pulled him back.

"Leave it, Sim," she whispered, dragging him to one corner of the room.

"But this is horrible."

Freda checked nobody was paying attention to them. "Horrendous and not our problem. Focus on the bloody mission. The terrorists are all that matters. The longer it takes to find them, the greater the risk of another atrocity."

Sim wanted to interject, but Freda talked over him. "If a few turtles have to die to catch these slippery bastards, so be it. We do what it takes."

Having double-checked the faces of the crowd at the turtle race, they left and racked their brains for the next strategy.

"How about the medical records?" said Sim. "We all got our bio passports checked on entry to Marinus. There must be a file of all recent entries, presumably linked into the medical centre. If we break in there, hack the system, we might be able to track down our quarry."

"Good idea. I hope your IT skills are as good as David's. Computers never were my strong point."

Sim thought about the time he had re-programmed a hover camera to snoop at the window of the girls' changing rooms back at school. He smiled and nodded to Freda. They went back to their room, grabbed their autographers and some other kit then changed into stealth cloth. It was now three o'clock in the morning and the corridors were deserted. But they knew that there would be guards at the entrance to the main building on the rig – where the medical centre was – from the tour earlier in the day. The agents climbed the stairs inside the rig's leg as before but this time stopped a few steps below the level of the main hallway.

A tiny periscope poked up over the lip of the floor. Freda could see two sentries standing next to the door they needed to access.

There was another corridor leading off to the right. She reached inside her jet black jacket and pulled out something that looked like a wind-up mouse. There was a tiny programmable screen underneath and Freda tapped out some commands. The mouse hummed into life; she reached up and placed it on the floor of the hallway. It zoomed off into the corridor on the right and then started emitting smoke and strobe lights, drawing the sentries away from their door. The two agents raced across the hall and got through the door while their pet mouse led the sentries on a merry dance.

On the floor above, the medical centre was easy to break into, but the computer system was heavily protected with password and palm print technology. Sim went to work, patching in his roll-tab and running a number of routines that took a few minutes to scrape away the protective layers of the medical system's network. Freda kept guard while Sim finished the job and started searching the medical records for the two men they were after.

"Look, Freda. They arrived the day before us, as we suspected. Not using aliases at this stage, that's encouraging. Wait, hang on, it says they left yesterday. Crap!"

"Let me see," said Freda, coming over to Sim and peering at the computer screen. "Does it give us their destination?"

"Don't move a muscle. Step away from the desk and put your hands on your head. Do it. Now!"

Freda slowly turned back to the door she was supposed to be guarding. The sentries that had been distracted by their mouse were standing in the doorway pointing automatic rifles at the British agents.

CHAPTER 12

A growing population and a shift in taste towards meat-based protein amongst the Asian middle class had put an incredible strain on grain production in the early 21st century. Over-intensive farming had caused soil erosion and led to increased reliance on fertilizers to promote crop yields. Phosphorous and potash fertilisers became highly valued.

OD Training Manual Section 2d

3½ years earlier, a mining settlement in Eastern Morocco.

Robert d'Estaing was sweating. He was stuck in a cramped hut at the end of a long, hot day. The stale odour of his clothes mixed with the metallic tang of the phosphate soil invading his nostrils. A drop of water beaded on his forehead and then fell onto the map that was spread out on his desk. The sweat mixed with the orange dust that lay on all the surfaces in his hut. Two more drops fell onto the map, turned dark orange and glided slowly down the creases of paper. A river of blood wending its way across Morocco.

There was an angry mob outside the mining settlement. The banners and chanting had been peaceful for the first few days. The gang leader had wanted to meet with Robert as the man in charge of operations. He spoke fluent French and had let Robert know of their peaceful intentions. But today a flaming sunset seemed to have infused the mood of the protesters with a lust for revenge. Protest songs had morphed into abuse and insults directed at the foreigners. Makeshift weapons were brandished in the air. To make matters worse, the marines who were supposed to be ensuring the safety of this French operation had disappeared on a training exercise at dawn and still had not returned. As he peered out from the hut's tiny window, Robert could see the mob starting to clamber over the wire fencing, and a large truck was nuzzling up to the main gate, like a bull testing its strength on the gate to its field. He didn't think the gate would win this contest.

"*Espèce d'idiot!*" he muttered to himself. Why had he let the Finance Minister talk him into this mad scheme? It was a few months ago, but he remembered everything about that morning when he had met the minister in secret. The honour of a personal call to meet him and the illicit thrill of the subterfuge used to make sure nobody else knew about their meeting.

"Do come in, have a seat Robert, please. Coffee? Croissant?" The room was elaborately furnished with gilded chairs around a mahogany table, beautiful scrollwork on the framed mirrors and a 17th century carriage clock sitting on a side desk. The bulk of the rotund, balding politician placed a strain on one of the antique chairs. The minister had set the ball rolling in that meeting. Right now it looked like that ball was a giant boulder and it was about to crush the life out of Robert.

Robert's company – Excavo - was a mining and chemical conglomerate, with operations all over the world. The minister had suggested in their meeting that he look at a potential take-over of Morpot, a small mining company based in Morocco. It had mining rights to a very tiny portion of that country's phosphate reserves. Robert's Chief Financial Officer had run her beady eye over the accounts. It was run quite efficiently, making a small profit each year, but showed very little potential for turn-around or asset sweating.

He looked out of the window of the hut and saw the security guards being beaten by the mob. The raised clubs, the kicks aimed at heads, these were not designed to intimidate but to kill. Where the hell were the marines?! Robert checked the lock on the door to his hut and hauled a heavy filing cabinet across the entrance. He closed and bolted the shutters on his window, then started recording a message onto his vid-watch.

"My darling wife. I'm so sorry. To end our marriage like this, hundreds of miles apart. If you ever get this message, please try to forgive me and know that I love you forever. If you want revenge for my death, then you must tell the world about what the government has done here. Not the Moroccan government, but our government, the French authorities."

He proceeded to summarise that first meeting with the Finance Minister and then continued. "At the second meeting with the Minister I explained how little value there was in Morpot. I was surprised to hear him agree with this assessment. But then he said, 'How much do you think the company would be worth if it had *exclusive* mining rights to all of Morocco's ore reserves?'

"They were worth a fortune, more than the rest of the Moroccan economy put together. But the government would never sign over control to a foreign-run company. Not without taxing it out of existence. 'Leave that to me,' the Minister had said without elaboration. I should have walked away there and then but he sweetened the deal, offering Excavo a special tax-break and me the prospect of a Legion d'Honneur if the deal went through. Hah! As if I'll ever get one now."

Robert jumped as the door was rattled from the outside and then hit with something large and heavy. He paused the recording for a moment, waiting to see if his makeshift barricade would hold. Fortunately for him, his hut was built better than the wooden boxes that the local workers had to put up with. He wedged a chair behind the filing cabinet that was blocking the door. He was safe for a while, long enough to finish his recording, he hoped. He pressed the record button again.

"The take-over went smoothly, the shareholders of Morpot were delighted to sell out at a generous premium to the market and the French papers barely even noticed. But the next instruction from the Finance Minister made no sense: 'Aggressively expand operations. Begin mining outside of your licensed area.' I refused at first, but the Minister can be very persuasive. He said his department had found some irregularities in our family affairs, threatening to drag your name through the courts over some bullshit charge of tax evasion. What choice did I have?

"So I did what he asked and, *quelle surprise*, the Moroccan authorities objected. They imposed a big fine, slapped an injunction on the company and even arrested the chief operating officer. When I went to see the Minister he wasn't even worried. 'Relax Robert, this is going according to plan.' He then asked me to go to Morocco and personally oversee further expansion plans. 'You must be mad if you think I'm going there. And the board is never going to allow further expansion after what the Moroccan authorities have said.' 'Don't worry, I assure you, you're in no danger. Provided you follow the plan.'

"I told him that I would rather fight the tax charges in court than keep going with this insane idea. 'Oh I don't think you need to worry about tax charges, Robert,' he said. 'You should be more worried about what the police might find on your roll-tab. Do you know how easy it is to remotely plant some child pornography on an unwitting victim? That must be a terrible fate to befall a father, don't you think?'

"So here I am. Stuck in a hut in Morocco with the barbarians at the gate. And the stupid marines the Minister sent to protect us nowhere to be seen."

There was a crash of breaking glass as somebody outside starting attacking the window to the hut. The shutters started to buckle. Robert clicked off the recorder, and rushed to wedge a drawer from his desk behind the shutters. The battering from outside stopped. Every muscle in his body was knotted with tension. Robert sank down on his haunches and wept. Without warning the hut was plunged into darkness. He could hear chaos outside still. Chanting, glass breaking, an occasional scream of pain. Robert was glad that he could not see what was going on.

After an hour or so the noise started to die down. Nobody came to test the door or even the shutters on the window. Had they forgotten him? *It must be dark outside by now if the mob has destroyed the generators or the floodlights on site. Probably both.* Robert did not dare click on his torch in case it showed through a crack in the shutters. He quietly felt around the hut, finding a snack bar and a half-finished drink that he gulped quickly and then regretted not savouring. The temperature outside was dropping fast and the hut did not provide much insulation. Robert stuffed some papers inside his clothes and lay down on some cardboard. It took him some time to slip into an uneasy sleep.

The door burst open, sending Robert's barricade thudding to the floor. He sat up groggily, bracing himself for the inevitability of the lynch mob. Light streamed in through the opening which his eyes could not cope with after hours of pitch darkness. Arms reached forward and hauled him outside. He was dazed and confused. As his eyes adjusted to the brightness he could see that the mining site was in ruins with some parts still smouldering from last night's fires. But he wasn't being mis-treated.

"*Ça va? Tu es blessé?*" A French voice inquired after his health. And then the person in front of him snapped into focus. A soldier. A Marine. A French Marine. They had returned too late to save the site, but Robert owed them his life. A microphone was thrust in front of him.

"Monsieur d'Estaing. This is France 24. You are live on national TV. Can you tell us what happened here? How many people were killed by the mob? Are you the only survivor?"

Robert was still too dis-orientated to answer any questions, but the reporter did not seem to care, firing away with some more.

"Is the company going to allow terrorists to dictate what happens to your mining operations? Is it true that the French government are sending a battalion of Marines to ensure the safety of all your Moroccan sites?"

Robert managed a "no comment" from his parched throat before the soldier helped guide him away from the reporter and towards the medical hut for a quick check-over. There were two other employees also being treated for injuries, but what about the rest? The site had a roster of 35 people, including the security guards. Did that mean 32 people were missing or dead? Robert could not believe it. There had been protests at the other mining sites already, but nothing as violent as this. He couldn't quite be angry with the marines; they had saved his life after all, but had been too late to save the others. No, there was only one person who deserved his full wrath.

A fortnight later he was back in Paris for another meeting with the Minister.

"So everything OK now with the extra marines? The further expansion plans going alright, no? I must say the media reaction has been splendid: how dare the Moroccans commit such atrocities! I like this one: our mining sites, our people, our rights! I'm sure the Moroccan government would like to disagree, but the technicalities are behind us now. We have troops on the ground protecting the mining operations; we can do what we want."

The minister was practically giggling like a child. Robert put down his coffee cup with a force that cracked the delicate porcelain saucer beneath it.

"Do what we want? Do what we want?! Did you even notice how many people died during that riot two weeks ago? Tell me Luc, you wouldn't happen to know why the camp was devoid of French troops on that fateful night, would you? Or whether there's any truth in the rumour that the mob had been incited by the French secret service?"

"Come, come Robert, sacrifices have to be made in the name of progress."

"So you did know it was going to happen."

"Nobody will ever be able to prove anything. Your shareholders are happy. The nation's shortage of fertiliser has been solved. The Legion d'Honneur is headed your way. Is that such a bad outcome? We all have to whore our way to the top you know. The trick is to be able to look in the mirror and tell yourself you're still in control."

Robert had to get out. He glanced at his watch, thanked the Minister for his time and left. Outside the ministry building he turned off the recording device in his watch. *We'll see who's still in control.* Robert made his way along the Rue de Bercy and at the Gare de Lyon bought himself a beer and sat down opposite an African man.

"Jember Abdi? I have what you need. Let's take these bastards down."

CHAPTER 13

Torture is an occupational hazard for an Overseas Agent. Techniques will be taught to help one resist, but the main job is to delay conveying accurate information for as long as possible until a recovery operation can be mounted.

OD Training Manual Section 8e

The agents were dis-armed, stripped of their autographers and other equipment. They were bound and gagged before being taken to the small holding cell they had seen earlier in the day on the guided tour. En route, Freda's right leg dragged painfully on the floor. After the guards had locked them in, Freda tried to wriggle out of her hand-ties. No success.

"Anything useful in that walking stick of yours?" said Sim.

"What, like a sonic screwdriver? Not last time I checked."

"So this is it. We're going to die."

"Don't be so melodramatic. There's plenty of time for us to negotiate our way out of this. Just let me do the talking when they come to interrogate us, OK?" said Freda.

Sim's stomach was rumbling with hunger by the time they were escorted to the office of Elsa Greenwood, the leader of Marinus. Standing behind her desk as they were thrust into the room, she was a striking woman, at least 6 feet tall, with long grey hair and skin stretched too-thin over sharp cheekbones. Even more remarkable was the hawk perched just behind her. The bird gave a cry and stretched out its 50-inch wingspan.

"Her name is Acky, a Northern Goshawk. Isn't she beautiful, Mr Goodall and Ms White? Or should I say, Ms Brightwell and Mr Atkins?" The agents were pushed into seats in front of the desk, strapped down and then ungagged. The guards discreetly fell back.

"Just wait outside, will you boys? I'll holler if our guests become troublesome. Thank you so much. Now," she said, turning back to Freda and Sim, "let's not have any nonsense or denials from you two. What are you doing in Marinus and why did you hack into our medical records?"

No reply.

"What's the matter? Cat got your tongue? Did Freda tell you, Sim, what happened to her last partner at OFWAT? How old was he when he was killed? Twenty-five, wasn't it, Freda? Same age as Sim. The accounts that we uncovered are a little hazy; was it his first mission?"

Sim looked across at his boss. She wouldn't hold his gaze, but her eyebrows looked like they were ready to throttle Elsa. Sim didn't need to ask Freda if it was true. A thousand other questions burst forth. He chewed the inside of his cheek so hard he drew blood.

"We are a pair of OFWAT agents who happen to be lovers. Inter-office relationships aren't allowed, so we've come on holiday to Marinus in secret," said Freda. Sim tried to suppress the look of surprise on his face.

"Then you should have been in bed humping, not hacking into the medical systems."

"Yes, well, actually we were trying to get me a free boob job. Alter the systems so it looks as though I have a platinum medical policy. You know, the sort that includes plasto-work. Too expensive on a government salary." She thrust her chest forwards. "Don't you think I'd look better in a D cup?"

"Nice try but not very convincing. I better get some truth from you or this conversation is going to get awkward." She rolled her letters like an actress enjoying the sound of her own voice, whilst stroking Acky. Elsa took the lid off a box containing bloody chunks of chick carcass; the smell hit Sim like a slap across the face. The elderly stateswoman dipped her ungloved hand into the goo, drew out a dripping lump of flesh and fed her hawk.

Freda looked across at Sim and sighed.

"OK, look, we *are* on official business. Tracking down a pair of terrorists who fled London after blowing up a Salt Camel and we think they came here. Obviously our superiors know where we are and if we don't report back soon they'll send more agents to check up on us. I doubt your residents would appreciate a Royal Navy frigate clogging up their precious marina, would they?"

"That's the only reason you're still alive!" shouted Elsa. Her sudden outburst caused the bird to become agitated. It flapped its wings again, screeched and then lifted its tail feathers before defecating in the litter tray below. "I'm well aware of the repercussions of two agents disappearing while visiting our Sea State. But accidents happen at sea. One of you could, for example, fall out of a window at any time." She went across to the small window in her office, opened it and stared down at the inky void of the sea far below.

Elsa left the window open and walked around the table to stand behind Sim's chair. She rubbed her fingers across his cheek and down his neck, leaving a trail of bloody slime from the hawk's food. Sim strained to pull himself away from her touch. He thought of the smell of this blood and the sharks in the water surrounding Marinus. He felt his bowels loosen and wondered if the hawk would mind sharing the litter tray. The look in Elsa's eyes as she conducted the unholy baptism was even more un-nerving than the thought of the sharks.

Elsa composed herself and turned to Freda. "I have no interest in protecting terrorists – it's not as if they pay anything extra, and we're not exactly overflowing with space. We like to run a clean operation here. Even the upper decks are kept clear of seagull droppings because of the hawks. Acky is the alpha female, of course."

"How can you stand there, showing off your bird of prey and allow that barbaric sport to take place onboard Ivey?" said Sim, his mouth almost foaming. "Those wee turtles are an endangered species. Feeding them to vultures - it's worse than the bloody Romans."

"Come now, Mr Atkins, boys will be boys. I have to turn a blind eye occasionally. Allow people to let off steam somehow. This is a cramped environment; being cooped up can be bad for one's health. You must've seen how many distractions there are for the bored rich here. You've just scratched the surface. There are places you can go for sex, for snowballs, even for suicide if you're tired of life. It really would be pointless to try to ban it all," replied Elsa with a bored smile.

"Does it bother you," asked Freda "that you've ended up becoming the government all your residents are supposed to be fleeing from? You have more power over who comes to this place, what they're allowed to do onboard and how much tax they pay than any democratic government. Doesn't that hypocrisy keep you awake at night?"

Elsa fed her pet some more food and pursed her lips. "Well somebody got out of the wrong side of bed this morning, didn't they Acky? What's the matter with the grumpy little woman?" Sim noticed Elsa was smiling, seeming to enjoy the banter. Her eyes kept lingering over him as she paced the room and then she sat opposite him before looking across to Freda.

"Really Ms Brightwell, it's nothing like that at all. I'm elected merely to carry out the wishes of our residents. If they don't like what I'm doing, they can vote me from office or join another Sea State. Now. What to do about you two? Britain is one of the major sources of new residents here. I'd hate to lose that special relationship over a couple of silly people. What is a girl to do?" Elsa drummed the fingers of her left hand on the desk, while her right hand dropped below the table top and worked its way between her thighs. With her head cocked to one side she stared hard at Sim, mimicking the hawk behind her.

"I have it! You can buy the whereabouts of the terrorists from me."

"We don't exactly carry a Bank of England cheque book around with us. If you want to negotiate a fee for this information, you'll have to let us go and get in touch with our superiors," said Freda.

"I wasn't speaking to you," replied Elsa. "Sim can buy the information from me in return for a small favour. Though not too small, I hope."

There was a pause as the two agents processed what she meant. Freda looked across at Sim. "You don't have to do this."

Could he trust Freda any more? What other secrets was she keeping from him? Sim glanced briefly at his boss. What had Freda said earlier – get the mission done, whatever it takes? He turned his gaze back to the older woman. "I'd be happy to oblige."

Elsa smiled at Freda and called for the guards to take her back to her cabin. Then she hitched up her skirt and sat astride the captive young man. Sim was pretty sure that the training manual didn't cover this. But he was grateful for the small mercy of not having to do his duty in front of his boss. Elsa started slicing open his top with a letter knife while grinding her hips over his groin.

Sim tried to think of Rosie, but that just left him feeling guilty. He closed his eyes and breathed deeply. Eau de litter tray with overtones of dead chicks. Was that really an aphrodisiac for this mad woman? He managed a wry smile for her as he realised that the only time he would happily come as quickly as possible was the one occasion it simply wasn't going to happen.

CHAPTER 14

The Litani River is an important source of water running through Lebanon. It passes very close to the Israeli border before veering sharply westwards towards the Mediterranean Sea. Its control has changed hands between the Lebanese and the Israelis several times during the past 50 years.

OD Training Manual Section 5b

3 years ago. Israel-Lebanon border.

Freda was lying on her front, peering through a pair of binoculars. Next to her was Max, her partner, drawing a sketch of the view on his roll tab. A slit of vision squeezed between the white powdery rocks on the ground and the heavy camouflage netting above them.

Freda glanced across at what he was doing. "Why don't you just take a picture? Or even better, let the autographer video it for you?"

"Meh, where would the fun be in that? Besides, it uses up some time while we wait for something to happen."

"Don't be so quick to want some action, Max. We're here because this is a flash-point. If something happens, it's gonna be ugly. I'll be quite happy to lie here doing nothing for two weeks and get back to Blighty bored out of my mind."

She looked through her binoculars again. A digital read-out of distances and an infra-red overlay of information displayed in her field of vision, while sounds from directional mics played in her ear piece. The dust caked her nostrils and the heat was warming up the rocks just enough to give off a faint metallic smell.

She pressed the second button on her intercom device. "Day five, still no movement on the border. Temperature climbing, cloud cover minimal. Chance of precipitation zero."

As darkness fell, the two agents took it in turns to crawl out of their hide-out, relieving their bladders and aching muscles. Freda shivered as she stood outside the tent, pulling on a jumper. A crescent moon, barely two days old, cast a faint icy glow over the landscape. The few splashes of colour from vegetation or abandoned houses blanched out: even without her star scope, Freda's vision had become monochrome. She looked up in the sky and then down into the dip near the river.

The valley of the crescent moon. I wonder if we will find the cup of everlasting life here?

Freda huddled down into her sleeping bag, while Max assumed look-out duties. Freda yawned. "You know, for your first mission, you've adapted to life in the field very well, Max."

"Don't tell me, this is the moment when we have a heart-to-heart, right? You tell me about the day your dog got run over, have a cry and then we put the world to rights?"

"Shut up. I was just saying you'd made a good start, that's all. Wake me in four hours, OK?"

A gentle shake of her shoulder. Eyes snapped open and then blinked shut again. Daylight had started to creep into the camouflage tent.

"What time is it?"

"About 6am. You seemed tired so I did an extra shift."

"Max, you need your rest too. A tired agent is a danger to their partner as well as themselves. Don't do that again." Freda propped herself up and took a slug of water from a canteen. "Have a bit of sleep now, I can do the morning shift on my own."

Max started to roll out his sleeping bag, while Freda went to relieve herself. When she came back, Max had already closed his eyes. She lay down in the observation slit and trained her binoculars on the border. Movement. A dust column over the horizon, maybe a couple of klicks from the river. She flicked her foot at Max's sleeping bag.

"Max, get up."

"Hmm, what? Already? That only felt like two minutes."

"It was. There's something happening. Vehicles approaching the border, I think."

Max roused himself and got out his roll tab, starting to jot down a mission entry.

Date: 20.4.25. 0612z. Israel-Lebanon border, Litani River. Co-ordinates 2513-1378
Vehicles approaching border.

"Can you count how many?" said Max.

"Not yet. Hang on. Yep, here they come. I see three Merkava mark IV battle tanks. IDF alright. Moving in standard squad formation. Then another squad behind them. And… yep some minesweepers. This is serious."

Max tapped away on his keyboard. "Any markings?"

"Looks like 53rd Sufa Battalion."

"Makes sense, part of the 188th Barak Armour Brigade. That's who I'd choose to lead an invasion."

Freda looked across at Max, as he typed this all into his report, nodding her head. "Pass me the sat phone, will you?"

They continued to observe the armoured column approach the far bank of the river. The tanks fanned out, forming a defensive ring around a patch of clear ground that shelved gently down to the riverside. A few soldiers deployed from the rear hatches and took up position between the tanks. After the minesweeping vehicles had patrolled the area, more vehicles appeared. Soft-skinned trucks, carrying more troops and engineering equipment.

"Look at those pumps and generators. They are definitely tapping the river," said Max.

Freda punched in a number on the sat phone. "C.O.R. C.O.R. This is O.D. six, over."

"O.D. six, this is C.O.R. Receiving you. Encryption begins. Report please."

"We have an incursion and asset-strip happening right now at our location. Visual on several tanks, a platoon of infantry and engineers. Permission to call in airstrike?"

"Negative, O.D. six. Record and prosecute. That is the mandate of your mission. Zero engagement, unless under direct fire. Understand?"

"Message received C.O.R." Freda pressed a button and put the phone down.

"What a bunch of pussies," said Max. "Prosecution always takes months, even with direct evidence like this. I thought the *Club of Rome* would've learnt after the cock-up over the Renaissance Dam."

"You may be right, Max, but orders are orders. Come on, let's file this report."

Freda took the first night shift this time. The Israeli forces seemed to have set up a few tents near the water pumps, inside the defensive ring. Generators had cut in as the sun set, replacing the solar panels, and a faint smell of diesel wafted over from across the river. As the camp settled into a noisy stillness, and the thin moon peeped between broken clouds, Freda heard a loud whistling sound sail over her head. Within a second the camp was lit-up by an explosion that sent debris and soil raining down over the whole area. Freda clicked her autographer into record mode just as a second whistling shell flew overhead and detonated between two of the tanks. A horrible scream followed a couple of seconds later and Freda could just make out a flaming body stagger towards the river, collapsing on the bank just short of its destination.

Soldiers started rushing around the camp. One person seemed to be standing still and pointing commands. Two more rounds exploded as the Israelis ran for cover inside the Merkava tanks. The shelling continued for another minute or two and then stopped.

Silence.

And then the crack of small-arms ammunition rounds exploding in the flames. The diesel generators could not be seen any more, and the pumps were sticking up in a tangled white mess next to the river, inert like the festering corpse of a beached whale.

Max looked across at Freda. "Did we get the airstrike after all?"

Freda shook her head. "I think this was a local attack. Artillery. Must have been short range to be that accurate from the very first round. The Israelis won't take this lying down."

"But they're the invaders. What do they expect?"

"IDF standard tactics. Crush any resistance. There'll be hunter-killers here by morning. You'll see. Now get some sleep."

The low morning sun glinted off another platoon of tanks that joined the original force the next day. Some armoured engineering vehicles had begun digging entrenchments and laying concrete blocks by the time Freda and Max had finished breakfast.

"Seems like they are getting ready for a long stay," said Max. "They must know how long prosecutions take at the UN these days."

A pair of jets streaked across the sky at low altitude. The camouflaged tent in which the O.D. agents were hiding shook violently.

Freda craned her neck up to the sky through the narrow slit in the tent. "That will be the Israeli ground attack planes, seeking out the Hezbollah ordnance."

An explosion sent another shock wave through the tent. Freda raced to the flap at the back and peered through. There was a billow of smoke rising from just below the horizon and a parachute in the sky.

"What the? That looks like one of the Israeli pilots. Hezbollah are packing some serious kit if they can take down an F-16 these days."

The tinny retort of many rifles being fired began and the pilot's body jerked several times, while the parachute began to disintegrate under the hail of bullets.

"Poor bastard."

"How can you say that, Freda? The Israelis are the invaders, they are the transgressors here."

"Still. Not a nice way to go, looking down at your killers, knowing you can't do a thing to dodge those bullets."

Some of the tanks started moving out from the Israeli camp, heading for the main bridge over the Litani river.

"Come on, let's tail them," said Freda. "We can leave a camera in the tent recording anything while we're gone." They armed themselves with automatic pistols and slipped on their liquid armour vests. "If we get split up, head back here at night fall."

"Don't shoot unless targeted by enemy fire. Destroy the autographer memory stick if in danger of being captured. Code for emergency evac is Golf Tango Alpha. Blah, blah, blah. I know the script, Freda." Max checked the clip in his gun, thrust it back into place and slipped out of the tent.

Crouching low, the pair of agents ran between small clumps of cedar trees until they found a tributary stream of the river. They splashed through the trickle of water, using the channel as cover, moving parallel to the tanks' route. They would have stood no chance of keeping up with the tracked vehicles, except for the extreme caution being used by the Israeli tank commander. At every building and junction in the road, he would order a halt and send off a tiny surveillance drone to investigate potential ambush spots.

Freda and Max stayed in touch with the tanks as the vehicles made their way along the road, weaving between makeshift homes. Doors hung off hinges. Flimsy curtains fluttered in windows without glass. At one point, one of the tanks rotated its turret towards the agents and they had to dive for cover into a little dip in the ground next to one of the buildings. The dip was lined with faeces and the stench filled their nostrils as they lay still in the night-soil listening to the buzz of flies lingering in the heat. Freda could feel the bile building in her throat and tried to fight off the urge to retch.

Once the tanks had moved on again, Freda and Max crawled out of the shallow cesspit and continued to tail the Israelis. They had covered another kilometre or so when the tanks stopped at a major junction. The road here was a little better defined than the dirt track they had been following so far. And some of the buildings dotted around seemed less flimsy than others they had passed. Once again the tank commander sent a hover drone to investigate the buildings. The sun glinted on its tiny yellow propellers as it whirred forward like a bee in search of pollen.

Before the drone reached the buildings, there was a roar of flame and a whoosh as a missile was launched at an Israeli tank. Freda thought it sounded odd, as if there were an echo. The tank immediately responded with a shot-gun blast from a tiny dome on top of the main turret. It didn't seem to make any difference. The missile slammed into the hull of the tank, just above the left tracks. The explosion lifted the tank, tipping it onto its right-hand side. More rockets were fired at the exposed belly of the beast. Flames started licking around the tank and a very unpleasant smell wafted over to Freda's concealed observatory. The other tanks opened fire, slamming high explosive rounds into all of the buildings. Machine gun tracer bullets flew in all directions.

As Freda and Max watched the battle unfold, the rear doors of the Merkava tanks opened. As the soldiers disembarked, Freda noticed that the terrain around the back of the vehicles was shifting. Little shrubs, bits of discarded furniture, even the ground itself, all were moving. A child appeared from behind a rusty oil barrel. He ran forward towards one of the tanks and threw a grenade in through the open door. The troops were slow to react, almost disbelieving this source of attack. The bomb went off, shaking the tank from inside, before the infantry outside realised what was happening and turned their guns on the child. The small body was flung backwards by the impact of the bullets.

More children appeared from carefully concealed hiding places. One was gunned down as soon as she stood up. Others managed to throw their grenades towards the tanks before diving for cover again. But now that they had been spotted, the cover wasn't adequate. Not against high velocity machine guns. Freda bit her lip and tried to blink away tears.

Max got up and unholstered his pistol. "I'm not standing by to watch this slaughter."

"Max, don't!"

Max starting running forwards, raising his pistol in both hands, level with his eyes and firing at the Israeli soldiers. He shot one before others noticed this new assailant. Bullets stung the ground near Max's feet before the first round found its mark. His vest absorbed the hit, though the jolt caused Max to lose his balance. His feet slipped on some loose gravel and then the second bullet hit him, skimming the side of his neck where he had no protection. As Max was falling a third round slammed into his body, this time smacking into his hip.

Freda stayed crouching, assessing the distance between her hiding place and where Max lay. The battle between the Israelis and Hezbollah continued for a few minutes. Another tank was hit by a missile. The remaining tanks were spewing thick white clouds from their smoke generators. The IDF infantry seemed to be running in haphazard directions. Eventually the Israelis began to retreat.

Freda crawled forward. "Oh Christ, Max, what've you done?"

His eyes were closed. Blood, still seeping from a gash on his neck, had pooled beneath his head. Freda grabbed a medical dressing from her trouser pocket and pressed it into his wound. Max groaned. Freda surveyed the rest of his body. She couldn't see any other wounds, but as she slid her hands down the underside of his torso she felt more blood. Moving round to his other side she could see where the bullet had penetrated his trousers at the left hip. She cut the trousers open and gasped as she saw the shattered bone piercing the skin and the very large pool of blood that had collected in his clothes.

"Shit!" She pulled the sat phone out of her utility belt. "C.O.R. C.O.R. This is O.D. six requesting immediate emergency evac. Golf Tango Alpha. I repeat Golf Tango Alpha. Emergency medical evac required."

"O.D. six, copy that. Helicopter will be dispatched. E.T.A. is twenty minutes. Hold tight."

Freda tried to take Max's pulse. She couldn't find a beat in his wrist and his neck was in too much of a mess to try there. "Stay with me, Max. Evac is on its way. You hear me. Just hold on." She leant over him, holding her cheek next to his mouth, hoping to feel a breath, while her eyes scanned down his torso looking for a rise and fall. She waited for twenty seconds. Nothing but the smell of dried faeces on his clothes.

"Fuck!" She pressed her hands together, interlocking her fingers, and positioned her body directly over his rib cage. She pressed down twenty times in quick succession, then wrapped her lips around his mouth, pinched his nose and gave a rescue breath.

"Come on, Max! Don't you dare do this."

She pressed again, another twenty dips followed by a rescue breath. Again and again.

And again.

CHAPTER 15

The human body can survive in water for several hours, provided that the temperature of the water is not below 10 degrees centigrade. But exhaustion or unconsciousness will kick in much sooner, so a life jacket is essential to extend the chances of an agent being picked up before drowning occurs.

O.D. Training Manual Section 7d

Sim walked back to his cabin, rubbing his wrists where the handcuffs had chaffed. As he crossed the hatchway between the oil rig and the cruiser, with the grey shifting sea matching the colour of the sky, Sim could tell it would be another hour or two before the sun rose. He passed a couple of cleaners, some of the nocturnal staff who busied themselves while others slept. Sunken eyes stared out at him from sallow faces.

Sim entered the cabin softly, wondering if Freda would still be awake. She sat up in bed as soon as he approached.

"Sim, I'm sorry I didn't tell you about Max, my first partner." She focused on a loose thread on the bed covers.

"S'OK" He sat on the bed with his back to her and took off his shoes.

"I still blame myself for what happened. But I didn't think it was relevant to our mission."

The room was silent except for the faint sound of machinery far off in the ship and the hum of a fan whirring just outside their window.

"Well?"

Sim looked around. "Well what?"

"Did she give you the info she promised?"

Sim couldn't hold Freda's gaze, he turned again and removed his socks. "Yes – she gave me a contact in America. The Captain of a NUCL barge."

"And?"

"And what? Did I enjoy it? No, of course not. Did I do whatever it takes? Yes, I bloody well did."

Freda tutted. "That's not what I was asking. I meant did she give you any extra information? Like how this Captain was tied in with the terrorists? Would he help us, or he is a threat too?"

Sim shook his head and turned towards his boss. Before he could reply, the door to the cabin banged open. Three huge men squeezed their way through the opening. Sim recognised the first one, the ass-grabbing Tomas.

"I was on a promise, you little bitch," the barman said.

Freda and Sim got to their feet. Tomas' two companions were nearly as big as him. Standing side by side they cut off any possible escape route.

"Look, there's been some misunderstanding," said Freda.

"That's right," said Tomas. "You misunderstood who you were messing with. You rub yourself up against me in the bar, begging for it, and then think you can just piss off to spend the night with some runt, eh?"

"It's not what you think. He's not my lover."

"I'll tell you what else he isn't. He isn't staying on this boat any longer. Bezo, Mark take him for a long walk off a short plank. Me and the little lady have some unfinished business." Tomas reached for his belt and started to unbuckle it.

Sim punched and blocked as best he could, but the other two

men had longer reaches and were simply too strong. They grabbed him around the neck and legs and started carrying him out of the cabin. Sim tried to call out to Freda, but the arm pressing into his throat cut off any sound. It was difficult enough to breathe, never mind speak. Freda threw a karate punch at Tomas' midriff but it just bounced off.

Sim was hauled into the corridor, being held horizontally. Doors to other cabins, containing sleeping tourists blissfully unaware of the violence happening metres from their beds, passed closely in front of Sim's face. He couldn't get an arm free to bang on a door or make any sort of noise to alert some fellow passengers. His fear was mixed with anger at the thought of what Tomas might be doing to Freda back in their cabin.

He thrashed his legs and twisted his arms in a desperate effort to get free. But the arm around his neck just squeezed even tighter until Sim's throat began to close and his vision started to blur.

Sim woke up and spluttered as cold water trickled down the back of his throat. He tried to look around but could not tell which way was up. He breathed in, not realising he was still underwater and convulsed once again. After a few seconds that seemed to last minutes he bobbed to the surface and was able to cough the water out of his throat and take a deep breath. The cruise ship loomed above him like a cliff of steel. He couldn't see anybody on deck from down here and in the gloomy light before dawn it was doubtful that anybody would spot him even if they did happen to look over the edge of the ship.

He tried yelling but the wind was whipping his cries away as soon as they left his mouth. Waves were slapping against the side of the ship and making it difficult for him to hold his position steady in the water. There were no openings at sea level on this side of the cruise ship. He would have to try to swim around to the other side of the vessel. He might be able to climb onto one of the oil rig legs, or even onto part of the algae farm. But the sea was rough and he already felt exhausted after a night without sleep.

He started to swim towards the stern of the ship, which looked a bit closer than the bow. Unfortunately, this meant swimming into the wind. The water seemed to take Sim's efforts as a personal affront and kept slapping him across the face. Every other breath seemed to coincide with a wave searching for a way into his mouth. The salt water stung his nose which was bleeding from the fight back in the cabin. He was forced to pause frequently for extra breaths even before he had made it to the end of the ship. He had to hurry. Freda needed him.

Coldness was beginning to turn his hands and feet numb. He looked up again to see how close he was now. There was something on the surface of the ocean, not too far away. His heart lifted momentarily. A boat, perhaps? Had somebody seen him fall in and organised a rescue? He looked again. No, too small to be a boat. It was grey and triangular. *Triangular*. His mouth, in spite of his surroundings, felt very dry. His nose bleed had just become more than a mere inconvenience.

He trod water while he tried to figure out if he could get around the stern of the ship before the shark cut him off, or whether he would have to try to go back along almost the entire length of the ship, hoping that the shark would not follow. Neither option seemed particularly appealing. There was a loud splash in the water behind him. He turned to see Freda bobbing up to the surface with a dagger between her teeth. He swam over to her.

"Are you alright? How did you get away?"

"Never mind that, we've got company," said Freda. "May as well meet it head on, come on." And she started swimming towards the shark.

As they reached the end of the ship and could finally see a place where they might be able to haul themselves out of the water, the shark cut across their route, almost as if it knew where they wanted to go. Freda put her knife in her right hand and trod water again, trying to keep herself between Sim and the predator.

"Sim, help me keep track of it. Call out every time you see it change direction or when it dives then re-surfaces."

No reply.

"OK Sim? Did you hear what I just said?" Freda couldn't turn around to look at Sim, she kept her eyes focused on the shark all the time. But Sim's eyelids were drooping and his limbs were becoming increasingly numb.

As Freda turned to see what was wrong with Sim, the shark surged forward. Freda managed to twist and kick at the last second and the shark's teeth closed around nothing but water. It circled around once more, forcing Freda to keep manoeuvring to protect Sim, and then it attacked again. This time Freda was well prepared. As the shark's snout rose out of the water, she reached out with her knife and drove it into the shark's eye. The shark's teeth sliced into Freda's other arm but failed to catch and snare her. It swam off, and this time didn't turn to circle the two swimmers.

The sudden attack had jolted Sim back to full alertness. In the dull glow from lights on the oil rig, he saw tendrils of red spreading from Freda's left arm. "Quick, we need to get out of the water before that shark comes back."

Freda winced and tried to press the wound closed with her right hand. "Take the knife, Sim."

One of the oilrig legs, only one hundred metres away, had a metal ladder that rose out of the water and ended at an access hatch. But the swimmers' progress was slow. The waves were bigger now they were out of the lee of the ship. Sim was near exhaustion. And Freda was having to propel herself mostly with just her legs because she was using her right hand to try to apply pressure to her wound. They had managed to cross half the gulf between the end of the ship and the sanctuary of that rusty metal ladder when a shape just below the surface of the water moved across their path. Then another one. And another.

Freda and Sim stopped swimming and looked at each other.

"I've got nothing," said Sim.

"Split up. You swim to the ladder and I'll keep them occupied."

Three fins broke the surface of the water and started to circle them.

"I'm not leaving you here to get eaten, Freda."

"You've got valuable information that HQ needs to know. Stop being a hero and start doing your job."

Sim hesitated and looked around for a third option. There had to be some way out of this for them both. He thought he saw some lights deep below him in the water. Was he hallucinating? There they were again, only this time brighter and bigger. The sharks pulled back, alerted to the presence of some massive object underneath their intended prey.

The conning tower of a small submarine rose up out of the water right next to the pair of British agents. A hatchway in the top was quickly opened and a man armed with a rifle lifted himself out of the submarine. He scanned the water for the sharks, spotted one and steadied himself for a shot. Sim could see the rifle was fitted with a scope and silencer. A puff of smoke escaping from the barrel was the only evidence that the trigger had been pulled. Sim looked across to the shark and saw a pool of blood spreading out from the stationary body. The other two sharks pounced in a frenzy of snapping teeth.

The marksman turned towards Sim and Freda. "Anybody hail a cab?"

Inside the submarine, one of the crew attended to Freda's injuries while Sim sat wrapped in a silver blanket, drinking from a steaming mug.

The Captain of the vessel spoke. "Wardle asked me to keep an eye on things. You didn't think we'd let you take on the whole of Marinus by yourselves, did you?"

"First rule of agency work, Sim; always have an exit," said Freda.

"But how did you guys know we were in trouble just now and not, say, twelve hours ago?" asked Sim, thinking back to their interrogation in Elsa's office.

The Captain reached across to the knife Freda had used on the shark, examining the handle. He flipped it around and holding the blade, handed it over to Sim. "O.D. standard issue, basic maritime survival kit. The knife has a locator device in the handle – starts transmitting automatically on contact with water."

"I think you need to brush up on your training manual, Sim," said Freda.

"So, what now? You need to get back into Marinus?"

"No, we've got what we came for," said Sim. "But we don't have any clothes, false passports or equipment any more. They're all back in our cabin."

"I suspect they've already been stolen actually," said Freda. "We need to get to America as quickly as possible. We have a contact to pursue, but not sure how long we've got before the trail goes cold."

The Captain looked at the pair. "Best thing we can do is get you back to the nearest landmass – Cape Verde – and have another agent meet you there with new IDs and kit. I'll send the message and get you there overnight. Why don't you two catch up on some sleep?"

CHAPTER 16

Rigor mortis is the stiffening of the body between one to seven hours after death and occurs due to muscular tissue hardening as myosinogen and paramyosinogen coagulates. The process starts in the smaller muscles and works its way down the body into the larger muscles. Rigor mortis usually disappears between 20-30 hours after death. The human body loses around 1.5 degrees centigrade per hour (dependent on environmental factors), so temperature can also be used to ascertain time of death.

O.D. Training Manual Section 7f, Assessing a crime scene

2½ years earlier, a small road east of Lhasa, China.

Rabten was sitting next to his master, watching the hindquarters of the mule that was pulling their cart rock from side to side. They were taking a supply of crops to one of the villages near the monastery.

"How many more trips will we have to do this year, master?"

Wangdue looked at his pupil. "As many as it takes. You know the villages are struggling to grow enough crops, whereas we are blessed with an abundance. Four trips a year should help bide them over. Which means one more after this one. Be mindful of your impatience, Rabten."

"Yes, master."

The mule plodded onwards over the rocky road. Rabten took a sip from a bottle of water, noticing the shifting shades of green wind-blown bamboo either side of the track. As they turned a corner, the path was blocked by a fallen tree.

Rabten tutted, wondering if the pair of monks would be strong enough to haul it out of the way.

"What do you see?" asked Wangdue.

"A tree has fallen and it's blocking our path, master."

"Look again."

Rabten looked at the tree. Dark brown, mottled bark. A cavity in the trunk near the right-hand end. The other end, where the roots should be. *Where the roots should be.* He looked at the ground either side of the road. No hole where the tree might have been growing. Instead just drag marks off to the left.

"It's been put there on—"

A man stepped out from behind a bush and drew a large sword from his belt. "We need your food. Get down from the cart. Nobody needs to get hurt."

"But people will get hurt if we fail to deliver these crops to the village," said Wangdue.

"I don't care. Hand it over, before I lose my patience." The bandit advanced another few steps closer and several companions emerged from behind the surrounding trees. Two of them were armed with bows, while one had a threshing mace and the other a two-handed scythe.

Wangdue got down from the cart. "Protect the crops and watch your back," he whispered before approaching the swordsman. "I respectfully decline your offer."

"I didn't say you had a choice." The bandit signalled to his archers who loosed their arrows at Wangdue.

The monk knocked one arrow to the ground in mid-flight as if he was swatting a mosquito. And just as the other arrow was about to pierce his shoulder, he caught it. Holding it up to his face he examined the barbed tip carefully. "Very nasty. You should be more careful with these."

The swordsman leapt forward and slashed at Wangdue. The monk dodged the blow easily. Another thrust with the sword, but this time Wangdue not only side-stepped the attack but also grabbed the bandit's arm and twisted it until the sword fell to the ground. The monk kept twisting until there was a popping sound from the bandit's shoulder and he yelped like a puppy.

Rabten was watching the fight closely and almost didn't hear the noise of shoes crunching on the path behind the cart. He turned just in time to see another man, armed with an iron-tipped staff, climb on board the cart. Rabten leapt up and punched the man in the face before he could swing his staff. The would-be thief toppled backwards into a pile of turnips and stayed down.

The rest of the attackers turned tail and ran off into the trees and bamboo on either side of the track. Wangdue picked up the sword and prodded the leader up the backside with the arrow. He limped off, clutching his arm.

"Come on," said Wangdue, "we still need to make the village before dark."

The villagers welcomed the two monks with joyous waves as the sun was just starting to dip below the western hills. The harvest was carefully stored in one of the larger buildings while the mule was rubbed down, fed and watered. Wangdue and Rabten were shown into the village meeting hall, but none of the village leaders greeted them with smiles.

Rabten looked across at his master, who shrugged and sat down at the table.

"Not your usual welcome, this time. Why the long faces?" asked Wangdue.

Rabten thought of a funny joke about the mule's long face, but decided to keep quiet.

One of the village elders cleared his throat. "We have grave news, Master Wangdue. Murder has come to our humble village."

"Somebody's been murdered? Who?" Rabten stood up. "When? Where?"

Wangude glared at his pupil, who immediately sat down again. "Forgive my disciple's outburst. We are sorry for your loss. Please, if we can be of any assistance, we would be only too happy to help."

"Thank you, Master Wangdue. We would prefer to keep the authorities out of this scandal. The fewer excuses they have to interfere in our affairs, the better. We would feel much happier if you could investigate the crime. Xiaodan will show you the scene of the barbarous act and will fill you in on the details." The village elder indicated a young woman standing in the corner of the room, who came forward and bowed to the monks.

The smell of death invaded Rabten's nostrils as soon as the door to the bedroom was opened. Flies buzzed in the corner of the room, and the lantern light caught on a pool of something that reflected back like sparkling rubies.

"The power to the house was down when we found her," said Xiaodan. "Throat has been slit. Looks like a roll tab has been stolen. At least we can't find one here."

Wangdue entered the room, watching where he placed his feet. "Who was she?"

"A geologist from the University of Chengdu. She came here a few weeks ago to complete some studies in the hills west of here. She kept herself to herself really. Seemed pleasant enough. Can't think why anybody would want to harm her."

Wangdue bent closer to the body, which was lying face down on the floor with thick, dark blood pooled around her head. The corpse was wearing a simple t-shirt and pair of jeans, typical of a student but somewhat unusual in this rural setting. "No sign of interference, I presume?"

"Not unless the murderer got her dressed again afterwards."

"How long ago did this happen?" said Rabten.

"She was discovered this morning. A neighbour noticed that the door was open and went to see if everything was alright."

"So, it likely occurred last night, sometime. An autopsy would help us establish a more accurate timeline and check for sexual abuse. But I presume the village council would rather avoid that route?"

Xiaodan nodded.

Wangue turned to his pale-faced pupil. "Why don't you get some fresh air and then go talk to this neighbour?"

Rabten agreed and quickly left the room, breathing deeply as soon as he was outside. He crouched down to steady his legs and then went to find the person who had discovered the corpse.

Rabten came back into the student's room cautiously and was pleased to see that the body was no longer there. Wangdue was searching through the woman's possessions and kept shaking his head. He looked up when Rabten arrived.

"Any luck?"

"Nothing much to report. The neighbour remembers hearing a brief scream just before he went to bed but nothing after that. He had presumed it was the woman getting scared at a rodent or the TV, and just ignored it. He remembers that there was a window open when he found the body and as Xiaodan said, the front door hadn't been closed properly."

Wangdue nodded and went to check on the windows in the other room. When he came back, he was shaking his head. "Something doesn't quite add up. There are plenty of valuable items left here – so robbery can't be the motive. She's fully clothed so rape seems out. I've been looking at her books and posters. No obvious radical beliefs, so I can't think she had any political enemies. What if there's something missing that we don't know about, because we're not even thinking about it?"

"You've lost me, Master."

"How do we know that it wasn't robbery and that there isn't a gold bar missing from her room? We presume she didn't have one, so we presume it's not missing."

"But that could apply to anything, Master. How does that help our investigation?"

"Look for signs of its departure, Rabten. Act like a scientist looking for quarks – detect their presence through their influence on things that we can see."

Rabten scratched his head and then yawned. "I see," he lied.

"Come on, let's get some sleep and see if a new day helps to inspire us."

Rabten woke up expecting to hear the sounds of the monastery bustling around him. Then he remembered where he was, and what he had to do that day. Images of red fountains and spectres had filled his dreams. He could tell from the light creeping past the curtains that he had woken very early. Master Wangdue was still asleep on the other bed. Rabten got out of bed slowly, picked up his shoes and padded out of the room.

Once outside, he stretched, farted and put on his sandals. He looked around the village. The milky whiteness of the sky suggested a sun that was still an hour from rising. Nobody else was up and about yet. A dog and some chickens wandered among the buildings freely, scratching, sniffing or pecking at anything of interest.

Rabten walked in no particular direction, vaguely following one of the chickens. As he turned the corner towards the murdered woman's building, he heard a grunt and the scrape of metal on metal. He ran towards the noise and spotted a person trying to climb through one of the windows leading into the building. The man stopped and turned to look at Rabten. He paused for a moment and then dropped to the ground before sprinting off towards the forest on the edge of the village.

Rabten gave chase, sprinting through the dirt in his sandals. His feet skidded and stumbled in the gravel, and he was still at least 50 metres away when the man disappeared into a part of the forest thick with undergrowth. Rabten kept running but as he passed the third tree trunk, a large branch came swinging through the air and smacked straight into his face. Blood started streaming down his nose and his vision blurred. He was vaguely aware of somebody approaching and tried to blink away tears as he formed a defensive posture. Then, another cry from behind him, somewhere near the village and the man in front of him turned and fled.

"Has the bleeding stopped yet?" said Wangdue.

Rabten was sitting with his head hung low, pinching the bridge of his nose. He sat up straight, let go of his nose and sniffed gently. "I dink so."

"Where did he come from?"

"I spodded him climbing into the student's building. Or at least, I dink he was climbing in. Maybe he had already broken in and wad coming out again." Rabten looked up to the ceiling and tried to replay the scene in his head.

"Did you notice anything about his clothes?"

"Very dark. Bladder than bladd, almost as if the light wad being absorbed. He wad certainly quick in those drainers."

Wangdue paced the room. "Sounds like he was wearing nano-cloth which probably means he was government. Let's assume he was the murderer. If he was coming back to the scene of the crime, it must mean there was something he'd left behind, or something he couldn't find the first time. Come on, we need to search her room again."

The student's room was a mess. Every drawer had been emptied and the contents lay strewn across the floor. Book shelves were bare, and the carcasses of ripped-open hardbacks littered the floor like feathery bones.

"I think we can safely say he was leaving, not entering when you disturbed him," said Wangdue.

"I'm sorry, Master, I should've stopped him."

"Everyone else was asleep, including me. Don't blame yourself."

Rabten looked around the room. "You know, for a student who had come here especially to do research, there isn't much sign of any work."

"That's it, of course. The absence we didn't detect. Her research. What if she'd discovered something in the hills that the authorities didn't want anybody else to know."

"Worth killing for?" asked Xiaodan.

"Apparently," said Wangdue. "Come on, while we figure out how to find her research, let's have some breakfast. I'm famished."

As the three of them went outside, they noticed a pair of kids squabbling on the far side of the village square. A control pad clattered to the ground and then there was a crunch of plastic against wood as a hover drone crashed into the roof of a building.

Wangdue stopped and stared. He wandered up to the children, who were pushing and pulling each other for possession of the control pad.

"Namaste. I wonder if you boys can help me. Some research equipment has gone missing from the bedroom of the lady who was living over there," he said pointing to the building he had just come from. "You wouldn't know anything about that, would you?"

The two boys stopped fighting, and then shook their heads while shuffling their feet in the dirt. The boy who had ended up with the control pad held it behind his back.

Xiaodan joined them. "Come on Han and Liu, Master Wangdue is here on very important business, helping the village elders. If you know anything, you must tell him."

The boys looked at each other, nodded and proceeded to explain how the lady had let them play with the drone last week. And then yesterday, when they went to ask to borrow it again, there had been no answer at the door. The door was open so they had gone in and found the drone by the front door. They had only borrowed it and they were going to bring it back, but then they had heard what had happened to her and didn't know what to do.

"It's OK, boys, nobody is blaming you," said Wangdue. "But we need to take the drone back now."

Once the drone had been retrieved from the roof it had crashed onto, the monks accessed the memory card in its camera. Playing back some of recordings showed a vast swathe of trees in the western hills had been felled and undergrowth cleared. The path through the hills and forest was like a livid scar, perfectly straight, stretching for miles to the west.

"They're building something, for sure," said Rabten.

"I thought they'd given up with major infrastructure projects, especially out here. Maybe there were some more clues on her roll-tab. But what's so important that they'll murder a person over?" Wangdue shook his head. "I'm sorry Xiaodan, but I don't think we'll be able to capture the culprit. He could be miles away by now. Tell your elders what we've found. We need to report this to the Grand Master. Come Rabten, let's get the mule hitched up to the cart."

CHAPTER 17

The New Union Canal Lattice – or knuckle – was conceived as a grand infrastructure project to kick-start the ailing US economy, while simultaneously helping with rising sea water levels and delivering a more energy-efficient transportation system. Ground was broken on the first new canal in March 2018, but it took a full eight years for the whole system to be completed.
O.D. Training Manual Section 4e

May 3rd, 2028, Brasilia, Brazil.

"I've gone right off the natural world," Sim said. He was staring at an advertising screen, luring tourists to the local zoo. In between clips of elephants and jaguars, there was a bird of prey that looked a bit like the one in Elsa's office and then a picture of the aquarium, which was full of sharks. Sim shivered in the air-conditioned coolness.

Freda and Sim were in the terminal at Brasilia airport, on their way to the USA, having taken the first flight west to the Americas from Cape Verde. Waiting for their connecting flight they stretched their legs through the huge shopping mall. Every other shop seemed to be a designer outlet full of people spending money. Sim glanced up at the departure board to check if their plane was boarding. The screen showed that there were flights to every major capital on the planet. They walked on a little further, past a section of the terminal that was closed for improvements. The airport was being expanded and the Brazilian water company, Sabesp, was sponsoring this latest building project.

"Look, I know that thing with turtles was pretty nauseating, but you nearly flipped out twice back in Marinus. I need to know you can keep calm in a tight situation."

"Well you don't need to worry about me being over-confident now. Would it hurt, man, to give me the occasional piece of praise?"

"Sim, if you're going to work in the field you need to learn how to control your emotions."

Sim stopped walking and turned to look at Freda. "When exactly were you going to tell me about your previous partner?"

"How would that've helped us? The past is past. You need to stay focused on the here and now," replied Freda in a quiet voice.

He turned away and walked off again. Just at that moment a young Brazilian woman strolled past him, her breasts apparently attempting the samba inside a low-cut top. Sim's eyes followed her along the passageway until, not looking where he was going, he stumbled into a potted tree.

Freda caught up with him and smiled. "Busted. Literally. I thought you'd be more of a leg man, myself. You certainly spend more time looking at my legs than my tits."

Sim picked himself up, feeling his cheeks flush hot. "Sorry." He stole one last glance at the disappearing distraction and then focused on his boss. "I should stop staring at your leg, you're right of course. It's just I *am* curious, what did happen?"

There was an announcement over the tannoy.

"That's our plane, come on, Sim." And with that Freda slung her bag over her left shoulder, tapped the ground in front with her walking stick a couple of times and headed for the departure gate.

They boarded the VARIG plane destined for Memphis. It was one of the latest designs – a wing wedge – that only the most upmarket airlines could afford. The whole plane was built like a v-shaped wing, with the main fuselage contained within its thick arrow-head shape. This meant less turbulence, less drag and much more floor space according to the infommercial that ran on repeated loop as they boarded the plane. It took a bit of getting used to the idea of an aircraft with 30 seats across each row. The agents settled into their comfortable seats and prepared for the journey.

Freda turned to Sim. "The training manual has a good section on the NUCL; probably worth your while reading up on it."

After Freda and Sim had cleared border control at Memphis International Airport, they hired a car and bought a large-scale map of the area that covered the address they had been given for Captain Rogers. He would have information on the whereabouts of the two terrorists, if what Elsa Greenwood had told Sim was true.

They were tired after the too-short overnight flight but nevertheless they set off straight away, stopping just briefly for an unhealthy breakfast of coffee and 'donuts'. It was a surprisingly cold start to a bright spring day. The baked-brown and barren countryside zipped past their car windows; regular droughts in recent years had re-created the dust-bowl conditions of the 1930s. But as they approached the town Pine Bluff there was an oasis of green. Clearly there was no ban here on hose-pipes and automatic sprinklers. Freda tutted loudly as they passed acres of perfectly watered lawns. A couple of hours after they had left the airport, they tracked down the 'subs' where the Captain lived on the outskirts of the small city.

Sim looked at the unusual homes and piped up. "I remember watching a documentary about these. Some scientist had claimed that the best way to insulate your home and protect it from the ever-increasing tornadoes was to dig down and bury your home in the ground. One homebuilding company believed in him and built a neighbourhood of these houses in a town in Arkansas. The town got hit by a whopper shortly after the new homes were finished. The tornado devastated most of the town, but this small group of underground homes was left virtually scratch free. They passed the test with flying colours. The news channels carried footage of the town and its group of un-damaged homes throughout the country. Demand sky-rocketed and suddenly the 'subs' had been re-born."

"Proper little encyclopedia, aren't you?"

"What? It was a good programme. There's a part of me that still thinks I should've become an architect. The part labelled Mum and Dad."

The agents pulled up outside the Captain's house.

"Let's see who's home. I'll pose as somebody from the Guild, you cover my back." Freda hobbled across the road and down the small flight of steps to the front door. She got out her OFWAT badge, carefully placing her fingers over the parts of the ID that showed where she really worked, and knocked on the door. Sim stood at the top of the stairs squinting down. After a long wait there was a shuffle of somebody's feet approaching the entrance, a key was turned and a slight lady with silver hair and wrinkled skin opened the door.

"Hi there, honey, what can I do for you on this fine morning?"

Freda mimicked the accent. "Howdy ma'am. Me and my partner are from the Guild of Lightermen." She flashed the badge quickly in front of the old woman's face. "We're doing some routine check-ups on Captains' licenses and paperwork. Is Captain Rogers around?"

"Well no, ain't that bad luck, you just missed him. His barge is sailing today."

"Do we have time to catch him before he casts off?"

"Doubt it."

"Would you know where he's headed? I could check with the Guild but it'd save us time if you could oblige us."

"Hang on, I have it written down somewhere. Won't be a moment." The old lady shuffled back into the house. Freda turned to give Sim the thumbs up, but when she turned back to face the door she was staring down the barrel of a gun.

"Just because I have grey hair don't make me stupid. You think I'd fall for that fake ID, missy? What you want with my husband?" said the grandma. Her lips were pursed and she was holding the gun firmly, finger on trigger, safety catch off.

Sim drew his gun and aimed at her. Freda held her hands out to both people.

"Now hold on, there's been a mix-up. No need for anyone to get shot over this," Freda said.

"Tell your boyfriend to drop his weapon or you're gonna be chewin' lead!"

"Sim, do as she says."

Sim acquiesced, placing his gun on the floor in front of him with a careful, exaggerated gesture. As the old lady concentrated on what Sim was doing, Freda whipped out her taser and shot the probes into the woman, sending a violent burst of electricity through her aged body. Muscles spasmed and as she fell to the floor her index finger tightened around the trigger. A shot burst forth, narrowly missing Freda and ricocheting off the floor near Sim's feet. The old lady convulsed on the floor for a few more moments and then slipped into unconsciousness as the electric charge dissipated.

"Don't suppose she's going to tell us much now. Better put her in the recovery position while the effects wear off. Come on Sim, help me carry her inside."

They put the old lady on the sofa and looked around the lounge. A painting of a dragon dominated one wall. Above the fire place, an adjustable 3D photo of a bearded man in a uniform.

Sim pointed. "Look, that must be the Captain on board his barge."

"There's a ship's name in the background," said Freda. Her fingers felt for the control buttons on the frame. "If I can increase the zoom on the photo, rotate it around a bit, refocus... There! The *Ahab*. How very original."

"But how are we going to intercept it? We don't know where it started or where it's headed."

"Have a look around – the old lady might have something written down," said Freda. After carefully searching in the hall, Sim then proceeded into the kitchen and found a stick-screen on the fridge door. It scrolled across a message: *May 5th Hyatt Regency Wichita, 316 293 1234, May 6th back home.*

"Well we know where he's due to stay at the end of his two-day journey. If we can figure out his starting point, we should be able to intercept him," said Freda.

"I could break into their car and look up where they last drove to. It should be stored in the on-board system."

"Wow, you did have a mis-spent youth, Sim. Hacking PCs, stealing cars. We missed that on our background check."

"It doesn't show up if you don't get caught," said Sim with a smirk. After he had done something clever with the car locks and something even more clever with the car's systems, they knew that Captain Rogers had been dropped off at Fort Smith around two hours ago.

"So it's half past ten now, it'll take us two hours to get Fort Smith Chubby, which gives the Captain a three-hour head start. That should give him time to do, say, 60 klicks. Our speed net of his progress, taking account of the roads being less direct than the canal, should be around 40 kilometres an hour. So we should catch him around mid-afternoon, somewhere near Muskogee."

Freda looked across and grinned. "Not bad for a rookie."

"I used to do a lot of orienteering in the Territorial Army. What about you and your US accent? That was very realistic."

"Come on, we better get after the Captain before this conversation gets mushy."

Sim's estimate turned out to be too optimistic. Their progress was delayed by the stray bullet from Captain Rogers' wife; it had punctured the front left tyre on their rental car. After that was sorted, Freda tried to drive aggressively but every time she pressed hard on the accelerator, the engine kept fading out.

"What's wrong with this bloody heap of a car?"

"We must be on the NASCON," said Sim.

"The what?"

"The National Automatic Speed Control grid. Tiny sensors in the engine bounce a signal off the central strip which tells the car how fast it can go. Even I can't over-ride this."

It was an extra 50 kilometres, and getting close to dusk, by the time they caught sight of the Captain's barge.

Even though Sim had read about these behemoths, the sight still forced a "wow" out of him. As they turned the final corner and emerged from behind a row of trees, the barge was at least 500 metres away and yet it rose up from the horizon like a floating football stadium. The silhouette of a huge ship was completely incongruous in the middle of this vast continent. And yet there it was – the *Ahab* – a white-hulled VLB-class vessel, 250 metres long, 60 across and 20 metres high. The only obvious super-structure was the bridge at the stern of the barge, adding another 20 to 30 metres to the height of this looming giant.

Freda drove up the small road that ran parallel to the canal, until she was within shouting distance of the boat. She got out of the car and was about to holler across when something caught her eye. She motioned to Sim to keep quiet and stay low as he too got out of the car and came towards her.

They could just make out in the gloom that some of the crew were being frog-marched towards a pair of lifeboats with their hands tied behind their backs. The boats were ready to be lowered over the side of the barge just opposite the bridge. The lights on the barge were still not switched on – strange in itself – so it was hard to tell exactly what was happening. As far as Freda and Sim could see, it seemed as if the people in charge were wearing the same uniforms as the prisoners. Was this piracy or mutiny? There was no sign of an obvious leader amongst the captors or the captives. Maybe the Captain was still on the bridge, oblivious to what was going on immediately below him.

"We need to get on board and fast," whispered Freda.

"There's a bridge a few klicks further on from here. If we can get there in time and abseil down from the span, it might work," said Sim. "Not sure how we're going to pull this off without being spotted though," he mumbled to himself. They got back into the car. As they caught up and overtook the barge they could see the lifeboats, now full of men and cast adrift, bobbing up and down vigorously in the wake of the barge's huge propellers.

It only took a few minutes to reach the elevated bridge; its span was some 60 metres above the level of the canal to ensure the barges could pass underneath it. It would be another couple of minutes before the barge reached them. Freda parked the car in the middle of the bridge's span. The passing traffic was not impressed by having one lane blocked by some idiot in a rental, and many of the drivers weren't afraid to show their feelings on the matter. When there was a gap in the traffic, Freda reversed the car out into the middle of the road, so it was now facing directly along the canal in the direction the barge was coming. She then mounted the kerb until the car's nose was practically dangling over the edge of the bridge. There was a low metal fence marking the edge that was now nuzzled up against the car's front bumper.

The two agents got out some lightweight rope that ended in a karabiner; these were looped around the front axle of the car's wheels. They donned their Teflon gloves – the sort Freda had given Sim many days ago at Biggin Hill – and wrapped the rope round their torsos while letting the spare dangle over the edge of the bridge. The prow of the barge drew level with the agents while the back of the barge, where the pilot was presumably sitting in the steering room, was still at least 200 metres away.

Sim had done this sort of exercise several times before in the parachute regiment but never with such a makeshift set of equipment. "I have a bad feeling about this."

Freda leaned into the car and flicked on the full headlights, hoping that the bright xenon lights would dazzle whoever was in control of the barge and allow them time to slip on board unseen. "Now," she shouted as she leaned over the edge of the bridge and allowed the rope to start racing through her gloved fingers. They felt utterly exposed during the drop to the deck of the barge. It only took a few seconds but seemed to last minutes.

They ended up on the port side, still quite near the prow. As soon as they reached the deck, they extricated themselves from the rope and pulled out their firearms, with Freda also unclicking her extendable walking stick. They looked around to gather their bearings. There was an entrance hatchway off to their left in the middle of the ship's beam about level with them. Further aft of that the majority of the ship's deck was taken up by a low-level structure that contained openings to the vast holds of the barge. As they crept towards an entrance hatch, four men jumped out from around the corner and pointed their automatic rifles at the pair of agents.

"Errr, parley?" said Sim.

CHAPTER 18

Thorium is a safer alternative fuel to uranium for use in nuclear reactors. India, blessed with abundant reserves of the element, pressed forward with plans for thorium reactors in the last decade and was the first to come up with a working model. It has zero risk of meltdown and produces no fissile material for use in nuclear weapons.

O.D. Training Manual Section 2d

The Captain roared with laughter. His massive frame, unbowed by his advanced years, dominated the ship's bridge. Twinkling eyes shone out from the deep creases of a whole murder of crows' feet. His thick silvery beard contrasted sharply with the ruddy complexion of a face that had spent many years on the deck of a boat. "Parley?! Did you hear that on some crazy pirate film, Jim lad?"

Sim was tied by the ankles and handcuffed to a chair. Freda had been treated with slightly more care due to her crippled leg. Her hands were still tied to the back of her chair, but she was at least allowed to stretch her legs out.

"Why did you board my boat? Did you really think that stunt with the headlights would fool us? What're you up to? Come on, we haven't got long, I want some answers."

"Haven't got long for what?" asked Freda in a low voice.

"You'll find out soon enough. Now answers, not questions."

"We wanted to ask you some questions about a couple of men we've been tracking for many days now. We believe they committed an act of terrorism near London last month, and we were told you might know where they are," said Freda.

"Really? What are their names?"

Freda gave him the names of the terrorists.

"Well in the circumstances, it don't matter much. Them men are right behind you – they're part of my crew."

Freda twisted in her seat and looked up at the two men pointed out by the Captain. "Then I presume they acted on your orders, yes? We saw what you did to the rest of the crew, so I guess you're planning another attack imminently."

"Clever girl. I ain't denying it. And who told you I knew where they are?"

Freda refused to answer.

"Look, you're going to die pretty soon. Why make those last few minutes full of pain? Answer me and I won't have to cripple your other leg."

Freda still refused to answer. The Captain went over to a red box on the wall at the back of the bridge. He opened the box, took out a flare gun and loaded a fat cartridge into the pistol.

"Ever seen what happens when one of these is fired at somebody's kneecap from close range? Me neither. I can't wait to find out." The Captain took aim at Freda's left leg.

"Wait! I'll tell you," said Sim. "We got your name from an informant back in London. He overheard your men talking about the job at Biggin Hill, and one of them mentioned your name."

The Captain turned around to look at Wyploz and Fields.

They simultaneously blurted out: "But it wasn't me, boss, it must've been him who sang." They pointed fingers at each other, eyes wide and brows arched.

Captain Rogers looked at each of them in turn, raised the flare gun and shot Fields in the stomach. Sim was glad that the man, writing in agony, was just out of his field of vision. The screams, while lasting only a few seconds, etched onto his memory like acid leaving a trail on glass. Rogers' face glowed red from the flare; baring his teeth, he looked like a member of Dante's sixth circle of hell.

"Anybody else been blabbing about me?"

The bridge fell silent and then the Captain ordered the body to be thrown overboard.

Freda wriggled in her seat, her eyebrows knitted in concentration. "But I don't understand what links this barge to a Salt Camel?"

"Maximum possible pain for big corporations. You realise what those scum get away with? The largest corporations in the US pay just ten percent taxes while the average household pays forty-five percent. And the fat cats running these firms earn two hundred times what the workers earn. How can that be fair? I have to work another five years for my pension now that the retirement age has just been extended. For the third time this decade. Because the government cannot afford it? Or because they're too chicken shit to tackle these big firms? I'm sick of it."

"You're a proper Marxist, aren't you, Captain Rogers? I'm still not sure what that has to do with blowing things up," said Freda.

"We'll keep up the attacks until the workers of the world start getting a decent wage, and governments start charging companies a fair tax. Unions all over the world are getting ready to strike back. There's a storm coming. One way or another we will get our fair share." He paused to let his rhetoric sink in. "Did you notice, by the way, before you jumped on board my ship, what cargo we're carrying?" asked the Captain.

Sim and Freda looked at each other. "Err, no actually," admitted Freda.

"Thorium, two thousand tonnes of it. Interesting stuff, thorium." The Captain picked at some dirt underneath his nails. "All this technology was developed by the Americans about fifty years before the Indians came up with their prototype. Even back then thorium was known to be a safer fuel than uranium. But it didn't suit the big cats who had backed designs for uranium plants. And the military wanted uranium of course to help develop their nuclear warheads. So they squashed the thorium idea, hid the results and spent millions promoting their own plans. And hey presto, mankind has been paying the goddam price ever since: Three Mile Island, Chernobyl, Fukushima. Bastards got rich on the scheme as usual."

"I dare say you have a point, but how exactly does blowing things up help? The corporates just claim on their insurance and repair the damage, which will line the pockets of another firm by the way, or they charge their customers more to pay for the damage. Or maybe the firm goes bust and then all of its workers lose their jobs. Not to mention what happens to the ones who get killed while you are playing at demolition man."

"We have our orders. We've done a deal to ensure we don't have to keep slaving away. Now, no more monkeying around. Time for you to shut your trap and die. Matt, are all the charges in position?"

"Yes, Captain, timed to detonate at 21:00."

"Good. Brett, how's our ETA looking?" asked the Captain, turning to another crew member.

"Right on schedule. A steady nine knots should get us there just before the clock strikes nine. Hehe, tick-tock, mother-fuckers!"

"Nice. Right, get everybody on board the last of the lifeboats and fire her up. I'll just make sure the *Ahab* is on course for its rendezvous. Then we high tail it back up the canal. While our friends here," he said, leering at the tied-up agents, "enjoy the fireworks display."

The crew shuffled out. Sim and Freda could just hear their footsteps on the metal ladders down, and then the put-put-put of an outboard motor starting up.

"So what are we going to crash into? If I'm going to die, I would at least like to know where," said Sim in a calm but sad voice.

"There's a major flight of locks coming up in a mile or so, one of the busiest in the whole NUCL. It connects to both the Rockies section and the Great Lakes. Will screw the network up for quite a while, clearing up the mess this little beauty is going to leave behind. Did I mention that thorium ignites on contact with water? Should be a swell bonfire."

There was a pause while the Captain stared along the canal. "I'm going to miss her," he said, stroking the steering wheel and giving the console a pat. "But sacrifices must be made." His voice tailed off as if he might be having second thoughts. Then he shook himself, lifted his chin and pushed his chest out. "I can just make out your destination, so this is where I leave you. It's a nice straight run, should only take you a couple of minutes. See ya. Wouldn't want to be ya." And with that he opened the bridge door and scooted down the steps to the waiting life boat. The engine immediately fired up to full throttle and the sound faded into the background.

Sim turned to Freda and opened his mouth to say something, but just left it open. Freda was standing up, the chair still tied to her wrists. Sim's eyes flicked between her foot and the redundant walking stick lying on the floor next to him. Freda flipped the chair upside down, rested it on the floor and then tucked her body between her elbows and the chair, finally slipping the ropes off the chair legs. She was free.

"I don't have time to get you out, Sim, this is going to be close enough as it is." Freda yanked on the engine's controls, putting them into full reverse. In a barge this long and with such a huge mass, it would take some time before that made much difference to their speed. She angled the steering wheel slightly to starboard and then hobbled out of the bridge, slid down the ladder in one jump and took off along the starboard deck towards the bow hold.

At first Sim panicked, thinking about what had happened to her previous partner. She was abandoning him to his fate! He could just see out of the bridge down to the forward part of the deck from his enforced sitting position. After 15 seconds of sheer terror, he saw Freda trundling along in a lob-sided jog. *How was that even possible with her disability?* Sim realised she was not abandoning him, but heading for the explosives that the crew had left behind. It was set for detonation at 21:00. The red figures of the digital clock on the bridge glowed in the dim light, showing 20:59:20 – this was going to be mighty close. The radio on the bridge burst into life – the controller of the lock was trying to get hold of Captain Rogers. Sim couldn't reach it to answer.

"Rogers, answer the radio, you idiot! You're coming in too fast. Full reverse, I repeat, full reverse!! All hands prepare for crash. This is not a drill. I repeat, all hands prepare for crash."

Sim watched as the figures on the clock ticked on towards 21:00. His pulse quickened, nausea kicked in, and a series of blurred images flashed through his mind as his brain desperately sought some past experience that could possibly help. Nothing. 20:59:56, 57, 58, 59. 21:00. Silence. Sim waited for a moment and then released his breath, relaxing every muscle in his body. The barge was still in motion and at that point Freda's nudge on the steering wheel came to fruition. The boat kissed the side of the canal. It was only travelling at 3 knots, but the momentum of such a massive object colliding with an edifice of stability was never going to end well. The noise was horrendous, as if an army of giants was scraping their finger nails down building-sized chalkboards. The floor Sim's chair was resting on buckled and he was thrown sideways. His shoulder took the brunt of the fall, but his right temple still received a knock that split the skin.

Eventually the barge came to a halt. No explosion. *Freda must have got to the bomb in time.* Sim lay on his side, still strapped to the chair and unable to get back up. He waited, hoping Freda would not be long in coming back for him. His head throbbed and his already bruised shoulder was taking most of his weight as he lay there immobilised. *What was taking her so long?* Some blood trickled into the corner of his eye and his nausea was getting worse. One of Sim's recurring nightmares as a youth was of falling asleep drunk and drowning in his own vomit. The paranoia started to edge back into his thoughts as his stomach prepared to empty its contents. He managed to twist his face towards the floor and retched.

Why isn't Freda coming back? Had the bomb been booby-trapped? Had she sacrificed herself to save me? He had narrowly avoided being blown up by a terrorist's bomb; he should be elated but his mind was full of thoughts of guilt and gloom. After several minutes of waiting a wave of extreme tiredness washed over him. He fell asleep.

He was woken by a person gently shaking his shoulder.

"Can you hear me? My name is Ben, I'm with the emergency services. I'm here to help you. Open your eyes."

Sim obeyed and looked up into a smile and a moustache. He was lying on his back, and his bonds had been untied. There were several people moving rapidly around the bridge of the ship, but

Sim couldn't really tell what they were doing. He saw a machine gun in the hands of somebody standing nearby, watching over the medic and Sim. He had the distinct impression that person was guarding him. Sim sat up abruptly.

"Freda!"

"Who?"

"My colleague. British woman, red hair, down the other end of the barge."

The medic turned to look at the man with the machine gun, seeking answers on Sim's behalf.

The soldier replied. "It's a bit confusing. One of the teams discovered a female terrorist, she seemed to be trying to detonate a bomb. They shot her, I think. Can't be too careful with suicide bombers."

CHAPTER 19

The islands lying 70km east of Taiwan are known as the Senkaku Islands by the Japanese, the Diaoyu Islands by the Chinese and the Tiaoyutai Islands by Taiwan. Their sovereignty is disputed by all three countries with various vaguely worded treaties over the past 120 years leaving ample room for disagreement. What is not disputed is that the Japanese currently occupy the islands and that the Chinese would like to change the status quo.

O.D. Training Manual Section 5c

2 years ago, the East China Sea.

The cliché was right: it was, for once, a dark and stormy night. Kurihara-san stood at the top of the bluff on Uotsuri-Jima, the largest of the Senkaku Islands, remembering the stories his father used to tell him as a child when frightened by a storm. His father had sold the islands to the Japanese government 14 years earlier. But when it was decided to build a small outpost on the largest island, Kurihara-san had volunteered to be one of the few permanent residents. There was not much to do on the island, though it was blessed with a rare breed of albatross, some unusual herbs and an endangered species of mole. Kurihara-san loved dramatic weather as much as he loved flora and fauna. And that was why, at 3 o' clock in the morning, he was stood outside on the highest point of the island watching the black clouds bubble up and the forks of lightning streak down to the ocean.

Raijin is angry tonight, he thought to himself. The Shinto god of thunder had plenty of reasons to be angry.

At each strike of lightning the sea was briefly illuminated. Kurihara-san was just about to return to his warm, dry bed when a flash of light revealed a set of small boats approaching fast. He stood in puzzlement as the boats drew closer. Another flash of lightning and Kurihara-san could make out that each boat held a few men who in turn were brandishing weapons and wearing helmets. He ran to warn the other residents on the island even though he knew there was nothing they could do. There was no garrison defending this lump of rock in the middle of the East China Sea. The hood of his coat flew back as he raced between doors, not waiting for a reply to his banging. His faced was drenched and his hair was matted to his skull as he burst into the communications room.

"Come in Tokyo, come in Tokyo, this is Uotsuri Jima base. Please respond. Tokyo, Tokyo, this is Uotsuri Jima base, we are under attack, I repeat, we're under attack. Please acknowledge."

There was no reply. Kurihara-san tried to check the power to the radio equipment. He checked for any loose connections but could not find anything amiss. It was too much of a coincidence to think that some vital part of equipment had broken down on this particular night. The more likely and more worrying alternative was that something nearby was preventing the equipment from working. If it was the latter, it implied a level of planning and resources that meant the boats about to land were not just some pirates come to rob them but something much worse.

♦

Five days later, the Japanese Self-Defence Force High Command received an urgent message from a coastguard plane. It had been patrolling the seas at the western end of the Ryukyu Islands when it received a warning from the Chinese navy not to approach Uotsuri Jima. The coastguard plane was asking whether it should continue with its usual patrol route or turn back.

"Get me Uotsuri Jima at once," ordered the Naval chief. "We need to find out what's happening there."

A couple of minutes later, a radio operator confirmed that Uotsuri Jima was not responding.

"The recon planes need to scramble. Let's get some eyes on that island. Order them to adopt full stealth mode and prepare for hostile airspace. This is not a drill."

Two hours later a pair of F-35 jets from the 5th Wing of the Air Self-Defence Force conducted a high-speed low pass over the Senkaku Islands. Thanks to the jets' stealth capabilities and low-altitude flying, hostile anti-aircraft batteries on the islands were unable to get a lock on either plane. The photos from the reconnaissance flight clearly showed the presence of Chinese soldiers. There was an entire company of commandos and some heavy ordnance such as anti-aircraft missile batteries visible on the photos of the main island. And the other smaller islands had become the temporary home of more platoons of Chinese soldiers. There was no sign of Japanese civilians; at least they were not being used as human shields. But whether they were still on the islands or had been taken back to the Chinese mainland was a mystery.

The Chinese navy had formed a cordon of small vessels around the island consisting of several frigates and one ordinary looking fishing vessel. Japanese intelligence had analysed the recon photos and seen the greater-than-usual number of antennae and radar dishes on this boat. Inside it was likely packed with the latest electronic observation and jamming equipment and was the probable reason that Uotsuri Jima had been unable to raise the alarm.

The Japanese government formally requested that the Chinese vacate the islands and return all Japanese civilians safely to their homeland. Even as the Ambassador in Beijing delivered his government's message to the Chinese authorities he knew it would make no difference. But these things had to be seen to be tried.

Behind the scenes the Military High Command was preparing a response to this invasion. Admiral Nagai was pushing for an overwhelming response. "This is our chance to show that we can stand on our own two feet. If we cannot demonstrate our potency now, how can we justify our budget to the people?"

Ever since Shinzo Abe had been appointed Prime Minister of Japan in 2012, his intention had been to kick-start the Japanese economy through expansionary monetary and fiscal policy. The latter had included a near-doubling of the military budget.

"But why not let the Americans help us? The islands are included within the Treaty of Mutual Cooperation and Security. They are duty-bound to offer us assistance." The Admiral was in danger of being over-ruled by the Minister for Defense.

"With honour and respect, Minister. If we rely on the Americans, we will just prove to the whole world that we are still in their thrall. The Abe government did not abolish Article Nine so we could continue to hide under the skirts of American soldiers."

The Minister took his glasses off and placed them on the table. "Yes, I do know the significance of Article Nine, thank you Admiral. But these are after all just a few small islands of no economic significance. The newspapers will have a field day if we incur massive casualties over some useless lumps of rock. What's the minimum force you think we could use to re-take the islands?"

"That will depend, Minister, on what the Chinese Navy use to counter our task force. It would take very few ships and aircraft to defeat the current occupying force, but we have to intimidate the Chinese so that they concede defeat."

Five days after the invasion had been discovered, there was a large Japanese naval task force heading for the disputed islands. There were none of the logistical difficulties faced by the British in 1982 when they had had to travel several thousand kilometres to re-take the Falkland Islands from the Argentine invaders. This was the largest military action undertaken by the Japanese in over 80 years of passive defense. The weight of the nation rested on the shoulders of a few thousand sailors, pilots and marines.

◆

In the CIA satellite department, an analyst called Bo Brunswick was watching developments around the Senkaku Islands with interest, discussing them with his team leader.

"This task force that the Japanese have assembled is pretty awesome. Two missile cruisers, seven destroyers and two minesweepers as well as a troop-carrying vessel with landing craft stowed. Our sonar buoys are also picking up a pair of attack submarines and constant air cover is being provided by sorties from bases back on the mainland."

"First rule of war: always attack with overwhelming odds to minimise your casualties," replied his boss.

"As if that is not enough, it looks like they have moved up numerous Anti-Shipping Cruise Missile stations to the western tip of the Ryukyu Islands."

"No doubt to provide protection against any retaliation from the Chinese. This could be a real hum-dinger if they each keep throwing extra assets into the area."

After a brief military engagement – watched over screens from thousands of miles away like some reality TV show - Bo could tell that the disguised fishing boat had been sunk by one of the submarine's torpedoes. Two Chinese frigates had been sunk by the Japanese cruisers, with the rest fleeing. And the Chinese commandos had surrendered shortly after enduring a vicious bombardment from the destroyers' five-inch guns.

Now to see how the Chinese will respond to this task force, thought Bo. The People's Liberation Army Navy was much bigger than Japan's in terms of numbers of ships and could have quickly gathered a huge armada to attack and probably defeat the Japanese. But at what cost? If the CIA knew about the Anti-Shipping Cruise missiles, the Chinese almost certainly did as well. Moving so many ships to one small part of China's territorial waters and potentially losing several of them would place a significant constraint on its Navy's ability to continue projecting its presence elsewhere.

Two days later, Bo got his answer. It would seem that in the eyes of the Chinese upper echelons the cost of defeating the Japanese was indeed too high. A high-ranking Admiral in the PLAN was forced to apologise publicly for his blunder in ordering the invasion and was imprisoned. Back in Japan there was jubilation in its defeat of the Chinese and a new surge in pride and confidence that would soon show up as an increase in the birth rate for the first time in nearly 40 years. The two warring governments agreed to exchange prisoners in a deal brokered by the Republic of Korea.

But something was bugging Bo. However he pieced it together, something did not add up in this Chinese invasion. He went to see his boss again. "Why invade in the first place if you know you're not going to try to keep hold of the islands? The Chinese would never have risked this invasion only to back down immediately unless that was their intention all along."

"You're not making any sense Bo. What does it matter? The invaders have been defeated, the status quo is restored."

"But what if the Chinese *deliberately* lost the battle to keep all eyes on this coastline rather than somewhere else? What if they're up to something in another part of their territorial waters or inland somewhere?"

"Bo, you're a good analyst. But you have to realise that sometimes, people screw up. The Chinese under-estimated Japanese resolve. When they realised how quickly the fight might escalate, they chickened out. End of. C'mon, get yourself a beer and lighten up. It's Friday night for Christ's sake."

CHAPTER 20

The CIA satellite department is based in Langley, along with the rest of the Agency. Satellites have always played a crucial role in the CIA's work, but when the Great Flux started, there was a need for a separate department to deal with their few remaining satellites. Joint operations between the CIA and OFWAT overseas division have been uncommon but not discouraged.
O.D. Training Manual Section 1b

May 5th, 2028. Near Amarillo Chubby, Texas.

The FBI turned up in a helicopter while Sim was still reeling from the news about Freda. Every fibre of his body was willing it not to be true. The soldier was not sure what had happened; maybe he had been mistaken. Sim wanted to run to the front of the barge to see for himself, but the FBI agents insisted on keeping him here while they questioned him.

"Who did this? How many are there? Where are they now?" the FBI leader asked. Sim paused, wondering whether he could burst past them and make a dash for where Freda was.

"Come on, answer me. We need to start a manhunt for them as soon as possible."

"There were seven of them, no wait, six. One of them was killed. They left the barge in a small boat, maybe a kilometre back up the canal." Sim looked at his watch. "An hour ago, I would guess."

"Any names?"

"Captain Rogers was in charge. One of the others was Wyploz or Fields."

"What were you doing on the barge?"

"My boss and I were chasing the perps of a terrorist bombing at Biggin Hill, a couple of weeks back. We're with OFWAT Overseas Division. Please, I need to know if my partner is OK – somebody said she'd been mistaken for a terrorist. Shot."

"I'll get someone to check for you, but right now we need you to come with us and help identify this group. If we can catch them up."

Sim tried to protest but was bundled off the barge and into the FBI helicopter that was waiting on the bank of the canal. Not exactly a prisoner, but he certainly wasn't going of his own free will. The chopper rose, twisted and then dipped its nose as the pilot sent the craft tracing back along the canal at maximum speed. The sliding doors to the helicopter were left open and an FBI agent armed with a high-powered sniper rifle was leaning out of the cabin for a better view. Sim had been given some headphones to communicate with the FBI agents sitting with him.

"Yell if you recognise anybody or the boat they used to get away."

They sped along the airspace above the canal. The pilot was about to fly straight under the bridge which Sim and Freda had abseiled from, when Sim remembered the cables would still be dangling in their path.

"Go over the bridge, not under!" he shouted. The pilot pulled back on the joystick, powered up the collective lever and just got the aircraft up and over in time. The FBI leader stared at Sim and then saw the cables as the helicopter descended back down on the other side of the bridge.

"Nice call."

The sun had set a couple of hours ago and below the edges of the canal there was very little light. Without his goggles the dark surface of the water looked, to Sim, like a fissure in the Earth leading to a subterranean void. But after a few more kilometres the pilot, using his helmet's night vision, spotted a small boat making fast progress up the canal.

The boat had no lights, so it was hard to tell who was onboard, or even if it was the craft they were after. But it did not take long for the helicopter to catch up. The spotlight from the aircraft revealed a small rib boat, with four men on board. The FBI sniper put a bullet through the right side of the hull which rapidly deflated and the crew were quick to surrender. Sim stared at the men's faces as the helicopter got closer; it was soon obvious that the Captain was not among them. Sim did, however, recognise the face of one of the men he had been chasing since Biggin Hill.

While the crew were being processed and taken into custody, Sim gave the FBI a detailed account of what had happened on board the barge. He was still desperate to hear news about Freda; the uncertainty was almost worse than knowing for sure that she had been killed. The FBI leader radioed through to HQ.

"Seems like there was a mix-up. Your partner wasn't shot. She was found next to the bomb. Looks like she had defused it, but was then knocked unconscious. Come on, I'll take you to the hospital where she's being held."

Sim hugged the FBI leader when he said this. The American stood there stiffly until Sim let go.

Sim reached the hospital room where Freda was recuperating. The FBI leader explained to the two police guards outside the room who Sim was. Inside there was a male nurse checking some forms and noting a few readings from machines that were connected to Freda. It was 5am, and Sim had been on the go for 24 hours, with very little food, severe bruising to his shoulder and a throbbing temple. He caught his reflection in a mirror and saw that he looked as bad as he felt. He gazed at his companion lying there peacefully, and gently brushed the hair away from her face. He slumped down in the chair next to Freda's bed, hoping for a quick nap until she came round. As he sat down, her eyelids flickered and she woke up.

"Eee, turned out nice again," said Freda.

The medic looked alarmed and turned towards Sim. "Is she alright? Still concussed?"

"George Formby," she said. "1940s. You know. Ukulele man. Leaning on a lamp post?"

"Don't worry, Doctor," said Sim with a laugh, "she does this sort of thing all the time." He reached out to hold her hand, then withdrew it almost as quickly. She tutted and reached for his hand, giving it a squeeze.

"I'm not infectious you know. You look as bad as I feel. How long have I been out?"

"Only a few hours."

Freda looked over at the medic. "Can you give us a few minutes alone please?" The attendant made a note on Freda's medical records, nodded and smiled towards Sim before withdrawing. Freda rolled over onto her side to face Sim directly.

"So what happened on the barge?"

"I might well ask you the same question, Wonder Woman! Running off to defuse the bomb – neat trick for somebody with a crippled foot. Afterwards, there was a lot of confusion – I must've passed out. When I came to, I was told you'd been shot as a terrorist!"

"And what about the Captain and his crew?"

"We got some of them but the Captain is still at large." Freda tried to sit up but Sim put his hand out in protest. "Don't fret.

They have a full manhunt going on; it shouldn't be long before he's behind bars."

Freda rolled onto her back again and gave a sigh of relief. "We'll have to speak to head office to see if they want to deport the surviving Biggin Hill perp. I'm sure the politicians will want him to face justice on British soil."

Sim continued. "You saved my life. You just saved lots of lives not to mention a two hundred million dollar ship. And the canal got away with only minor damage. How does it feel?"

"Sore."

"That thing with your leg. How did you do that?"

Freda sat up and looked at him with a tinge of red in her cheeks. "Ahh, that, yes… well I guess you were bound to find out sooner or later. Have you ever seen the film *The Usual Suspects*?"

Sim shook his head.

"Typical… another classic missing from your education. Well, Kevin Spacey plays this disabled criminal who… oh, never mind, it's a complicated plot." She paused and looked out the window. Her shoulders dropped. "I woke up with a sore leg the day after my mother died. It got worse and worse. By the time of the funeral I couldn't walk without a stick. I got more sympathy that day over my leg than I did about my mother. And the worst thing was, I enjoyed the attention. How pathetic is that?"

Freda asked for a tissue to blow her nose, then continued. "There is something wrong with my ankle, something un-operable, but the physios said with the right exercise it'd be fine. Instead of following their advice, I exaggerated the problem and have used a stick ever since. Still, saved our lives, didn't it?"

Sim sat there for a moment. "You mean you've spent the majority of your adult life pretending to have a club foot?"

"Well it's also been an interesting social experiment to see how people react around disability. And I dare say it helped open doors for me in my career: 'Ooh, let's hire the girl with the funny foot, that'll look good on our diversity form.' Anyway, I'm glad you know the truth now, should make the journey home a bit easier."

"Well there's bad news on that front; we're not going back to Britain just yet."

"What do you mean? Surely once the FBI has nabbed the terrorists we only have a bit of paperwork to do?"

"I'm afraid not. Look, we might have caught the guys who blew up the Salt Camel at Biggin Hill, but the original assignment was to investigate the disappearing satellite, remember. We presumed the attack at Biggin Hill might be related, but I've been thinking."

"Careful."

"Ha. Look, it's seems clear to me that Captain Rogers and his crew are nowhere near capable of taking out a military-grade satellite."

Freda lay back on her bed. She closed her eyes again for a few moments. After a while, Sim touched her on the arm to see if she was still awake.

"Sorry, still a bit woozy. I guess you're right Sim. But we'll have to head back to headquarters to start the trail afresh, won't we?"

"Not sure. Apparently, the CIA is sending somebody here to go over what happened on the barge again. The FBI is putting us up in a safe house nearby. We can get in touch with Wardle and see if he has any new leads back home."

Freda spent the rest of the day resting some more, while Sim went for a wash. The FBI had bought them both clean clothes. That evening Freda was released from hospital and taken, with Sim, under armed escort to the safe house. A conventional two-storey house in the outskirts of Amarillo. Freda walked from the car to the front door clutching onto Sim's arm. "Sorry, I've been using that walking stick for so long, I feel a bit naked without it."

They were shown inside and found that their luggage from the boot of the abandoned rental car had been retrieved for them. Armed guards would be outside the house all night, and first thing in the morning an agent would come to talk with them.

Freda looked out through the curtains of the sitting room at the suburbia outside. An old lady was walking down the street on the opposite side of the road, a bag of groceries following behind her on a hover trolley. A jogger went past in the other direction, his black sweaty skin glistening under the street lamps. A sentry appeared right in front of the window, making Freda jump. He motioned for her to close the curtains.

"Are the FBI guards here for our sake or for theirs?" said Freda as she returned to the sofa.

Sim looked up from his TV channel hopping. "Hmm?"

"Try the front door. I bet it's locked."

Sim got up and tried to open the door, without success. "What the?"

"There's gratitude. Under virtual house arrest after foiling a major terrorist attack on a very important American asset."

"Maybe they're just worried about reprisals from the Captain's gang. They still haven't found him, remember. I imagine he's pretty, what do they say here, pissed with us."

"I've been lying in bed for twenty-four hours, I want to get out in the fresh air. Let's see if we can sneak out the back."

Freda went towards the back of the house. From one of the windows she could see that the yard led onto a dimly lit alleyway with a series of lock-ups facing the house. There was a brief spark of light in the shadows and then something moved up the alley. Freda went to fetch her night vision goggles and from one of the bedroom windows surveyed the street.

"Sim, come look at this."

Sim went upstairs and saw what Freda was pointing at. A young man was shaking a can of paint and spraying something onto each of the roller doors of the lock-ups. Every time it was the same. The letters 'TF' in black paint, enclosed in a red circle.

"I know this symbol, I've read about it somewhere," said Freda. She pressed her fingers into her bruised forehead. She winced and then cried, "That's it. The Terror Formers. A well-funded anarchy group; claimed responsibility for a lot of attacks on American soil. They could've been behind the Captain's stunt."

"We should warn our guards," said Sim.

"What, and let the FBI take all our credit? No way." Freda went downstairs and dialed for a pizza.

CHAPTER 21

There are six main systems of aqueducts and infrastructure that redistribute and transport water in California. Lacking reliable dry-season rainfall, water rights have always been among the most divisive political issues of the state. The rising frequency of droughts after 2010 forced the state to expand its desalination program. The infrastructure has been the target of numerous terrorist attacks in recent years.

O.D. Training Manual Section 4e

One year earlier, down-town Los Angeles.

I walked past the prostitutes, ignoring the various carnal offers being described in vivid detail. Not tonight. I had more important business to attend. Past the titty bar where the neon lights reflected in the puddles left by this afternoon's rain. Somebody tried to make a grab for the holdall I was carrying in my left hand. Big frickin' mistake. I hauled on the handles, dragging him closer to me and punched him in the throat. Hard. He let go of the bag pretty quick, staggered backwards unable to breath and fell on his ass.

Onwards to a drinking establishment where the owners clearly had a dim view of wasting money on the exterior décor. I squeezed between two large bouncers – why are they called that? – and pushed open the entrance door. A shot of rye later, I settled onto the bar stool and surveyed the clientele. No worse than I expected at this hour.

My contact was either late, or scrutinising me before they approached. How the hell would I know which it was? No description, just a place and a time. Better keep my wits about me. So far, more slugs in my revolver than in my stomach; I hoped to keep it that way tonight. I toyed with my second drink and eventually got the tap on my shoulder.

"You must be BB."

"BBB? Sounds like a low-grade bond." That was funnier than it meant to be. "But yeah, that's me."

"I'm Smith."

I tried not to roll my eyes. Sure you are. Still, if he gave me what I wanted, what did I care about his false ID?

"Let's talk at the back," he said, walking over to the table furthest from the bar. I followed, eyeing up the exits as I wandered over.

"Do you know what you're getting yourself into? These dudes are bad news." He arched his eyebrows and swigged from his bottle.

"No point in meeting with them if they aren't," I replied.

"I need re-assurances that you ain't gonna do nothing stupid."

"What do you mean?"

"See, someone I know put this guy in touch with them. He turns up and tries to off the leader. Didn't succeed, of course. But the middle man, just for sending him their way, sure had trouble walking for the next year. I'm kinda fond of my legs the way they are now, thanks very much. So?"

"I have a bag full of re-assurances, they're green with a President's head on them. And I don't have a death wish so, no, I won't be doing anything stupid."

He glanced around the bar, looked me up and down once more, and then paused while some mental calculation was going on behind those beady eyes. "Alright. Here's the address you need. Fridays at 11pm. However bad you think it's going to be, it'll be worse."

I left my holdall under the table, grabbed the slip of paper and left the bar.

An industrial estate, just off the Santa Ana freeway, near Buena Park. Plenty of buildings that all looked the same. Some places working night shifts, so lights, noise, traffic even at this hour on a Friday. Good choice; these guys aren't dumb. That was a relief. My plan, maybe even my neck, relied on them not being dumb.

I parked up well out of sight and walked the last 400 metres. A welcoming committee at the entrance barred my way in.

"Get lost, punk."

I looked up at the eloquent giant. "I'm here to join the TF."

"Who sent you?"

"Smith," I replied, hoping the name wasn't as lame as it sounded.

He patted me down and quickly found my Ruger. He emptied the cylinder of all five bullets and handed it back to me.

Patted me down again, more carefully this time, checking for spare rounds. I was pointed out the stairs to the basement and told to go see Jake. As I walked away, I spat out my last round and descending the stairs, slipped it into the first chamber of the revolver.

At the bottom, the basement stretched ahead and to each side for ten or twenty metres in either direction. The place smelled of locker rooms. Furniture was sparse and the lighting industrial. A group of men stood around two people sparring lightly, while off to the right was a threesome enjoying the only trappings of comfort that I could see.

Jake was a funny guy. Well, the women draped on both his arms laughed at every joke he told, so it must've been true, right? He didn't stop the wise cracks when he saw me approach.

What have we here? A new recruit? Look at this everyone. Dead man walking. Ha ha hah."

I tried to look cocky and smiled back. But, truth be told, my cheeks were tight enough to start a fire if anybody had bothered to put some kindling between them. This part of the plan was not watertight, no siree. If I got paired up with the wrong guy, it would be all over for yours truly in the next five minutes.

"The name's BB. I wanna join," I said.

"You know you gotta get through Punch Bowl first, right?"

"That's why I'm here."

He looked across at all the other men present, who were starting to congregate around us. He asked me: "You know the first rule of Punch Bowl?"

An old movie popped into my head. I offered: "Don't talk about Punch Bowl?" There was a ripple of laughter around the room.

"*Don't lose.* We don't like losers here. If you don't win your first fight, you get to go home. Just not necessarily in one piece. Or, as Mr. C. Darwin esquire would've put it, survival of the fittest. Ain't that right, homies?"

There was a murmur of agreement and some nodding heads. If this bunch were the fittest LA could offer, Gold help us all.

Jake looked around and pointed to a tall guy near the back. "Lex, come give our visitor a real friendly welcome." Then he turned to me. "Let's see what you can do. No weapons, remember. Even an empty gun is a good club. So I'll look after your piece for you."

I handed it over as casually as I could manage in the circumstances and turned to face my opponent. I was pleased to see that he wasn't the strongest looking man there. But his hands seemed to droop near his knees and, with his height advantage already, I figured his reach was going to be 50% longer than mine. I would need to get up close and personal with this one.

I shuffled forwards with my fists raised defensively. The other people in the room formed a natural ring around us. Lex came forward and jabbed from too far back. And yet it still connected with my nose. Jeez his reach was long! And now my eyes were watering. Another jab. I felt something squish in my nose this time and warm liquid tricked onto my top lip.

I danced sideways trying to stay out of his reach while I blinked the tears from my eyes. I crouched low and charged at his midriff, like a line backer taking out the quarterback. He smashed both his fists down onto my back. That hurt, but I had too much momentum to be stopped and the collision pushed him backwards. I got in a couple of kidney punches. Heard him gasp so knew they must've hurt too. I followed up by scraping my foot down the front of his shin, ending in a stamp on his foot. While it was pinned, I used a karate punch on his chest. He lost his balance and couldn't get his right foot beneath himself quickly enough. Like a pine tree he toppled. I jumped on top of him and pinned his arms with my knees. A couple more smashes to his face and he stopped struggling. I got up and turned back to Jake, wiping the blood from my nose and mouth.

"Nicely played," said Jake. "At least we know you can fight. Now let's see if you have the *cajunas* for the TF. Dispose of Lex for me, will ya?"

I looked across at the man I had just been fighting. His eyelids had puffed up already but I could tell he was awake and paying attention. He groaned and tried to get up. Shit. I had been hoping to avoid this. Can't afford to look weak. I rolled him over and wrapped my arm around his throat, yanking his hair with my spare hand to expose his throat some more. I leaned in close, squeezing hard and whispered into his ear.

"Stop struggling." Eventually, he did exactly that. I hoisted his body onto my shoulder and carried him upstairs. At the main door, I dumped him on the floor and told the welcoming committee that I would be back with my wheels in a minute. Once I'd brought the car round the front, I flipped the trunk open and went to retrieve Lex. When he was in, I drove the car around the corner where it had come from and then strolled back to the Punch Bowl.

"So when do I get to meet the TF?" I asked Jake when I had returned to the basement.

"Woah, not so fast, cowboy. Getting into the Bowl is a piece of cake compared with the TF." He leant back and took a swig out of his drink. "If you're serious about this, you better come with me."

Jake led me towards a dark corner at the back of the basement. There was an industrial lift I hadn't noticed before. We got in and Jake pressed for the top floor. His eyes shifted across my body as the gears and cables trundled the elevator upwards. I tried not to fidget.

On the top floor we were greeted by two more heavies. One of the them took my revolver and placed it on a desk. My hand involuntarily went towards my weapon, only a tiny flinch, but I wondered whether Jake had noticed. The second heavy told me to hold my arms out and spread my legs, then he ran a small black rod up and down my body and along my limbs. Silence.

Jake showed me to a large chair that looked like it belonged in a dental practice. Directional lights were shining straight at me and left me only vaguely aware of other people sitting opposite. Clamps flicked out of hidden recessed in the armrests and the bottom of the chair and wound themselves around my wrists and ankles. These guys sure were cautious. Thankfully my plan took that into account. Relied on their precautions, in fact.

A female voice from behind the lights. "Welcome to the Terror Formers. Changing the world, one scream at a time."

I'd heard the motto before, of course, but it still made me smile. Gotta hand it to these dudes, they had better PR than most of the Wall Street listed companies.

"We're flattered by your interest in our group. And, of course, you've already passed the Punch Bowl trial. But we have some further tests to run. Don't worry about the clamps, they're just there to help you keep still."

The woman speaking had an accent I couldn't quite place. Not American, probably a European who had lived here some time. Maybe French? A man approached and took a digital scan of my finger prints as well as a drop of blood. Then he placed an over-sized pair of goggles on my eyes. Except there weren't the sort to look through, these ones shone a light into my eyes.

Madame piped up again. "Try not to blink. Keep your eyes open for as long as possible. That'll speed up the test, thank you."

After a minute or so somebody pulled the goggles off me. The clamps stayed around my wrists and ankles. But at least the lights had dimmed and I could make out two people sitting on the far side of a desk, facing me.

The woman was sitting on my left, tapping at the surface of the desk and reading a screen. "So. Let's see who you really are… Ahh yes, here we go." She was younger than her voice sounded. Shaven head but features so pretty that the lack of hair just emphasised her beauty. "Bo Brunswick."

"That's me," I said.

"You see, the thing is that our records never lie. We have access to almost every database on the planet. And they tell us that you work for the CIA." She tilted her head to one side and smiled in a way that didn't seem all that friendly.

"Well of course they show that."

"It's just that from where I'm sitting, it seems that you're an under-cover agent trying to infiltrate our organisation. Call me biased if you will, but I make it a company policy never to let government spies join."

"You really think that if I'd wanted to go undercover the firm wouldn't have erased all my ID links back to them? Please give us *some* credit. Your databases show that I work for the CIA because I wanted you to know."

"Really. And why would that be? Do you like pain?"

"No. I've come to offer you my services." I paused to let that idea sink in. "I can be your man on the inside. Keep you one step ahead of the government. Help identify weaknesses."

The woman smiled. "What makes you think we don't have one already?"

"Because if you did, I wouldn't know about the phosphorous plan. You know, the one where you pour chemicals into all the LA reservoirs and turn the water green with toxic algae."

That one hit home.

She stood up and came closer, bending over me, her breath sweet and warm on my face. "OK, you got my attention. Now tell me *why* you want to double-cross your country."

"I have this habit. It's kinda expensive. Not the sort that a government salary covers. So I figured you might be willing to supplement my pay checks."

The woman clicked her fingers and the man who had done my tests came forward. "Blood sample shows high traces of coke and PCP. He's a user alright."

I tried to shrug my shoulders but it wasn't easy still clamped to the chair.

The woman went back to her desk and pressed a button, releasing me from my bonds. "You have a deal, Mr Brunswick."

I drove the car away and after about ten minutes pulled up at a gas station. Lex, the ingrate, was hollering away in the trunk wanting to be let out. Not here, not now. I went over to the phone booth and dialled in a number. An automated voice asked for a code which I keyed in and then a password. Eventually, I got a human.

"Line is secure, go ahead."

I looked around the garage forecourt. "It's me. I'm in."

CHAPTER 22

GPS tracking devices lost their effectiveness after the Great Flux destroyed the network of satellites that formed the basis of the global positioning system. New versions relied on short-range radiowaves. Passive RFID tags are powered by the readers and therefore do not need an independent battery.

OD Training Manual Section 8d

The pizza delivery drone arrived in extra-quick time. The guards at the front of the house were too busy checking the contents of the pizza boxes to notice a window at the back being opened and two people squeezing themselves out.

Sim and Freda, wearing their stealth-cloth again, ran into the alley at the back and disappeared into the shadows. They moved up the line of TF signs towards the freshest paint and when they got to the end scanned the streets for any sign of the sprayful youth. There was another alleyway with lock-ups a couple of hundred metres away and more TF motifs. Sim looked behind him as he heard sounds of doors slamming and shouting from the backyard of the safe house.

"Sounds like they know we're not at home," said Freda. "C'mon, let's try over there." She led the way towards the other lock-ups, keeping away from the street lights. As they reached the end of the alleyway they just saw the graffiti artist turning right at the far end. "Shit, quick!" She hobbled along as fast as she could while Sim ran on ahead.

This road was much broader and busier than the others they had sneaked along. There was a series of food and entertainment venues in a cluster at the top of a small slope. Sim watched the youth dump his spray cans in a rubbish bin, then enter a ten-pin bowling arcade. Sim retrieved the cans and waited for Freda to catch up.

Inside the bowling venue there was a party of loud ten-year old kids occupying two lanes off to the right. Balloons, cans of coke and cake festooned their area. Some of the middle lanes were busy with men wearing wrist guards who lovingly polished their ball before each throw. In the far-left lanes there was a group of youths who had draped themselves over the seats and did not seem too interested in the balls or pins.

Freda nudged Sim and pointed left towards the young man they had been following.

"What's the plan?" asked Sim.

"Angry neighbour," said Freda. She walked over to the youths and stood with her hands on her hips. "How dare you spray your silly little logos on my garage. Don't you look all innocent at me young man. I saw you do it. Now either you come straight back to wash it off or I am phoning the cops." Freda had edged closer to the graffiti artist and was wagging her finger at him.

The other youths started laughing at first, but when Sim approached too, they rose from their lounge-lizard positions and formed a line facing the two British agents. The accused remained seated, behind the defensive barrier.

The tallest youth spoke up. "What you talkin about, crazy bitch?"

"I ain't nobody's bitch," said Freda. She pulled a small can of deodorant from her pocket and pulled the top off. She pressed the button and two tiny arrows shot out of the nozzle and stuck in the tall lad's torso. A stream of electricity coursed down micro wires from the can into the youth's body. His faced contorted into a gruesome grin and his limbs stretched out rigid. He fell to the ground and twitched for a few seconds and then became still.

"Jeez, the woman is nucking futs!" The youth who had been spraying the graffiti stood up as he saw what Freda had done to his friend and ran up one of the bowling lanes towards the pins.

"After him, Sim. I'll deal with this lot," shouted Freda. She dropped the taser can on the floor and adopted a martial arts pose. She beckoned the other youths closer with the fingers of her leading hand.

Sim ran down the nearest bowling lane and then leapt across the gulley to the next lane. He saw the youth dive forwards as he reached the end of his lane and slide into the pins, which went flying. The lights for that lane lit up for a Strike. The youth didn't reappear so Sim carried on running down his lane and slid feet first into his set of pins. Sim banged his head on the overhang and was momentarily dazed. The heavy metallic arms of the machine came down to clear away the pins that had been knocked over. Sim only just recovered his wits in time to crawl into the mechanic's gangway behind the lane before the machine crushed him.

He squeezed through a round opening on the far side of the pins and caught his pullover on a piece of gearing. He pulled hard and eventually the cloth ripped and he escaped the machinery. There was a narrow corridor running perpendicular to the bowling lanes, dark and quiet compared with the front of the bowling alley. Off to his right there was a fire exit whose door was just swinging closed. Sim ran for the door and out into the cold Texan evening.

The back street was dimly lit, with several rubbish bins as big as cars on small rubber wheels huddled around green fire exit doors like fat groupies awaiting the star after a performance. Sim wished he had his autographer with him, tracking his prey would have been much easier with night goggles. He heard a screech of tyres from the main street off to his right and saw the youth nearly cause a traffic accident as he darted out, in front of a car. Sim turned and set off in pursuit.

He crossed the road more carefully, trying to keep an eye on the traffic as well as the youth who had headed straight down the nearest residential road. As Sim glanced to his side, he thought he recognised the driver of one of the trucks approaching. He didn't know anybody in this part of America, how could that be possible? Then he realised that it was one of the guards from the safe house. Coincidence, or were they tracking him? He ran down the residential road after the youth while he thought about what he was wearing.

Another screech of tyres and the roar of an engine behind him suggested that the guards were on his trail alright. He felt inside his trouser pockets as he ran along and noticed a small hard nub in one of them. He turned his pocket inside out and managed to yank the little button away from the material, ripping the pocket in the process. He was just about to throw it away, when he had a better idea.

After a burst of speed and two more streets, he managed to catch up with the youth who was by now wheezing badly and barely able to continue walking. The youth turned to look at his chaser and put his hands on his knees. "What the fuck you want with me, man?"

Sim grabbed hold of him. "We need to have a serious talk. We know you're involved with the Terror Formers. What do you know about Captain Rogers?"

A truck screeched to a halt just in front of Sim, and the guards from the safe house got out, pointing guns at Sim. "Hands in the air where we can see them. Step away from the kid, Mr Atkins. Do it now."

Sim looked at the guards, then back at the kid and rolled his eyes. Slowly, he let go and raised his hands above his head. "You're making a mistake. This is a suspected terrorist, we need to bring him in for questioning."

"All we need to do is to get you and your partner back to the safe house before you cause any more trouble."

Sim dropped his hands to gesticulate. "But he's been spraying Terror Former motifs all over the neighbourhood."

"I don't care if he's been spraying black cocks all over the White House, Mr Atkins. Our job is to keep you at the safe house. Now get your hands back above your head before I have to shoot you." The first guard aimed his gun at Sim's head and advanced a step.

"OK, OK," said Sim.

Handcuffed in the back of the truck, Sim watched the youth walk away grinning. As the truck pulled off, the young man showed Sim the back of his clenched fist and then raised his middle finger. Sim smiled back then turned around in his seat. The passenger at the front of the truck tapped a few times on the screen of his roll tab and called up a map of the local streets with a flashing icon on it.

"Looks like she's still at the bowling alley. Come on, let's get this thing contained before the boss finds out."

After a short journey, they pulled up outside the entertainment venue. There was a pair of police cars outside, blue lights silently rotating on the roof of the vehicles, but nobody inside. One of the guards opened the back door of the truck and beckoned Sim to get out. He was marched into the bowling alley with one guard holding his upper arm and the other leading the way.

Inside, two police officers were trying to restore calm. Two of the youths who had been hanging out with the graffiti artist were clutching injuries, while Freda was arguing with the manager of the bowling alley. The lanes were not working and angry customers were complaining to any member of staff that they could find. One of the guards strode forward and showed the cops a badge. They stepped aside and let him approach Freda. The guard said something to her that Sim couldn't hear. She looked over at him and her shoulders sagged. She was handcuffed too.

But before the guards could lead the British agents away, another man turned up. He was tall, black and exuded an air of calm that belied the chaos around him. He showed his badge to the cops, the manager and then to the guards. The guard next to Freda jabbed his finger at this new source of authority but the black man just placed his hand on the guard's shoulder and shook his head. The cops left, while the manager started getting his venue back up and running. The youths walked past the black man; he high-fived one of them and the rest gave him a friendly greeting.

"This is bullshit, man," said one of the guards to nobody in particular as he undid Sim's handcuffs.

The black man wandered over to Sim as the two guards left. He held out his hand. "You must be Sim Atkins. I'm Bo Brunswick, CIA." The voice had a surprisingly English accent.

Sim looked at the man's hand and then into his eyes. "What's going on, here?"

"Don't worry, I've called off the goon squad."

"Those youths seemed to know you."

"They're good kids really."

Sim tutted. "And the man we identified spraying Terror Former motifs all over the neighbour. What about him? I managed to slip the FBI's tracking bug into his pocket. Shouldn't we follow that up?"

"Believe me, I'd know if the Terror Formers were mixed up with Captain Rogers. There is no connection," said Bo. He turned to Freda. "Where are my manners? How do you do, Miss Brightwell?"

"Pleased to meet you," replied Freda. There was a momentary pause as she stared at him, resulting in the handshake lasting a little too long for a formal introduction.

Bo looked into her eyes and smiled. "I always knew you Brits liked shaking hands."

"Looks like we've earned an upgrade. What's the news? Is it related to our missing satellite?" asked Freda, letting go of his hand at last.

"We think so. I work in the CIA's satellite section. We too have recently lost satellites in mysterious circumstances, and it's happened to the Japanese and the Indians too." He led Sim and Freda over to a small table. "On the day your D.O.W. disappeared we happened to have a surveillance plane passing over the Arctic. It managed to take some photos of a surfaced submarine that had some strange equipment on its deck. It's possible that this submarine was used to attack your satellite."

"Really?" said Sim. "I didn't realise Russian subs carried missiles capable of achieving that sort of altitude."

"I've said too much already. Look, the Feds are pretty embarrassed that a pair of Brits just turned up on our soil – unannounced I might add – and prevented one of the worst terrorist atrocities this century."

"Well, excuse us for doing your job," replied Sim.

"We were just lucky," said Freda. "Can't you share more information with us to help us on our way?"

"Don't get me wrong, I'm very glad you were there to stop the Captain. But we've talked enough in this location; it isn't secure. My commanding officer reckons a collaboration of our two agencies would be beneficial. This is bigger than just a British satellite disappearing. And we have something very interesting to show you. How do you fancy a trip to Alaska?"

Sim turned away from Bo and leaned close to Freda. "Can we trust this fella?"

Freda looked over Sim's shoulder. She smiled at Bo. "I think we should give him a chance."

CHAPTER 23

The High Frequency Active Auroral Research Program, or HAARP, was started in 1993. Conspiracy theorists have long linked this research to some sort of super-weapon, or a device to control the weather. But in reality its study of the ionosphere was primarily focused on enhanced radio communications. Recent developments are less well known, however, and it is possible that the conspiracy theorists might actually be right for once.

O.D. Training Manual Section 6

"Have you been with the firm long?" asked Freda.

Bo looked up from his airplane seat. "A few years. I started on the Asia desk. That went a bit crazy for a while when China tried to invade the Senkaku Islands. Then we had a re-organisation and I ended up in water."

"Hot water?"

"Ha. I've spent a fair amount of time up in Alaska so you could say quite the opposite."

Freda turned to face him directly. "How come you speak with an English accent?"

"My father's job took us to the UK when I was growing up. I boarded at Marlborough College. Hard not to copy the Queen's English when you are surrounded by it for five years. Fortunately none of my fellow boarders seemed to fancy my black ass so I never got buggered."

The other two shifted in their seats, not replying, while Bo smirked at their embarrassment. "Oh come on, guys, lighten up. That was a joke!" he said, breaking out into a deep laugh and giving Sim a hefty slap on the shoulder. Freda started sniggering while Sim did his best to look amused.

Bo explained that they were heading for the base that was used to develop HAARP, and Freda admitted that her knowledge of the project was slim, so Sim recounted what he could remember about it from his course at university. He explained that conspiracy theorists had originally blamed HAARP for all the satellites that fell from the sky during the Great Flux.

"Nobody believed that guff, did they?" asked Freda.

"Sure they did. Folks'll believe anything if the government denies it ain't true," said Bo, slipping out of his English accent. "Besides, HAARP is used to beam high intensity beams up into the atmosphere. So you can see why the web is full of rumours about this stuff."

"I presume missiles are the only reliable way to bring down a satellite from the ground?" said Sim.

"There aren't many missiles that can reach an altitude high enough to take out a satellite, Sim," replied Bo. "Lasers will work but only if they're mounted on something also up in orbit."

"So which of you clever clogs is going to tell me what did actually bring down our satellite?" asked Freda, smiling as she shifted her gaze between the two men. Sim was sitting upright while Bo was lying back in his chair.

"A high-frequency pulse beam. Somebody must have copied our research," said Bo.

"Ahh, so you have been using HAARP for weapons development. Red-handed, man!" said Sim, finally flopping back in his chair and folding his arms.

As they flew over Canada Sim looked out of the window and noticed a huge blemish amidst the beautiful scenery. It looked as if a giant pot of grey ink had been spilt across the countryside. And just to make it worse, somebody had driven an enormous tractor across the same patch of land over and over again. He nudged Freda and pointed it out to her.

"That's one of the Athabasca Tar Sand Mines. Huge reserves of bitumen in one of the few places in the world where surface mining makes economic sense. But it takes a lot of water to separate the oil from the silica."

Sim pulled a face as if he had just swallowed some tar. "They're allowed to get away with this crap?"

"Oh, there've been protests about all this for years but to no avail. The Canadians probably have more freshwater per head than any other country in the world, and plenty of empty country. So why should they care? The bloody idiots."

When the plane landed in Alaska they were met by some more CIA people who drove them to the HAARP centre near Gakona. The road wound through tracts of pristine ever-green forests still lightly dusted with the last of the winter's snow. Spring came late in this part of the world, but here and there Sim caught sight of flowers blossoming. A gap in the trees highlighted a flying squirrel emerging from a winter shelter. It stood stock-still as the SUV roared past, then leapt across to the nearest tree trunk and disappeared from view.

The government base was a sprawling mass of utilitarian low-rise buildings topped with numerous radar dishes. There was an array of large antennae arranged in the shape of a Christian cross. The whole complex was encased within a high-security perimeter fence. It reminded Sim of a high-budget version of the little OFWAT centre at Wilkhaven. His last visit there was only a fortnight ago, but it seemed a distant memory.

Once inside the main building, out of the cold, Bo took them into a conference room and introduced them to his boss, Diane Butler. She was in her mid-50s, with shiny cheeks and a ready smile.

"Pleasure to meet you, Agent Brightwell, Agent Atkins. Seems like you've already had quite an adventure during your brief visit to America. Good work on spoiling the Captain's plan – we had him down as a crack-pot, but not a terrorist."

"How is the manhunt going?" asked Sim.

"Good and bad news. The FBI tracked him down eventually. But the snatch was bungled. The Captain managed to swallow a suicide pill before our agents could subdue him. I hate it when they do that. No interrogation and no public display of justice being served. Still, our government has no objection to extraditing the survivor responsible for the Biggin Hill attack back to Britain."

"That's good to know, thank you," said Freda.

"But that's not why I asked you to come up here. We have something much more interesting to discuss. I believe Bo has told you about the submarine that we were lucky enough to photograph just before your latest satellite disappeared. And I'm sure you're at least vaguely familiar with the research conducted at this facility, no?"

"That's right, Sim gave me a crash course on the flight up here, with Bo's help," replied Freda, smirking as Sim shifted uncomfortably.

"So assuming that the submarine sighting was not a coincidence, and that some country has replicated our HAARP technology in a machine that can be transported by sub, what else strikes you about this potential chain of events?"

Sim piped up, slowly at first, as his mind raced ahead trying to join the dots. "If you have a submarine under the polar ice cap, you can pop up, destroy a satellite passing overhead, and disappear again before anybody realises. It makes it very difficult to trace the source of the attack – a land-based version would be much easier to track. So whoever is doing this wants to remain anonymous. Hmm, what else? Of course, the other interesting thing about these attacks is that they are all on polar-orbit satellites."

"Go on," said Diane. "Why is that important?"

"Och well, geo-stationary satellites just stay in the same place all the time of course, by definition. But polar-orbit satellites will pass over every part of the Earth eventually. As the Earth rotates underneath them each south-north pass that they trace out is along a different longitude. So if a country wanted to stop prying eyes from passing over their territory, they would need to destroy the polar-orbit satellites."

"Exactly, and if that's true, then somebody has an awfully big secret to hide."

"But how are we going to figure out *which* country?" asked Freda.

Diane stood up and placed her hands on her hips. "What I'm about to tell you is highly classified. I'm trusting you two because I think our agencies are going to have to work together on this, but if I find out that either of you has blabbed to your British colleagues about it, I *will* haul your asses back here to stand trial, understood?" Her smiley face had hardened into a steely stare and Sim began to realise how this plump jolly woman had risen to her elevated status at the Firm.

"Sure, of course, we promise to keep it to ourselves," said Sim, eager to hear about secrets from his favourite research lab.

"Well as you know, the USA has been deploying unmanned drones in war zones for many years, helping to spy on terrorists and insurgents as well as conducting airstrikes when possible against identified targets. These light aircraft have generally used their long-range capabilities, small size and quiet engines to avoid detection. Less well known is the fact that we've also been researching how to benefit from the small, light body of an unmanned aircraft in another way. Hypersonic travel."

"Wait, you mean, like more than five times the speed of sound?" said Sim.

"Precisely. We call them Hypersonic Drones or Hydras for short. Once you strip out the weight of the human pilot, and all the extra instruments and equipment necessary for that pilot, the whole aircraft design becomes a lot easier to focus on the important part. With some improved engine technology, the only thing holding back hypersonic travel in un-manned drones has been the problem of relaying remote-control instructions from the handler back at base."

"How did you get around that problem?" asked Sim.

"The answer came from Artificial Intelligence; making sure the onboard computer could make a series of smart operational decisions based on the parameters given to it at take-off. It turns out computers are much better than human pilots at flying hypersonic planes with small wings anyway, so we killed two birds with one stone."

"But what's this got to do with the missing satellites and the mysterious polar submarine?" said Freda.

"On the day in question we were preparing one of the Hydras for a test flight when the surveillance plane informed us of the unidentified sub that had surfaced. So we quickly re-programmed the drone to seek out this sub and try to take some close-up photos. The mission was a complete success. It got there in about 30 minutes, circled the sub while evading all attempts to shoot it down, and returned to base with a belly full of high-definition photos."

"And? What did you discover?" chorused Sim and Freda together.

"We've never seen a submarine like this before. We think the Russians and Chinese have been collaborating on a new design. The crew were all masked up so we couldn't get any facial details. Russia has the easier access to polar waters, but we've had difficulty keeping tabs on Chinese subs ever since they started taking over the West China Sea. So we're still not sure which. We were hoping you might've found something during your mission to suggest either way?"

Sim looked blank.

"China," said Freda.

"What makes you so sure?" asked Bo.

Freda waved her right hand in the air as if trying to touch something just out of her reach. "The Captain. He said they were following orders and had just done a deal; he must be working for them. Right before he left, he said something weird about not monkeying around. I thought it was odd at the time."

"So?"

"Well, it's the Chinese Year of the Monkey. And he had that painting of a Chinese dragon in his house, do you remember, Sim?"

Sim nodded. "China? Wow. They must have a lot of top-secret stuff going on. God knows how they're coping with the water situation."

"I knew those guys were up to something when they aborted their invasion of the Senkaku Islands," said Bo.

"But if it is China, that brings its own problems, doesn't it? I mean, much as I like to think our department is top class, China is an *awfully* big place for two OFWAT agents to investigate. Anything else to go on, or are you just going to send every single

CIA operative to help us scout the entire bloody country?" asked Freda.

"Now, now, Ms Brightwell, we're not at home to Mr and Mrs Sarcasm in this neck of the woods."

Bo grabbed a file from a pile of papers at the end of the conference table and flicked through it. "We do have something else to go on. It's here somewhere. Yes. One of our agents, based in India, has been monitoring the outflow of the Brahmaputra. She recently reported a massive flooding of the river which quickly subsided. That river starts in Tibet."

"But isn't the Brahmaputra prone to flooding when the Himalayan snows melt?" Freda asked.

"Yes but this report came through in April, long before the snows melt. And it stopped too quickly to be a natural melt flood; it must have been man-made. I think the Chinese must be interfering with the flow of that river." Bo tapped on his keyboard and a map of the region flashed up on the conference room screen.

"I thought the Strategic Foresight Group had brought together the countries of that region to agree on shared access to the Brahmaputra," suggested Freda. Sim looked at her. He realised how little he knew about the global water situation compared with his boss.

Diane shook her head. "That was over twenty years ago and it was an agreement reached between hydrologists, not politicians. Even if we don't know exactly what's going on, there are two things I'm sure of. First, the Chinese won't hesitate for a moment to commandeer water from this river if their situation is desperate enough and they think they can get away with it. And second, the Indians won't take this lying down. They too are in a desperate state, ready to lash out like a cornered tiger. If the Chinese are stealing water from the Indians, we could be on the verge of full-scale war in Asia."

"That is not good; the Indians have already been antagonised by Pakistan," said Freda.

"And with a nuclear arsenal to back up their conventional forces this won't be no cat fight," said Bo.

Diane stood up and leant forward, placing her hands across the table. "We need to get a small team deep into China and investigate what is going on; top secret, top priority."

CHAPTER 24

India and Pakistan were established as separate countries by the partition of British India in 1947. There have been many wars between the two countries, most of them involving the disputed region of Kashmir. Both countries suffer from level 4 freshwater poverty (see Section 2c) as a result of climate change and population growth, which has added to the regional tension.

O.D. Training Manual Section 5c

9 months earlier, New Delhi, India.

There is panic on the streets of Chennai,
Delhi, Mumbai, Srinagar.
I wonder to myself.
Burn down the thorium.
Hang the blessed rain god.
Because the monsoon rains that constantly fail
Say nothing to me about my crops
Hang the blessed rain god.

"That's *Panic* by the Singhs, a re-worked version of a UK song from the 1980s, doing very well in the charts this month. And we have the lead singer, Muralidhar, coming into the studio next week, so make sure you're tuned in at 8am on Tuesday. In the news today, the government has banned the export of wheat and rice as stockpiles fall to dangerously low levels. The miners' strike in Andhra Pradesh has now entered its tenth week with no sign of either side compromising. At least there's something to cheer about in the cricket, where India have beaten Australia by five wickets to take a 2-1 lead in the Test series. Over to Ishita with the weather report."

"Yes thank you, Harini. Well I'm afraid there's still no sign of the monsoon rain. We're halfway through the rainy season, and only a tenth of the water that we would normally expect to reach us has arrived. Looking into next week, there's a chance of some very heavy precipitation, but with that comes the risk of localised flooding. We'll keep you updated with that forecast, of course, as the weekend progresses."

The Minister for Home Affairs, Vanya Kumar, was sitting in the back of a chauffeur-driven government car, on the way to an emergency meeting of the Union Council of Ministers.

"Turn that radio off will you please, Sanjay. There's enough bad news in my life without hearing it repeated every hour by the radio stations. How long until we get to the Secretariat Building?"

"About another thirty minutes, madam, I'm afraid. Traffic is always terrible at this time of the morning. There aren't even any back routes I can use, everywhere is clogged up."

"Why don't people use the trains more? Did we spend those billions of rupees for nothing?"

"To be honest, madam, I think the trains are so crowded that people can't get on. And the safety record is still, ahem, not exactly spotless. If you don't mind me saying so, madam."

"If I want your opinion on the state of our rail infrastructure, I'll ask for it. Otherwise, shut up and drive."

The rest of the journey was completed in an awkward silence, not helped by an over-turned lorry causing a further 15 minute delay. Eventually, the car pulled up outside the Secretariat Building and the Minister bustled inside, clutching her confidential papers and muttering dark oaths against her driver. Once inside, she joined the rest of her cabinet colleagues. The meeting had only just started. The Defense Minister was speaking:

"Intelligence reports suggest that Pakistan forces are massing on the border. As best we can tell, there may be up to four divisions of infantry and two tank divisions in the immediate vicinity. We're not sure about the risk of vertical envelopment. I'm afraid we haven't been able to ascertain any recent data about their air force activities. Our current forces in the region should be able to defend their positions for some time against an invasion of this magnitude, but we will struggle to defeat them outright. And if their air force commits in strength, then the region could fall. Best-case scenario is a repeat of the Kargil War of `99 – a minor incursion and we force them to retreat after a few weeks. Worst case scenario is a re-run of the War of `65, with major casualties on both sides. Already we're having to deploy the army throughout the country to quell protests and riots. Can we afford to send more troops to Kashmir?"

The Prime Minister responded. "Can we afford not to? If the masses think we've lost the ability to defend our borders as well as the ability to feed our citizens, well, we should just hand the country over to the rioters now. General, make sure every spare unit is denied leave until we know what Pakistan is up to. And get that intel on their air force by the end of the week. We cannot fight this battle blind. Smt Kumar, see if you can do something useful to get these riots under control – you are supposed to be the Home Affairs Minister, aren't you? If you were doing your job properly we wouldn't have to tie up all these soldiers on domestic duties."

Vanya cleared her throat but the PM continued: "OK, now what news about the power cuts and brown-outs?"

This time it was the turn of the Minister for Mines to speak.

"The miners are still refusing to come to the negotiating table unless we improve their working conditions. But we don't have enough spare water."

"Why do they need water at a coal mine?"

"Well, first to keep the dust under control. It's extremely hazardous to work in an environment of fine carbon particles, so I'm told. Second, to wash clean the extracted deposits. It's too bulky to transport unless it has been stripped back to the pure coal, and won't burn properly of course. And third, to prevent the men from dying of thirst. It's extremely hot down in the mines. The litre of water a day we're providing barely lasts until lunchtime apparently. And local prices are so high that the workers refuse to pay for any extra themselves. Ironically, we've had to suspend operations at our Iron Ore mines because they have contaminated the ground water."

"Ironic Iron Ore, ha ha, yes very good." The PM erupted into a corpulent belly laugh, but all that came out of his unhealthy lungs was a quiet wheeze. The others forced out a laugh too.

The PM continued. "We *must* improve the electricity supply. The situation is intolerable. The economy is collapsing. Our popularity is plummeting in the polls. If the opposition forced through a vote of confidence, we wouldn't stand a chance. What happened to our master plan to develop thorium nuclear power plants? I thought that was supposed to solve all our power problems?"

It was the turn of the Minister for Atomic Energy. "Err, yes Prime Minister, the th-th-thorium is helping enormously. If it weren't for that, our economy would be c-c-crippled already. But we cannot build the plants quickly enough to replace all the coal-powered per-per-plants. And the hydro-electrical dams... This lack of rain is a c-c-curse on our country."

"What does the meteorological office have to say about the rest of the monsoon season?"

The Science and Technology Minister piped up. "Well, of course, long-range forecasting is always tricky. They do expect that we'll get a lot of heavy rain for the next two weeks, but for the first week it will just bounce off the rock-hard ground and cause flash flooding. After that, well it's just guess-work really but they reckon we'll end up with maybe fifty percent of the usual monsoon rains. Reservoirs will be perhaps a third full by October. Enough to get the hydro-electricity back up and running but still only maybe half of what they were designed to provide."

"OK, so where does that leave the harvest? Is the Agricultural Minister here?"

"Yes Pradhanmantri," said a small, young man from the far end of the Cabinet table, partially obscured by a very large colleague who was eagerly leaning forward over the table. The Agricultural Minister was the youngest by far at this meeting, in fact the youngest ever appointed to the full Council. His supporters liked to think that this proved how brilliant he was, a future Prime Minister for sure. Other, more cynical, observers pointed out that the job was a poisoned chalice and was only ever handed over to expendable members of the administration.

"As I'm sure you heard we've had to ban the export of wheat and rice for the rest of the year to protect our diminished stockpiles. The rain, of course, is the main factor causing a problem. A lot of the less developed regions are having trouble accessing groundwater reservoirs. Uttar Pradesh and the Punjab are the worst hit areas. East India is still relatively well served by the Brahmaputra River. But in most parts of the country the water table has simply dropped too far for ordinary wells to reach it now. Our trade agreements with Kenya and South Africa will provide us with an emergency supply of food if the harvest turns out to be even worse than predicted. We're trying to encourage more consumption of fish as this is the only food source that doesn't require any irrigation, but of course the electricity problems mean refrigerators don't always stay cold enough to store the fish. So there has been limited success with this campaign."

"Well I'm sure you are doing your best, thank you. Now Smt Kumar, do you think you could do anything useful to help the Agricultural Minister? Release some funds to help with the wells, or to improve the fishing supply chain?"

Vanya felt like she was getting picked on and was beginning to fear for her political future. She dabbed at her forehead with a large tissue. "Certainly Pradhanmantri, I'll do what I can. Let me consult with my deputies and report back next week."

When she got back to her own Ministry later that day, she did indeed 'consult' with her deputies. This mainly involved a lot of shouting, accusations of uselessness and urgent requests for some positive news in time for next week's cabinet meeting.

But before the Cabinet could meet up again, the news they were dreading arrived. Vanya was sufficiently senior within the Cabinet to be included in the Python committee that handled all emergencies. She arrived at the secret bunker and joined the rest of the committee for a de-brief from the head of the Armed Forces.

"Pakistani forces crossed the Line of Control at midnight, and have cleared the border minefields in two broad swathes through Azad Kashmir. We think they are heading for the Vale of Kashmir and the City of Srinagar. Our army has responded forcefully with all locally deployed units but we've not been able to gather sufficient weight of numbers to hold back the advance of the invaders. The worst news is that the Pakistan land troops have been joined by a large-scale deployment of paratroops on the far side of Srinagar, cutting the city off from reinforcements."

"Oh, so that's what vertical envelopment means," muttered Vanya.

"Something you'd like to share with us?" asked the Prime Minister. The Interior Minister shook her head.

Over the next couple of days, the Python committee was in almost permanent session. Military Intel kept giving updates. The invasion force was estimated at six divisions. Cut off from reinforcements, the defense forces at Srinagar did not last long against the three Pakistani divisions that had been tasked with gaining control of the city. One of the other divisions had swung left towards the Wular Lake, sealing the gap between the border and Srinagar. The other two divisions turned right to form a defensive shield at the Chenab River.

The Committee braced itself for news of atrocities against the local population. The government prepared a blanket ban on media reports from the area, but their own feedback contained few shocks. This was no genocide mission apparently; no repeat of the 1971 atrocities of East Pakistan. Civilian casualties were high in the fight for Srinagar, but where possible the invading army had tried to allow civilians to flee the battlefield according to eye witness reports that were relayed to the Python committee.

The committee was informed of the Indian Army gathering its forces for a counterattack, but everybody knew that there would be little chance of quick success, with the invading forces well dug in to a very defensible corner of Indian Kashmir.

"I need some results! I need to show the people how we deal with invaders. I don't need excuses, General."

"Of course, Pradhanmantri, but we're still not sure what Pakistan's next move might be. It seems odd that their objectives are so limited. Why risk all-out war over such a small part of the disputed region? There's no sign of their forces preparing to advance. Why? Are they waiting for reinforcements? Is this a bluff?" The General charged with debriefing the committee was doing his best to be honest and realistic as well as diplomatic.

"I don't care," replied the Prime Minister. "Just get me a victory to announce to the country."

The Armed Forces had to take the battle with Pakistan to sea. It was their only chance of gaining a quick victory and appeasing the Prime Minister. The Admiral of the Fleet was highly ambitious and was happy to get involved, even though his advisors warned that the outcome of a sea battle between two evenly matched foes was hard to predict.

At the next Python committee meeting, Vanya could feel the tension in the room as the committee awaited news of the naval clash. She was pleased to be out of the spotlight for once. The Admiral came into the room, with a jumble of emotions showing across his face. The attack in the waters near Karachi had resulted in a Pyrrhic victory; each side losing a frigate and a submarine. The Prime Minister was able to announce a counter-strike on the accursed invaders but the battle resulted in 300 lives lost at sea and no tactical improvement in the situation.

Three hundred lives and the PM is going to broadcast it like a victory! thought Vanya. *I remember a mudslide killing three hundred people in my village when I was growing up. I knew every name that was read out at the commemoration.* She stood up in front of the committee and all eyes turned towards her.

The Prime Minister's smile slid off his face like the mud that fell off that mountainside. "Yes Smt Kumar, you have something to add?"

Vanya breathed in, stuck out her chin and then shook her head, deflating as she spoke. "No, Pradhanmantri, it can wait."

Across the border in headquarters near Islamabad, the Pakistan High Command was debating their next move. The Chief of Staff was summing up their progress and options from here. "All has gone to plan so far. We caught the Indians under-prepared. Invasion of Kashmir completed with minimal casualties. Our forces have now formed a defensive front around the city of Srinagar. We can hold out there for several weeks, but we will need to open up a second front if we're to make further inroads into Indian territory. The Indians have amassed a substantial force to block our advance and more troops are arriving daily. They'll be strong enough to launch a counter-attack soon."

"The second front should've opened up by now," the head of Military Intelligence said. "The Chinese have promised ten divisions. They too were to invade Jammu and Kashmir, cutting off the remaining Indian forces in the area and presenting a second front for the rest of India to deal with. But this is taking longer than expected. Our spies suggest that there are enough Chinese troops near the border to fulfill their half of the bargain, but there is very little sign of operational readiness. I'm afraid we have to contemplate the unpleasant possibility that they will renege on their promise."

"And if they don't invade, our troops will have to start a fighting retreat soon if we're to avoid being surrounded ourselves. Based on current reinforcement rates, the Indians will have a two-to-one advantage in the area by next week," replied the Chief of Staff.

"But what you're contemplating is political suicide! The government will fall if we have to admit that the invasion has been a total failure. You must give the Chinese more time. We'll seek assurances from Beijing forthwith. Hold your ground at least until Saturday," said the Defense Minister. That was going to be cutting it fine to get the troops out if there was not any help from the Chinese. The Chief of Staff's protests were waved away like an annoying insect.

Three days later, finally granted an audience, the Pakistani ambassador in Beijing protested vehemently with the Chinese government about the betrayal of trust.

"You promised us ten divisions," said the Ambassador to the Chinese Minister for External Affairs.

"I'm afraid you must have mis-understood our prior communications, your excellency. We promised to support your invasion, not join it. We have maintained international silence on these developments while others have condemned your invasion. We haven't offered aid to the Indians, while others have. So you see, from a certain point of view, we've been supportive of your actions. Our defense industry will be only too happy to help you replace any lost ordnance. At very favourable rates, of course." As the Pakistani Ambassador stormed out of the meeting, the Minister tried hard to suppress a smirk. He picked up the phone to speak to the Chinese Premier.

"Phase three of the Gangotri Plan proceeding according to schedule, Sir. India's attention is now firmly on its neighbour to the west rather than ourselves. I imagine there'll be a change of government in Pakistan soon, so there might not even be much souring of relations between our two countries."

The Pakistani forces were being slowly beaten back by the sheer numbers of Indian units pouring into the area. The delay in the order for a full retreat back across the border, while they awaited confirmation of China's intentions, was as costly as the Chief of Staff had suspected. Four infantry brigades were sacrificed to ensure that the withdrawing troops had some cover, with a thousand killed and the rest of the men left behind surrendering after two more days of fierce fighting. Nearly 7,000 prisoners were paraded in front of the Indian television cameras.

The jubilation within India at this military victory – the repulsion of the long-time foe - had a great unifying effect on the civilian population. Riots and protests against food rationing or power cuts were considered unpatriotic and quickly subsided. The government's ratings in the polls surged. And even Vanya Kumar, Minister for Home Affairs, enjoyed a brief surge in popularity.

CHAPTER 25

In December 1942, twelve commandos set off on Operation Frankton, a daring raid on German ships harboured in Bordeaux. The men became known as the Cockleshell Heroes thanks to the simple canoes they used to sneak deep into enemy territory. Modern canoes are still a viable form of silent transport that agents can use, in the right circumstances, to slip undetected into foreign states.

O.D. Training Manual Section 7b

May 8th, 2028, Gakona, Alaska.

"Sunny side up, with French toast and lashings of maple and bacon, just the way I like them," said Freda.

Sim was having breakfast with his boss at the HAARP centre. Yesterday's revelation about the Chinese sub and the potential conflict between China and India over the Brahmaputra River had given the two OFWAT agents plenty to think about overnight. Sim could sense a change in Freda. Whether it was the fading effects of her concussion, the sugar-infested American breakfast she had just consumed or something else he wasn't sure.

"Somebody sure is in a good mood," he said.

"What's not to be happy about? I've finally stopped using that bloody walking stick. And we get to go on a joint mission with the CIA. To China. Tickets like this don't come along very often."

"Chasing a couple of bad guys across London for blowing up a dirigible is one thing, but taking on the Chinese government... I don't know. I sorta feel out of my depth. Up until last month I'd spent most of my career stuck behind a PC terminal."

Freda reached out across the table and gave Sim's hand a

squeeze. "You've done great, Sim. Truly. For an agent's first time in the field, you've certainly exceeded my expectations."

"Judging from the first time we met, I think it would've been hard to undershoot those expectations. I just don't think I'm big enough to save the world."

"Napoleon was only five foot five and he conquered the whole of Europe."

"Ha ha. That's not what I meant, man. What difference can a couple of OFWAT agents make in a super-power conflict like this?"

Freda's face contorted with a flash of anger. "That's just the sort of shitty attitude that has got the planet into this mess. Too many people presume that they cannot make a difference and give up without even trying. It's just a pathetic excuse because they don't want to admit they're not in complete control of their destiny." Her face softened. "They wouldn't even admit they were scared."

She fell into a brooding silence while Sim tried to process this outburst and sudden change in attitude. That last sentence seemed to refer to some specific people.

Sim looked at Freda for a moment, mentally rehearsing his next question. "Boss, you've been in the job for, what is it now, over fifteen years? Why did you join OFWAT in the first place?"

There was a sigh from the other side of the table. "I was about your age when I joined the agency. A year prior to that I was engaged, thinking about quitting work to start a family. But something happened and the marriage never took place."

"What was it?"

"Howard was a lifeguard. Not at a swimming pool, the other sort. He worked for the RNLI, keeping an eye on the beaches near St Ives. There was a storm one night in the autumn." Freda paused, pulling her legs up to her chest and wrapping her arms around them. Sim sat silently, waiting for her to continue.

"It was a real bad one – a spring tide combined with low pressure and there was a lot of rainwater draining off the land. They say the water was five metres higher than normal, but the wind was whipping it up, sometimes to twice that height. Howard wasn't working that night but had been out for a quick beer with some friends.

"When he came out of the pub there was a crowd of people gathered on top of the long breakwater protecting the bay there. A man had fallen in and was drowning on the far side of the breakwater. Howard didn't stop to think, he just jumped in. The man was hysterical, fighting Howard's efforts to rescue him in a blind panic. The people standing on the breakwater just watched. Just watched.

"They were interviewed afterwards. Each of them said they thought there was nothing they could do, the water was too dangerous. Every single one just stood, frozen to the spot and watched both men drown. Not ten metres away around the corner there was a life-buoy and rescue line. Nobody even checked – they just assumed somebody else had been to look already."

"Crap, I'm sorry, Freda. That must've been awful." Neither of them spoke for a minute.

"So don't ever tell me there's nothing you can do. I joined OFWAT a few months after that because I wanted to make a difference."

"But. What about your ring? You're still wearing it."

Freda held her left hand up and wiggled her third finger. "I couldn't take it off. I needed it to remind me of Howard. It's too precious to me."

"What about other relationships? I mean after you'd mourned for Howard. Surely there's more to life than just the Agency? I don't think I'm willing to become a singleton forever just for the sake of a job."

"Oh sure, there have been a few one night stands along the way, but nothing serious. That's not the point." At that moment Bo entered the room and started walking over to them. "The point is, errm, the point is... The point is that you can make a difference. We could be the two agents that help stop World War Three."

"As if that's going to happen, boss. That's just for books and films."

Bo came over to sit with them, mug of coffee in one hand and a plate of cherry pie in the other.

"Sim was just explaining to me that he doesn't want to go on this mission to China," said Freda.

"Oh really?" replied Bo. "That's too bad. The plan worked better with even numbers. I guess we'll just have to see if the CIA can rustle up another field agent."

"Hang on a minute," said Sim. "I didn't say I wouldn't go, just that I had my doubts about our chances. Anyway, why does the plan need even numbers? And who is going to partner you, Bo?"

"Well the first part of the mission – the insertion – involves a set of two-person canoes. My partner will be Chung Lennox, third-generation Chinese. Speaks fluent Mandarin and looks the part obviously. Should be quite an asset to the mission. I'll introduce you guys later."

"Wardle sent us on a mission together, Freda, and I'm not going to abandon you now. I'm not scared of anything the Chinese can throw at us." Sim stood up to leave. "And I'm bloody good in a canoe."

The OFWAT agents got in touch with HQ, explained what was going on and their next course of action. The CIA provided all the equipment and there was an intensive phase of training. The canoes were pretty sturdy but ultra-light weight. Even fully laden with all the equipment needed, they could be carried over obstacles or around impassable parts of a river for short distances. Each of the participants was issued with four gold sovereigns, tucked safely into a discreet compartment in their belts. High value, small and waterproof, the coins were there in case they needed to bargain their way out of trouble.

Freda and Sim got to know Bo a bit better, and were introduced to Chung. In age and height, he was somewhere between Sim and Bo. He was much stockier than either of the other two – and most of it was muscle to judge from the power he could put into a canoe paddle. Bo's long arms acted as very effective levers, while Chung relied on brute strength. Freda and Sim's canoeing was just as effective but came mostly from good technique and timing. Sim had done some canoeing while in the Territorial Army and Freda -inspired by the canoeing gold medals Britain had won at the 2012 Olympics – had taken it up in her youth.

Halfway through the week's training – a mixture of canoeing practice and memorising details of the Chinese region – Sim found himself sitting down with Chung over lunch. The food here at the base was pretty simple. Fresh salmon with some rice and steamed vegetables – a good combination of protein and carbohydrate to make up for all the calories they were burning out on the water. Sim knew it was good for him, but he could have murdered a burger with all the trimmings.

"So Chung, Bo was telling me you used to be part of the space program. That must have been pretty awesome."

"Hmm, well I was going to get involved in the REMU, but it didn't work out in the end."

"REMU? You mean the Rare Earth Moon Unit?" Sim's eyes

widened. "I've read about that. Is it up and running now? I heard that they started construction a couple of years ago."

"Yep, phase one was completed last year. It took them a few months to build a proper base, with a regular stream of spaceships delivering new materials. It's pretty basic but it still counts as mankind's first colonisation of the solar system. You'd think the US would make more of a thing about it, but to be honest I think they're getting so much flak for commandeering the moon's resources that they're trying to keep it low-key. Anyway they are well into phase two now, building the huge excavators that will mine the rocks. I was due to become one of the regular pilots on the shuttle missions to and from the moon base, but I failed the medical."

"You? But you're as fit as a butcher's dog. How did someone like you fail the test?"

"A butcher's dog? I ain't no dog. My physical fitness was fine and mental aptitude I passed with flying colours. But one of the cardiogram tests picked up a very slight anomaly. It turns out I have a congenital heart defect. Can't really tell there's anything wrong with me in normal gravity but they reckoned in the stress of high-G take-off and re-entry I might just suffer a cardiac arrest. I tried to persuade them it was fine, I would test out the risk in the high-G training equipment. I was desperate to get on the program but they wouldn't change their minds."

"Too bad. Still their loss is our gain, heh?" said Sim. Chung didn't smile. He mumbled an excuse and abruptly left the dining table. *Bit rude*, thought Sim.

The following evening, the four agents were spending the night outdoors to get used to their equipment and brush up on their field-craft. Sim had got the fire well stoked, with plenty of spare wood for later, while Chung was heating up some basic field rations and making hot drinks. The sun had set a couple of hours ago and with the canopy of the trees cutting out much of the twilight, darkness had fallen quickly on the campsite.

The sky was clear; in between the trees Sim could see a multitude of stars not spoiled by any nearby light pollution. Even compared with the Scottish night sky, this was a truly majestic sight. As twilight gave way to a pitch black night, Sim could see the broad sweep of the Milky Way appear like a brushstroke of icing powder. The evening chorus of birds settling down to roost had given way now to the hoot of a nearby owl. Bo went off to do his business in the woods; a loud farting noise cut through the quiet of the forest.

"Jeez, Bo, at least make sure you're downwind of us," Freda called out to the darkness.

Sim laughed and then smiled as memories of tins of baked beans around a campfire in Scotland came flooding back. As he was cleaning his pistol, Sim heard the snap of a twig in the darkness. He was just about to accuse Bo of having heavy boots when the noise was followed by a deep growl, and something nearby sniffed the air. He turned to see the faint outline of a bear ambling closer to the camp, blocking Bo's path back to the rest of the party. Sim raised his pistol and aimed. Freda urged him to shoot it, but he couldn't pull the trigger. The bear stopped advancing, swaying its head back and forth, sniffing the air some more. Chung grabbed a burning branch from the fire and started walking towards the bear, swishing it about and shouting. The bear hesitated as if mesmerised by the flames, then it turned and left at a gentle gait while Bo ran back to the camp, looping behind Chung.

"Thanks for nothing Sim," said Bo.

An awkward silence was broken, for once, by Chung. "My grandfather used to tell me a story about Chinese water shortages in ancient times. Would you like to hear it?" The others nodded.

Many years ago, the Chinese believed there were five sacred mountains: Mount Kunlan - the abode of the gods - Huashan, Songshan , Hengshan and Taishan. Now there was a village near Hengshan that had been suffering from a drought for over a year. The crops had failed and the previous year's harvest had been used up. Many of the villagers' cattle and pets had perished and the villagers were starving. A small, deep well gave them just enough to drink but not enough to irrigate the fields. The elders of the village decided that a sacrifice must be made to the Dragon Yinghong who lived at the top of the mountain and who controlled the rains. The elders knew that they had nothing of true value to offer to the Dragon, so they devised a wicked plan:

'If we send one of our strong youths up the mountain, the Dragon might accept the boy as our sacrifice. The boy won't go willingly, so we'll have to give him a token to take. As a pretence of a sacrifice.'

In a mock ceremony, the elders chose a brave boy named Lin Chong whose parents beamed with pride, not realising what the elders had in store. Lin Chong was clever and fit, and set off on the long walk up the mountain almost straight away. He was allowed to take one of the warriors' spears to protect himself against creatures that lived on the mountain, and he was given a small ornate necklace to offer to the Dragon. On his back he carried a modest bamboo basket with food and water to last him for several days. He wore a traditional wide-brimmed hat to protect him from the fierce sun and strode out of the village looking, and feeling, like a young man.

After an arduous trek through the foothills of Mount Hengshan the boy made camp and settled down for the night. But he could not sleep, dreaming of his forthcoming encounter with the immortal Yinghong. Would the Dragon take the form of a man to meet him, or remain as a mighty winged lizard, bigger than a house? As he dozed lightly, a snuffling noise and a scrape of claw on rock made him sit bolt upright and grab for his spear. Encircling his camp were ten huge wolves. Their bared teeth glistened orange from the firelight and their eyes were full of hunger. The boy knew he could not fight off ten of them, even with fire and spear, so he turned to the biggest wolf, who was a little closer to him than the rest.

'Oh mighty wolf, who comes upon my camp looking for flesh and bone to chew, I implore you to hold your jaws lest a terrible fate befalls you. The Dragon Yinghong has sent for me: I carry important information and a gift for the exalted one. If he discovers that you have prevented me completing my mission, his terrible wrath will be brought down upon your pack.' It was the best the boy could come up with on the spur of the moment but the wolves stopped advancing.

'Show me the gift' demanded the biggest wolf. The boy held up the jade necklace for the whole pack to see.

'Now tell me what information you are taking to the great dragon,' growled the pack leader. The boy was about to make up some secret and blurt it out, when he realised the wolf's trick. If he told him the important information the wolves could eat him and give the dragon the gift and message themselves.

'I cannot tell anybody but Yinghong himself. I have been sworn to secrecy. I would rather be eaten by wolves than face his wrath for betraying his trust.'

The pack leader sized up the boy. He growled and turned away, leading the pack in search of an alternative meal.

The boy found it difficult to sleep for the rest of that night, fearful that the wolves would return, but there was no sign of them. At dawn he resumed his climb to the top of the mountain. The air was pure and thinner than down in the valley of his village. Everything seemed to sparkle with an inner radiance: the winter snow that remained in shaded parts, the green moss that clung to the cracks in the rocks, even the mountain itself as the sun caught the façade of crystals embedded on the surface.

As Lin Chong neared the top, just when he was beginning to think that there was nowhere for a dragon to reside up here, the ground began to shake and suddenly Yinghong himself appeared. The boy was utterly frozen to the spot, beguiled by the dragon's great eyes, pools of fire bluer than the ocean. The lizard's front two legs ended in paws that could have flattened a barn and huge talons as deadly as any scythe. Between his front legs, Yinghong's chest stood proud and broad as the Great Wall itself. The scales of his armour-plated skin shone like aquamarines in the morning sun.

'Have you brought that spear to kill me, boy?' asked the Dragon in a mocking voice.

'Even if I had a thousand spears and a thousand mighty warriors to heft them, it would be folly to think we could penetrate your magnificent scales, oh exalted one. I brought it merely to protect myself on the journey.'

'Hmm, a sensible answer for one so young. Maybe you are worth listening to. You seem to know how to talk to a Dragon. What brings you to my domain?'

'Our village in the valley below is suffering terribly from a drought. I am sure your mighty powers would barely be troubled to send us some rains, but we would not dare to ask you without suitable recompense. My elders gave me this precious necklace as a token of our offering.'

Yinghong peered down at the tiny necklace that would not have stretched around even his smallest toe, and roared with laughter.

'This necklace has no worth, boy. Your village is either poorer than you realise, or the elders have played a trick on you. They have offered me yourself as a sacrifice, not the jade bauble. How low you petty mortals will stoop in your hour of need! I have a good mind to eat you and make the drought last another year to teach your elders a lesson.'

Lin Chong gulped and involuntarily took a step backwards. He knew there was no point in trying to flee, so his mind began racing for something else to say.

'It is true, oh master, that our necklace is a mere trinket. However, I was not sent here as a sacrifice,' he lied, 'but as a challenge to entertain you. I am the village's best player of games. If I can beat you at a game of your choosing, you must promise to send us rains. And if I lose, as undoubtedly I will, you can do with me as you please.'

The Dragon looked down at the little boy and was intrigued by his tempting offer, for if truth be told life as an immortal lizard on top of a mountain could be boring at times. He licked his lips and smelt the crisp morning air.

'Very well, we shall play Go. I hope you are as good as you say, for your sake as well as your village.' The Dragon shrank himself down to human form and led the boy to a cave whose scruffy entrance belied the opulent interior. Numerous oil lanterns hanging from the walls, Persian rugs on the floor and a scattering of silk cushions transformed the cave into a room fit for a King. Wine, fruit and a bejeweled Go board adorned a large central table where the two opponents sat facing each other and the game began.

Go is like trying to play five games of chess simultaneously. Each part of the board becomes a separate battle for territory where any false moves can quickly lead to defeat. The boy's only hope was that the Dragon would be over-confident of victory and not take the boy's strategies seriously. So he continued to ply Yinghong with compliments which the lizard lapped up while carelessly playing through the first few rounds of the game. The boy even made a few deliberate mistakes in the early game, allowing the Dragon to capture some small territories, while laying a long-run trap that might just win him the game if his opponent failed to spot it in time.

Eventually the trap worked. The Dragon stretched his pieces too far, and the boy pounced. A cascade of increasingly large captures ensued. The Dragon's eyes flashed with blue flame, but there was nothing he could do. Finally, he slammed his fist on the board and swept the pieces to the floor.

'Alright, you win,' said the Dragon. 'Give me the word and I will end the drought to your village. But know this. The water I send to your people will divert from somewhere else. By your deeds will you condemn another village to the same fate that befell yours.'

The boy hesitated. 'Then they will have to find somebody who can best you. My duty is to my village alone. Please, o mighty Yinghong, send us water that we may grow our crops.'

Chung looked at his colleagues. "What would you've done in Lin Chong's place?"

Sim shrugged. "He did what he had to." Bo nodded in agreement.

"What about a compromise? Offer to help the other village by sharing? Djeez, you guys are so black and white."

"And yellow," said Chung, wagging his finger at Freda.

Later in the week Diane laid out the basic plan to them during one of the many briefings they had to sit through. She had given the mission team a codename, *Rodger's Rangers*, after the British leader who had led a surprise raid on St Francis by canoeing along the Saint Lawrence River during the Canadian Seven Years' War. The rangers were experts at guerilla warfare and at survival in harsh conditions, she explained. She did not think it was worth mentioning how many of the Rangers made it back alive from that particular raid.

"You will be transferred to the *USS Nimitz* in the Bay of Bengal and from there a helicopter will take you to the Assam region in India. Remember, you are trying to keep clear of the Indian authorities, we don't want to arouse their suspicions. Then you travel up the Brahmaputra and cross the Chinese border in secrecy. After you have travelled far enough away from the border, you should be able to ditch the canoes and pose as conventional tourists with Chung pretending to be your guide. Get yourselves a faster boat, but one that blends in with the normal river traffic. Once you have done that, well, just keep following the river to its source until you discover what's going on."

"If we do discover something big and need some back-up, or need to be extracted, how do we get in touch with HQ? We can hardly just phone up and ask for a ride home," said Sim.

"This is a high priority mission. You will have full back-up available from the Nimitz. Bo will be carrying one of the military's sat phones. And failing that, as a last-ditch measure, you can always use a thumper." Everyone nodded except Sim, who hadn't a clue what a thumper was. He doubted it was a turbo-charged dildo but felt too embarrassed to ask now.

PART
THREE

Be careful what you water your dreams with.

Lao Tzu, 6th century BC

CHAPTER 26

The Chinese Water Diversion Project began just after the new millenium started. Three routes, Eastern, Central and Western, aimed to bring billions of litres of water from northern rivers in China to the arid but more populated southern regions. But by the time these huge aqueducts were completed, the north was not able to spare as much water as first hoped. And the needs of the south had become even more pressing.

O.D. Training Manual Section 4d

4 months earlier, 100 kilometres north of Ordos, Inner Mongolia.

The government officials stopped just outside the village. There was a sign on the side of the road that read: *Xinjie, closed until further notice.*

"That's the tenth one this month. We may as well admit it. The Water Diversion Program isn't working," said the first official. "Our only hope is the Western Route."

The officials made their way into the centre of the village. A few stray dogs were fighting over the bones of a horse carcass; they scattered as the black government car drew up. The men got out and inspected the well near the village square. One of them leant over the edge and dropped a stone in. After several seconds the stone clattered into something metallic and sent the noise reverberating back up towards the surface.

"Just like all the others."

"Inspection records show this well started out only 20 metres deep," said the other official, consulting a roll-tab. "It must be three times that depth now."

"You have to give the villagers credit for sticking it out this long.

I'd have given up on this well years ago."

"We could give more help to these villages. Send civil engineers with the right equipment. This well could go a lot deeper with proper know-how."

"What, and have hundreds of badly monitored wells tapping the aquifers? You know the score – force them to move into the cities where we can control the supply of water and ration it for their own good."

While they had been talking the pack of dogs had started to re-gather. The low growl of the pack leader alerted the officials to the animals. The desperation of these dogs was obvious from the all-too-visible ribcages – some of them looked striped like zebras. There was a fierce light in the pack leader's eyes: the officials were on the menu today.

Before the bodyguards could reach the officials, the first dog had leapt for the throat of the man nearest the well. He put out his hand to defend himself and the dog's teeth latched on to his forearm. The momentum of the animal forced the man backwards until he staggered into the wall around the edge of the well. Gunshots rang out as the bodyguards killed the rest of the pack, but they could not risk a shot at this last dog. For a moment the man and dog teetered over the black abyss. The walls of the well reached out like lips as if the earth was hungry for a meal of its own. Then a yelp from the dog. It let go of the man's arm and dropped into the void. The knife the man had pulled from his jacket was still protruding from the animal's chest.

"Damn! That's my army blade. Been through some tough times, me and that knife."

"It must be getting worse if the dogs are turning on humans now," said the other official.

The injured man was not listening. His attention was on the

bodyguards rushing to tend to his wound. "If you useless pieces of shit ever let a single dog, let alone a pack, get anywhere near me again you'll be turned into dog food, you hear me?"

One of the bodyguards went to get a dressing from the car to wrap around the wound and some spray to clean it. The other guard fetched the official's pack of cigarettes from the car and lit one for him. After a few deep drags, the bite wound had been dealt with and they walked out of the centre of the village into the fields nearby, where most of the villagers had tried to scratch a living.

The second official bent down and rubbed some dust between his fingers. There was barely any soil left. He shook his head. "Not a tree in sight. Guidelines clearly state that all farmland must have at least twenty trees per hectare to protect the soil quality."

The first official flicked away his finished cigarette. "They never fucking listen. Too busy burning the trees for fuel or lining the well with planks. Soil in these fields isn't much better than the desert. The idiots get what they deserve."

The Gobi was spreading across the country like an infection, seeping into every field and hillside where the water had dried up and the soil had crumbled to dust. On the horizon, the officials could make out a sandstorm heading in their direction.

"The Gangotri plan's our only hope. How is progress up there?"

The first official rubbed the bandage on his arm. "I haven't been to check in person for quite a while. The cold air plays havoc with my sinuses. But seems to be going fine. Engineering is coping with the temperatures, but the cover-up is complicated. I can't help feeling there are too many loose ends. Are we sure that nobody in India, or in the West even, is going to be able to figure out what we're up to?"

"Of course not. The Indians are fixated on their border with Pakistan. And the Diaoyu diversion was a master stroke, even though I say so myself. It took a lot of persuading to get the Premier to agree to that. You worry too much, Guozhi. I guess that's why you're such a good civil servant, ha ha ha. Come on, let's stay ahead of that dust cloud."

◆

Drepung Monastery, Tibet.

High up in one of the monastery buildings Lama Kunchen Jamyang was floating through the air enjoying the breeze of a warm spring day on his feathery body. He dived down into a shimmering lake and joined a school of fish; thousands of bodies twisting and turning as one. He had not stopped being a bird, but he was a fish as well now. He leapt out of the water and became a young antelope too, taking its first faltering steps on the grasslands. He reached out to nibble some grass but as he did so the pool he was standing next to turned silver. The pool transmogrified into a mirrored snake that sprang at him and wrapped itself around his slender neck. It squeezed until he could breathe no more. His vision blurred and then he passed out.

He came around from his afternoon meditation with a gasp. He looked around his sparsely furnished room and saw his student waiting patiently for him to speak. "The silver serpent is strangling the world. It has to be stopped," he rasped as if his neck was still in a vice-like grip. Jamyang's vision was reported to the council later that day and was interpreted in various ways, depending on who did the translating: pollution, climate change, a preparation for Jamyang's eventual reincarnation.

"Why can't you see it? The meaning's obvious. We've all witnessed the government building these new pipes across the land. *Silver* pipes. The pipes bring death. We must find out how and why." Tenzin Wangdue was making his case to the council for direct action, not for the first time.

The monastery was no stranger to controversy, having been shut temporarily twenty years ago as the monks led a protest against the Chinese rule of Tibet. But the implications of this vision could lead to violent conflict. There was a small minority on the council, led by Wangdue, who felt that conflict was inevitable and that the monastery could not shy away from its duty no matter what the cost.

The Grand Master of the council sought out a more pragmatic, peaceful response. "We must broaden our minds, Master Wangdue. Seek knowledge and understanding."

Wangdue pressed on. "Over the past year, the authorities have been building a large network of buildings and pipelines through the region. When we observed one of the construction sites, it turned out that these aren't normal pipes. And there have been no recent announcements of new gas or oil fields being found in the Tibetan plateau. Is the government deliberately trying to keep quiet about a geological discovery?"

"Why does everything have to be sinister, Wangdue? Isn't it possible that the authorities are building these pipes for peaceful reasons?" asked the Grand Master.

"I might've been ready to believe that if I hadn't heard Jamyang's vision. And the murder of that student I investigated a few months ago. The four silver pipes feed into this new complex and then carry on out the other side. We don't know what happens there. But whatever the reason, security is a priority. Even during the construction phase there were armed guards all over the place. And whatever this building is for, it needs a lot of power. They have a local sub-station within the development and what appears to be a diesel generator as back-up. These are no ordinary gas pipes."

"Maybe you're right and there is something suspicious about all this. But I urge caution. Don't do anything hasty. I will make enquiries through the official channels. This council is adjourned. *Namaste.*"

Jamyang could not return to the same enlightened state to get any answers, even though he tried nearly every day. The Grand Master continued to counsel pragmatism and peace, though his inquiries to the Chinese authorities were ignored. Wangdue secretly gathered a group of his closest allies and prepared for direct action.

On the evening of Tuesday 28th March, a group of eight monks gathered under a moonless night sky just outside the monastery. They were dressed in warm dark clothing, with rucksacks of equipment on their backs. Accompanying them were four of the monastery's guard dogs – huge Tibetan Mastiffs. These were not the more common nomad type, but the heavier Tsang Khyi variety. Nearly 80cm tall and 80 kilograms in weight, these dogs were bred to confront wolves and leopards. The monks had chosen the four dogs with the darkest coats so the whole group blended easily into the dark night.

After an hour of hiking they approached the construction site. It was bitterly cold, and snow had started falling. The black outfits did not seem like such a good idea any more. The site was surrounded by a 3-metre-tall fence topped with razor wire. The only gates into the complex were well lit by floodlights and had at least four armed guards manning the entrance. Inside the perimeter fence it looked as though there were at least two pairs of guards patrolling on foot with torches.

The monks approached the perimeter fence at the point furthest from the gate and one of them started snipping a hole through it with some wire cutters. He had to stop and retreat into the cover of darkness at one point when two guards passed nearby, but the hole was soon complete. Two monks and two of the dogs stayed outside, guarding the escape route, while the rest squeezed through. They ran to the nearest building and hid in its shadow, watching to see where the sentries were. The generator building and the guards' accommodation were off to the right. A communication building and a storage shed were to their left, while the building they were using as cover was the electrical sub-station. Wangdue could hear and feel the slight vibration of a large-scale transformer inside. The main building ought to be just behind this one.

The guards were tracing out simple and predictable loops just inside the perimeter fence. After a few minutes, one of the team of guards popped inside the accommodation building – no doubt for a hot drink to stave off the cold – which meant that the remaining pair of guards was leaving a large gap between circuits. The monks capitalised on this and easily sneaked around the sub-station to the main building without being spotted. The side door they had reached was locked, but it was not all that sturdy and one of the monks managed to kick it open. They scrambled inside and shut the door behind them, hoping that the guards would not notice the broken lock in the darkness.

They were in a black corridor. Reaching for their torches, they followed the passageway towards some sort of control room. There was a series of monitors across one wall, and a bank of computer keyboards, instrument gauges and telephones. All of the equipment was still inert. This plant – whatever it was – was not yet fully operational. Passing beyond the control room they came to the main chamber of the building. It was here that the four silver pipes from outside penetrated the western wall at about waist height. These then fed into a large circular vat that seemed to resemble a huge hot water tank, complete with thermometer on the outside. There was then a pipe which led out of the vat into a series of four turbines that drove the liquid along into four more silver pipelines and out through the eastern wall.

Wangdue noticed that built into the top of each of the pipes on their way to the vat were inspection hatches. Although the machinery was clearly not operating, he could hear liquid running through the pipes. He opened up one of the inspection hatches and peered in with his torch. The liquid inside was colour-free and odourless. He poked it with an object to make sure it was not acid, and then dipped his hand in. It felt like cold water. He tasted a drop or two. It *was* cold water. *All of this effort – the buildings, the huge pipeline across the Tibetan plateau, just to transfer some water! But where is the water coming from in the first place? There is no excess water up on the plateau or in the mountains to feed into these pipes.*

He whispered his discovery over to his colleagues, but at that moment, the lights in the main chamber were turned on. From three different directions armed guards ran into the room, raising their rifles and pointing them straight at the monks. The mastiffs sensed the danger and immediately launched themselves at the nearest guards. Rifle shots rang out from all directions and one of the dogs fell, instantly slayed. The other dog had one guard by the throat and pinned to the floor. The monks scattered in the confusion, using the vat and pipes as cover from the bullets. A stray round ricocheted off the metal casing of a turbine and punctured the lung of one of the monks, who collapsed in agony. Four of the monks headed for the doorway where the surviving mastiff had opened up a gap. The other guard at this door was aiming for the dog, and didn't notice the flying kick from one of the monks until too late. He collapsed in a heap and they all leapt over him, calling for the dog to follow them down the corridor towards the exit.

But Wangdue had been left behind in the confusion. He had been too far away from the exit the other monks had used, with the machinery in his way. Though the guards could not get a clean shot at him immediately, he knew he was surrounded. He had to give his friends time to get away. He reached into his backpack and retrieved two flasks of oil. He threw one of them on the floor and set fire to it with a lighter he had in his pocket. The pool of fiery oil spread under the pipes and towards the vat but lacked anything flammable to catch onto. He shook his head. Then he poured the second flask over himself from the top down and took a deep breath. He sparked the light against his clothing. The flames took hold immediately. Screaming in pain, he ran for the corridor back to the control room. Shocked at the sight of a burning man, the guards momentarily lowered their rifles. Wangdue made it to the control room and collapsed on the desk – his final act of defiance to cause as much damage as possible.

The retribution meted out to the monastery was as swift as it was violent. Three of the monks who had escaped were rounded up the following day and executed by firing squad. They had been followed back to the monastery at a distance, and CCTV images had captured their faces from inside the water treatment complex. The monastery itself was shut down for three months.

The Grand Master of the council took all of this in his stride. "Our friends have continued their journeys in another form. We should pray for the Lord Buddha to look over their souls. *Namaste.*"

Meanwhile Jamyang, whose vision had started off this chain of events, had another, more violent, version. He was lying on top of the world and the silver serpent was coiled around his body and limbs. It reared up its head and bared its fangs at him. The venom dripped into his eyes and he screamed and writhed in agony. The whole world shook beneath him, splitting and cracking. As it did so fires sprang up from the fissures. He awoke again. "The Silver Serpent brings poison to the world. Nations will rise up in arms against each other and the earth will burn."

Wangdue's student, Rabten, who had survived the incident at the water plant, heard this new vision and felt he understood what had to be done. He packed a bag of simple possessions and clutching a note that Master Wangdue had left for him, he abandoned the holy order, heading for Nepal.

CHAPTER 27

Vast tracts of the delta that makes up most of Bangladesh had become flooded as sea levels rose. The huge cost of moving millions of households to safer, higher ground was too much at a time when the economy was shrinking. Eventually, the Government had to seek external aid and the Chinese were the first to volunteer. Although this magnanimous gesture was widely applauded, it came at a cost. The Chinese authorities gained a say in the internal affairs of the country, which they never relinquished even after the situation had been stabilised. Bangladesh had effectively become a puppet state of the Chinese.

O.D. Training Manual Section 3c

May 17, 2028, Bay of Bengal, Indian Ocean.

"So Chung, what's it like to be going back to China?" Sim was shouting at the CIA agent over the roar of the helicopter's rotor blades as they were ferried from the US aircraft carrier *Nimitz* into India.

Chung looked up from cleaning his gun. "Mixed feelings."

"Why's that?"

"I think Grandfather regretted leaving his homeland."

"Did he struggle to find work when he came to the USA?" asked Sim.

"He didn't have to open a laundry or a take-out, if that's what you mean. There are some very skilled professionals who emigrate from China to the United States, you know. Under-appreciated, but highly skilled. You Brits are as bad as the East Coast Americans, always assuming you are fricking superior." Chung glowered at Sim and went back to checking his equipment and gun for about the tenth time.

Pardon me for breathing, thought Sim, as he fell back into thoughts of the mission. *Glad I'm not sharing his canoe.*

The team of agents and their equipment – canoes and all – fitted easily inside the cargo hold of the grey Sikorsky Sea Dragon they were travelling in. The helicopter's flight path to the Indian state of Assam had to go over the corner of Bangladesh to avoid a time-wasting detour of several hundred klicks. To gain permission to fly through Bangladeshi airspace, the US navy had pretended that the helicopter was full of aid workers to avoid any repercussions with the Chinese authorities. But nobody had informed the bandits living in the flooded delta that this was a mercy mission.

The huge helicopter banked sharp left as a hail of small arms fire streaked up towards the aircraft. Equipment was sent hurtling across the width of the hold, some spilling out of packing cases. Sim grabbed hold of his seatbelt, keeping one hand free to fend off any flying debris. He heard the sound of small fireworks being set off as the co-pilot deployed chaff in case these bandits were armed with something deadlier than a machine gun. Sim could see the smoke trails and intense glare of dozens of tiny decoys. Another volley of bullets. Some of them found their mark this time, rapidly drumming the outer skin of the helicopter. The Sikorsky was built to withstand small calibre bullets. The bandits were quickly left behind and the passengers breathed a collective sigh of relief.

"All clear," said the pilot in a quiet voice as if they had just passed through some inconvenient turbulence.

As pulses and blood pressures returned to normal, Sim was starting to lap up the view from the helicopter's window as it followed the path of the Brahmaputra upstream. The verdant banks and glistening ox-bow lakes were beautiful, especially for someone like Sim who had not travelled much before.

"Stunning, isn't it?" said Freda as she leant across him to share the view. "Pity we won't have time to enjoy it, it's one of my favourite parts of Asia. Strange to think it could all be ravaged by war before long, if we don't figure out what's going on. This region's likely to be the frontline of any land-based campaign."

The Sikorsky landed near Dibrugarh, the largest town on the river before it entered the disputed region of Arunachal Pradesh. Sim pictured the briefing maps they had memorised back in Alaska. The Brahmaputra is shaped like a squashed question mark, with its tail ending in Bangladesh. The bottom of its hook starts in Assam where they had just landed. Then it crosses through Arunachal Pradesh before turning west, traversing the bottom of the Plateau of Tibet. Although Arunachal Pradesh is part of India, the Chinese claim the region as their own and subject it to heightened observation. Diane had felt the mission would be safer and attract fewer enquiring officials if it started in Assam.

"Right come on, let's get this gear shifted into the vans before we invite too many prying eyes," said Bo. As they lifted one of the canoes out of the helicopter they noticed a round hole in the bottom of the hull. One of the bullets from the earlier attack must have penetrated the aircraft's armour.

"Shit. What we going to do?" said Chung.

Bo bent down and examined the gash. "We can't wait for a replacement canoe. We'll have to patch her up. We've got repair kits, we've practised this. Come on, let's get hustling. Chow down later."

"Why aren't you in charge of this mission, Freda? Surely you can pull rank on the great big puddin'?" whispered Sim.

Freda shrugged. "CIA is providing the kit, the transport and the back-up, so they call the shots."

By the time the repair had been done, the kit had been loaded onto the vans and they had made the short road trip to the banks of the

Brahmaputra, it was almost dark. The US attaché who was acting as their liaison had rented out a simple house where they could rest overnight before starting on their river cruise.

Sim was sitting opposite Freda, in the main living room, enjoying a drink. He picked at his lips. "Can I ask you something?"

"Sure."

"Do you get nervous? I mean before the start of a mission like this?"

"Not really, the adrenalin and testosterone kick in. We're here to do a job to the best of our ability and that's what we're going to do. No point in worrying about stuff we can't control. Funny thing about testosterone: it makes me horny."

Sim's beer bottle stopped mid-way between the table and his lips. He tried to focus on the bottle, gulped down more than he had planned and started coughing. An image of Freda getting undressed in Marinus popped into his head. And then one of Rosie, smiling at him from behind the bar at Dornoch, her hand wrapped around a thick beer pump. He felt his cheeks redden slightly as the crotch on his trousers tightened.

When he looked up at Freda, he could see she was smiling, but whether she was enjoying his embarrassment or actually making a pass at him, he couldn't tell. He put his beer down, said he needed the loo and left the room in a hurry. He went upstairs to his room and opened the window to let in some cool air. He stood there looking out at a jumble of dark, unfamiliar shapes and tried to make sense of his feelings for Freda.

After a while he headed back downstairs into the main living room. As he entered he saw Freda and Bo sitting close together on the sofa. There was something about the movement of their bodies away from each other and the position of their hands, almost touching, that suggested they had been doing something intimate just before Sim came in. The realisation made him pause and then he barrelled on into the room, grabbing his beer and quickly taking a slug.

"Some weather we're having, huh?" He winced inside, realising the inanity of his question, but he couldn't think of what else to say.

Bo leant back in the sofa and smiled. "Sure is hot."

Freda finished her drink and got up. "I'll see you in the morning, Sim."

Bo watched her leave, then turned to look at Sim. "What a day."

"Yeah, you could say that, man," muttered Sim through gritted teeth.

"I can't help feeling there's some tension between you and me, Sim. What wrong have I done? I can't remember offending you at any point. If the mission is going to be a success, I need to know the whole team's pulling together."

Sim looked at Bo and weighed up the benefits of honesty versus diplomacy. "Well, I can't help wondering why they put you in charge instead of Freda. It seems to me she has far more experience in the field and would make a better leader."

Bo grinned and leaned forward. "And that wouldn't have anything to do with your feelings for Freda, would it?"

"I don't know what you mean."

"Oh come on Sim, I've seen the way your gaze follows her around the room. The way you wait to have your lunch until Freda's started hers, so you can sit opposite her. You two have been through a lot together."

Sim took a slurp from the beer, while waving his free hand around. "You're a fine one to talk. Waltzing around in your designer clothes and smooth accent. As far as I can tell, I'm not the only one who wants to get inside her kn…" Sim stopped himself abruptly.

"Hah, you see, I knew I was right!" beamed Bo.

Sim fiddled with the top of his beer bottle, trying to flip it like a coin. But his fingers felt fat and clumsy; the bottle top pinged on the floor.

The American was unfazed; he leant back again, took a big gulp from his beer and looked at his watch. "I'm going upstairs now. No hard feelings, huh?" He held out his hand for Sim to shake.

Before Sim reacted to Bo's offered hand, Chung entered the room wearing a mask and night-vision goggles.

"What the—?"

Chung signaled for silence. He indicated an enemy outside the house and crept out of the back door. Sim and Bo went to get their side arms to cover the front door. There was the noise of a brief struggle outside and then something heavy being dragged across the verandah at the front of the house. Chung opened the front door and pulled a body inside. Once the front door had been closed again, he took off his goggles and mask.

"Indian NIA, I think. We can't take any risks with him reporting back on our presence."

"You idiot! Now they have a dead agent they're bound to investigate what our aid mission is really about," hissed Bo, trying not to raise his voice.

"Relax, we can easily cover this up. We get the attaché to report an attack on our aid mission. You know, local gang tried to steal all our supplies, there was a fight etcetera, etc."

Bo was still annoyed but eventually agreed to this. The corpse would be dumped in the middle of the night by the attaché in a cluster of nearby trees. Sim stared at the body, the crimson stain over its heart where Chung had slipped the blade between ribs. It was the first time Sim had seen a combat victim up close. This person had not even been a true enemy, just somebody who might have compromised the mission. What had Freda said to him on Marinus? Whatever it takes? That was certainly Chung's philosophy too, but Sim was struggling to accept it.

Later, the men went upstairs. Sim forced himself not to watch which room Bo headed for.

The next morning, they all rose at first light, checked their equipment one last time, stowed it carefully in their respective canoes and got ready to set off on the mission. The corpse had disappeared as agreed. Freda and Sim stood next to their canoe in silence. Sim waited for Freda to get in first, but she appeared to have something on her mind so he gave up waiting. As he moved to enter the canoe, Freda did so at exactly the same time and they bumped heads. A quiet apology was exchanged and then they co-ordinated their embarkation.

"Rangers, ready to rock?" said Bo as he wriggled into his rowing seat.

Bo was at the front of the first canoe, with Chung behind him. The Americans had insisted on taking the patched-up canoe – they tested it for leaks and it seemed fine. The difference in height between the two Americans made their stroke lengths different. Because of this the lead canoe was a little wobbly, but they had plenty of power. Freda was sat at the front of the second canoe, with Sim bringing up the rear under strict instructions to crane his neck round occasionally to check on any river traffic behind them. The canoes were each fitted with small electric propellers that were powered by solar-panels built into the decking. There was plenty of sunlight available at this time of year, and the gentle addition of a few knots per hour helped tremendously on a long-range expedition like this.

The first couple of days were easy going and uneventful. The four canoeist quickly developed a routine that involved a couple of hours of paddling, a rest for drink and food, then two more hours of paddling and so on. At this point they were more interested in preserving rations than secrecy so would stop near settlements where Bo could wander into a village to buy victuals for the team. If it had not been for the thought of what lay ahead, this really would have been a very pleasant holiday.

The broad river glistened in the sunlight, the banks teemed with lush long grasses. White-headed ducks swam in and out of the reeds. Sim saw a dark brown hispid hare dart back into the undergrowth as the canoes approached. A naked child shouted when he saw the canoeists and nudged his friend. They waved and then dived into the river; emerging with huge grins on their faces. The canoes passed a herd of elephants bathing in the waters.

Elephants in the wild! If only my old fella could see me now, *thought Sim.*

As their journey entered the region of Arunachal Pradesh there was a perceptible change in the atmosphere. The wildlife was scarcer, there were fewer children playing and the river was noticeably more turbulent. Still, they continued to make good progress and seemed to be attracting little attention even when they stopped for sustenance. After a week of paddling blisters were starting to develop on everybody's hands and their back muscles were starting to groan under the continuous strain. As they got closer to the Chinese border, the blisters and tiredness were made worse by the weather clouding over, cutting the effectiveness of their propeller units. The pleasant river cruise had given way to stress and tension as they drew closer to enemy territory.

On the 28th of the month, they pulled into shore just a mile from the border. There were still a few hours of daylight left, but the next part of the journey would have to be done under cover of darkness. They rested and dozed lightly after feasting on the last of the Indian food they would be able to forage. Chung volunteered to keep guard while the others slept.

Sim and Freda were woken by the noise of a scuffle in their camp and the squeal of a high-pitched Indian voice. Grabbing for his gun, Sim leapt up and saw that Chung had caught hold of a young boy who was holding something in his hand. Chung was trying to place his hand over the boy's mouth but the youth was kicking wildly and managed to sink his teeth into Chung's hand. Chung reached for his knife and was about to plunge it into the boy when Freda intervened.

She grabbed the child from Chung and yelled. "What the hell do you think you're doing? He's just a boy." She opened his hand and showed Chung the food stolen from their rations. "He's hungry." Freda gave the child a few notes of local currency and sent him on his way.

"Christ, Chung. What a nutter!" said Sim.

Bo stepped into the middle of the group. "OK all, let's just calm down. It was dark, hard for Chung to tell what the kid was up to. We're all on edge this close to the border." He looked at the black expanse of the broad river, perhaps a kilometre across at this point. "We have to choose between the relative safety of staying near the bank using the cover of any trees and shrubs. There's more risk of people on the bank seeing us go past. Or do we choose the middle of the river? No natural cover except for the near pitch-black conditions. The river is more turbulent and less safe mid-stream."

"I vote middle of the river," said Freda. "We're experienced enough to cope with some choppy water, but if we're spotted it's game over."

"I agree," said Bo.

Chung just nodded and Sim shrugged. "I have a bad feeling about this."

Bo slapped Sim on the shoulder. "Come on, let's get to it."

They covered up the solar panels on the canoes, blacked up their faces and hands, added some camouflage netting to their outer clothes and then pushed out and paddled towards the centre of the river. It really was very, very dark – Freda was struggling to keep an eye on the outline of Chung's back in the first canoe even at a distance of just a few metres. After paddling for only ten minutes or so, their hearts sank when they saw the searchlight of a large boat flashing along the middle of the river, coming almost straight towards them.

"Quick," shouted Bo in a hoarse whisper as loud as he dared, "get in the log position." All four of them stopped paddling and leant forward pressing their chests and heads as close to the top of the canoe as possible. The camouflage netting on their backs and the colour scheme of the canoes helped with the subterfuge. Closer inspection in full daylight would have shown them up quite clearly, but in this darkness they had a chance. Having to stop paddling left them at the mercy of the river's current, which meant they were drifting downstream away from their goal, but they did not dare move as the boat came closer and closer.

The flashlight on board the boat swept across the river's surface 100 metres ahead of the craft but there was a lot of river to cover and the captain was not going slowly enough to do a thorough job. The canoeists relaxed as the light passed over their heads, but they were not yet out of danger. They still did not dare to start paddling and were drifting into the path of the oncoming patrol boat. The agents craned their necks, trying to judge how close this was going to be. Bo and Chung looked to be safe, but the boat was getting ever nearer to Freda and Sim's canoe. At the last moment Freda sat up and gave a few big pulls on her paddle, just getting out from under the boat's prow. She dropped back down into the log position and as the boat's stern passed by Sim could feel the spray from the engines' outlets on his back. There were no shouts or cries of recognition from on board the patrol boat – they had got away with it.

"Phew," said Freda, "that was far too close for comfort."

"I think I might need some clean underpants," said Sim.

They carried on paddling upstream and after half an hour reached the official border. They could tell from the lights and fencing on either bank that it was an actively guarded check-point. There were a couple of police boats tied up to a small jetty on the right-hand side of the river, but they were either resting between patrols or only brought into use when the alarm was raised. The canoeists praised their luck and kept grimly paddling on up the centre of the river. The water was becoming more turbulent and progress was hard work. But they knew they could not turn towards the calmer waters near the bank yet.

The border had started to disappear behind them in the gloom when the turbulent water became a thrashing, heaving monster underneath their canoes. It lashed out at them with its foaming white tentacles, stinging their faces and tipping their canoes left and right. One moment they were paddling hard just to keep still, the next moment the front of the canoe dipped alarmingly as they were plunged into an eddy. Freda and Sim had more experience of rapids and knew that the best option was to keep a steady rhythm and focus on balancing the canoe. Bo and Chung were struggling, with their uneven strokes and relative inexperience causing panic to set in. Freda tried to shout over helpful instructions, but the noise of the water drowned out her voice and she was too busy fighting the river herself to carry on yelling.

Freda and Sim kept paddling with all their strength. One of the blisters on Sim's right hand had burst and was turning into a bloody mess, while Freda's strokes seemed to be getting shorter and less frequent. After what seemed like an hour, the water turned calm and flat again as if some giant had taken hold of both edges of the river and pulled it smooth. They paddled on a little further to be sure they were out of the danger zone and then turned to look for Bo and Chung.

They waited and waited. With every passing minute a ball of lead grew in Sim's stomach; in all likelihood the other two had capsized and been swept away, perhaps drowned. They waited longer than they should have, not willing to let go of the faint hope that any second now the two Americans would re-appear out of the gloom with a smile and a wave.

Eventually Sim tapped Freda on the shoulder and said: "Come on, we should head for the bank. Find somewhere to hide before it starts getting light again."

They paddled slowly on and made their way over to the right-hand bank where there appeared to be a little more cover. Finding a small grove of juniper trees, they hauled the canoe out of the water and covered it up with some vegetation. A pale moon peeped out from behind dispersing clouds, casting a grey hue over the landscape. They stripped off their wet clothes but did not dare light a fire. The comrades huddled together in their sleeping bags, cold and exhausted.

CHAPTER 28

Tibet was invaded by Chinese troops in 1950; a year later China's sovereignty over the region was formalised. Sporadic rebellions were defeated by the Chinese People's Liberation Army. After the Lhasa uprising of 1959, the Dalai Lama fled to India. The position still retains some influence as the head of state for the Tibetan government in exile.

O.D. Training Manual Section 5c

The day before the British and American agents headed off to Assam, a Tibetan monk had walked into Kathmandu. Rabten had been Wangdue's student and was trying to fulfill the last wishes of his now-dead master. He was looking for a certain man, somebody his master had asked him to seek out should anything happen to him.

The sun shone white-hot against a pale blue sky and the temperature was creeping up towards 30 degrees centigrade. Rabten stopped for a drink at one of the rivers which flow through the Kathmandu valley, bringing cold, silt-laden grey water down from the Himalayas to this sub-tropical climate.

He was no longer wearing his monk's robe, but his shaved head might still mark him out as a Tibetan Buddhist. He wore a modern hooded top to hide this fact, but every so often a gust of wind blew it off his head. Several times he caught people staring at him as he quickly pulled it back over his bald pate. Rabten felt as out of place in this city as the ice-cold water from the mountains. He'd read that the Nepalese authorities had assisted in curbing anti-China protests from the Tibetan Diaspora, and so as Rabten passed through the outskirts of Kathmandu he felt like he was walking into a bear's cave.

The city was a vast sprawling mess, home to millions of people, much bigger than Rabten had realised. He had very little money left and had not eaten all day. As he passed a modest home, he noticed a local woman putting some scraps of food into a bowl outside her front door. As she closed the door a scrawny dog with no collar and some sort of skin disease trotted up to the bowl and started eating. Rabten's stomach rumbled and he thought about shooing the dog away but shook his head and moved on.

His master had suggested a bar called the True Tarpan where Rabten might be able to find the man he was looking for. The person in question was a Ghurka called Gopal Limbu. It was not much to go on; the name of a bar and the name of a man. There was no picture to identify him and not even an explanation of why this person would help. But his master had sacrificed himself for a cause he believed in, and Rabten would not dishonour his memory by failing in this mission.

Eventually the student made his way into the centre of the city. There was an open area called Basantapur Square in the corner of which stood an ancient wooden two-storey pagoda – the Kasthamandap. Just opposite, on the other side of Ganga Path, was a collection of other temples, some in ruins after the Earthquake of 2015. The square was full of tourists at this time of year which helped Rabten blend in. There were Chinese and Indian families, rubbing shoulders in this neutral ground between the two states that would not be possible anywhere else. There were Westerners too, some visiting to enjoy the culture of this ancient city and others using the capital as a stop-over before heading up into the mountains.

Rabten needed money and information and he was running out of daylight. He saw plenty of street entertainers - fire-eaters, jugglers, a snake charmer and a singer - dotted around the square, trying to persuade tourists to part with a few coins. Perhaps that might work? He put down his backpack, placed his tin cup a couple of meters in front of him and started doing some of the hardest yoga poses he knew. The first few he tried, such as the King Pigeon Pose or the Eagle Pose, were tricky to do well, but did not look all that impressive. Some American tourists walked past and barely glanced sideways at him. He changed tactic and tried some more ostentatious poses, such as the Standing Split, the Upward Facing Two-foot Staff Pose and the Peacock pose. People were stopping to watch now, even gasp, when Rabten's back bent at an un-natural angle or when he balanced on his hands. A few coins started to drop into his tin cup with a satisfying rattle.

Rabten was enjoying the attention – he had always practised his yoga in solitude at the monastery, or at best with a teacher and a few fellow students. He tried even more elaborate poses such as balancing upside down on one hand that would not have looked out of place in a circus. But the larger crowd now watching him had caught the attention of two policemen who were patrolling the square. Rabten's hood had flopped down during one of his poses so that his shaven head was clearly visible. He was just taking a breather between poses when he caught sight of the approaching policemen. He grabbed his bag and cup and dashed off in the opposite direction, weaving between the pedestrians who were strolling around the square. The policemen gave chase. Rabten turned left and right at random down alleys he barely noticed. Everybody he raced past turned to stare at him. How could a city this big feel claustrophobic?

His heart was strong but he was feeling light-headed from the lack of food. The crowds were thinning out, making it easier for the policemen to see him. But they were not as young as Rabten and their incentive to capture him was less than his survival instinct. Eventually after a few streets their half-hearted attempt to chase him was over.

Rabten came to a stop in a secluded spot and smiled as he saw the large pile of coins in his metal cup. He wanted to spend them on food, and anyway wasn't sure he had enough for accommodation. Up on the mountains it wouldn't be sunset for another hour but down here the temperature was dropping quickly and the light was beginning to fade. He still had to figure out where was the *True Tarpan*. For some reason the name rang a bell even though he had never been to this city before. He walked a little further out of the centre, looking for somewhere not frequented by tourists that might sell cheap food. Each time he spotted an inn his pace quickened until he saw that the name above the entrance was not the one he needed.

By now it was close to ten o' clock at night and his stomach was beginning to cramp with hunger. He had drifted into a part of the city that did not seem to have any places to eat, at least not ones that stayed open late and that he could afford. But as he turned the corner into a main thoroughfare known as Tribhuvan University Road, some men passed him, talking about heading for a drink at the horse trough. That's it! He remembered what a *Tarpan* was – a Mongolian wild horse.

He followed the men across the road and there at last was a picture of a prancing pony outside a large building. The men went in. He ran to the entrance of the bar, brushed himself down in an attempt to improve his appearance and pushed open the doors.

Inside, the *True Tarpan* was a busy, noisy establishment. It was surprisingly large on the inside, stretching a full 30 metres right to the back and at least 15 metres wide. The bar itself, situated in the middle of the room, was a circular counter with several bartenders. They were each busily pouring drinks, tapping out bills on the till and taking money, dodging past each other without looking, in a graceful choreography that involved no rehearsal but a seemingly telepathic level of understanding. Off to the right, a little further back, beyond the bar there was a small raised dais on which a quartet of musicians was playing some strange instruments. The resulting tune was not unpleasant though a little alien to the monk's ears compared with the religious chanting that made up the usual sounds of his monastery.

Rabten went up to the bar to order a drink while he tried to figure out how to find this Gopal Limbu without bringing attention to himself. He asked for *Raksi*: a strong alcoholic drink made from rice that he had had before and remembered was a Nepalese speciality.

Somebody tapped him on the shoulder and Rabten turned to see a large local man staring at him. Relieved that it was not a policeman, he nodded and turned back to his drink but the local grabbed his shoulder painfully and twisted him round to face the man. "My friend doesn't like you."

"I'm sorry," said Rabten in an awkward accent that would no doubt mark him out as a foreigner. He could speak Nepali but not like a native. He did not want any trouble and tried to avoid making eye contact with the hairy brute in front of him.

"I don't like you either," continued the aggressor, jabbing the monk in the shoulder, determined to pick a fight. When Rabten failed to react to this provocation too, the local took a swing at him anyway. He may have been a bit taller and much broader than the monk, but attacking a White Crane martial art expert, especially after a few too many drinks, was a big mistake. The ruthlessness, or *Chan*, that is taught as part of the martial art kicked in and so instead of simply dodging the clumsy punch, Rabten caught the man's arm and punched his elbow so hard it popped right out of its socket. There was a scream of pain and he fell to the floor clutching his dislocated joint. His friend tried to smash a bottle on the monk's head. Too obvious, too slow. Rabten side-stepped the blow and brought his knee up rapidly into the second attacker's stomach, making him double up, gasping for air. A sharp blow to the back of the head left him dazed, sprawling on top of his friend.

The monk stepped back, looking round and wondering if another attacker would appear, but the rest of the bar crowd just backed away from the two injured men. For a moment there was silence and then the chatter and clatter of bar life resumed as if nothing had happened. Rabten bowed to the bartender and apologized for the fight. He took his drink and hastily retreated towards the back of the saloon where it was darker and less crowded. He sat down at a table, put his backpack down next to him and started to sip his Raksi. A couple of tables away an older man sat on his own, nursing a large glass of beer. He looked up at Rabten, stared him straight in the eye and asked him where had learnt to fight the White Crane method.

"I don't know what you mean," he mumbled.

"It's okay, I'm not going to tell anyone where you come from." The man got up and brought his drink over to Rabten's table. "Besides, I promised my friend Wangdue I would look out for somebody like you if anything ever happened to him."

The monk was confused. *Why was this man looking out for me? How did he know that something had happened to Wangdue?* Eventually, he held out his hand. "Gopal Limbu, I need your help."

The Ghurka explained that he had known Wangdue for a long time. He knew that oppression had been getting worse in Tibet for many years and that even Nepal was becoming a hostile country towards the monks. He had wanted to offer his friend shelter and protection but Wangdue would not abandon his native country. Instead he had asked that the Ghurka should look out for a student of his who would one day come looking for him in their hour of greatest need.

"I read about some monks who had been executed a few weeks ago for acts of terrorism, so I figured Wangdue must've been involved. I'm very sad to hear that, but not entirely surprised. That old fool never could learn to sit back and do nothing, if there was some wrong to be righted." Gopal sighed and took a big swig from his beer.

"How do you know my master?"

"We used to be in the British army together. Did he ever tell you he was a soldier before he became a monk? He wouldn't listen to my warnings about the Chinese government. You know once, when we were stuck in the desert, he tried to lift a two-ton truck onto his back so I could fit a spare tyre. Wouldn't wait for the repair team. Strong as an ox, stubborn as an ass."

Rabten smiled at the description. "Our Grand Master called him a shield of oak. Defender of the weak, incapable of flexibility."

"I guess now that you're here, I'm going to have to do something stupid too, aren't I? I made a promise to my friend and I'm not going to break that now."

Rabten explained about the silver pipelines that were running through Tibet and the processing plant that the monks had spied on with fatal consequences. He also talked about the visions of Jamyang.

"*Jhaarpaat*! Don't talk to me about visions. In my experience there are only two types of visions. One happens after taking drugs and the second is when a soldier gets delusions of grandeur on a battlefield. Neither ends well. Stick to horoscopes Rabten, you'll live longer."

"Wangdue is convinced, was convinced, that the Chinese are trying to hide some massive secret up in the Himalayas. Moving huge quantities of water across the country somehow. But where they're getting the water from, and how, is a mystery. It can't be legal."

"If they're stealing water from the Indians, they're not going to be able to keep it a secret for long. And when that happens, the shit is really going to hit the dog bowl. Not sure what we can do about it, but we have to try for Wangdue's sake. We need to get up into the mountains and see what's really going on. I've some companions who are no friends of the Chinese; they'll come along to help."

"Great," replied Wangdue, barely listening as he watched a waitress carrying a large tray of food across the room. He closed his eyes as the smell of spiced lentil soup wafted towards him.

"But first, let's get you some decent clothes and a warm meal – you might fight like a White Crane but you are as skinny as one too," said Gopal.

Later that night, with his belly full after the first decent meal for days, Rabten soaked in a hot bath while Gopal made a few phone calls to his friends. The monk closed his eyes and let his mind wander back to memories of his teacher. *I did it, Master, help is on its way.*

CHAPTER 29

A taser uses electric current to disrupt voluntary control of muscles, causing incapacitation. While it is a highly effective non-lethal tool for subduing a target, it can only be used in specific circumstances. The maximum range is around ten metres and it only has a one-shot cartridge. The electrodes fired can penetrate thick clothing but not body armour.

O.D. Training Manual Section 8c

Sim woke up cold and in pain. His neck and back muscles were in spasm, after the exertions of the previous night's canoeing. Falling asleep still slightly damp and on hard ground had not helped. He was spooning with Freda – not for the first time – but sex was the last thing on his mind. The pair of them were stuck in China. Half of the team had been lost, perhaps drowned, and that included the one who spoke Mandarin. Was there any point in carrying on? Perhaps they should just give up now and sneak back across the border to explain what had gone wrong.

Freda woke up, stretched and started rummaging about in the kit bag for some rations. She was humming a tune to herself as if this was still just a camping trip. Sim sat up, shivered, and went for a pee. Freda looked up as he came back.

"While you've been attending to your bladder, I've been thinking about what to do next," said Freda.

"I thought you were trying to sing an annoying tune," said Sim.

Both of them fell silent while they ate a cold, meagre breakfast.

Sim looked up from his food and saw Freda was already looking at him.

"Sorry," they muttered simultaneously.

"I think we have to go back to the border—"

"We can't go back now, what about the mission? What about Bo and Chung?!" said Sim.

"If you'll let me finish, I was going to say that we should go back to the border to see if Bo and Chung are being held prisoner there. Look, we know they're both good swimmers. If their canoe capsized last night they would've had a decent chance of making it ashore. But the current would've taken them back towards the border, and the odds are that one of the guards would've spotted them. If that's true, then they're probably being held in a police station somewhere not too far from here."

"What about the mission? Didn't you once tell me that was all that counts?"

"Sometimes the needs of the few outweigh the needs of the many, as a wise Captain once said. Besides, we're not likely to get far on this mission without Chung. I cannot see us paddling up the whole length of the bloody Brahmaputra... and I don't know the Mandarin for 'Please can we hire your boat?'"

Before attempting a rescue the agents assessed what equipment they had left. In the canoe they had rations for two to three weeks at a push, a small gas cooker, some rope, torches, wire cutters, several charges of explosive and timers, and a thumper. On their person they each had a 9mm automatic pistol (with four clips of ammo), a couple of flares and a large knife. Freda also had a taser in one of her jacket pockets.

"What about the sat phone?" Sim asked.

Freda looked down the river. "That was with Bo in the other canoe. Hopefully it's now at the bottom of the river. If they found that sort of equipment on him there'll be hell to pay."

Leaving most of the rations and the canoes where they were, the rest of the kit was packed into bulging jacket and trouser pockets. Sim and Freda set off for the border, moving through the vegetation along the river bank.

◆

Bo was floating through the air in a see-through bubble. He looked down at the ground far below him – his view was distorted by the prism effect of his sphere. Then he realised that the bubble was made out of water and that he couldn't breathe. He thrashed and kicked, bursting the bubble. He sucked in the air, desperate for a breath, and promptly dropped ten metres down onto the ground. There was a sickening thud as one of his ankles crumpled on landing and then he woke up. He was manacled to a chair, stripped down to his pants. His head hurt and his left ankle was sending shooting pains up his leg. He looked around the room, struggling to focus, and saw Chung sitting in a chair like his a couple of metres away. There was a single door out of the room, which was green and looked very solid except for a small section at eye level that could be slid back to look into the room. There were no windows. A single light bulb hung from the ceiling. There was an empty chair in one corner near the door and a bucket that smelled of stale urine.

"Hey Chung," he whispered. He tried again, a bit louder this time. Chung stirred.

"Oh, hey Bo, I must've dozed off. Been waiting for you to wake for the past few hours. Quite a bang on the head you took when the guards captured us. You were out cold."

"Do you know where we're being held? What happened to Freda and Sim?"

"No idea about the Brits. I think we're in a police station on the border."

The observation panel in the door slid back and a pair of eyes stared at the two CIA agents, who fell silent. The eyes continued to stare, far longer than was necessary given how little there was to look at. The door was unlocked and a squat, over-fed Chinese man strode into the room, with an armed policeman behind him. The plump man was dressed in a suit and tie and he carried a pair of thin reading glasses on a piece of cord around his neck.

He shouted at Bo in heavily accented English. "You come with me, now, and tell everything."

Half an hour later, Bo was dragged back into the room by two guards and hand-cuffed to the chair once again. His face was bruised and his bottom lip was split and bleeding. His legs had welt marks across his shins where a cane had been used to beat him. His body glistened with sweat and his injured ankle had started to resemble an aubergine, swollen and purple.

"What happened?" said Chung. "What did you tell them?"

"Nothing," replied Bo, shouting the word at an unseen guard outside. He sucked at his lip and spat blood at the door.

"That's good," said Chung. "Not that we have much to tell them if truth be told, right? Just a hunch here, a possibility there. I mean, a river cruise up the Brahmaputra, it's like looking for a needle in a haystack." He paused to see if Bo would reply, then carried on. "Diane didn't let you in on any secrets, did she? You know, for your eyes only. Did she?"

"Hmm, what?" Bo was feeling groggy again from his beating. Chung leant forward, listening for his partner's reply. "No, nothing," said Bo before slipping back into unconsciousness.

♦

Freda and Sim had made their way towards the border and found what appeared to be the most likely holding facility. It was a chunky, low building, with little obvious security on the outside, except for a lack of windows and a couple of police officers stationed outside the main entrance. The police station was on the main road that ran along this side of the river, together with a few basic establishments: a restaurant, a grocer's, a butcher's and a bakery. There were a few very simple houses scattered around too. Most of the road traffic was either bicycle or cart being pulled by a donkey or ox. Beyond this tiny conurbation there was a small airfield off to the left. Off to the right, a mile or so away, a much more impressive set of buildings, searchlights and very tall fencing as far as the eye could see marked the official border between China and India. But it seemed that not much crossed the border these days. The area was pretty quiet even in the middle of the morning.

"So, how are we going to do this?" asked Sim.

"I don't think we can afford to wait until night-fall. For all we know they're being tortured in there. Or they might be taken away at any moment, flown to Beijing or something. We need a distraction to get inside, and then once we're in, just hope that the building doesn't have too many places to search for prisoners." She explained the outline of a rudimentary plan to Sim, using a stick to draw a simple map in the dirt. It brought back memories of Territorial Army weekend exercises. He wondered what Rhys would make of all this if he could see him now.

"Right boss," he said, snapping back to the present day.

The pair of them sneaked around to the back of one of the shops opposite the police station. Freda took her knife and pierced the top of the cooking stove she had brought, letting out a tiny jet of gas from within the canister. She placed it as close as she dared to the entrance to the shop and then retreated a few metres.

She pulled out one of the flares, struck it and as it burned bright orange in the alleyway, she threw it at the gas canister.

Phakoom! The canister exploded instantly and a great ball of flame leapt up, setting light to an awning at the front of the shop. There were gasps and shrieks from passers-by and people who were in the shop. Freda and Sim sneaked around the back of the shop and re-appeared on the far side of the building from the fire, watching the entrance to the police station. The two guards outside the station immediately rushed over to help put out the fire giving the agents their chance to dash into the police building.

Inside the entrance there was a reception desk. The policeman who usually sat behind it had got up to see what was going on outside. Freda burst in catching him off guard. The look of surprise on his face was nothing compared with the grimace when 50,000 volts from Freda's taser coursed through his body. He fell to the ground, twitching uncontrollably. The agents raced past and dashed down the only obvious corridor they could see. There was another policeman, also surprised to see some Westerners running around the station. Freda's taser had not recharged, so Sim pointed his gun in the face of the shocked policeman and used basic sign language to tell him to keep quiet and lie down. He was not armed so they just left him there. An alarm started wailing inside the station. They were running out of time. They ran on again and turned a corner, reaching what they judged must be the back of the station – the obvious place for any prison cell.

Bo awoke when the alarm rang out. A guard was coming into the room and approaching Chung. He proceeded to unfasten Chung's handcuffs and said something to him in Chinese. Chung arose from his chair, patted the guard on his back and then pulled a knife from some unseen pocket. He twisted the guard's head to one side and drew the blade across his throat. The body crumpled to the floor, bubbles of blood escaping from the throat of the dying victim. Chung turned to Bo.

"I don't understand," Bo said. "Why did he release you?" His addled brain was trying to piece together hints and clues that might have been easier if he did not have a splitting headache. "Come to think of it, why didn't they ever interrogate you?" No reply. "Was it even the water that made our canoe capsize last night?"

Chung grinned at Bo. "In the words of one of your Presidents, I cannot tell a lie. It was me." And with that he bent over the helpless spy and slipped the blade between his ribs. Bo's mind flooded with fire. He tried to hold the gaze of his assassin as long as he could, wishing he could fight back with just his eyes like the Gorgon of legend. But there was no fight left in him and slowly his eyes closed.

Freda burst open the cell door and rushed in with Sim close behind. Chung managed to flick away his knife towards the dead guard before they noticed and turned to the pair of would-be rescuers.

"Freda! Sim!" he said. "Thank goodness you got here just in time. This guard attacked Bo, but I managed to over-power him. I think Bo's hurt real bad. See what you can do for him while I keep an eye out for more guards." And with that he slipped outside into the corridor.

Freda quickly glanced at the guard – he wasn't going anywhere – and then moved on to Bo whose head was lolling on his chest. Blood was seeping out of a deep wound on his left-hand side and his laboured breathing was fast and shallow. Freda knelt down in front of him and desperately looked for something to staunch the loss of blood. There was nothing to hand so she tore a strip off the bottom of her cotton t-shirt and pressed it against the wound.

Bo winced as she applied the pressure. He opened his eyes, looked at Freda in desperation and whispered, "Chung."

"Don't worry, he's safe. Come on, we need to get you out of here." Freda started trying to work out how to get him out of his manacles.

Bo shook his head and looked angrily at Freda, the wild exasperation that comes when your partner in a game of charades keeps guessing *Star Wars* when you are clearly miming *Star Trek*.

"Chung. Is. One. Of *them*," he said, gulping for air. He fell back with the exertion. He closed his eyes for one last time as his heart slowed into stillness. Freda froze.

Sim had heard what Bo said and his mind was racing. Chung was a traitor? What was he doing outside in the corridor? Betraying them? His boss was not moving; he had to take control for once. He pulled at Freda's shoulder.

"Come on, we have to leave right away. The only thing we can do for Bo now is to avenge him."

After a couple of interminable seconds, Freda's brain kicked into gear. She grabbed the Saint Christopher that Bo wore around his neck and the pair dashed outside into the corridor with Sim leading the way. A bullet thudded into the wall just beyond him as a policeman at the other end of the corridor shot wildly. Sim rolled forward, aiming his gun in one motion and shot the policeman in the leg. The agents carried on sprinting for the only exit, ignoring the Chinese man who had dropped his gun and was now writhing in agony on the floor. Luckily for the British pair, the confusion of the explosion outside the station, their attack on the way in and Chung's rapid exit had led to mayhem. There were three policeman outside the station attending to the fire, three were incapacitated (one taser, one bullet and one karate punch from Chung) and the rest were all doing different things at once. One was yelling down the phone, another was trying to move people away from the entrance of the station and a third had started donning some riot gear by the front desk.

Freda and Sim ran out into the street, not even attempting to stay hidden. They just caught sight of Chung a few hundred metres ahead of them as he turned off the main street, heading towards the airfield.

"C'mon," said Freda, looking back at Sim. "We must get to him before he commandeers a plane and gets away." They ran through the street, dodging and weaving through innocent bystanders who were starting to throng towards the commotion near the police station. Sim was pulling ahead of Freda. He glanced back towards her a couple of times and could see she was limping on one ankle, then put his head down as he broke into a full sprint, just keeping Chung in sight.

As Sim got closer to the airfield, he tried to use whatever cover he could: a shed or hut here, some trees there, a parked vehicle. Freda caught up. They got as close as they dared to the area of the landing field where the planes were parked. This was no high-security area, the runway was not much more than a flat strip of closely mowed grass and the perimeter fence was designed to keep out cattle, not secret agents.

Most of the small aircraft had tarpaulin covers over the cockpit and engines, with chocks under the wheels. No chance of a fast getaway in one of those. But there was one slightly larger plane which was unencumbered. The paintwork was flecked with dirt and the propeller casings were tinged with rust. It was a twin-engined Harbin Y-12 aeroplane, with a stubby nose and high-mounted wings above a stocky, dirty-white fuselage. Freda could make out somebody in the cockpit starting up the engines. It *had* to be Chung.

"We've got to get on board somehow," she said to Sim over the whine of the starboard engine as it sparked into life. They sneaked around at some distance until they were directly behind the plane's tail and then made a dash for it. There was a hatchway into the cargo hold at the rear of the plane. Freda tried the handle - it wasn't locked. The port engine roared into life. The noise was deafening. Sim looked at Freda as if she were crazy, watching her clamber into the cargo hold. The plane started to move off. Sim gave an almost imperceptible shrug of the shoulders and hauled himself in too, pulling closed the hatch behind him. A minute later the plane took off, with Chung at the controls and Freda and Sim curled up in a very small cargo hold.

"I don't suppose there's in-flight service on offer is there?" asked Sim, trying to get his breath back.

CHAPTER 30

A glacier is a persistent body of dense ice that is constantly moving under its own weight. Most of the Earth's glacial ice is contained within vast polar sheets but glaciers are also found in mountain ranges. Glacial ice is the largest reservoir of freshwater on the planet. Climate change has caused some glaciers to retreat as their melting season starts to outweigh the accumulation period each year.

O.D. Training Manual Section 2b

The cargo hold was pitch black and very cold. No matter how much he wriggled, Sim always seemed to end up with one of Freda's knees or elbows in the small of his back. His muscles were aching, stuck in a foetal position and unable to stretch out, and he had not eaten for several hours now. He was about to make some quip about their plight when he realised that he could hear Freda sniffing and feel her shoulders shaking. He tried to reach out and hold her hand in the darkness. It was the first sign of weakness he had ever noticed from his boss.

"Hey Freda, what is it?"

"I can't stop thinking about Bo. No one deserves to die that young. Captured in a foreign land, at the hands of a traitor... God, it's just horrible."

"But there's nothing you could've done about it. We didn't abandon him, we went back, risking our own lives to try to get him out. None of us even suspected Chung. There was no way of knowing."

"They teach you a lot of things in Overseas Division, but dealing with death... No doubt I'll get some bloody offer of counselling when we get back. If we get back. I have a bad feeling about this."

"Hey, that's my line," said Sim. The plane lurched downwards and banked hard to the left. "Seems like we might be coming in to land. I wish Chung was a better pilot, I'm not looking forward to this touchdown."

As the plane started to slow and glide downwards, the flight got bumpy in more ways than one. With no seat belts, no warning about the next sudden movement in the plane and no space to stay apart they kept accidentally kicking or elbowing each other. Whether the turbulence was due to Chung's incompetence or bad weather, the two British agents could not tell from inside their cramped cocoon. After a few minutes more, the rear wheels banged down hard onto the tarmac of a runway, sending an uncomfortable jolt right up through Sim's spine. The plane taxied along the landing strip for what seemed like ages and then eventually came to a halt and the engines were cut.

With no visual clues to go on, Sim was trying to estimate some basic parameters to ascertain where they might have landed. Duration of flight he knew from the cheap illuminated watch he wore. Approximate airspeed of an old propeller plane like this he could estimate give or take 15%, so that gave him distance from the take-off point. Six hours at around 250 kilometres an hour makes 1500 klicks. The descent had been quite brief, so presumably they had landed at altitude – certainly the temperature had not improved much since landing, suggesting that outside was very cold. And the length of the runway seemed pretty big given the length of time spent taxiing so it was not a small field in the middle of nowhere. He pictured a map of Asia in his mind: there were a lot of places in a radius of 1500 kilometres from where they took off. Beijing was probably out of reach, but there were plenty of other Chinese cities it could be. Not many at altitude, though. Unless they had gone to Mongolia? Ulan Bator was a capital at quite high altitude, he seemed to remember.

"We'd better wait a while before we sneak out of here," said Freda. "There's still probably a couple of hours of daylight left. And there's bound to be ground crew sniffing around the plane to refuel it or something." Sim was desperate to get out and stretch his aching limbs, but he knew she was right. Then he had another thought.

"But if this is a busy airport how will we pick up Chung's trail? If we give him a two-hour lead we may never see the fella again."

"Damn, you're right. We're gonna have to risk it." They listened carefully to check if they could hear any movement immediately outside the plane. There was nothing except the howl of a strong wind, pulling and tugging at the plane's wings and tail. Sim opened the door to the cargo hold a little and peeked through the gap. A rush of cold air forced its way in. No sign of people but plenty of snow on the ground; after several hours stuck in the pitch black of the hold it was dazzling. He opened up the door some more. As it stopped supporting his back, gravity took over and his limbs were too stiff to react. He tumbled out, landing in a heap onto the snowy tarmac.

Freda stuck her head out of the entrance. "Oh bravo, Mr Bean, nobody will've noticed that."

Fortunately the airfield seemed quite deserted. Sim's deductions had been right on all accounts except for one thing – the long runway was not a sign of it being busy and large, but instead it was remote and spread out. They were very high up with a range of imposing mountain peaks stretching all along one side of their view, and it was bitterly cold even at this time of year. In the other direction, the runway stretched out for some way along rough uneven ground before disappearing over the brow of a ridge to some unseen point in the distance. There was no sign of natural life up here, neither flora nor fauna.

Sim started shivering almost straight away. He rubbed his arms and stamped up and down. The thought of all their spare clothing residing in the bottom of a canoe at the side of a river, some 1500 kilometres away now, was maddening. They would have to get inside a building soon or die of exposure.

There was a small hangar nearby but no signs of any other structures or settlements in the distance. Surely Chung would not have flown to such a desolate spot if there was not something else here? They approached the side-door to the hangar with guns drawn, crouching low using some oil drums for cover and listened hard for signs of anybody inside. Nothing. They tried the door, which was not locked, and crept into the gloomy interior.

The hangar was not actually dark inside, but having gone from pitch black to bright snow and then to a grey interior, their eyes were struggling to adapt. Sim panicked for a moment as he peered in, unable to tell if he was already being scrutinised by somebody better adapted to the light conditions. He held his breath, waiting for the shout or crack of a gun that would seal his fate, but there was none. His eyes relaxed and he could make out what was inside.

There was a plane similar to the one Chung had flown up here. It was parked to one side, leaving enough room for the other plane to be brought in out of the snow. Towards the back of the building there was a large tank of fuel and a small tractor with a plough attached to help clear the runway and a hook to tow the planes in and out of the hangar. There also seemed to be a small workshop with a range of tools next to the tractor. In the far left corner there was a room walled off from the rest of the hangar. There were lights on in there and the faint sound of music drifting out.

Freda signaled for them to approach. She crept up to the window that looked out from this room to the rest of the hangar and peeked through. There was a man sitting at a desk with his back to the window, filling out some paperwork. In front of him on the desk was a powerful radio communication set, presumably used to talk to incoming pilots, but right now tuned into a music station. The man was tapping his pen on the desk as if he were playing the drums. He did not hear the door click open, nor the pad of Sim's soft steps as he sneaked up behind him. There was a thud as Sim brought the butt of his gun down hard on the skull of the man, who fell to the floor unconscious. Freda quickly tied him up and gagged him.

"Shouldn't we try to bring him round and question him?" asked Sim.

"Not much point unless you have a babel fish handy."

Sim's eyebrows converged and then relaxed. "Oh, yeah, good point."

They looked around the room and in a cupboard found warm outer garments. As they were putting these on and luxuriating in the return of some warmth to their limbs, they heard a noise from the far side of the hangar. Looking out from their inner room, they saw some men in cold-weather gear climbing out of a trapdoor in the floor of the hangar. The men's peripheral vision was impeded by their goggles and the large hoods on their jackets so they failed to see Freda and Sim peeking out at them. One of them proceeded towards the tractor while the other two went to open the hangar doors. The agents could probably sneak past them down the tunnel, but then the workers would almost certainly find their colleague tied up and raise the alarm. So, more people to subdue and tie up; it was the safest option.

The taser accounted for the tractor driver before he had even moved the vehicle. The pair of agents moved around opposite sides of the hangar until they were close to the other airfield crew. They jumped out and pointed their guns at the unarmed workers. One of them surrendered immediately but the other, nearest Sim, threw his wrench at the agent forcing Sim to drop to the ground, allowing the escapee to duck behind the hangar door he had been opening. Sim's gun retorted, but the bullet bit into the edge of the door, sending a harmless shower of splinters to the floor. Freda ran outside and saw the crew man sprinting towards an intercom system on the outside wall of the hangar. She raised her pistol, aimed and pulled the trigger. The barrel jammed. The workman had almost reached the panel now. Freda glanced around and saw one of the lids of the oil barrels was loose. She picked it up and using it as a frisbee, hurled it towards the Chinese man. The discus clattered into his knees and sent him sprawling, allowing Freda to catch him up and pin him to the floor before the alarm could be raised.

The tractor driver and two crewmen joined their colleague in the radio room, bound and gagged. Sim searched them and found security swipe cards in their pockets He also took the goggles and gloves from them.

Freda and Sim followed the steps down through the trapdoor and along a well-lit tunnel that was about three metres tall and the same distance across. It curved round to the left and then went on for at least 200 metres, alarmingly straight. There was a security camera covering the length of tunnel. At least they vaguely looked like the ground crew from a distance, wearing the borrowed clothing and with goggles to hide their faces.

The agents walked on as calmly as possible, fighting the urge to break into a run. That would make it obvious something was amiss. But what if somebody appeared at the far end of the tunnel? The tunnel gradually turned up towards the end; they were out of sight of the camera at last. But instead of leading to another building the tunnel just ended back out on the mountainside. It was starting to get dark, but there was no missing the enormous industrial plant a few hundred metres ahead and to the right of them, lit-up like a tourist attraction in the snow.

They had not been able to see this from outside the hangar because of the ridgeline blocking the view of the end of the runway. There was a set of large silver pipelines leading from the plant away to their left and disappearing off into the distance, following the easiest path eastwards. The industrial complex looked like a cross between a power plant and a chemical refinery. There were plumes of smoke billowing out of a broad, tall chimney stack as well as hundreds of metres of pipework clinging to the outside of the building like mercurial ivy. Beyond the complex the horizon was dominated by mountain peaks, but there was a gap in the line. In between two massive spurs of rock there was a glacier. It looked as if a dam had burst and the water had frozen while spilling through the breech. Freda and Sim could see some activity at the foot of the glacier, but they could not quite make out what was happening at this distance, particularly in the gathering gloom.

They crawled a little closer, peering over the ridge. A group of workers seemed to be spraying something at the foot of the glacier, like the high-powered jets that are used to mine China clay in Cornwall. Whatever they were using was considerably hotter than the ice because vast clouds of steam were rising from the face of the glacier.

"This must be it, Sim. This must be what the Chinese have gone to all these lengths to hide from the rest of the world."

"But what is it?"

"I don't know yet. Maybe it's not water-related after all. Chemical weapons perhaps?" She pulled out a small telescope from a pocket and peered down it.

"What can you see?" asked Sim.

"It looks as though the slush they are creating is collecting at the bottom of the working area into some sort of drainage system."

Sim rubbed his chin. "Are they clearing a tunnel? Fashioning some sort of base hidden in the middle of the glacier?"

Freda shook her head. "Seems too indiscriminate for that. Hmm... maybe the Chinese are trying to steal the Himalayas."

"What you haverin' about? How can you steal an entire mountain range? And steal it from who?"

"Whom, Sim, not who. Look, I don't mean the whole mountain range and I'm just guessing, but what if you had a large power plant at one end of a glacier and melted the ice, spraying it with warm water and then piping it away to help irrigate your land? At the other end of the glacier the ice would start retreating, leaving less to melt and flow down the far side of the mountain towards oh, let's say, India."

Sim rolled over onto his back. "Crap, no wonder they don't want anybody to find out about it. That really is going to lead to war if that's right. There must be trillions of litres of water locked in that glacier."

Freda squashed her telescope back into itself and pocketed the instrument. "And who knows if this is the only plant? There are several other glaciers on this plateau where they could be doing the very same thing right now. If the Indian rivers start drying up there's going to be bloody millions dead."

"That would certainly make the Indians desperate enough to reach for the nukes. Crap. What're we going to do?"

"Come on, let's try to sneak into the base and confirm what's happening. See if there's any info on other bases. But first I think we'd better deploy the thumper. If anything happens to us, I need to know that this secret won't stay hidden."

"Umm, Freda... suppose for a minute that I didn't get round to reading the chapter of the training manual that deals with thumpers. Can you remind me what one is?"

"Hah, OK. It's a bit noisy so we'll have to move away from the base first." Freda eventually found a slight depression in the rock a few hundred metres from the tunnel and the complex. "Look, first you deploy the tripod feet and secure them into place. Then you activate the drill. After it has reached a certain depth, the drill is retracted and then a high-powered explosive is detonated at the bottom of the shaft, creating a chamber deep underground. Then the thumper uses that chamber to send a faint but regular pulse through the ground. The geological monitoring stations will pick up the signal and should be able to pin-point it fairly quickly. E.T. phone home, if you like."

Sim looked at her without reacting.

"Not another classic you haven't seen! Didn't you waste any of your childhood in front of a TV?! Sheesh, what do they teach kids these days..." Freda activated the thumper and the drill sprang into motion. The first few minutes were incredibly noisy but the wind was carrying the sound of the drill away from the industrial complex. There was a loud crack from the rock that made them jump and then the noise from the drill abated as it penetrated deeper into the ground.

"OK, time we tried to sneak in and see if my hunch is right."

"Yes, boss."

CHAPTER 31

Avalanches are deadly. They cannot be out-run. If you are caught in one, try using a swimming motion to stay near the surface of the snow and jettison heavy gear if you can. As the snow begins to solidify around you, your priority is to maintain an air pocket in front of your face. Most victims of avalanches suffocate before rescuers can dig them out.

O.D. Training Manual Section 7d

A week earlier, Kathmandu.

A beaten-up Toyota Hi-Lux inched its way out of Kathmandu, trying to avoid the mopeds that were weaving in and out of the potholes. The truck contained four men, a small arsenal of rifles and pistols and in the flat bed under a tarpaulin, a heap of climbing and camping gear. Gopal had persuaded two former comrades to join him and Rabten on their quest to the mountains of Tibet.

"What's the plan?" asked Rabten from the back row of seats.

Gopal glanced in the rear view mirror at the monk. "We head to Simikot, and then find a way across the border to Mount Kailash."

"Why there?"

"It's the source of four of the biggest rivers in the continent, and the Chinese sealed off the area to tourists a few years ago. If water is what lies behind all this, it can't be a coincidence."

"How long will it take to get there?" said Rabten.

"The drive to Simikot should be pretty straightforward, provided we avoid any checkpoints on the road. Then it gets interesting. A week-long trek across the border to the mountain, avoiding all the obvious passes that will be guarded."

"Will we actually have to climb the mountain?"

Gopal held up his hand. "Don't worry, Lach and Thaman are very experienced, they'll help you."

"That's not what I meant. Kailash is *rinpoche*, precious. It's sacred to Buddhists. Walking around the base of the mountain is the path to righteousness, but setting foot on the mountain itself is sinful. It's said that death comes to those who break the taboo." Rabten looked across at Lach, who was sitting on the back seat with him.

"Well you can believe what you want to believe. First, let's get to the area and see what we find. We may not have to climb the mountain itself," replied Gopal.

Thaman leaned out of the front passenger's window and banged on the roof of the truck. "Jam, jam!"

The cyclist in front, barely visible under a heap of vegetable sacks ignored the exhortations and continued to weave slowly between stray dogs and water-filled pot holes.

It's going to be a long drive to Simikot, thought Rabten.

The monk was jolted awake sometime later as the truck left the road and bounced along a deeply rutted dirt track. The sun was low in the sky ahead of them. "Why are we leaving the road?"

"There's a security check up ahead. Not sure they'll believe we're on a hunting trip and your lack of ID papers will be awkward."

"I'm sorry," said Rabten, "I shouldn't have dragged you into this."

Lach leaned across and softly punched the monk on the shoulder. "Don't worry, we were getting bored back home. Time we got some blood coursing through our veins again. Just like '19, hey Tham?"

Thaman turned round and grinned. "You mean the time I saved your life or the time you got shot in the backside?"

"I took one for the team, and you're wrong. I saved your life. Remember, when that—"

"Quiet!" rasped Gopal. He had slowed the truck down to a crawl. The dirt track had turned back close to the road and although there was a line of bushy fig trees between them and the road block, noise could still give them away. Gopal killed the engine and told the others to get out and start pushing.

It had been raining recently and the mud on the track made it difficult for the pushers to get any grip. They slowly advanced along the path until they were roughly level with the roadblock. The track dipped sharply down at this point and the truck started speeding up, sliding over the mud. Rabten lost his balance as the vehicle ran away from him and fell flat on his face; the others couldn't keep up and had to stop pushing too. As the monk got up and wiped the mud from his eyes, he saw the truck had slid some fifty metres further on but then had stopped as the track started to climb steeply out of this depression. The vehicle had lost all momentum and there was no way they would be able to push the Toyota up that slope in the mud.

Gopal opened his door and whispered for the others to get in. "We'll have to risk the engine." He started it up and put the truck into gear. The wheels span helplessly on the greasy surface. Revving the engine achieved nothing; the wheels just span even faster.

Rabten looked out of the rear window, towards the trees that had bordered the roadblock. Some movement between the dark glossy leaves. "Hurry, I think they heard us."

Gopal looked in the rearview mirror. An armed guard appeared through the trees and shouted towards them. Gopal put the truck into reverse and started slowly moving the vehicle back towards the guard.

"What you doing?" asked Thaman.

Gopal waited until he had edged back twenty metres from the steep incline and then put the Toyota into second gear and pressed the accelerator. As soon as the guard realised that they had stopped reversing, he shouted out again and raised his rifle. On the flat the vehicle was able to gain some traction and this time when it reached the foot of the slope it had enough momentum and grip to climb the bank. A volley of bullets smacked into the tailgate of the truck, then it was up and over the incline and out of sight.

"Shit, they'll be coming after us," said Gopal.

"Don't worry about the guard." Lach had his hunting rifle lying across his lap. There was a large sniper's scope on top. He pulled back the bolt and ejected the empty cartridge. "He ain't going to tell any tales."

Rabten looked across at his fellow passenger. He hadn't even heard Lach get his rifle out. "I'm glad you're on our side."

After a few miles they re-joined the main road. The sky had long passed from pink ribbons into black velvet by the time they reached Simikot, but they did not head into the town. They skirted around the settlement and then after a few more miles found a small wood where they pulled in and camped for the night. Lach and Thaman pitched the tents while Rabten went to gather firewood. When the monk came back he saw Gopal over by the Toyota, stroking the tailgate and poking a finger into the bullet holes.

"What's she called?"

Gopal turned and quickly dropped his hand from the truck. He stood silently for a moment, shifting his glance from Rabten to the vehicle and back again. He patted the Toyota and sighed. "Joanna and I have been through a lot together. She never lets me down. I want to return the favour."

"That's exactly how I feel about Master Wangdue."

In the morning they continued on towards the Tibetan border. The road climbed upwards as they entered the beginning of the Gandise mountain range. There were still banks of snow in shady patches either side of the road where it had been brushed aside by a plough.

"This time of year, the road ought to be busy with tourists. Now look at it, nothing in sight thanks to the border closure," Gopal said. "We're going to have to hide Joanna somewhere and start walking soon."

Three hours later, Gopal edged the Toyota into a thick copse of Himalayan pines, well away from the road. As he got out of the truck, Rabten shivered; the spring thaw had only just begun here. The monk breathed deeply, filling his lungs with the first taste of truly clean air since he left the monastery three weeks ago. Gopal unrolled a camouflage net over the vehicle while Lach cut down some thin branches from the evergreen trees to add to the effect. The men divided up the camping and climbing gear as well as the weapons; the three ghurkas slung rifles over their shoulders and a pistol was handed to Rabten. Weighing it in his hand, the metal grip felt cold and prickly. He tucked the gun into the back of his trousers.

The sun was exactly overhead when they set off. Gopal said they would stick to the forest to begin with; although there was no clearly defined path to follow, they were far less likely to encounter other people here. The branches of the pine trees knitted together above the hikers, shutting out noise and weather, while the fallen pine needles formed a soft carpet beneath. Was the land giving them one last hug before sending them out into a maelstrom of snow? Through the occasional gap in the trees Rabten could see a clear blue sky above them. A wisp of high cloud swirled slowly like the smoke of incense candles he used to light for his master.

By nightfall they had left the forest far behind them. Gopal had found a path running alongside a stream – whether by luck or some innate knowledge of this region, Rabten couldn't tell. Snow was lying thicker here even in the sun. There was running water in the stream, but in places the clear liquid disappeared under bridges of ice and snow.

The new hiking clothes that Gopal had bought for the monk were keeping him warm, but they chafed. Rabten used the pain to help keep himself awake. "How much further before we camp?" he asked.

"We need to get across the border in darkness. Four more hours at least. You want another rest?" said Gopal.

"I can keep going as long as you need."

The pace slowed as the group picked their way along the path in near total darkness. The quarter-moon cast an occasional pale shimmer across the landscape but was mostly hidden behind clouds. A featureless Gopal turned to Thaman and pointed upwards. "System closing in – it'll be bad tomorrow."

"Might work in our favour. Nobody stupid enough to follow us up."

Lach grinned. "Ever the optimist, Tham."

In the morning, they huddled round a gas burner that was heating their water. Then cold hands clasped the warm mugs lovingly while faces hovered in the steam. Gopal showed them a battered old map of the region.

"The main tourist path is here between the two lakes. It's the shortest route to Mount Kailash and likely crawling with guards. We go round the east side of Lake Manasarovar, but first we have to cross the base of Gurla Mandhata."

"What's that?" asked Rabten.

"The ruddy big mountain behind you," said Thaman, pointing. "Stick close and you'll be fine."

"Provided there aren't any avalanches," said Lach.

"Don't listen to him, he's just grumpy because I left his coffee jar behind. Not a morning person."

They set off in full mountain-climbing gear. Thick cloud cover ensured there was no sun to warm them. Rabten was breathing more quickly now, even at a slow walk, sucking in the thin air. He couldn't hear the others puffing loudly so he used his yoga training to try to breathe deeply but quietly. Even with no sun, the reflection off the snow was starting to hurt his eyes until Gopal reminded him to put his tinted goggles on. That prickly feeling he had got when walking through Kathmandu as an outsider was starting to spread over his skin again.

Rabten's feet and thighs ached after three hours of climbing but the path required no special skills, much to his relief. The clouds sunk lower and the snowflakes, instead of fluttering gently past, started to push themselves into every crevice of clothing they could find. Rabten's neck got cold as flakes that caught on his chin started to melt and crawl down his body as if they were seeking somewhere warm to hide.

Gopal stopped and called back to the others. "We need to rope up."

"We need to go back," said Lach, shouting over the wind.

"No, we have to press on while we can. Nobody can spot us in this."

"Rabten, attach the karabiner here." Thaman showed him the best attachment point and gave the rope a yank to make sure it was safe. "You should get your pickaxe out and use it as a walking stick. No good stuck in your rucksack in an emergency."

"Thank you."

Rabten was barely able to see Gopal up ahead at the front of the chain. All of them were struggling to keep their footing as the wind swirled and tugged at their centre of gravity while the snowed piled higher. The wind seemed to be talking to Rabten. A fell voice. "Gooo. Gooo."

"Go… jump in a lake," he replied, leaning forward and quickening his pace a little.

They stopped for a rest when they got into the lee of a small outcrop of rock. With snow clinging thickly to their clothes and goggles over half their faces, each of them had become nothing more than a mouth, gratefully slurping at a flask of hot soup.

Rabten thought he saw a movement in the snow below them. *Don't be mad, what could be up here?* Then it moved again. A hump in the snow was rising up and coming closer to them.

He pointed. "What's that?" As the others turned around, a metallic dome reared up out of the snow. The dome rotated until a camera lens pointed straight at them. Rabten could have sworn it blinked.

Lach reacted first, diving forward to try and grab the machine, but he missed. The robot rose further out of the snow and backed away from the prone Ghurka. An aperture appeared above its lens and then something shot out at high speed with a 'thum' like a firework. They lost sight of the projectile as it flew up into the cloud. A moment later there was a huge bang on the mountainside above them. Silence for a moment and then an odd noise, as if a huge wedding cake was being sliced.

"Avalanche," shouted Gopal, running towards the outcrop.

Thaman grabbed Rabten and pushed him up against the rock. "Hold your arms in front of your—"

A wall of white fury cut off Thaman's words. Rabten felt himself sliding, tumbling and yet unable to move voluntarily. An insect caught in white amber. And then silence. He opened his eyes but there was nothing to look at. Snow pressed up against his face. He had managed to get one arm up across his mouth thanks to Thaman's half-formed advice. Rabten used his fingers to dig a little hole in front of his mouth, breathing shallowly. Oddly peaceful, trapped in cotton-wool silence.

The hollow in front of his face grew as his warm breath melted the snow. Then it collapsed down into his mouth. He spluttered and tried to claw the snow away from his mouth again. Then he realised that he could see something. His head was right at the surface of the snow, and the little amount he was able to push aside with his hand was just enough to reach fresh air. He twisted his head from side to side and back to front, clearing more room. Inch by inch he was able to free up his face, his hand, then his shoulders. Sweat dripped down the inside of his clothes, mixing with the ice-cold melts of snow. He called out to the others but heard no reply.

Eventually he freed himself completely. Clambering out of the newly formed slope of snow he couldn't see any sign of the outcrop to orientate himself. He scanned the surface. There! A trail of rope. He rushed over, pulled it taut, and started digging with his hands where it disappeared into the snow. He quickly got to Gopal - stuck in a foetal position with an air pocket between his limbs - and helped him out. Movement in the snow a few metres away startled Rabten. He grabbed his pistol ready to shoot the droid sentry, but there was no metal dome this time, just the beaming face of Lach.

"Thank Buddha it's you."

"Where's Tham?" asked Lach.

"He tried to protect me." The monk looked away. "We got separated."

They fanned out and started probing the area with tent poles, calling out for Thaman and then straining to hear any response. The weather was hampering their vision and hearing. After twenty minutes of further search they found something. Lach launched himself into a frenzy of digging, clawing at the snow with his hands. But it was too late. His friend had suffocated.

"It's all my fault, all my fault," Rabten kept repeating, while the others dug Thaman's corpse out of the snow. The weather improved enough for them to rest a while after their exertions.

"We should give him an air burial," Gopal said and the others agreed. Thaman's clothes were carefully removed and his naked body was laid out on the rocky outcrop. "Come, mountain birds, and feast on our friend. Release his spirit and let him soar among the peaks with you." Gopal looked up into the cloud-filled skies and stretched out his arms in supplication to the unseen birds.

After, they spent some time uncovering equipment that had been buried beneath the avalanche. Another moving mound of snow started to approach them, but this time Lach was ready. As soon as the droid lifted its dome above the snow, Lach swung his climbing axe and cut off the robot's camera lens. He swung again and buried the axe deep in the robot's head, sending a shower of sparks reflecting blue off the whiteness all around. Another swing, and another. There was little left of the dome on top of the droid's cylindrical body by now but Lach kept swinging and smashing. He dropped to his knees and slowly pulled his axe out of the mangled metal in front of him.

Gopal touched him on the shoulder. "Come on, it's time we moved off."

Rabten was now at the back of the chain and feeling like the mountain was pressing down on him.

The next day they found what they were looking for. Four silver pipes stretched across the landscape like an impossibly large electronic circuit.

"These are what I saw in Lhasa. They must originate somewhere near here," Rabten said.

They followed the pipes for another two kilometres until they came to a peak that led down to a complex of buildings in the distance. The three men lay down in the snow, peering over the top of the mountain spur.

Gopal focused his binoculars and relayed to the others. "There's some sort of a base down there. Very high security – fences, search-lights, guards on duty – but it doesn't look like barracks. Some sort of chemical plant?"

"What would that be doing up here?" Rabten asked.

"Wait. There are two workers off to the right, well away from the base. They seem to be drilling into the rock with some weird device. Lach, what you reckon?"

Lach unslung his rifle and settled it into the ground in front of him, squinting down the scope. "One thousand metres. Strong cross wind. Should be easy to get one. Will have to be quick to take out the second before they realise what's happened."

"Do we have to? They might just be innocent people trying to earn a living," said Rabten.

"You can't climb a mountain without stepping on a few ants. We need their IDs if we're going to break into the base. Take the shot, Lach."

Lach adjusted the crosshairs on his scope for distance and wind, settled back into position and took three deep breaths. Just as he squeezed the trigger the wind suddenly changed direction. The bullet ricocheted off the ground at the foot of one of the workers.

"Damn!" He looked up from his scope to feel the wind. "What's it doing now?" Lach waited for the gusts to die down and re-adjusted his sight.

Gopal watched through his binoculars as the two people stopped attending to the drilling machine and started to move away. "Wait! Hold your fire. Something's not right. The way they're moving. It's like they're trying to stay hidden from the base, sneaking."

"I'll never get them both now," said Lach.

"Don't worry. I have a feeling they're on our side. Come on let's see what they get up to."

CHAPTER 32

The rule of threes: you can survive three minutes without air, three hours in a harsh environment without shelter, three days without water and three weeks without food. So as long as you can breathe, prioritise shelter, water and food in that order. A sharp blade can mean the difference between life and death in the wilderness.
O.D. Training Manual Section 7d

Breaking into the base's outer perimeter should have been easy with the use of the swipe cards Freda and Sim had obtained from the ground crew earlier. There was a locked gate that would presumably open on insertion of a card into the security reader. But there were two guards present. Even if they could subdue them silently, the guards' absence would soon be noticed. Sim and Freda's other prisoners might not be discovered for several hours, but if these guards went missing the alarm would quickly be raised. The agents watched the guards' movements to see if there were any gaps in their vigilance.

One of the sentries was stamping his feet and flapping his arms, either less well insulated or less stoic than his companion. He said something to the other guard and dashed back to the building. One down. The remaining sentry started a circuit of the base, walking along the perimeter fence.

"This might be our only chance," said Freda as she made a dash for the gate from their hidden observation point. Sim followed. The cards worked. Once inside the gate, they had a choice to make. It was a large complex and they had no idea where other guards might be stationed, or even where they might bump into local workers. Directly ahead of them, across a short path dusted with snow, was a doorway into the main building which the first guard had used. It was the obvious way in, but also probably led to a busy part of the complex.

Freda ignored the path, heading off to her left and towards some large pipes that climbed up and over the main building like a ribbon wrapped around a Christmas present. Just as they reached the pipes, the door they had avoided swung open and the itinerant guard hurried across the path towards the exit gate, clutching a steaming mug. Freda and Sim ducked behind the pipes and watched him take up his station at the gate, staring beyond the fence for potential intruders.

"Phew, that was lucky. Should have plenty of time to snoop around now," said Sim.

Freda shook her head. "They'll still find their colleagues in the hangar before long. Come on, we have to move fast."

They continued to sneak around the left-hand side of the main building, ducking under pipes and sticking to the shadows until they reached another door. It was not guarded and had the same swipe-card entry system.

Freda approached the door. "No tracks in the snow outside this door; let's try in here." She led the way in and found herself in a room full of smelly large bins.

"Pew!" said Sim. "I don't suppose they have a weekly collection around here, do they?"

On the opposite side of the room was a pair of swing doors that led through to a corridor into the heart of the complex. Freda and Sim shed their outer clothes, hid them behind one of the bins and crept down the corridor with gun and taser at the ready. There was a jumble of junctions to explore; above each one there were Chinese characters which might have been helpful if either of the spies could read the language. Freda looked to Sim for suggestions. He dredged up some memory of how to navigate a maze from his childhood love of puzzles.

"Keep your shoulder brushed up against the same side of the corridor at all times. You can't get lost that way."

She acquiesced and moved off. Sim followed behind and had a flash back to playing games on his console at home. He could not help feeling that he was in the most dangerous first-person shooter he had ever played. There was no resurrection point or start-again option if this went wrong.

They came to a junction with a set of swing doors on the right, and corridors going straight on and to their left. There was a faint smell of food wafting from the swing doors. Ignoring those, they kept going straight on. The corridor was coming to a dead end, but there were two doors ahead, each on the right-hand wall. The first one had a sign next to it with the symbol of a radio mast and some Chinese characters, while the second one had a white cross on a red background.

"We should go for the Comms room first; maybe get out a distress call and cut off their communications too," whispered Freda. The door was locked and their swipe cards did not work on this one. They were just about to move on to the medical room, when the door in front of them was opened from the inside. Chung stood in the doorway. His eyes opened wide in surprise. He reached for a gun, but Freda was too quick for him.

"Drop it, you fucker."

His grip on the gun relaxed and it clanged loudly on the floor. Sim winced and turned to look down the corridor. Chung stared down the barrel of Freda's gun in a state of shock, but he quickly regained his composure.

"Well, well, fancy meeting you two here."

"Give me one good reason why I shouldn't shoot you right now!" demanded Freda, her face contorting in anger.

"Oh I can think of at least two. First, because the gunshot will bring a hoard of guards rushing in this direction which will inevitably lead to your capture and probable execution. And second, because if you kill me now you'll never know the answer to all those questions swirling round your head. So why don't you lower your guns and ask me what you want?"

Freda kept pointing the gun at the double-agent. Her fingers loosened and then re-tightened on the grip of the pistol several times. She reversed the gun in her hand and brought the butt of it smashing across Chung's face. His round cheek split open like a peach. She pushed him back into the communication room and raised her gun again. Sim checked the rest of the room - nobody else. He put his hand on Freda's shoulder.

"He's not worth it, Freda. Think of the mission. We still have an out, as long as you don't kill him." For a moment she did not react, and then Sim felt her muscles relax and she lowered the gun.

"Why did you become a traitor?" she asked.

"My family were the ones betrayed!" fumed Chung.

Freda took a step back, and the snarl disappeared from her face.

Chung continued. "My grandfather came to the United States as an IT genius. He got a job at one of the big companies, solved all their glitches, designed some new program that earned them hundreds of millions. And what did they do for him? Sacked him. Just like that. He was still just an immigrant: no rights, no comeback. That project was the culmination of a lifetime's work. They broke his heart, not to mention swindling him out of a fortune."

"That does sound harsh, but hardly a reason to betray a country or start a nuclear war."

"The American system is very good at rewarding those it wants to and looking after those with influence. That's not something I could live with." There was a pause while Chung chewed on the inside of his mouth. "And when those mothers at NASA turned me down for the moon project, that's when I knew the USA would never be my homeland." He spat the last words out as if they left a bitter aftertaste in his mouth.

"How was any of that Bo's fault? Becoming a double agent... that truly is a whore's life," said Sim.

"Well at least the Chinese government treated me with some respect. You Brits are no better than the Americans, with your fancy accents and acting as though the Empire still existed. How dare you come poking your noses into business that's no concern of yours! Here you are on the other side of the world from home, trespassing in a perfectly legitimate Chinese government building."

Freda closed in on Chung and jabbed a finger at him. "If I'm right in thinking that you're trying to steal that glacier out there, then yes I have a right to stick my nose in. There are international conventions dictating the use of water resources. As you well know."

"Ahh, so you have figured it out, well done Freda. You know we have five more of these plants dotted along the Himalayan range, tapping into the many glaciers up here. All of them sending lovely, clean, fresh water into the Chinese interior." Chung smiled at the thought.

"But you've no right! India needs this melt water too, only they let mother nature take its course. They don't use some bastardised mining technique."

"Hmm, what an interesting perspective on international rights you have. The British government would be proud of you. We have no right to this water, you say? But of course the Americans are allowed to take all the rare earth they want from the moon base? And how about what the French did in Morocco?"

Sim looked across at Freda in silence.

Chung continued. "Why did nobody lift a finger when Egypt invaded Ethiopia? International rights are just a convenient excuse for you Westerners to keep up your colonial supremacy. One rulebook for the rich and one for the rest of us. Well, we're not putting up with it anymore. China will take what it wants from now on."

"The game is up Chung, once HQ knows about these plants, they're going to be shut down permanently. Face it, the plan has failed."

"No Freda, the Gangotri Plan is working. It has taken years of planning and the presence of two British Agents isn't going derail us now. Nobody will ever find out about it because you're not escaping from here. You should've shot me while you could."

A squadron of guards burst into the room. Sim wheeled round, drawing his gun, but he had too many soldiers to cover. Freda grabbed Chung by the shoulder and pulled him between herself and the guards. Her gun barrel pressed hard into his neck. The guards were pointing assault rifles at Freda and Sim, shouting something in Mandarin at them.

"That means drop your weapons, in case you weren't sure," said Chung, struggling to speak with Freda's gun pressing on his vocal chords.

"Tell them I'll shoot you if they don't drop their weapons," said Freda. Chung said something in Mandarin but the soldiers did not react.

"It's no good, Freda. In the grand scheme of things, I'm expendable and perfectly happy to die for the cause."

"Bullshit."

"What about your toy boy? Are you willing to sacrifice him?" Freda paused for a moment to look at Sim, and then to look around the room.

Sim scanned the area for something over-looked, a way to create mayhem and mischief. Nothing. He was stood in the open, facing certain death from a dozen armed guards. He looked across at Freda, his eyes and shoulders trying to convey an apology. She slowly lowered her gun and released Chung from the arm lock she had been using on him. Sim mumbled something to himself and lowered his pistol too.

Ten minutes later the agents were in a locked room, with their hands tied behind their backs and stripped of all weapons and equipment. It was a small room, barely three metres square, with only one door, no windows and no furniture. They were sat on the floor, leaning back-to-back with extra straps pressing them together as if they were Siamese twins.

"I don't suppose you have any tricks up your sleeve? A hidden knife, or a double-jointed wrist to get us out of here?" asked Sim.

"There is always hope, Sim, always. Do you know what time it is?"

"I can't see my watch, no. If I hold it up behind me can you see it?" He struggled to shift his arm upwards. "Why do you want to know anyway? Late for an appointment?"

"What's keeping them so long? Why can't they hurry up?"

"Personally I'm in no rush to face the firing squad, Freda. Maybe they are leaving us until the morning. 'Shot at dawn.' That's what usually happens, isn't it?"

"No, no, not the Chinese you dolt! The Americans. They must've picked up the signal from the thumper by now."

"But even if they have, how can they help us here in the middle of the Himalayas, thousands of kilometres away from an American base?"

Freda tutted. "Honestly, Sim, anybody would think you'd eaten slow pills for breakfast. The Hydras are on their way. The first one may have already done a recon pass in whisper mode. The attack drones should be here soon."

Sim breathed a sigh of relief and smiled. But then he pictured the drones circling the base outside. "How exactly is this going to help us? I mean don't get me wrong, I'm glad that the secret is out and the Chinese are going to be stopped. But. Aren't we just going to get blown to smithereens along with the rest of the base?"

"Maybe," said Freda, not displaying the level of gravitas that Sim thought the situation deserved. "But you never know what chaos may ensue."

She leant her head back against his, gently rubbing his scalp with her hair. "I'm glad you're here with me at the end, Sim. Come on, get to your feet, we may need to spring into action at any moment." It took them a couple of attempts to get up from their awkward position without the help of their arms, leaning back against each other in mutual support. At least they could hobble about now if there was a chance to escape.

"See if you can reach my engagement ring," said Freda. His fingers caressed her hand.

"Got it."

"Try to work it loose, the edge of the diamond might be sharp enough to cut our bindings."

Sim's digits strained and tugged at the ring. Freda gasped as the ring squeezed over her knuckle. Now for the really difficult part – using the sharp edge of the large precious jewel to work away at their bindings. Sim's hands were at an awkward angle, and his fingers were cramping but he dared not weaken his grip. If the ring fell, they might not be able to pick it up again. Strand by strand the main cord tying them together started to fray. Beads of sweat glistened on his forehead while his fingers began to feel numb from the pressure he was trying to exert. Inside their cell, Freda and Sim heard a double crack of thunder loud enough to wake Thor himself. The room gently shook.

"That must be the other Hydras. Not bothering with the subtle approach this time," said Freda.

Almost immediately the agents heard the sound of an explosion somewhere outside the base, and then a klaxon sprang into life. The alarm in their room emitted a painful wail, rising and falling with Sim's laboured breathing. More explosions – at least one of them must have hit the building as the walls shook again. Freda let out an exasperated sigh. "In true American style, shoot first, ask questions later."

"Almost there. I think… I can feel… the cord… beginning to give way."

The explosions were getting louder. Whichever section of the base they were in was now the point of attack. There was a huge retort from behind the back wall of their cell and part of the partition blew inwards. The shockwave knocked them off their feet as the cord holding them together finally gave way. Sim knocked his head as he fell and dropped Freda's ring. Freda sprang up and looked through the hole in the wall. There was utter devastation. Whatever had been in the room next door no long existed, smashed into unrecognisable pieces that were smeared on the walls. There was a hole in the ceiling and bits of light debris, still on fire, were gently floating down to the floor. The exterior wall had disappeared, replaced by a crater at the bottom of which was a burning heap of wreckage.

"Come on, get up," urged Freda, seeing Sim still dazed and groggy on the floor. "Now's our chance." She bent down and tried to grab Sim's collar with hands that were still tied behind her back. It was not much help, but Sim started to come round and managed to get himself up again.

"Your ring," he managed to grunt as she pulled him onwards. Freda hesitated for a moment then carried on running through the smoking chaos of the other room. More explosions crumped into different parts of the building. Sim was vaguely aware of human cries of pain in the distance and somebody barking orders in Mandarin. The agents gingerly made their way through the burning crater to the outside. It was dark and cold outside the building, contrasting sharply with the heat and light of the bombed-out wreckage behind them. They couldn't tell what part of the base they were in or where the outer gates were. They just blindly stumbled away from the building as quickly as possible.

Some of the Chinese workers at the base were doing the same thing, running out into the night in a panic, trying to get away from the explosions. Sim barged into one of the workers. Both stumbled then got up, staring into each other's eyes momentarily united in a common fear. The worker ran off, leaving Sim to catch up with Freda.

A few of the guards were still showing some signs of discipline. A couple of them were firing assault rifles in the general direction of the Hydras, while one had managed to locate a Surface-to-Air missile launcher and was trying to get a lock onto its target. And then two of them spotted Freda and Sim trying to escape and shouted to the others. There was no cover this time and they couldn't even run fast. Sim was waiting for the hail of bullets to cut him down when he heard the guards starting to cry out. He turned to see the Chinese soldiers fall, bodies flung backwards, splatters of blood darkening the snow. Sim was so confused he stopped running, trying to figure out who was attacking the Chinese. Bullets from an unseen sniper, not missiles from one of the Hydras. But how?

"Over here."

Where did that come from?

"This way. Come on!"

Yes, there it was again, a voice shouting out in English! Freda had heard it too. The pair of them changed direction and started heading towards the source of this unexpected help, even though they still couldn't see who it was.

They were getting closer to the shouting now and could make out a small group of armed men who were kneeling in cover next to a gate they had clearly forced open. One of them shouted something and pointed behind the pair of escapees. Freda and Sim turned to see Chung in a doorway of the building with an assault rifle in his hand. He raised it to his shoulder and fired. The ground next to Sim's feet flew up as the bullets bit into the earth just in front of him. Before Chung had a chance to correct his aim a rocket detonated against the wall a few metres to his side. He was knocked to the ground and the outer wall collapsed on top of him. Freda stopped to check he wasn't getting up again and then carried on jogging towards their rescuers.

One of the group – a man with a shaved head – untied their hands, releasing a welcome rush of blood back into the ends of their arms. The leader motioned for them all to withdraw further away from the base into the darkness. Sim thought he recognised a kukri on the soldier's belt – the curved dagger of a Ghurka.

What was he doing here? Another explosion made him turn back towards the base.

The building by now was mostly rubble and fire. Those parts that were still standing had lost most of their structural integrity and looked like they would soon collapse too. The Hydras had stopped attacking, probably having used up all of their missiles and rockets. After a couple more passes over the base, the drones headed back towards the coast, accelerating noisily to hypersonic speed.

As the Ghurka dug out some spare clothing for Freda and Sim there was a rumble in the distance as the Hydras set off avalanches on their way over the mountains. Freda looked at Sim and flung her arms around him.

"We did it," she whispered in his ear.

He just stood there enjoying her embrace without saying a word. After a long hug, he turned to their rescuers. "Thank you for saving us, whoever you are."

Rabten clasped his hands in front of him and bowed to the English pair. "It is we who grateful. You have defeated silver serpent. My master rest in peace now."

One of the other men said something in a language Sim couldn't understand. "What did he say?"

"I'm not sure how to say name." Rabten pointed to a mountain peak where plumes of white powder showed an avalanche in process. "He said mountain of doom is shaking fists at us. We need leave."

"Come on," said Gopal. "It's a long walk back to Nepal from here. We'll have plenty of time for introductions later."

CHAPTER 33

Commercial attachés stationed in Embassies and High Commissions throughout the world are trained to respond to certain coded messages from agents working undercover. Once activated, they will provide all the aid they can and offer asylum to any stranded agents. If you are cut off in enemy territory, they are your best hope.

O.D. Training Manual Section 8e

It took them just over a week to hike back to Kathmandu. The Ghurkas were skilled mountaineers and, aside from Sim's stumble down a crevasse, they kept everybody safe despite the bad weather. Rations were pretty meagre with two extra mouths to feed, but once they had descended back below the snowline, there was plenty of scope for hunting and foraging. When they were back in the capital, Gopal led them to his house on the outskirts of the city, away from prying eyes. He lived in a modest region where simple wooden houses were crammed together. You could practically shake hands with the neighbours if both sets of upstairs windows were open.

Gopal's home was full of inexpensive furniture and well-worn rugs. But after the exertions of the long trek, and the canoe trip before that, it felt like a five-star hotel. A log fire in the sitting room was not really needed at this time of year, but it had been lit at Freda's request and she spent the first evening in the house mesmerized as the flames danced across the burning wood.

Rabten had not shaved his head for nearly a month now and his fuzzy growth made him less conspicuous. But Freda and Sim, as Westerners, still attracted attention. Freda asked Gopal to trade in one of her gold sovereigns for plenty of local currency and with the proceeds paid for a huge feast in a local restaurant to thank their rescuers.

Freda offered the other sovereign to Gopal. "It's the least you'd get paid for an expedition like that into the mountains."

He shook his head. "We didn't do it for the money."

Freda shrugged and pressed the shiny coin into his hand. "At least give it to the family of your dead friend. It's no compensation I know, but it will help tide them over the next few months."

Gopal looked down at the lump of metal and closed his hand around it.

The next day, Freda tried to get in touch with OFWAT HQ via the British embassy in Kathmandu. She wore some traditional Nepalese clothes Gopal had borrowed from one of his female neighbours and made her way to the embassy.

"I would like to see the commercial attaché. Please tell him that his cousin urgently needs to organise a family re-union." The receptionist looked rather puzzled at first but relayed the message over the phone. The commercial attaché, a young man with a goatee and an ill-fitting suit, came bustling out after a few minutes.

"Hello, pleased to, err, meet you. Can I see your I.D. please?"

"I lost it on active duty," she replied.

"Oh, well I'll need to take down your details." He was sweating profusely despite the air conditioning and his hands trembled slightly as he jotted down her name and mission code. After he had checked something on the system, he escorted Freda into an office near the back of the embassy, and sat down opposite her. "So, umm Agent Brightwell, how can I help you? You'd like to get in touch with HQ, I understand? You'll have to forgive me, it's been quite a long time since anybody has invoked the protocol in this part of the world. Could you give me a minute while I confer with London?"

Eventually, a secure line to Centre City Tower was established and Freda reported to her Head of Division, Wardle. Afterwards, she thanked the attaché for his help, and walked back towards Gopal's house. She doubled back a couple of times just to make sure she had not picked up a tail from her visit to the embassy. It was a pleasant, sunny morning and the extra-long walk was refreshing.

Sim lay in bed, staring out of his window. The moon was still visible, pale in the morning sun. A white, mottled disc slowly crossing his blue rectangle of sky. He tried to time how long it took the moon to move the width of his outstretched thumb and wondered if you could see the Rare Earth Moon Unit through a powerful telescope. Would any of this have happened if Chung had passed his medical? The moon drifted across his thumb. Freda's return jolted him alert. He threw on some clothes and dragged himself downstairs.

"Where are the others?" she asked.

Sim shrugged. "Not sure, I was asleep most of the morning. I heard Gopal say he was going to try and get in touch with a contact in China to see if the incident in the Himalayas had made the news. But the others were already gone by the time I got up."

"I doubt Gopal will hear anything on the Chinese side of the border. I'm sure the authorities will cover it up or simply deny it ever happened. I gave HQ our Sit Rep. Wardle was delighted to hear we're both safe. He'd been in touch with the Americans and feared the worst with us being out of the loop for so long. The Hydras continued their reconnaissance trips throughout the

Himalayas and found the other five bases. They met the same fate as the one we discovered."

Sim smiled at her. "That's good."

"The Chinese won't be trying to steal any glaciers again I shouldn't think. So, congratulations and promotions all round. I'd be surprised if Wardle doesn't offer you a post in Overseas Division when we get back. That's the least you deserve after a mission like this."

"Hmm?" said Sim. He was staring out of the window at the top of a mountain just visible from the sitting room of the house. "Oh, that." He paused and shifted his weight. "To be honest, Freda, I miss home. I'm not sure I'm cut out for O.D. work. I tried to tell you back in Alaska, but you were pretty persuasive at the time. I used to dream of working for O.D. but now that I've tried it, I think I prefer the quiet life."

Freda frowned. "What, and miss out on all this adventure and excitement?! Doesn't it make you feel alive and on top of the world knowing what you can achieve?" She twirled around the room.

"I wouldn't have achieved much if it hadn't been for you. Besides, I'm quite content knowing that I do a good job at Sat Division. And if I can make a couple of birdie putts on the golf course at the weekend, or take my bike for a spin along the A9 to Wick, well that's enough for me really."

"I'm surprised, Sim. I thought this mission around the world would've opened up your eyes to the possibilities of the planet, and to your potential."

Sim thought about it for a moment. "No, man, it just made me realise there's no place like home."

"Oh, so you do know some of the classic films after all," she said. Sim looked puzzled and Freda was just about to say something when she heard a click from upstairs as if a window frame was being opened or a door handle turned. She put her finger to her lips and felt for the gun she kept tucked into the back of her trousers. It was not there. She had left it in her bedroom when she had gone to the embassy. And her room was upstairs, possibly where the intruder was. She looked around the sitting room for a weapon and grabbed a poker from the fireplace. Sim ducked next door into the kitchen and got the biggest knife he could find.

There was the faint sound of footsteps on the stairs – somebody trying to creep down silently but not quite succeeding due to the old wooden boards. Freda positioned herself just behind the door into the sitting room, with the poker raised ready to strike. Sim crouched behind an old leather chair, also ready to leap out. The shadow of a figure appeared in the doorway and a hand holding a black revolver was tentatively aimed into the room. Freda brought the poker crashing down onto the wrist of the intruder. There was a howl of pain and the gun fell to the floor. Freda jumped out from behind the door to press home the attack with her poker.

Her assault was temporarily halted with the surprise of seeing Chung in the doorway. There was pain and anger in his eyes, and a deep, livid scar across his forehead that did not used to be there. Freda's momentary hesitation was enough for Chung to turn defence into attack. He launched a high kick at Freda's left shoulder, knocking her off balance, and followed up with a grab for the poker in her right hand. There was a brief struggle, but even using his left hand Chung was much stronger than Freda and wrestled the weapon out of her grasp.

Now there was fear in Freda's eyes, facing a stronger opponent and without the advantage of a weapon. She retreated from the doorway. Chung advanced and swung the poker at her head. Freda partially blocked the blow with her forearm, but there was a loud crack as her radius bone snapped. And despite being much slowed down, the poker's momentum still carried it on towards her face, glancing her forehead. She reeled backwards and collapsed, blood welling up from a deep cut on her right temple.

Sim leapt out from his hiding place and slashed at the arm Chung was using to hold the poker. The knife cut through Chung's sleeve and bit deep into the flesh. Chung yelled out in agony and dropped the poker. Now his left arm was bleeding and his right wrist was almost useless from the initial blow of the poker. Sim tried to advance, though his footing was tricky as he stood over Freda's inert body trying to protect her. Chung aimed a kick at Sim's midriff, winding him. As Sim paused in his attack, Chung reached down to his boot and grabbed a small blade of his own. Sim remembered their training together back in Alaska; even injured Chung was probably a better fighter than him. Chung glanced down at the body on the floor and Sim swallowed hard, knowing that he would have to protect Freda as well as himself.

He immediately advanced again, trying to keep himself between Chung and Freda. The two knives clashed as Chung lunged and Sim parried. There was a cry of pain as Chung's deflected blade caught Sim's knuckles on the way past. Chung pressed the attack and instinctively Sim started to retreat. As he stepped backwards one of his feet caught on Freda's limp leg. He lost his balance and started to topple over. Chung used a high heel kick to finish the job, landing a blow smack in the middle of Sim's chest. The British agent fell backwards, crashing to the floor and dropping his knife in the process.

Chung continued to advance, but instead of trying to finish off Sim, he bent down to grab Freda by the hair and raised her floppy head. Her long neck was pale and vulnerable. A shaft of sunlight streaming in the window just caught her exposed flesh and for a moment Sim saw it glistening brightly like a goose ready for the butcher. He struggled to get his feet. A rush of hatred and anger filled him as a renewed dose of adrenalin coursed through his veins. Digging deep into inner reserves of strength he launched himself at Chung in a full dive, grabbing the Chinese man around the shoulders and knocking him backwards. Sim landed awkwardly on top of Chung, trying to pin him to the ground. Their two faces pressed closer together. Sim could smell his enemy's breath. Then Chung's face broke out into a smile and suddenly Sim's world was full of pain. Looking down he saw Chung's left hand, still holding the knife whose blade had slipped between two of Sim's ribs. His arms collapsed as Sim's strength left him and he rolled off to the side.

Then three things happened all at once. As Chung pulled the knife out of Sim and was getting back up, Freda started to come round. And at that moment Gopal came running into the room. Seeing Chung's gun lying on the floor in the doorway, he stooped to pick it up. Cocking the revolver and aiming it at Chung in one smooth movement, he squeezed the trigger. It was not an especially powerful gun but it jerked in the Ghurka's hands like a beast trying to escape from its captor. Chung toppled backwards clutching at a heavily bleeding stomach wound. He struggled to get back to his feet, but a second shot from Gopal was aimed straight between the eyes and killed the double agent instantly.

Freda was still groggy and in agony from her broken arm. But the retort of the gun firing twice quickly brought her to her senses. As she looked around to see what had happened, she let out a yell of anguish as she saw Sim lying on his back with his right hand pressed over his ribs. She crawled over to see if he was conscious and breathing. Sim's eyes were just about open but he was staring at the ceiling and did not focus on Freda as she knelt over him. His breathing was fast and shallow.

"Oh Christ, not again. Sim, Sim, it's going to be alright. It's me, Freda. Stay awake, Sim. Look at me!" She turned away. "Gopal, quick, go and call for an ambulance."

Sim gradually opened his eyes wider and looked at Freda, recognising her face at last. He smiled weakly and then started to cough. Some blood came up and the effort of spitting it out of his mouth exhausted him.

"Sim, I need to roll you over onto your side. This is going to hurt, I'm afraid."

His breathing became much shallower and faster and now there was a wheeze coming from his torso every time he gasped for air. Bubbles of red blood started foaming up around the wound, like some sick new brand of washing-up liquid. Freda rolled him onto his right side, tilting his head into an approximation of the recovery position, hoping that Sim could cope with just one lung to keep him going. She looked around for something to plug the wound with, all the time shouting at Sim to stay with her.

"Where is that bloody ambulance, Gopal?" she screamed.

"A few minutes yet, I'm afraid. We don't exactly have air ambulances in Nepal, you know. I have some old army medical kit in my bedroom, I'll see if there's anything useful in that lot." He sprinted upstairs.

Sim could hear the shouting from the other two people but could not make any sense of it. He felt incredibly tired. Just a little nap, yes, that was what he needed. He would feel much better after a rest. He closed his eyes and his breathing slowed until eventually the red bubbles foaming from his punctured ribs ceased.

CHAPTER 34

All agents are eligible for death-in-service benefits. Three times salary is awarded to the next of kin and pension benefits are transferred to the agent's spouse, if any. The department will make all practical efforts to repatriate the body.
O.D. Training Manual Section 8a

Fairfax county was dull and overcast, unusual for that time of year, as if the sun was too embarrassed to share this day with people in mourning. The gathering at the cemetery was clad in monochrome colours. As drops of rain began to fall, umbrellas were raised, like black daisies opening their petals to welcome the grey sky. The patter on the taut material beat out a gentle drum roll to welcome the Marines carrying two coffins to the burial site. Inch by inch, the soldiers lowered the deceased into the ground next to each other. The stiffly folded stars and stripes flag sat proudly on top of each coffin. The sergeant major called the Marines to arms, and barked out the orders for three shots. The metallic retort reverberated through the group of mourners, a physical shock numbing the senses and forcing the people to retreat within themselves. Bo Brunswick's mother stood with her head bowed, barely hearing the words of the service, as the tears fell from her cheeks and merged with the raindrops. Around her neck she was wearing the St Christopher that Freda had rescued from the Chinese police station. Mrs Brunswick reached out her hand to the other mother who was burying her son that day. Mrs Lennox, Chung's mum, looked up and managed a weak smile.

◆

Just outside the Bullring Shopping Centre in Birmingham there is a Victorian church with a tall pointed spire. It stands in marked contrast to the ultra-modern curved exterior of the armadillo-like department store next door. Freda looked at the two buildings; the religion of the old and the new perfectly contrasted in a single snapshot. It was late Monday morning in the middle of July. The sun was high in the sky, shining extra brightly today as if to mock the workers returning to their offices at the start of the week. Freda entered the church of St Martin's through a door in the North Transept. She passed beneath the magnificent Burne-Jones window awash with vibrant tinctures. She wished it had been raining. She did not want colours today.

She went to the side altar and, placing a deposit in the money box, lit a prayer candle and bowed her head in memory. This was the tenth time she had come here to mourn the anniversary of her fiancé's death, but perhaps it was the last time she would follow this ritual. It was time to move on. The ring had gone, buried somewhere near the top of a mountain on the other side of the world. Her finger was still pale where the ring had sat for a decade, signifying everything and nothing at the same time. All along she had been worried she would feel naked and vulnerable without it, but now that it was gone she felt liberated, as if a weight had been lifted from her shoulders.

After some quiet reflection, she left the church. It was nearly eleven. Today was her first day back at OFWAT HQ since she and Sim had set off on that fateful mission nearly three months ago. She was in no rush even though she knew Wardle, her Head of Division, was waiting for her. Punctuality did not seem very important any more.

Afterwards, she left the office, crossed over the road and entered the coffee shop where she knew Sim would be waiting for her.

"What're you having?" he asked as she sat down opposite him.

"I need something stronger than coffee. But I'll make do with an espresso."

Sim ordered drinks, dusted his coffee with cinnamon and sat down opposite Freda. He smiled at her and raised the drink to his mouth. Breathing in before taking his first sip, he accidentally inhaled a wisp of cinnamon dust, breaking out into a coughing fit. He winced in pain.

"Careful there, Sim, I'm not giving you the kiss of life again… well, not here in front of all these other people." She toyed with the sugar cubes in front of her, staring deeply at each one as if there were a secret hidden in the lumpy, mottled facets. Sim watched, trying to guess what was going through her mind.

She picked up a round lump of sugar and held it in front of her face, rotating it between her fingers. "Do you realise that we set off on our mission around the world exactly eighty days ago? We could've been back a lot sooner if Chung hadn't turned you into a colander, of course. But, doctor's orders, no flying with a collapsed lung. And they take quite a while to heal."

"Sorry to have been so holey at such an inconvenient time," he said. "But it was good of you to wait with me. It's so boring being stuck in a hospital bed."

"Least I could do. Besides, I had a broken arm to mend as well. And Wardle wouldn't let me come back without you. Still, eighty days, Phileas Fogg would've been proud."

Sim looked at her, trying to figure out who she meant. The name rang a bell, but he could not place it. He took an educated guess.

"*Star Wars*?"

"Not a film, a book!"

"Oh, *Three Men in a Boat* then?"

Freda grinned. "Strike two!"

"Well I give up," said Sim.

"*Around the World in Eighty Days*. Phileas Fogg and his servant Passepartout circumnavigate the world for a bet. They come back after eighty-one days and think they have lost the wager, but they've forgotten that they gained a day when they crossed the international dateline. You *must* know the story. Jules Verne ring any bells?"

"Isn't that the name of the World Cup trophy?"

Freda was about to explode in indignation when she caught sight of Sim grinning and she deflated with a smile.

"You are teasing me, Mr Atkins. Did you hear that Bo has been awarded the Distinguished Intelligence Cross?"

"But that's great, isn't it? At least his family have some recognition of his sacrifice. I've often wondered if it's the authorities who benefit most from posthumous awards: more volunteers for the next suicide mission. But I think it has to be for the family's benefit. I mean lots of parents bury their children prematurely, but not many have a piece of paper declaring them a hero."

"Well we got two more volunteers. Gopal and Rabten have just signed up to the service. They will ensure we have eyes and ears permanently in the area now."

"Sounds good."

"But wait 'til you here this." She glanced around the café to make sure nobody was within earshot. "The Indians still don't know about our mission and what we discovered. To help maintain the cover-up, it's been decided that Chung's defection and murder of Bo cannot be revealed either. He's been awarded the D.I.C as well! How messed up is that?"

Sim had a flashback to Chung's scarred, flushed face looming over him and smiling as the knife plunged into his ribs. Sim tried to physically shake the thought from his mind and looked at Freda. He knew there was more to hear from her meeting with Wardle.

Freda looked around the café again and then up at the ceiling. "I quit."

"But. You can't. You're the best agent OFWAT has."

"That's debatable… and immaterial now. No longer on the list."

"What did Wardle say?"

"Not much, he doesn't know yet. I just told him I needed some more time off. He was pretty upset as it was."

"What're you going to do?"

Freda gave no immediate response; she just sat there staring at the table.

"Come up to Scotland with me. I'd love to show you around, get to know you better. When we aren't trying to save the world." Sim paused, trying to find the right words, before continuing. "That night in India, when you… And I didn't reply. It wasn't what you think."

"Sim, it's in the past now. You're better off steering clear of me. First Howard, then Bo. I'm beginning to think I'm cursed." She held up her arm and traced the scar of the plate that had been used to mend her radial bone. "Some wounds heal. Others never will."

"I thought that once everything was back to normal, we'd be able to spend time together. Doing normal things." Sim's voice trailed off, like a child who knows the debate is not going their way.

"That's exactly what you should do, Sim. Go back to Scotland, do normal things, get a girlfriend, enjoy life. I have to get away from this job. Somewhere peaceful. That walking stick and that ring – I thought they were protecting me all this time, propping me up, keeping me going. But now I realise they were just holding me back. I don't have anything to prove to anybody. Howard's death doesn't mean I have to spend the rest of my life saving others. I don't know why it's taken me so long to realise."

"All the more reason to come up to Scotland," said Sim.

"You've forgotten the first rule of agenting. Always have an exit. I need a complete break. I have some family in New Zealand. It's high time I went to see them. The country's coping well with climate change, a haven from the mess we've created in this world."

Sim couldn't take it in. He was crestfallen, like a dog who doesn't understand why its owner is not taking it on holiday. Ever since the mission had finished he presumed that Freda would be part of his life back in the UK. Even if romance never flourished between them, at least good friendship. Now he felt hollow.

Freda said she hated long goodbyes. She hugged and kissed him. "Remember, the Overseas Division will always need people like you. You've got a lot more to offer than you realise. Good luck." And then she was gone.

Sim's motorcycle helmet was on the seat next to him. He picked it up and turned it over in his hands, looking at the scratched paint where he had nearly decapitated Freda sliding under the barriers at Biggin Hill airport several weeks ago. He headed out of the café, donned the helmet and headed South to Scotland. Lost in thought, he rode as if on autopilot: scenery and vehicles flashed by in a blur of lines.

As he passed through the shires of Scotland, his mood started lifting. He wanted to tell his friends about his exploits but knew he never could. He wondered if Charlie would notice a change in him. He stopped the bike outside his house, took off the helmet and breathed deeply; the coconut aroma of common broom in flower filled his nostrils. The smell of his childhood. Freda was right; normal stuff, that's what Sim missed.

His mouth went dry and he had a strong urge for a pint of beer in the local. *Rosie. Would she remember me at all*? He walked down the road and pushed open the door to the lounge bar. Rosie looked up and beamed at him.

He stood a little taller and smiled back.

NOTES FROM THE AUTHOR

I hope I have entertained you with the speculative thriller you hold in your hands. Sadly, the possibility of conflict over rare water resources is all too real, as the United Nations has warned. The US National Intelligence Council's report *Global Trends 2030* highlights that global demand for food, water and energy will grow by 35%, 40% and 50% respectively by 2030. By then, nearly half the world's population will live in areas of severe water stress. Africa and the Middle East are shown to be most at risk, but China and India are vulnerable too.

http://www.dni.gov/files/documents/GlobalTrends_2030.pdf

Two main factors drive this diagnosis.

First, climate change is reducing the availability of fresh water. Repeated droughts in places like California are an obvious example but more subtle ones abound. Flooding can reduce the availability of fresh water by overwhelming a region's infrastructure, contaminating the water supply with dirt and chemicals from the surrounding land. Rising seawater levels can render coastal water sources undrinkable by increasing their salt content.

Second, water consumption is expanding rapidly. Simple population growth explains some of this, but the situation is made worse by two factors:

1. Population growth is highest in parts of the world where freshwater resources are already severely constrained. See, for example, the map of the world produced by the UN (referenced below) for an illustration of how demographics will intensify water shortages in the Middle East and Asia.

2. Water consumption per person rises with income levels. As people become richer they use water more freely on washing themselves and their clothes, as well as for recreational purposes such as watering plants in parks and grass on golf courses. Diets also change as income levels improve. It takes 2,500 litres of water to produce a kilo of rice, but 15,000 litres of water to produce a kilo of beef. Switching from a vegetarian/subsistence diet to one enhanced with meat is a perfectly understandable response to improved living standards in Developing Economies, but the consequences for freshwater consumption are severe.

What, then, can we do about this? We can raise awareness of the issue as I am trying to do here. We can raise money for charities that are helping to bring clean, fresh water to some of the world's poorest people. It's easy to set up a monthly direct debit to support Water Aid – you can see the excellent work they do on their website www.wateraid.org.uk. In the United States Matt Damon is doing a great job as ambassador for a similar charity, Water.org. Those of you with some spare savings could consider crowd-funding research into technologies that will help improve the efficiency of our water infrastructure.

There are annual gatherings on water problems addressing these issues at a much higher level than I could ever achieve. World Water Week has been held in Stockholm annually since 1991, organised by the Stockholm International Water Institute. Every year, over 200 collaborating organisations convene events at the gathering and individuals from around the globe present their findings at scientific workshops.

http://www.worldwaterweek.org/

The United Nations produce a World Water Development Report annually now. You can follow their updates on twitter: @UN_Water. Their website also has some excellent statistics on water.

http://www.unwater.org/statistics.html

Circle of Blue was founded in 2000 by leading scientists and journalists and provides excellent information on the world's resource crises, with a focus on water and its relationship to food, energy and health. It publishes reports, free of charge, to help inform academics, governments and the general public.

http://www.circleofblue.org/waternews/

Resilience.org aims to help the world deal with the multiple challenges it faces ahead such as the decline of cheap energy and the depletion of scarce resources such as water. It is a network of action-oriented groups as well as a repository of information on these issues.

http://www.resilience.org/

The Watchers' website pulls together articles from around the world, "watching the world evolve and transform". It has a section specifically on droughts, floods and the water crisis.

http://thewatchers.adorraeli.com/category/earth-changes/water-crisis-earth-changes/

Freda is slightly obsessed with films. Most of the time, when she quotes from a film, she has to explain it to Sim, so the reader gets to share the source. But not always. For example, "the needs of the many are out-weighed by the needs of the few" on page 248. Many people will recognise this from *Star Trek III, The Search For Spock*. I have also used films as inspiration for several scenes in the book, not because I couldn't be bothered to think for myself, but because I hope it raises a smile with you, the reader, when you get the connection. It's my homage to the excellent TV series, *Spaced*. [Note to TV producers – why isn't this series repeated more often?] The films I have deliberately parodied, referenced or quoted from are shown below. See how many you spotted. Any film not mentioned here, and that you think is somehow incorporated into Blue Gold is the product of my addled sub-conscious. Kudos to you for spotting something I could not.

Chinatown (1974)
Cockleshell Heroes (1955)
Demolition Man (1993)
E.T. the Extra Terrestrial (1982)
Fight Club (1999)
Goldfinger (1964)
Highlander (1986)
The Magnificent Seven (1960)

Pirates of the Caribbean: The Curse of the Black Pearl (2003)
The Seven Samurai (1954)
Star Trek: The Motion Picture (1979)
Star Trek III: The Search for Spock (1984)
Star Wars IV: A New Hope (1977), referenced twice (at least!)
The Usual Suspects (1995)
War Games (1983)
The Wizard of Oz (1939)

OFWAT Overseas Division Training Manual Introduction, 2028 edition

OFWAT was established in 1989 after the privatisation of water utility companies. Its initial objective: good quality service and value for money for UK households and business.

Although Britain has been blessed with relatively abundant water resources and has not suffered from rising global temperatures, it became clear by 2020 that water security was a major global issue. Rapid population growth and changing diets are stressing the Middle East and Asia; meat needs 8 times more water than rice to produce. Climate change has affected weather patterns across the globe leading to more frequent drought and flooding. Rising sea levels from melting polar ice have also led to increased salinity of coastal drinking sources.

Many of the attempts to sustain high levels of energy supply such as fracking are very water-intensive. If the battle for the economic and military control of black gold - oil - was a dominant feature of the second half of the twentieth century, the control of blue gold - water - will be the key to the first half of the 21st century.

In 2022, following Egypt's invasion of Ethiopia, OFWAT's budget was tripled and the Overseas Division was set up to work alongside MI6 in monitoring and countering water-related terrorism and acts of war. This is where you, new recruit, can prove your worth in the most exciting civil servant's job in the country!

This manual is a crucial part of your induction into the work of OFWAT. Please read it carefully and learn everything you can from each of the sections. There will be a formal written exam on this manual at the end of your training course.

The timeline in Blue Gold is deliberately dis-jointed. Hopefully, it's a source of satisfaction to the reader as the pieces are placed in the jigsaw to form a coherent picture. For those of you who got to the end of the book and are still feeling slightly confused, here is the timeline in chronological order, including the dates of some events that are only mentioned in passing during the novel.

Timeline

Mar 2018	Work begins on the New Union Canal Lattice
Feb 2021	The Great Flux begins
Mar 2022	Egypt invades Ethiopia Chapter 2
Jun 2022	OFWAT is established
Sep 2022	Sim's friend gets shot on TA exercise Chapter 4
Feb 2023	Ataturk Dam is attacked See "A potable history"

EXTRACTS FROM:
"A POTABLE HISTORY OF W³,
THE WORLD WAR FOR WATER,"
A WARDLE

COPYRIGHT 2036.

Foreword by the author.

I spent many months travelling the world, interviewing key witnesses to and participants in key moments of the war. I have chosen to present each chapter in a dramatised fashion, not to downplay its gravity but to improve its readability and reach a wider audience. We must never let this conflict happen again. Notes to each chapter are taken from the OFWAT Overseas Division training manual. I had the honour to head this division during some of the pivotal years of the conflict.

Europe - 2023

The Guneydogu Anadolu Projesi (GAP) was one of the largest river-basin development projects in the world. It included 13 irrigation and hydropower schemes, involving the construction of 22 dams and 19 hydroelectric power plants on both the Tigris and the Euphrates. It provided 25% of Turkey's electricity as well as irrigation for agriculture in the area at the expense of water flow rates further downstream in Syria and Iraq.

The Secret Diary of Mert Yilmaz, aged 16 and 3/4. February 2023.

Tuesday 14th, 1am.
The moon shines pale, nine days since it was full. The sheep are restless. I wonder why? It is a fine evening, a little cold for me in this crappy sleeping bag in front of a fire that has almost gone out. But they should be cosy in their woolly coats. It's odd, they are not even herding - normally if something disturbs them they instinctively huddle around the elder ewes. But now they don't seem to know which way to go or who to follow. I have not seen that behaviour before, will have to ask Grandpa about it next time I see him. Even Bickin is whimpering - another first for this night. I scratch his ears and lie next to him to reassure him - he is a warm pillow.

3am.
WTF? How am I still alive? Ten minutes ago, I was jolted awake as the ground began to buck and shake. I was tossed out of my sleeping bag onto the fire. My jumper caught light but I was able to douse it in snow before it got too bad. Nasty burn on my left elbow. The ground continued to shake for three or four minutes; cracks appeared, turning into deep and wide scars on the hillsides. The sheep have scattered - it will take me ages to find them all again. Bickin went nuts. Grandpa has told me about earthquakes before, but this is the first big one I have felt. Luckily there is nothing to fall on top of me up here, but down in the valleys, in the villages, I fear something terrible has happened.

Wednesday 15th 9am.
After-shocks continue to hit and it freaks Bickin out each time. I managed to re-gather most of my sheep yesterday. I found one

bleating away, standing next to a crevice that had opened up the night before last. Three feet down its lamb had become wedged in and then suffocated. I pulled the carcass out and showed it to the ewe. After it left, I butchered the lamb and wrapped the joints carefully - I may need the food later.

Thursday 16th 11am
I have to stay up here in the hills to look after my sheep. It is my job, and I will not fail the family. The radio says the earthquake was huge. 8.1 on the Rikter scale - whatever that is. Apparently the electricity lines are down, the water pipes have burst, gas pipes have ruptured. I have heard several explosions from down in the valleys. Food and shelter are needed for tens of thousands, maybe more. I worry that people will come to steal my sheep, so I take them higher up in the hills to places not many people know.

Friday 17th 8am
I hope Talya is OK. I dreamt about her last night. It has been so long since I kissed her sweet lips and we laid together that my passion spilled out while I slept. Yuck, what a mess.

2pm
The radio says things are even worse now in Anatolia. The dam is leaking and has flooded some villages. Disease has broken out - there is no proper sanitation. I am better off up here out of the way and I must keep our flock safe. Grandpa says our people have gone soft since the G.A.P. brought easy irrigation and farming to this region. But not me, I can survive the whole winter up here with only my sheep and Bickin for company if needs be. I eat some lamb cutlets and drink sheep's milk. A shepherd's banquet!

Just before midnight

It is another cold, clear night but quite dark. The moon has nearly gone now. I am woken by the sound of airplanes overhead - not fast jets but transport planes with propellers. I feel my chest vibrate, as the deep heavy thrumming noise passes overhead. At first I thought it must be our air force dropping supplies to the isolated villages. But when I look through Grandpa's binoculars – the ones he used in the army and gave me on my 15th birthday – I see troops piling out of the back of the planes, not supplies. Many, many paratroopers. The tails of the planes have markings on them, but they don't look Turkish. Very odd; I feel nervous without knowing why. Bickin growls, he does not like our visitors.

Saturday 18th 8am

I cannot believe the radio. There are people dying of starvation, disease, exposure down among the valleys. In our hour of need Iraq has invaded Anatolia. Shitheads! The planes I saw last night were just part of the attack. Paratroopers have landed near several of the big dams, and they have captured some of the small airports in the region. How could they?! The dams are all supposed to have air defence systems, but I guess all that got screwed by the earthquake.

I cannot sit around looking after sheep while my country is in need. I don't know what difference one person can make, but I am going to do something about this invasion. I have my hunting rifle, my knife and a 200lb Anatolian Shepherd dog. If I don't come back and somebody finds this diary, tell Talya I love her, I hope she's alright. And let Grandpa know I tried to make him proud.

Monday 20th 11am

I'm back, it's a miracle. I hiked towards the dam on Saturday, approaching the structure as night fell, smearing mud on my face to camouflage my white skin. Earlier in the day I had heard the muffled sound of several large explosions coming from the dam. More gas pipes rupturing? I hoped that would be our air force bombing the Iraqi bastards. But it turned out to be the enemy troops blowing up the machinery at the dam. They opened the gates full to let the huge reservoir drain and made sure there was no way to shut it off again.

They had established a perimeter about 500m from the dam, sentries who were easy to spot - some were even smoking. In the darkness, the cigarettes lit up their faces as they inhaled their nicotine, making my job a lot easier. I say job, but really it was my duty. I have shot lots of birds, even a few wolves but never a person before. As I crawled to within 100 metres of the first guard, I breathed deeply and squinted down the sight of my rifle. I looked into his face, glowing red from the cigarette tip as he inhaled. I thought of all my countrymen dead or dying in the aftermath of the earthquake and squeezed the trigger. He crumpled to the ground before he even heard the crack of the gun.

But the sound alerted two more sentries. I was still well covered in the darkness. Swiveling round I managed to get off another shot, taking down the guard approaching from my left. The other one was faster and smarter; he used the trees for cover. He had me pinned down, letting rip with his semi-automatic. Shit, I thought I was going to die. But then I heard a growl and a scream from the guard as Bickin bowled him over with one leap and started tearing at his throat. I've never realised how much human intestines look like sausages before. The fur around Bickin's face still looks pink two days later. I had to drag the dog off the lifeless body, grabbed the machine gun and we high-tailed it away.

I thought I better lay low for a few hours after that. As dawn broke I got myself into a good vantage point to watch the Iraqis' next move and figure out how to pick off a few more of the scum. But as I watched, it became clear that they had already left. Must have been while I was hiding up with Bickin. I searched through the wreckage of the plant at the dam and found the bodies of some of my countrymen – engineers who had worked there. I made some crude graves for them and then returned to the mountains.

Tuesday 21st 1pm
The sun is shining again and there is a rainbow in the sky. The radio says the Iraqis have left – flown back to their country from the small airports they captured. They have disrupted nearly all of the dams in the area – every gate has been opened, generators blown, all the infrastructure has been destroyed. The Tigris and Euphrates rivers are now in full spate, sending billions of litres right into the heart of their country. Now all our reservoirs are nearly empty, how are we going to farm Anatolia? And still no electricity. At night from up here in the mountains I can normally see the lights of villages down in the valleys, like I am looking at the reflection of the heavens above. The stars have all gone out.

I cannot afford to mope. Me and Bickin need to go and round up the family herd; I hope they stayed near where I left them or I could be up here all spring! Wait until I tell Grandpa about this…

Middle East - 2023

The Republic of Yemen suffers from one of the most severe water shortages in the world. The arid climate and extremely low income of the country contributes to a lack of natural resources and infrastructure. The capital city, Sana'a, sits on top of a 2300 metre-high escarpment, making it too difficult to raise de-salinated coastal water up to where it is needed most.

Karif Al Lawati entered the cafe in central Muscat, sweating even more than usual, and quickly looked around the tables. Near the back there was a tall, tanned European with a heavy moustache slurping mint tea and next to him a younger woman, who also looked European, sipping a coke. He wandered up to them.

"Monsieur Florette?"

"*Oui*, you can call me Jean and this is my colleague Amèlie. I recognise you from the photo you sent. Please sit down. You need our help, non?"

The man from Oman sat at the table with them, took a deep breath but kept his hands clenched tight. "Our village has been attacked by Yemeni bandits several times in the past year. The attacks are getting more frequent and more violent. We need some help - I was hoping to hire you and your associates."

"And your government isn't doing anything about this problem, Mr Al Lawati?"

"We have complained to the local police - they sent an officer, but he just fled at the first sign of the armed bandits. The police refuse to take our calls now. The Army claims to be too busy to spare any men to protect such an 'insignificant asset'. We didn't know what else to try."

"Before we decide whether to take the job, we'd like to know a bit more about your village and these bandits, if you please."

"Our village is a few kilometres east of the Yemen border, in hilly countryside. We are mostly farmers; the rainfall is modest but our irrigation system is much better than across the border. It started about a year ago - at first they wanted to trade the Khat they had grown in exchange for our fruit and vegetables."

"What's cat?" interrupted Jean.

Amèlie replied without waiting for the village elder to speak: "It's *Khat*, a tea plant grown locally that acts like an upper. You chew the leaves, very valuable."

"That's right," said Karif. "So at first we were happy to trade. But the next time they offered less Khat and demanded more food. When we said no, they drew guns and forced us to accept their terms. And after that they didn't even bother to offer us anything in return."

"How many usually turn up?"

"Maybe five or six, in two separate dune buggies each with a mounted machine gun. They visit every month now. Before we go on, can I ask you about your team? I mean, how do I know you can handle this task?"

"Fair question. Three of us are ex soldiers, one used to be in a Canadian SWAT team. Amèlie here was a surveillance expert from the DGSE in Paris - French equivalent to the CIA - and you don't want to know about the other two. But I assure you, we can handle ourselves in a firefight. I don't expect any trouble from these amateur thugs. $50,000 and all expenses is our standard fee. I trust that is acceptable."

Karif gulped. "We cannot pay that much. $20,000 is more than enough."

"This isn't a stall in a bazaar, we do not haggle."

"25 then, it is all we have. Take it or leave it."

"I said we don't negotiate."

"Then you leave me no choice. I will have to detonate the

bombs that are strapped to my chest. I cannot return a failure. I hope you are prepared to meet your maker." He opened his palm to show them a small device with a button on top and a thin wire that snaked up his sleeve. Amélie recoiled in fear, but Jean merely smiled and clapped.

"Hah. You sure drive a hard bargain. OK, *bien*, we accept – 25k."

The seven mercenaries hired a couple of 4x4 vehicles and drove the arduous 800km journey from Muscat to the village of Herweb near the Oman-Yemen border. When they arrived there was a small committee of village representatives to meet them, wearing the traditional dishdasha long gown and patterned mussah on their heads. Each of them carried ornate Khanjar - curved daggers - in their belts. Amélie explained to the rest of the mercenaries that such formal dress was a sign of great respect to their guests and she thanked the village elders in their native tongue.

After a brief tour of the village, which only consisted of a few dozen houses arranged around a simple square and spreading linearly along the crude roadways, Jean started handing out orders to the team.

"Bob and Pieter, get the kit safely stored in one of the barns on the east side of the village. Gopal, draw up a schematic of the village and main approaches. Ricard, you and Monty scout out the countryside to the west of the village and set up an observation post. Amélie, you come with me while we talk to some more of the villagers."

Ricard was a 30-year-old black man from Southern France who used to serve under Adjudant Chef Jean Florette in the Légion Etrangère. He was a sniper and well versed in the art of camouflage and stealth. Monty, his companion, was a French Canadian much older than Ricard. As an ex-SWAT team policeman he too knew plenty about firearms and the need for stealth in approaching an opponent. The countryside was less barren than they had expected. It was rugged certainly, rocky and hilly, but there were a few streams and plenty of vegetation.

"Hmm, many places to hide but few good vantage points. Everywhere we might set up's going to have blind spots in each direction. This could be tricky, *non*?" said Ricard.

They eventually settled on an elevated spot on the eastern bank of a small stream just before the water cascaded down a series of miniature waterfalls over a few large rocks. Monty went out into the countryside with a spray can while Ricard watched him from this spot and shouted out whenever Monty went into a blind spot. It was marked with a cross within a circle of black spray paint.

Back at the village, Bob, a short Scots man who had served time with both the Royal and Merchant Navies, was unloading the packs from the trucks. Despite his red hair, his twenty years of taking orders had left him with an even temperament, which was more than could be said for Pieter. He was a tall blonde-haired Afrikaan who used to specialise in cracking safes, or blowing holes in walls, and who definitely wasn't happy about helping Bob with the bags.

"Och man, don't worry, you'll have plenty of chance to play with your fireworks later, I'm sure of it," said Bob.

After an hour or so the team returned to the barn where they had set up HQ, except Ricard who was taking the first shift as lookout. Gopal, a Nepalese ex-Ghurka, showed Jean the detailed map of the village he had drawn up.

"OK, so the main plan is to give these bandits a nasty surprise next time they come for their monthly collection. That bit should be relatively easy. The tricky part will be anticipating what they do next: give up and go home, which I doubt, or come back with reinforcements." He spent the next couple of hours drawing up their tactics and alternative strategies if plan A went wrong. The following day Pieter went out to the countryside that Monty had marked and left some of his 'fireworks' as Bob had called them. Ricard chose one of the houses on the western edge of the village and set up his FR-F2 sniper rifle in an upstairs bedroom.

Jean spoke to the village elders and explained what he wanted them to do next time the Yemeni robbers came calling - they told him it would probably be another day or two before the next raid. Amèlie set up some remote sensors and trip wires across a broad swathe of approaches. Bob, with the help of some of the younger village men, dug some trenches and foxholes on the western edge of the settlement.

The following day, the team spent some time showing and teaching a few of the villagers how to handle their spare rifles "just in case". Amèlie had one final assignment on the roofs of some of the taller houses and then it became a waiting game. As predicted, they did not have to sit around for too long - around noon on the third day after they had arrived Gopal radioed through that he could see approaching vehicles.

There were two dune buggies racing along the dirt road towards the village, the first with three men in it, the second with just two. Each vehicle had a light machine gun attached to its roll bar. As usual the bandits drove straight into the centre of the village square, and the leader hollered for Karif. Jean stepped out from a nearby house wearing the traditional costume of a villager. The loose-fitting gown helped to conceal a bullet-proof vest and where the traditional curved dagger should be, he had a 9mm automatic pistol. He held out his raised arms in the international gesture for peace and walked towards the bandits.

"Who the hell are you?" the leader shouted. "Where is Karif?"

"My name is Jean, and I'm here to tell you that there will be no more food for you from this village. Please, leave in peace and never return."

"We'll take what we want. Why should we leave?"

"Because, my friend, that green dot on your chest is the laser scope of a sniper rifle ready to kill you if you don't co-operate. And we have an RPG ready to take out your other vehicle if your friends get any funny ideas. Turn your cars around and leave. Now."

The leader of the bandits looked down to see the green dot from Ricard's laser scope projected onto his left rib cage. He looked around the square but couldn't see the sniper or where the RPG launcher might be. After a brief pause he muttered something to his driver who started up the engines and drove off, with the other vehicle following.

"We'll be back!" he shouted over his shoulder at Jean and the dune buggies pulled away.

Jean tutted. *You should not have said that, mon ami.*

He nodded towards the building where Ricard was hiding and there were two loud cracks as the sniper rifle took out both rear tyres of the second dune buggy. It slewed to a halt as its occupants cried out to their colleagues. The leader in the first buggy looked round, assessed the situation and abandoned them to their fate. Before long they were bound, gagged and dumped into a small out-house attached to one of the village homes. The first vehicle had disappeared out of sight.

Jean went to interrogate the prisoners. They were emaciated and frightened, cowering in the corner of the hut where they were being held. Their eyes darted from Jean's face to the bottle of water he was sipping from.

"Tell me everything you can about the rest of your gang," he said. Silence.

"Tell me now or I will let Pieter loose on you," he shouted. Blank faces stared back; a slight shrug of shoulders the only sign that they had even heard him. Jean tutted. "Get Karif in here to translate for me." There was precious little information to be gained from them, even with the help of Karif's translation. Their colleagues numbered at least 30, there were several vehicles and machine guns, but no real hardware that worried Jean. He told Karif to keep the prisoners guarded and make sure the villagers did not kill them in revenge.

"The rest will be back. No harm in having some collateral to barter with," explained Jean to Karif. "Now we earn our pay."

They only had to wait twelve hours. Monty was stationed at the observation post, looking out across the dark countryside enhanced by his night vision goggles. A column of dust was being kicked up by several fast-moving vehicles. He radioed back to base.

"Here they come, maybe 10 or 12 vehicles. I can't tell how many people in each yet. No lights, looks they're using NV goggles. Amèlie will be pleased. ETA about five minutes."

The others took up their positions. Pieter came out to join Monty. Ricard resumed his sniper's position, while Amèlie ascended to the first floor of a house in a different part of the village. Gopal and Bob scooted out towards the trenches on the western edge of the village along with a few of the farmers who had shown themselves to be capable of handling a rifle. Jean went to the same house as Amèlie, but stayed just outside it, using the perimeter wall as cover.

As the dune buggies came nearer, Monty set himself with a Rocket Propelled Grenade launcher. He squeezed the trigger as the bandits entered the kill zone. The grenade detonated on the first buggy; the nose of the vehicle cratered downwards while the rear rose into the air and carried forward in a somersault. The blast killed the two occupants and momentarily blinded the driver of the vehicle behind in his night goggles. He failed to take evasive action and slammed into the over-turned buggy.

The other buggies left the road and scattered in all directions. Pieter sprayed his light machine gun at one of the vehicles that came close enough to the observation post, while Monty reloaded the RPG launcher. Several bandits hurriedly disembarked from their vehicles before he was able to take out another buggy. A couple of the bandits started crawling towards the observation post, keeping low and using dips in the ground as cover. As they stopped and paused for breath, one of them noticed a strange symbol painted on the rock they were hiding behind, but failed to spot a small patch of freshly dug soil beneath his feet. As he lifted his foot to move forward again, the anti-personnel mine detonated, killing him instantly and sending his compatriot sprawling forward.

The main group of vehicles had bypassed the observation post by now and was approaching the village. The mounted machine guns were indiscriminately spraying the houses on the western side of the hamlet without much effect. Gopal and Bob each launched an RPG, disabling two buggies but not killing all of the occupants. Ricard managed to pick off another driver with his sniper rifle. But there were still a few cars getting close to the trenches and several dismounted bandits picking their way cautiously forward.

Bob and Gopal had given away their position and were starting to come under heavy fire. A spray of bullets bit into the earth in front of the trenches. One of the villagers next to Gopal peered cautiously over the lip of foxhole. A lucky shot from somewhere out in the darkness went straight through his forehead and exited the back of his skull with an eruption of blood and brains. For a moment his body continued to aim his gun and then dropped to the ground as if somebody had cut the strings to a marionette. Bob knelt up a little more than he should have to launch another RPG and took a bullet to the left shoulder, which sent him sprawling backwards.

Monty and Pieter abandoned the observation post and managed to circle round the back of this main group of attackers, creating panic and confusion among the bandits. Things were looking more or less under control until Amèlie's voice cut in on their earpieces. "More bandits approaching from the left, looks like a larger vehicle with multiple occupants." Jean and Amèlie would have to deal with this new attack on their own for now at least.

This larger vehicle turned out to be a World War II German half-track, well-armoured and mounting a heavy machine gun. It was used to carry a dozen soldiers into battle. "*Merde!* Where did they get that antique?" muttered Jean, diving behind the wall just as the heavy machine gun opened fire. The large calibre bullets bit into the walls of the house where he and Amèlie were stationed; these flimsy building materials could not stand firepower of this sort for long. The rest of the occupants of the half-track fanned out and started crawling forwards.

Jean whispered into his mouth-piece: "Ricard, take out that fucking HMG before this wall I'm hiding behind disappears!" There was a pause and then a loud crack as the sniper rifle registered another hit and the half-track's gun fell silent.

"OK everyone, goggles off, *maintenant* Amèlie," shouted Jean. A moment later a set of floodlights switched on and bathed a large arc of the approaches to the village with high-powered flourescent beams. The oncoming assailants screamed as their night-vision goggles amplified the floodlights into something unbearably bright. Temporarily blinded, they scrambled to pull their goggles off. Jean leapt up from behind the low wall and sprayed his sub-machine gun, killing several of them with a burst of lead. Amèlie accounted for three more from her perched position in the first floor window and Ricard picked off another with his precision weapon.

But the floodlights did not stretch to the far right end of the attack and here, still under cover of darkness, some of the bandits had crawled forward to reach the trenches. Bob was struggling to remain conscious when a figure loomed up out of the darkness. Bob reached for his pistol as the bandit shot, catching the Scot once in the side of the bullet proof vest and once in the upper thigh.

Another bandit took aim at Gopal but his gun jammed. Dropping the rifle, he lunged at him with a machete. Gopal's own gun was out of ammo. He managed to deflect the thrust with his kukri. He aimed a karate punch at the man's throat, leaving the bandit helpless and gasping for air on the floor and then Gopal sprinted over to execute a flying kick against Bob's assailant. As he picked himself up off the floor a third attacker appeared and was about to shoot Gopal when one of the villagers grabbed him from behind and stuck a dagger into the bandit's back.

"Thanks," said Gopal. He picked up Bob's pistol, and cautiously peered over the top of the trench to see if that was the last of the attackers. It appeared to be, so he dropped back down to see what he could do for his injured colleague. Bob had lost a lot of blood and was struggling to stay awake. Gopal reached into a belt pouch and grabbed a dressing, wrapping it tightly round Bob's thigh wound in an attempt to stem the flow. He jabbed a shot of morphine into the upper arm of the Scottish sailor lying in front of him. Bob woke up briefly.

"Save your medicine, laddie."

"Come on Bob, stay with me. You're going to be fine," lied Gopal.

"Not this time. Who wants to live forever anyway?" And with that he slipped back into unconsciousness. The fighting around them had finished and the final score read Mercenaries 31, Bandits 2. A couple of the bandits had realised things were not going their way, so had slipped off into the darkness and back across the border. Another four had non-fatal injuries; the mercenaries did what they could to patch them back up before leaving them, along with the other two prisoners, in the care of the villagers.

Jean and his team buried Bob in the trench where he had fallen. The amiable Scot would be missed by them all, but tears were not their style. Each muttered a brief farewell and then packed up their kit. Gopal said he was heading back to Nepal, his homeland. Jean said goodbye to Karif, accepted the payment, and turned to his other colleagues. "Riyadh next, gang, I hear there's good money to be made in the security business this time of year. *Allez!*"

Asia 2024

Dubbed the Panama Canal for Asia, the Kra canal is a fifty-kilometre waterway that cuts through the peninsula at Thailand's narrowest point, connecting the Indian Ocean with the South China Sea. It means that ships do not have to divert around Singapore – through the crowded Malacca Straits – saving fuel and time. The project was financed by the Chinese government, keen to spread its influence throughout Asia.

The Captain of the *Groene Draeck* stood on the observation deck, surveying the Straits of Malacca with his Chief Officer. Within a square nautical mile there were twenty other oil tankers of varying size at anchor, each fully laden with Dubai-grade light sour crude.

The Captain knew they were all here for the same reason. The recent recession in China had caused an unexpected decline in global oil demand. The glut of oil supply had led to another sharp price decline – the first time a barrel had dropped below $20 for 25 years. To absorb the excess supply several countries had filled their strategic reserves, while the oil companies themselves had hired out a sizeable portion of the world's fleet of VLCCs to act as floating storage containers. As Captain Peeters puffed on his tobacco pipe, he could see the green and red night lights of at least a dozen other tankers between him and the brighter, taller lights of Singapore in the distance. The effect was enhanced by the lights reflecting off the calm waters, gently twinkling under a moonless sky.

"Not as good as a Christmas tree but not bad, eh, Jaap?"

"Indeed, Sir," said the Chief Officer with a deep sigh. The Captain knew that Jaap Boeckman had a wife and two young children at home in Amsterdam whom he missed terribly. They would be getting excited about the visit of Sinterklaas this evening. A bunch of pretty lights in one of the world's busiest shipping lanes was not even remotely adequate compensation. The skeleton crew had been stationed here for two months now; they knew the owners would likely leave the ship here for at least three more months hoping for a pick-up in oil prices next year. Shore leave was restricted to one day in ten – not enough to get back to the Netherlands, nor to justify the family coming to Singapore for that one day.

"Christmas is always tough, Jaap," observed the Captain. "Come on, let's see if we can find some schnapps to drown our sorrows. At least we're too old to worry about Zwarte Piet."

A few hundred metres away, on the seafloor, a group of frogmen were making slow, steady progress behind three mini-subs that were illuminating the depths with their floodlights. Even at the relatively shallow depths of the Malacca Straits there was no danger of the underwater lights being spotted from the surface. There were two men in each of the mini-subs and a further 12 following behind. The frogmen walking along the seabed were armed with a harpoon gun each, while the mini-subs were laden with high explosives and drilling equipment.

On board the *Groene Draeck*, Peeters and Boeckman had found a bottle of yellow juniper schnapps from Denmark and had toasted absent family, the ship, Sinterklaas and anybody else they could think of. On the bridge, the Second Officer was in charge and there were four armed guards permanently patrolling the ship's deck in case of pirate attacks.

Just before midnight, the divers started to drill two small holes through the outer hull of the oil tanker, one at each end. In between the two layers of a double-hulled tanker is a gap of around two metres filled with ballast water. Through these holes, the divers planted a small charge of C4 against the inner hull using a telescopic arm. The explosives would be powerful enough to blast through the inner hull while simultaneously bursting open the hole already present in the outer hull. Towards the middle of the ship's length, they also planted a magnetic mine to help ensure the tanker would sink quickly. The timers were set for one hour, more than enough time to get clear of the blast area. They came to the surface just half a mile away from the tanker and clambered aboard the mini-subs to protect themselves from the blast shockwaves.

The mini-subs and divers momentarily appeared on the radar of the *Groene Draeck*. The Second Officer noticed the blip and was about to investigate but its significance was instantly forgotten as the ship lurched beneath his feet. There were three almost simultaneous dull crumping sounds and then sprays of water erupting from beneath the oil tanker. It immediately began listing to port as alarm bells blared out warnings from the control panel. The Second Officer grabbed hold of the captain's chair to keep his balance and then hauled himself across the bridge. His heart pounded double-time while the back of his neck flushed hot. He looked across at his fellow watchman who was lying on the floor.

"Kurt, are you alright? Get up, I need you."

The sailor got to his knees, rubbed his head, and then returned to his position next to the radio controls. The Second Officer assessed the damage reports while trying to maintain his increasingly untenable station on the tilting floor.

"A double-hull breech?! *Godverdomme!* What the hell hit us? Kurt, send out an SOS, give our position and tell them we are leaking oil too." He hit the abandon ship button on the console. "At least there aren't too many of us to get off. Now where is that roster sheet?" he muttered to himself. He grabbed the ship's log and donned his life jacket before heading out towards the lifeboats. It was hard work getting the boats launched given the tanker's severe list but after only a few minutes, two boats were in the water with all of the skeleton crew accounted for. The Captain and the Chief Officer had managed to salvage their bottle of schnapps but not much else.

"I guess Zwarte Piet got us after all," said the Captain with a weak laugh. He turned away from the sight of the sinking vessel, but couldn't block out the gurgling noise like a giant bath being emptied as the ship was sucked under. He took a swig from the bottle and rubbed his hand down his face.

One of the other nearby tankers had heard the explosions followed by the SOS signal and had started to manoeuvre towards the stricken ship. The mini-subs and divers disappeared back towards the seafloor and started repeating the exact same procedure on this second approaching tanker once it had stopped to pick up the Dutch crew from the *Groene Draeck's* lifeboats. This was a slightly smaller, Korean ship but still received three charges of explosives; once each to the forward and aft oil tanks and one amidships. The frogmen and subs retreated again and just after they surfaced half a mile away, there were three more underwater explosions, shortly followed by another SOS radio signal. Now there was a Korean crew as well as the Dutch crew going overboard into four lifeboats.

Chief Officer Jaap ended up in the same lifeboat as his Captain again. "Two accidents in one night is not possible. This has to be pre-meditated."

The Captain stared back at Jaap, and emptied the bottle of schnapps. "You think?"

Both sets of crew were more interested in getting away from the stricken vessels than figuring out what the motive might be. The spreading oil slick from the *Groene Draeck* had caught fire while the ship itself was mostly underwater. With the Korean ship also starting to sink the scene resembled the hellish aftermath of a World War II U-boat attack.

The rescue services were soon on their way: a pair of fast Vanguard VG7 lifeboats from Singapore that would be able to pick up the sailors with relative ease. There followed behind a series of slower fire tugs and salvage boats to see if there was anything they could do to stop the oil tankers from breaking up. It was a forlorn hope; both tankers were on the bottom of the shallow straits by the time these other vessels had arrived on the scene. The *Groene Draeck*, which had listed badly before sinking, lay on the bottom on its port side; its starboard flank was just a few metres below the surface of the water. The Korean ship had sunk more or else upright, with its flattish keel resting on the seafloor and a small portion of its superstructure, radar dishes and aerials poking up above the surface of the water.

But the mini-subs and frogmen were not finished there – they travelled a further mile or so along the seafloor and came up underneath another tanker in a different part of the Straits. At least the rescue services were close at hand when this ship – a Greek-owned Liquid Natural Gas tanker – was consigned to the same fate as the two oil tankers. It looked like a normal tanker but with five huge ping-pong balls cut in half and stuck on top of the deck. These ping-pongs did not float, however, and the boat sank just as quickly as the other two ships.

In the following days and weeks, there were endless inquests and investigations into who or what could have been responsible for these wanton acts of terrorism. Captain Peeters' observation to his First Officer had caught the attention of the world's press after he repeated it live on TV, and thereafter the attacks had become known as Black Peter's Day. Traffic through one of the world's busiest shipping lanes ground to a virtual halt. As well as the fear of future attacks, the relatively shallow sea was now difficult to navigate with three man-made reefs lying just below the surface. Even after the painstaking clean-up operation to salvage the oil and LNG in the tankers it would be several months before the rusting hulks of the ships themselves could be dealt with.

Meanwhile in Thailand the recently opened Kra canal was enjoying a surge in popularity. These attacks had given an extra incentive to try the new route. Conspiracy theorists had a field day with this convenient coincidence, but there was never any damning evidence to suggest that the Thai government had any involvement in the attacks.

North Africa - 2025

The Great Man-Made River in Libya is one of the engineering wonders of the world. There are four well-heads that descend over 500 metres into the earth below the desert and tap into the Nubian Sandstone Aquifer System, originally providing Libya with millions of litres of fresh water every day. The well-heads are connected to several reservoirs and then on to the major cities via a vast network of enormous underground concrete pipes. (See also section 3b)

The heat awoke Bigrahl at around 6am. The temperature had already climbed to 35 degrees centigrade in the first hour of daylight. The white-washed thick stone walls of his simple house provided some protection, but not much. The cheap Japanese air-conditioning unit had stopped working a long time ago and he still hadn't saved enough money to replace it. He got out of bed, wondering how his wife could remain asleep in this heat, and crept out of the room trying not to awaken their four-year-old son. In the other room of the house, which served as kitchen and living room, he gathered the tackle for his usual early morning fishing trip and carefully hid them in his rucksack. After a cup of strong coffee, he wrapped a hunk of yesterday's bread and a slice of chicken in a cloth for his breakfast and put those too in his backpack.

He left the house, situated on the eastern edge of the town of Ajdabiya, many miles from the coast, and got on his rusty old bike. The baked dust from the dirt tracks caught in his nostrils and on his tongue; he could smell and taste the heat as much as he could feel it on his skin. His destination was not the coast nor a nearby river but a reservoir that was part of the Great Man-Made River.

Allah be praised. Every day, Bigrahl still smiled to think that *his* country had built one of the largest man-made structures in the world.

The reservoir near Adjabiya was one of the most important. Although it was guarded by a perimeter fence and patrolled by sentries, Bigrahl had found a broken part of the fence where he could sneak in. The sentries were none too vigilant and the upkeep of the boundary was not a priority for public spending. At the edge of the reservoir near the gap in the fence a number of shrubs and reeds had grown up where seeds blown on the wind had happened to lodge and eked out an existence. Hidden from the sentries by these plants, Bigrahl had realised that this would be an ideal fishing spot. So many fishermen used their boats for ferrying migrants across the Mediterranean Sea that the price of fish in Libya had soared.

Spending some of his precious savings on a couple of dozen live fish, he had released them into the reservoir in the hope that they would start to breed. He came back every few months to check on his 'fish farm' and after 18 months reckoned it was safe to start fishing. Of course, if anybody had seen him sneaking in with fishing tackle in hand, they would have instantly started asking questions. So he only came here first thing in the morning, with his fishing rod disassembled and hidden in his rucksack.

On this particular day, Bigrahl was looking forward to his fishing more than normal – he hadn't caught anything last time and was desperate to bring a good catch home to his wife to show her what a wise investment this whole project had been. Her skepticism ebbed and flowed, not regular like the tides of the sea, but governed by the size of fish with which Bigrahl returned. As he quietly approached the perimeter fence, the fresh smell of water and clean air was like oxygen to an asthmatic. But something seemed out of place. The guards, who lazily patrolled the perimeter fence in a small jeep, were nowhere to be seen but their vehicle was parked just next to his secret entrance.

Bigrahl felt a knot of fear grip his insides. Had they discovered the hole in the fence? What would Henna say? As he crept closer he could see the gap in the fence was still there. It was then that he noticed a leg on the ground sticking out from behind the jeep. From where he was looking, he couldn't quite tell if it was still attached to its body or had been severed – perhaps some freak accident? He edged closer and manoeuvred round so he could see behind the jeep. One of the guards was lying on the ground, a leg sticking straight out, the other bent backwards at an unnatural angle. Judging from the bloody bullet holes in his chest, this guard was long past caring about a twisted ankle.

Bigrahl paused to collect himself and to make sure nobody else was around, then sneaked through the gap in the perimeter fence and approached the guard's body. No pulse. He looked around some more and noticed something floating in the reservoir. It was the body of the other guard, face down. There were bullet holes in the back of his uniform. Selfishly, Bigrahl thought of his fish – the dead body would have frightened them away from this spot for a while. Not much chance of appeasing his wife with a good catch today.

He thought about what to do. On the one hand, reporting this incident seemed the decent course of action – the guards' corpses would get the respect they deserved, and there had to be some villains out there who needed catching. On the other hand, he would have a lot of explaining to do about how he came to be here in the first place, and besides, somebody would notice that the guards had not reported in sooner or later. He chose the safer but less chivalrous option and rode back home as fast as his legs could pedal.

*

Four days earlier, just across the border in Egypt a small group of vehicles had assembled in the dead of night and set off west, heading for Ajdabiya. There were four large trucks, each with a covered flatbed hiding their cargo and all of them fitted with extra-large all-terrain tyres. There were 18 men from the elite Navy Seal unit, the Al Quwaat Al-Khaasat, and two women from the secret intelligence service. The trucks crossed the border near Al Jaghbub in a region that neither the Libyans nor the Egyptians bothered to monitor very closely. From there, the trucks had an arduous journey across several hundred miles of the Calanscio Sand Sea.

To begin with the journey was efficient but monotonous. The soldiers operated a shift system so that they could keep travelling almost continuously. While two of the crew drove and navigated, others slept in the back. There were inevitable stops when a truck got stuck in a difficult patch of sand, or for meal breaks and once a day to fill up with diesel from the barrels they carried with them. One truck lost a tyre on a particularly sharp outcrop of stone that lay at the bottom of a dip in the sand, but they had several spares on board. Getting the new tyre fitted was not easy, but one of the other trucks had some lifting equipment which helped enormously.

Towards the end of the second day, the navigator of the lead truck saw a plane appear in the distance, approaching from the west. He shouted out over the walkie-talkies: "Eyes in the sky! You know the drill, we've got a minute at most to get into positions."

The trucks stopped and everybody bailed out. From the back of each truck the crew unloaded a host of filming apparatus – cameras mounted on tripods, lighting screens, even a director's chair. The two intelligence officers who were already in civilian clothing started acting out a scene in the desert while some of the soldiers stripped off their uniforms and pretended to be filming the 'actresses'. The plane zoomed overhead – a few hundred metres up, then banked and came back for a lower, second pass. The women looked up as the plane roared over them, giving the pilot a cheery wave and their best smiles. The plane circled round and then climbed back to its original altitude and continued along the same route it had started on. There was a collective sigh of relief. Once the plane was out of sight the equipment was bundled back into the trucks and the journey resumed.

By midnight on the second day, they had reached the outskirts of Ajdabiya and stopped their trucks about half a mile away from the GMMR reservoir. A team of eight soldiers camouflaged their faces and donned night-vision goggles, body armour and helmets. They armed themselves with an assortment of pistols with silencers, a sniper rifle (also silenced), sub machine guns and stun grenades. Splitting into two teams of four, they approached the reservoir perimeter fence and cut their way in. One team headed for the guards' building – a basic accommodation unit with some communication equipment and monitoring devices in it – while the other team headed away from this building towards the two guards who were out on patrol in the jeep. The lights on the vehicle made it very easy for the commandos to track them down.

The guards out on patrol never knew what hit them. One had just stopped for a piss while the other was standing next to the jeep lighting a cigarette. A well-grouped burst of shots from silenced pistols at close range sent one sprawling next to the jeep, while the other toppled forwards into the reservoir. The other commando team crashed open a door and window simultaneously at the guards' building, throwing in four grenades. After these had exploded they rushed in, cleared each room and radioed for the trucks to approach the building while one of them went to open the gates.

The vehicles stopped next to the edge of the reservoir. The crew pulled off the tarpaulin covers from the back of the vehicles to reveal the cargo they had carried all the way from Egypt. There was a mini submarine resting on a cradle on each of the first three flat-beds, while on the fourth there was a large crane arm. This truck was stabilised with stanchions while six of the soldiers donned underwater diving gear.

Each of the subs was carefully hoisted into the reservoir where they bobbed on the surface a few feet from the water's edge while the crew ran systems checks. The exterior lights sprang into life and robotic arms twirled and stretched as if the submarines were waking from a deep slumber. The propellers started whirring and on command from an intelligence officer watching on the shore, the vehicles headed out into the middle of the reservoir and dived below the surface.

After a few minutes the divers had found the water inlet pipe for the reservoir. It was a vast tube – at least five metres in diameter – covered at this end by a mesh grille and some pivoting vents that could be used to shut off the water supply if the reservoir got too full. The first sub cut through the grille with an acetylene torch fixed to one of its robotic arms, and then descended into one of the arteries of the GMMR, closely followed by the other two submarines. The Intelligence officer in charge back at the trucks radioed "good luck" and settled down for a long wait. If all went to plan there would be at least twenty hours of radio silence before the subs returned. The soldiers set up a defensive perimeter and organised a sentry rota.

Inside the pipes the submarines made steady progress against the current of fresh water continually gushing out of well-heads hundreds of kilometers away. After a few hours one of the subs stopped moving and started to attach a series of explosive packages against the floor of the concrete pipe. A timer was set to go off in 24 hours' time, and then the sub turned around and headed back towards the original entry point, moving much faster with the flow of water now helping. It carried on past the point where it had entered the system of pipes and placed some more charges further down the network, co-ordinated to explode at the same time as the first set, before eventually returning to the waiting trucks.

The other two subs were carrying out similar assignments but at different points along the pipework. One branched off to set a charge at the entrance to the well heads at Sarir, while the first sub travelled the furthest away from the starting point before leaving its deadly package and started heading back towards the others. Halfway back to the reservoir at Ajdabiya, the engines on this mini-sub developed a mechanical fault and lost power. After gliding along it gently settled at the bottom of that section of pipe. There was no way to radio for help. Even if there was some way to get hold of the others, there was no possibility that they could be reached in time.

The two companions looked at each other in grim silence. Was this submarine going to become their tomb? They knew that the sabotage plan relied on Libya never finding out who carried out the attack, which meant that they were under instructions to self-detonate if they became stuck.

The more senior of the two commandos suggested a plan. "We don our breathing gear, set a charge on the mini-sub and swim back towards that inspection hatch we passed a few minutes ago. Once we are on the surface, we can figure out the next part of the escape."

Grabbing a few simple items of equipment they might need once on the surface they set the timer for ten minutes on their last charge of explosives. They braced themselves for the in-rush of water and opened the door of their sub. They swam towards the inspection hatch but when they got there, the handle would not turn. It was not easy to push or pull against the smooth inside of the pipework but even with both of them working together it simply would not budge. They were starting to panic when the leader had a brainwave. He began swimming back to the mini-sub, checking his watch to see how long it would be before the explosives detonated. This was going to be close.

He reached the submarine, prised off the acetylene torch from one of the robotic arms and swam back to the hatchway. Using the torch he cut open the lock on the entrance. The water from the underground pipeway surged upwards, filling the long tube that rose towards the daylight. As they got to the surface the commandos heard a dull thud as the mini-sub exploded far below them. Looking around they could see sandy desert in every direction. It was going to be a very long walk back to Egypt.

Just before six in the morning, the intelligence officer in charge of the operation gave up waiting for the final sub. The second one back had re-surfaced in the reservoir at Ajdabiya some time ago and had already been lifted back into its cradle on one of the waiting trucks. With everything safely stowed and covered up, everybody mounted up. None of them knew the fate of their colleagues but they assumed the worst. They paid their respects and the vehicles headed out of the reservoir complex.

Once on the public road, they passed a man cycling towards the body of water with a rucksack on his back. Then they headed off cross-country, retracing their steps back towards the border. At 7:30am local time the explosive charges detonated simultaneously at six different points on the eastern half of the GMMR network.

The four Egyptian trucks returned to base three days later to heartfelt congratulations from their superiors. The missing commandos turned up twelve days after that, having been saved by a caravan of nomads. With those loose ends tied up, phase two of the Duat Gamble kicked in: the Egyptian Ambassador went to see the Libyan Minister of the Interior.

"And you say that this accident took place three weeks ago? Why did you not appeal for help sooner?" asked the Ambassador.

"We needed to conduct a thorough examination of the evidence and assess how long it would take to repair the damage. Our Prime Minister felt it sensible to obtain all the facts to avoid unnecessary panic."

"I see. And you still have no idea how this happened? Has the secret service suggested any terrorist groups who might have committed this atrocity?"

"One or two possibilities, but there is no evidence to go on. We are clutching at grains of sand, frankly."

The Ambassador suppressed a smile. "It seems clear that you need humanitarian and financial assistance on an unprecedented scale. I have been instructed by my government to offer you everything you have asked for."

"Really? This is most welcome news. We—"

"I hadn't finished. We are willing to offer everything you need, on condition that all future output from the GMMR well-heads are split evenly between our two great nations."

The Libyan minister asked for the Egyptian Ambassador to come back the next day to hear the formal response to the offer of aid. He conferred with his Prime Minister and Finance Minister. The government finances were in terrible shape after years of diminishing oil output and the extra burden of caring for an ageing population. The Finance Minister explained that they had little chance of raising the funds to reconstruct the GMMR on the open market, without paying an exorbitant interest rate. The Prime Minister railed against the loss of face, and was even more upset at losing a significant share of future water supplies. But necessity prevailed, and the next day, the Egyptian Ambassador received the answer he had hoped for. The Duat Gamble had worked.

SNEAK PREVIEW OF *ROSE GOLD*

THE SEQUEL TO *BLUE GOLD*

ROSE GOLD will publish Spring 2018

with Urbane Publications,

ISBN 978-1-911583-40-0

Spoiler alert: do not read before Blue Gold!

PROLOGUE

The woman looked out through thick windows at the mountain range on the grey horizon, barren but beautiful like an Ansel Adams photograph her mother had once owned. A shaft of sunlight stabbed through the gap between two peaks. The woman squinted until the glass in the windows adjusted, and then she watched as the sun rose clear of the mountains.

She sighed. Hundreds of hours of unbroken sunlight that would soon send the surface temperature soaring above boiling point. She wondered if she would still be alive when the sun next rose, a month from now.

A small boy nuzzled into her leg. She looked down and put an arm around his shoulders, smiling. "It's going to be a beautiful day."

PART I

First Quarter

Chapter One

Sim rolled over in bed, post-coital endorphins flooding his flaccid mind. He glanced at the clock. 9:30am. He loved fuckin' Saturdays.

The next thing he knew Rosie had whipped the duvet away and he was getting cold. She was standing over the bed, fully clothed. Sunlight was catching the motes of dust from the duvet, circling in the air around her head like a halo. Sim's eyes closed again and he tried to nestle into the rapidly disappearing warmth of the mattress.

"Come on, up, you lazy sod."

He squinted sideways at the clock. 10:42am. "Ahh, Rosie, but the pub's not even open."

"You had more than enough this past night. We need to go shopping." She grabbed hold of a toe and twisted it until he yelped and hauled himself out of bed.

They strode into the small square that marked the centre of Dornoch. The little castle and miniature Cathedral both glowed amber in the early summer sun, beacons of beauty standing guard over the folks wandering about. Sim noticed that the moon was still just visible, hovering above the ancient fortification. He smiled at the contrast; to think of the people working up there, 380,000 kilometres away, in mankind's latest stronghold.

A woman approached them, pushing a pram. It was Helen. "Morning Rosie. Sim," she said with a beam on her face.

Sim leaned over the pram. "How is the wee man this morning? How are ya? Do you remember ya big Uncle Simon? Do you? Huh? Yes of course you do." He poked his finger at the baby and waggled it in front of large moist eyes. A whiff of unchanged nappy drifted up as he leant over; not good for a hangover. "Alright, Helen? He's growing quick – gonna be a fine flanker one day, just like his daddy."

"How are you two getting on?" asked Helen, looking at Rosie's waistline.

Rosie grabbed Sim's hand and dragged him away. "Can't stop Helen, we've got lots of shopping to do," she called over her shoulder.

They shopped in silence for an hour, and then walked back to their small house on the outskirts of town. Sim's fingers were pink and sore from carrying all the bags by the time they got through the front door.

He dumped the bags in the hall and rolled his shoulders a few times. "I was just being friendly, like."

"You don't have to go all gooey on every baby we meet. And did you hear her?" Rosie lips contorted into a sneer. "How are you getting on? Ooh, aren't I clever. Here's one I made earlier."

Sim frowned and shook his head. He looked up at the mic in the ceiling. "Kitchen. Put the kettle on." There was a click from the other room, and Sim bent down to pick up the bags again.

After he had disappeared into the kitchen, Rosie shouted after him. "That's right, make a cup of tea. Your answer to everything, isn't it?" She went into the lounge and Sim heard her tell the TV to switch on.

Tea made, he entered the room and saw the voice controller

lying on the floor, the back busted open and batteries spilling out. Rosie's eyes were screwed shut but tears were forcing themselves out anyway. The news on the TV was focused on one story. Prince George's wife was expecting a baby; the fourth in line to the throne.

Sim put the mug of tea down and knelt in front of his wife. He wrapped his arms around her and gently rocked. "It's OK. Everything's alright. We're gonna be fine. Whatever happens. You hear me?"

Rosie sniffed and smiled. "Sorry, just, you know, wrong time of the month. You going to bring me those choccie biscuits we bought earlier? Medicinal purposes, like."

Sim grinned and got up. They were going to be alright.

One packet of biscuits and three episodes of the latest Chinese detective show later, there was a knock at the door. Sim jumped. He wouldn't admit it to Rosie, but Chinese people still set him on edge. The scar had faded and his lung was fine now, but a Chinese man with a knife still haunted his nights.

Sim rose from the sofa and brushed the crumbs off his jumper. He went to the front hall, opened the door and froze for a second while he processed who he was looking at.

"Mr Wardle! What're you doing here? I'm guessing this isn't a social call?"

"Hello Sim, long time no speak. Still stuck in the satellite department, I hear. At least you have a few more to count these days."

Sim smiled and stood there for a second. His old boss had not come all the way from Overseas Division in Birmingham to discuss the ebb and flow of the Great Flux. Wardle had lost a lot of hair and gained many wrinkles since last they met. Sim tried not to stare so he looked at the person standing behind Wardle, a big chap wearing a black suit and dark tie. "Won't you come in?" Sim stood back and ushered them inside. "Rosie, we've got visitors."

"Sim, this envelope arrived for you yesterday at OFWAT headquarters."

Sim took the slim parcel. "I see it's been opened."

Wardle shrugged. "It contained a memory stick, which had a holo on it."

"A video message for me?"

Wardle nodded. "From the Moon base. We need to discuss its contents."

Sim showed him into the cosy living room. "Director Wardle, this is my wife Rosie. Rosie this is my old boss—"

Wardle stepped forward to shake her hand. "It's nice to meet you, Rosie, but I'm afraid I need to talk with Sim alone on a matter of some urgency." He ushered her towards the door that led into the kitchen, then turned to his colleague and nodded. The OFWAT worker pulled out a holo-projector from his bag and slotted in the memory card.

"Sim, you had better sit down," said Wardle.

The 3D video materialised showing a woman with long silver hair and a sharp nose. She was leaning towards the camera, obviously recording the message herself. She leant back and smiled. 'Hello Sim.'

Sim creased his brows and then looked across at Wardle. "Is that Elsa Greenwood?" He dragged his fingers through his hair. Memories of a bizarre erotic encounter came flooding back: a negotiation for information and a payment rendered. His cheeks flushed red and he glanced towards the kitchen door.

Elsa continued: 'I was voted from my office at Marinus shortly after we… met.' Elsa was being careful with her choice of words. This seemed unscripted but not unconstrained. 'Eventually I was offered the chance to become head of the new moon base. When the Americans opened up the Rare Earth Moon Unit as an international research centre four years ago *Adams Holdings* took control. They needed somebody with experience of running a small, self-contained community and so... here I am.'

Sim looked across at Wardle. "What's all this got to do with me? Why has that mad woman sent me a message from the Moon?"

"Keep watching," replied Wardle.

'Sim, I'm in trouble. I think the whole base might be. There's been a death, but I don't think it was an accident. There's a killer up here. Possibly a terrorist.' Elsa paused and looked around her office, as if the right words to say might be lurking in a corner somewhere. 'I don't trust anybody.'

"Still none the wiser, Sir," interjected Sim.

Wardle just pointed at the projection.

'I know you must be wondering why I've sent this to you, Sim. Why I chose you from all the hundreds of people down on Earth who might be able to help. I needed somebody I could trust.' She paused and took a deep breath. 'Wait there a moment.' Elsa disappeared from view and returned a few moments later holding the hand of a small boy. She sat down and perched him on her knee. 'Wave to the camera, James.'

Sim stared at the boy's face. That wide nose and those earlobes were familiar. That toothsome grin was just like a faded school photo his Mum kept on her mantelpiece.

Then the little boy spoke two words that made Sim's stomach shrink to the size of a peanut. 'Hello Daddy.'

The mug of tea in Sim's hand fell to the floor, bounced off the thick carpet then emptied its contents over the floor. He stared, unmoving, as the pool of tea spread.

"Shouldn't we wipe that up?" asked Wardle's assistant.

Sim looked up at the question and shook himself out of his stupor. He went to get a cloth from the kitchen. Rosie was standing at the sink. Her shoulders were trembling. Sim put his hands out to rub her upper arms. "Rosie?"

She shifted her stance immediately and twisted out from his caress. "Don't you touch me!"

"Hey, what's the matter?"

"What do you think's the matter, Einstein? I heard that, and I saw it."

"You weren't supposed to—"

"Go on, say it. I wasn't supposed to know. How long were you gonna keep me in the dark?"

Sim looked away. "That's not what I meant."

Rosie jabbed his shoulder, turning him back towards her. "I've been pissin' on a stick for two years, hoping to see some colour change. You've been having your way as often as you liked, all for the sake of *our* family." She looked away, staring out of the window. "When the truth is, you've already got one."

"Rosie, you have to believe me. I didn't know. This is a complete shock to both of us."

"Huh." She folded her arms. "You never did tell me what you got up to just before we started going out. When you disappeared for a couple of months. Travelling the world, you said. A girl in every port, was that it?"

Rosie's words were jabbing into Sim's solar plexus. He gasped for air. "It's not like that. I wasn't *allowed* to tell you. Something happened, OK, and… I… I had sex with that woman. Once."

"Oh well, if it was only once, then that's alright, isn't it? Proves you aren't shooting blanks. So it must be *my* fault we haven't had a baby yet. Great. I feel so much better now."

Sim grabbed one of Rosie's hands and enveloped it in his.

"Rosie, I want to tell you. It's not what you think. I was on a—"

Wardle pushed open the door from the sitting room. "That's enough Atkins. Any more, and I'll have you banged up for treason."

Rosie looked across at Sim's boss. Her eyebrows creased and her sobbing subsided.

"Sorry Sir," said Sim. He gave Rosie a thin smile and went back into the lounge with his boss.

Sim slumped down onto the sofa, while Wardle stood watching the young man fidget.

"I can't make you do this, Atkins. A mission like this is for volunteers only. All I can say is that the department, and the government, would be extremely grateful. You heard what Ms Greenwood had to say. You might be the only person she'll trust."

Sim was staring at the stained carpet. He nodded without looking up.

Wardle crouched down so he matched Sim's eye level. "It's a lot to take in, I know. But we need an answer tomorrow morning. If we're going to get you to that moon base, you'll need to do several days of basic training. The next rocket is due to leave in eight days' time. Promise me you'll think about it seriously. We need you, Sim."

Wardle stood up and moved into the hallway with his colleague. Sim followed him. "Can I watch the holo again, Sir?"

"Sorry, Atkins, but it needs to come back to HQ for safety. Newell has a letter for you." His colleague handed over a thick envelope. "It contains a transcript of the message and some basic information about the moon base and space training. I'll call you tomorrow morning to find out your answer." He turned and left the house.

Sim went back to the lounge. Rosie was not there. He looked in the kitchen and in the bedroom. She must have slipped out the back door. He returned to the lounge and slumped onto the sofa. He leant forward until his head was almost between his knees and retched. His mouth tasted of pain and guilt. And yet there was something else. Amidst the bile and the vertigo.

He didn't know what he could to help Elsa. He didn't know how he would patch things up with Rosie. But he did know one thing. He was going to the Moon, to see his son.

ACKNOWLEDGMENTS

There are many people I would like to thank for their help in making this book possible.

First and foremost, Matthew Smith for believing in my story and taking a chance on a debut author.

Louis Bacon and Elaine Crocker have provided me with support while writing has distracted me from my day-time job. Without their flexibility and understanding this book may never have been finished.

My tutor at the Faber Academy, Richard Skinner, for his advice and support even after the course had finished. And my fellow students on that course, for their encouragement and honest feedback. Sharing our hopes and frustrations over many a beer certainly helped smooth out the bumps and knock-backs.

Thanks are also due to Cornerstones Literary Consultancy for their professional and friendly editorial services. And to Steve and Gordon, my very early beta readers, for not hating that feeble first draft.

Most of all, thanks go to Fiona for her unstinting support throughout this eight-year journey. And to Amelie, for her love and laughter.

David was born in Cheshire but now lives in Berkshire. He is married to an author of children's picture books, with a daughter who loves stories. His working life has been spent in the City, first for the Bank of England and now as Chief Economist for an international fund. So his job entails trying to predict the future all the time. David's writing ambitions received a major boost after he attended the Faber Academy six-month course in 2014 and he still meets up with his inspirational fellow students. He loves reading, especially adventure stories, sci-fi and military history. Outside of family life, his other interests include tennis, golf and surfing. www.davidbarkerauthor.co.uk and twitter @BlueGold201